Green Fields #8

CATHARSIS

Adrienne Lecter

Catharsis

Green Fields #8

ISBN: 9781980333326

Cover art by S.Marko
Editing by Marti Lynch
Interior design by Adrienne Lecter

www.adriennelecter.com

Give feedback on the book at:
adrienne@adriennelecter.com

Twitter: @AdrienneLecter

First Edition February 2018
Second Print Edition November 2021
Produced and published by Barbara Klein, Vienna, Austria

To M

Because you're the light of my life.

Chapter 1

"You look like death warmed over."

I squinted at Burns, trying very hard to think of a witty reply, but came up blank. Every single cell in my body hurt—some more, some less; some that weren't even attached to me any longer. The harsh sunlight did a number on my already mushy brain, even though my eyes stung somewhat less than I was used to. That was one small reprieve, compared to...

I forced that train of thought to grind to a halt and focused on the most important thing: to not just stand there like a brain-dead zombie. I'd managed to get through the brief ride on the truck. I hadn't screamed my head off when I'd slid out into the snow, my feet having to bear my entire weight again. I was not going to let this get me down now.

"Gee, you say the sweetest things," I finally replied. The words came out just a little garbled although the cold had helped bring down the swelling in my jaws. Nate gave me a cautious, sidelong glance, but remained silent.

Jason and Charlie were still busy eyeing the truck behind us with distrust, while Tanner stepped up to Burns, Gita hot on his heels. All of them looked beat up from the fight with the wolves and zombies, but hypothermia seemed the greater concern. I had a solution for that either way. Maybe.

"Just telling it like it is," Burns pointed out. "We're between a rock and a hard place again, aren't we?"

I would have shrugged under different circumstances, but simply cocking my head to the side was hard enough. "What gave it away? Our little entourage, or the fact that they didn't give us our weapons back?" To be honest, I had my Beretta back in its sheath on my right thigh, all the good that it did me without ammunition—among other issues. I was still surprised that Red—Lt. Richards to those bothering to remember names—had only brought ten soldiers with him on our little trip outside the heavily reinforced fence of the base. Apparently, my ability to simply take off running into the snow-covered hills had been deemed nonexistent, and they knew that Nate would never leave without me. For once, I could have done with more of that usual underestimating of me going on, but that assessment was sadly very accurate.

"Some things never change," I offered, feeling the irony of that statement bite all the sharper. "We're heading to Europe."

Burns's eyes widened infinitesimally, but he took it in stride. The others, not so much, but after another round of staring at the soldiers no one spoke up.

Exhaling forcefully—and my, didn't that cause some nice spikes where my right kidney used to be... and half of my liver... and gallbladder… and other things—I went on, speaking in low, hushed tones now, trying not to make my voice carry back to our entourage.

"I should tell you that this is goodbye. We're caught up in this, but you're all free to go. And you should. Just turn around, hunker down for the winter, maybe pray for us if that's your thing." No one laughed. I hadn't really expected them to. "Fact is, I can't. We desperately need some backup because this is going to devolve into the shit storm of the ages. And I'm very likely going to be the one stirring it up. Even without that, I have a feeling it won't be pretty and will resemble a suicide mission more than anything else. They wouldn't be recruiting the heavy hitters if it wasn't."

Burns didn't bat an eyelash. "When are we leaving?"

I hesitated after opening my mouth to reply, having to shift onto my right leg to keep the pain in the left from becoming too overwhelming. A frown crossed his forehead, but Burns did a good job ignoring my obvious… issues. "Today."

"Where exactly in Europe?" A pause. "And how."

"Plane. Ship. Need to know, and we don't." My cut-off response clearly conveyed both my annoyance with the latter, and the fact that any further questions were futile. If not for the agony pushing away every other sentiment, I would have choked on my frustration.

Burns gave another nod, understanding. "I'm good to go."

I glanced at the others, not bothering to ask. Every word I didn't need to enunciate was a small blessing right now. Gita looked scared—smart girl—yet tried to hide it. The guys, mostly determined. "You're not getting rid of us again," Jason said, clearly speaking for the lot of them.

"Yeah, we never claimed to be very smart about this," Charlie agreed, trying for levity but failing.

I offered the most infinitesimal shrug I could manage, likely lost in the heap of winter clothes I was bundled up in. "Like attracts like." Glancing back toward the truck, I couldn't keep from adding, "And we'll be in stellar company."

Red didn't sneer back at me as I had hoped, still seeming way too relaxed about his babysitting duty. "Are you done being a drama queen yet?" he asked, his tone level. "We still need to select and pack your gear. The longer you spend standing around here uselessly, the less time you have for that."

There was no recognition in Burns's gaze, and bless him for the neutral look he regarded Red with. "He in charge?" he presumed.

I shook my head, hard-pressed to keep down the half-hysteric laugh that wanted to escape me. "Nope."

"Someone we know?" Burns asked, a hint of caution sneaking into his tone. The way Nate tensed next to me likely already gave the answer away.

"Yup."

"Who?" Bless him, but Burns wasn't yet tired of my singular answers.

"Bucky." No need to expand on that. They all knew who I was talking about.

The fact that Burns didn't react at all told me that he could easily read the clues right off Nate and me, no further explanation needed. The others didn't know us quite that well—and likely lacked a lot of background knowledge that even I hadn't been privy to until very recently—so their obvious confusion was only understandable.

"Why would you want to work with that damn bastard?" Gita voiced her obvious objection.

My snort came out wryer than I'd aimed for, my voice dipping into almost toneless territory. "Trust me, I really don't want to." That much had been true even before we'd reached the base. Now, it was like a creed, set in stone. Gita's mouth snapped open, obviously to ask why we still were, but I cut her off before our conversation could dip into dangerous territory. "I won't hold it against you if you'd rather not stay. You're still free to leave. All of you."

"We stay," Tanner insisted before anyone could say otherwise, his quiet confidence lending me a hint of hope. "We're in this together. You can explain the details later."

"You're not getting rid of us," Gita insisted, switching course. "You know that you'll need me. Us," she quickly corrected. The blank look on Tanner's face underlined that her slip was just that. My tongue burned with the need to question her about what exactly she knew, which, of course, was just another way of asking what Gabriel Greene had known when he'd deliberately sent her with us. I knew that her fangirl act wasn't just that, an act, but she might as well have proclaimed her mission statement right there. Instead, I nodded, the idea of having at least a hint of an extra security net in place a strangely comforting one. That was settled then, or so I'd thought.

"Actually, we're not done yet." Nate's voice was hard, raspy, and it took me hearing him say that to realize those were his first words since we'd left that conference room. His expression gave nothing away, but his body was singing with tension—never a good thing, but considering that I still remembered all too well how he'd shut down when they'd shot him up with that changed version of the serum, I'd take quietly stewing any day.

Of course, I always preferred no-nonsense, no-bullshit Nate to Broody McBroodface. The corner of my mouth twitched at that thought, sending pangs of pain up to my temple and all along my jaw. Still, worth it.

Once he was sure he had everyone's attention, Nate turned to Jason and Charlie. "You're not coming with us."

"Like hell we won't," Jason started to object immediately, but the look he cast my way was cautious rather than annoyed. Not quite sure where Nate was going with this, all I could do was stare back neutrally.

Nate grimaced, but his tone was far from apologetic. "I'm asking you not to, actually. I have a favor to ask of you. We struck a deal with them, for their head surgeon to try to help Martinez. They will try to get him up here as soon as possible. I would be much obliged if you would tag along and make sure that everything happens according to plan."

Jason looked mostly confused while a dash of hope crossed Charlie's face, but was quickly replaced by a frown. "From what he told me, that strut went right through his spine. Even before the shit hit the fan, that was usually a sentence for life. Their surgeons may be good, but that good?"

Jason cleared his throat before either of us could reply. "And not sure he'd appreciate you dooming yourselves for him."

Even though it hurt, I allowed myself a mirthless grin. Nate provided the answer, chuffing. "That was the carrot. Don't ask about the stick." I didn't miss how Burns scrutinized our entourage once more. Oh, I was sure that he could take a guess.

"And you trust them?" Jason nodded toward Red. "Not to hold Martinez hostage, or shoot us all the second we're out of sight?"

"Like hell," Nate grunted, but shut up when Richards finally abandoned his pretense that he wasn't listening to our every word and joined us. The difference between him in his perfectly maintained, camo-patterned fatigues and our ragtag assortment of gear couldn't have been starker.

"You can trust us," he insisted. He briefly glanced in my direction but continued to talk to Jason. "Contrary to what some may believe, we've never had a quarrel with any of the traders or scavengers. You're from the Utah settlement? If you want my superiors to get on the radio with Minerva to make additional assurances, that can be arranged. Or we can play this via Wilkes at the Silo. Your choice."

Jason looked at Nate instead, who shrugged. "I believe that he thinks he's telling the truth. That doesn't change my assessment in the least." He and Red did some staring that would otherwise have made me crack up, but my first impulse was to try to silently communicate to Nate to maybe not piss off the one guy who was trying to act diplomatic before we had a chance to get our weapons and ammo back. That offer about new gear had sounded genuine, and way too good to ignore.

Nate seemed to come to a similar conclusion, pretending like it was coincidental that he looked away first, not quiet acquiescence. "Besides, I need someone with Martinez who I can trust to have his best interests at heart. I have a feeling that whatever their first assessment will be, someone will stress that shooting him up with the serum is the best option. If he's had one objection all these years, it was that he'd never want that to happen. With us gone, that leaves you the perfect person for that."

Charlie slowly inclined his head, the look on his face solemn. "He mentioned that, once," he agreed.

Even trying to keep my face straight, my confusion must have been plain for everyone to see, making Nate smirk for a moment. "His faith. He made me promise him a long, long time ago to never elect him for a possible candidate because when it was time to go, he wanted to die only once, for good. Guess how great it must have been for him to come to grips that the entire world had gone to hell and now a single bite or scratch could easily destroy that notion for good."

I didn't know what to say, not that it was necessary. Jason still didn't look happy but finally gave his assent. "We'll take care that no one gets the chance to screw with his head. Might not hurt to have someone along who can give a firsthand account of what happened up here."

Red looked suspiciously pleased with that answer, but at least he kept his gloating at bay. "We are happy to either give you a ride with our next troop transport, or help you find other options."

Jason unabashedly grinned at the line of Humvees parked beyond the base fence. "Those come with heating?"

"I will talk to our quartermaster to make sure you will be provided a vehicle that does well in this climate and will bring you safely to whatever destination you have in mind. Once we're back inside the base, we can sort out the details," Red assured.

That was settled then. I didn't know how to feel about it. Relieved, sure, but I could have done without the dawning sense of just having signed their death warrants. Then again, they were likely a lot safer than the rest of us were about to be.

Nate took pity on me and heaved me back up onto the bed of the truck without having to be prompted. I was too numb with pain to care much, but as I'd feared, being so obviously incapacitated in front of my friends made my ego rear up once more, beaten and bruised as it was. Stupid, really, because if there were any people in the world who I could trust not to abuse my current situation, it was them.

There was a brief holdup when one of the soldiers bristled at the others of course bringing all their weapons with them, not just the packs. "Standard regulations for deserters and scum," the soldier groused. His name tag read, "Russell." How convenient that they had those. That one was going to be trouble, I knew it.

Red frowned, clearly at odds with his orders and common sense, or maybe he was annoyed that one of his men was acting like a petulant child. Nate turned to him, ignoring the soldier, giving Red a perfectly blank stare. "We're no good to you unless you arm us, so sooner or later you will have to give us guns with live ammo." I would have added a few expletives, resulting in immediate denial and subsequent issues. Nate, for once the wiser, clearly had a better grasp on how to navigate the situation. I could tell that Red was glad about that, and could proceed by telling his man to stand down. Russell looked less than pleased about that but followed his orders without objection, much to the smirks of several of his peers.

The others hopped up onto the back of the truck, sitting down in the middle of the benches lining the sides of the truck bed. We ended up wedged between the soldiers, shoulder to shoulder, the packs and weapons bundled up between our knees. I tried to keep my back straight but sagged right into Nate's side, incidentally giving Tanner a little more space. Burns, opposite us, eyed my every motion critically while keeping a—clearly fake—grin up as he pushed a huge bag toward Nate that I was sure hadn't been with us when we'd abandoned the wrecked cars. Inside were our sniper rifles—well protected in their cases—Nate's AK, and a heap of our other backup weapons that Nate had opted to leave behind when we'd set out toward the base, just the two of us… what felt like a million years ago.

Red looked on with vague interest—relaxed enough that I figured he trusted us not to be stupid and try to stir up some shit—but it was one of the other soldiers who couldn't keep his trap shut. Cole, if my part-time double vision didn't screw too much with me. "Aren't two of them a little overkill? Compensating much?"

Still keeping perfect control of his expression but as tense as a guitar string about to snap, Nate finished his brief check before he looked up. "Mine, and hers," he said, first pointing at the newer model, then the older. "A blood-thirsty rifle for a blood-thirsty gal."

It wasn't lost on me that this must have been the first time ever that he acknowledged—finally!—having relinquished ownership of his baby to me. I just couldn't appreciate it as much as I would have a week ago. Giving a shit about anything right now was hard. But it was something.

The significance was clearly lost on the idiot. "So you passed your old rifle on to your lady? Such a catch."

I almost laughed when I felt Nate stiffen even more, knowing exactly what part he took issue with.

"That's not just any old rifle. That's one of the finest pieces of killing hardware ever created. And it's seen quite some use."

Maybe he was just trying to defuse the tension, or jumping at a chance to learn anything from Nate's—usually tightly locked-away—background, but Jason asked, "Like where?"

Nate shrugged, although he tried to keep the motion small so as not to disturb me too much. He needn't have bothered; the vibrations of the truck alone were enough to make me want to continuously yip with pain. "Iraq. Iran. Afghanistan. Saudi Arabia. Qatar. Israel. Somalia. Liberia. Côte d'Ivoire. Sudan. Burma. Prague."

The last got not only my interest piqued. Burns let out a brief chuckle. "When did you off someone in Prague? Don't remember any official missions in Europe. Or unofficial ones." I doubted that anything any of the resident grunts had done in the past decade had been officially sanctioned by anyone. They'd probably dunked their mission reports in tar to make the redacting easier.

"Personal matter," Nate offered, guarded as usual. "Was just Romanoff, Zilinsky, and me." His tone was final enough, silently stressing that whatever had happened in Prague was staying in Prague. It sounded recent enough that I figured it had been part of preparing his takeover of the Green Fields Biotech building, and thus our not-accidental-at-all meeting. No swooning from being overcome with romantic nostalgia from me.

It was only then that something occurred to me that I probably should have considered much earlier, but I could see where my mind had drawn a blank on it before. "Shit. How am I ever going to shoot a gun again?"

I got a confused look from Burns that I ignored. Nate's small snort was comforting. "With lots and lots of practice," he offered, trying for a light tone but it held too much strain to be real. "You had no fucking clue how to hold a gun two years ago, either. We'll get you there before you need it." I tried not to, but of course couldn't help but look down at the thick, padded gloves that kept the bandages on my hands well hidden.

Fuck. Just fuck.

With no other way to vent the rising frustration inside of me, I let my body sag against the backrest of my seat. Pain exploded through the right half of my torso, making me sit more upright immediately, that damn whimper finally making it over my lips impossible to hold back. I could almost taste Nate's frustration with his inability to do anything to help. Burns, again, noticed, and this once didn't simply file it away for later.

"Exactly how bad is it?"

Considering Nate's surprise when Raynor had made me strip upon our arrival at the base, I guessed that none of my friends had a clue exactly how far my physical health had already deteriorated when we'd split from them, and I had absolutely no intention of giving a detailed answer now with too many ears around that had no business knowing. I was sure that Red had gotten an update complete with assessment from Raynor and her team, but I wasn't going to volunteer anything else. What I could be open about was the way more permanent change.

"Let's put it this way," I started, giving him a humorless grin. "If I thought I'd stand a chance in hell of you being able to knock me out if you socked me a good one, I'd be begging for it. But as that seems to be a thing of the past, I'll refrain. I'm bruised up enough as it is."

I didn't need to check with Gita, Jason, and Charlie to be aware of their confusion. Hell, I'd spent over a year traipsing through the post-apocalyptic world, barely knowing anything about the effects of the serum except that it made its recipients immune to zombie bites. No wonder my statement didn't ring a bell with them. For Burns, no further explanation was needed.

It was Tanner at my other side who let out a low whistle. "So they finally got you for good, eh?"

"Yup."

"Tried to sleep yet?" he continued. "Took me a good two weeks to manage, and over a month to get some actual rest. That shit's nasty to get used to."

So much more to look forward to. Just what I needed.

"Why?" Burns's question made me raise my brows at him, so he reiterated. "Why did they shoot you up with that shit? You'd think that if they wanted you there, they wouldn't risk the fifty percent conversion rate."

I briefly glanced at Nate, who'd once again fallen into silent fuming. "Guess they figured it was still better than the zero survival chance they gave me without," I offered. "Although I vaguely remember their overall optimism clocking in somewhere around thirty percent. It doesn't really matter as going without wasn't an option either way. I doubt I'd still be alive right now if they hadn't inoculated me, independent of any downsides." Which raised the question of what my body was running on right now, as I couldn't remember the last time I'd eaten anything. The infusions they'd given me couldn't sustain me for long.

The truck rumbling onto the base proper kept me from having to offer up further information. Instead of going back to the creepy-as-fuck underground complex that I now knew went far beyond the surface area of the base, it ambled toward one of the warehouse-sized buildings topside. As abandoned as the outside of the base seemed at a first glance, the interior was bustling with activity, people on foot and in smaller vehicles going this way and that. The lot of us was deposited by a growing stack of crates and bundles. The soldiers remained with us, because obviously we'd all been biding our time to infiltrate their home and now were about to rain fiery destruction upon them—for all of three seconds that it would take anyone to gun us down. In all honesty, I could understand why they wouldn't just let us wander off, but it was amusing to watch them watch us cautiously as Nate not only armed himself, but also made sure that all my backup guns were loaded. I got comfortable on the crate he deposited me on, careful to only lean my shoulders against the crate atop mine to remain in a somewhat upright position. It was warm enough inside that I could have ditched a full outer layer, but I still didn't feel the need to, nor was I particularly fond of the idea of taking off my gloves; getting them on had been bad enough. Gita and Charlie did the same, both still not quite recovered from the wolf attack.

Before Nate was done loading up, Red stepped up to us, ignoring the scowls of his men pretending to guard us.

"Hill over there will set you up with a radio so you can call whoever you want. Let me know when you're done," he told Jason before he turned to Nate. "We have about an hour left until the containers are loaded into the plane. If you got a minute to stop being needlessly paranoid, you might want to consider updating your gear."

While the offer sounded amicable enough, I didn't miss the slightly condescending note—and that wasn't aimed at Nate's penchant for stocking up on weapons. Unlike what I would have done, Nate didn't sneer right back into Red's face that we'd done a fine job dragging our weapons and tactical clothing out of every hidey-hole we'd encountered, but instead asked, "How much do we get?"

"Whatever you need," Red offered, looking toward the huge doors at the back of the building. "Over there are our stocks. Just don't needlessly ransack it, and only get what you can actually carry. There are washing machines on board the ship for the first leg of the journey."

I idly wondered if anyone would be interested in hearing my observations on exactly how long some people could make their underwear last before it fell off them in rags, but refrained. The swelling in my lower jaw had receded to a general state of puffiness without making me feel like I'd stuffed my cheeks with marshmallows, but talking remained uncomfortable. That still made it pretty much the least painful activity I could think of.

"Weapons and ammo, too?" Nate asked when Red made no move to leave. Good little soldier that he was, he likely had his pack ready for departure. Ah, to amuse myself with my own jokes…

Red glanced at the heap of weapons that Nate had dumped next to me before he answered. "Get as much ammo as you reasonably think you will need. Weapons only what you have to."

Nate wasn't exactly pleased with that response. "How shall I know what you consider reasonable when I don't have a fucking clue what you're setting us up against?"

For once, that gripe seemed to amuse Red. "Expect heavy opposition, damn hard to kill. About what you would have brought here if you hadn't had to bank on our goodwill to help your wife."

Nate didn't react to that jibe, but instead turned to Burns. "Fifty percent ammo, thirty percent for rations, twenty for clothes." That was pretty much what we'd been stocking last summer—or aiming for, never getting anywhere near those amounts of weapons or whatever they could shoot. Burns nodded, then grabbed Tanner and they headed toward the doors. Nate hesitated, giving me a downright uneasy look before he trudged after them. I had no idea what that had been about, and no intention of investigating.

Through the open doors, I got a pretty good look at what Red had described as their stocks. It looked like a mix between clothing storage and military surplus warehouse, at least the parts I could see. I figured this was where all the things that had been raided from the houses we'd checked in North Dakota a few months ago had ended up. They must have spent a lot of time dragging anything remotely useful up here.

As if he'd read my mind, Red noted, "We don't keep it all to ourselves. Most of the things we store are for the settlements. We only need so many teapots in the mess hall."

"You mean, the settlements that lick your boots and roll over the second you come anywhere near them," I grumbled.

I was starting to wonder if they'd selected Red to be our babysitter simply because it was impossible to get a rise out of him. Rather than get annoyed at my needling, he shrugged. "We help those that accept our offer, yes. We don't run a charity, and neither do you."

That rankled. "Yeah, but we don't raze them to the ground when they do something differently than what we think they should."

"No, you just infect them and turn them into walking bombs," he shot back. Ah, there was that annoyance that I'd been fishing for— only that it came with a rebuke that I couldn't quite refute.

Nate and Burns returning—bristling with ammo and weapons, what else?—prevented me from either having to go off in Red's face, or continuing to roll around in my ever-present guilt, freshly stoked as it was by finding out that, contrary to what was common knowledge, me infecting that asshole hadn't led to Petty Officer Stanton's death but only her severe mutilation. "Tanner says to come see what you need," Nate told Gita, waiting for her to leave before he dropped his load and turned to me. "I'm not sure if your shotgun will still be working for you, but any asshole can hit something with an M16. Think you can get used to that as your primary weapon? You like the M4 well enough."

I was tempted to tell him where to shove his sarcasm—and I didn't miss the slight chiding note in there, putting an end to our ongoing debate why I always grabbed the Mossberg when I could get away with it—but left it at a nod. "Idiot-proof sounds right up my alley." Was that the hint of a smirk I saw crossing Red's face? Impossible.

Nate went on as if he had assumed I wouldn't protest. "Most of your gear should be good but I'm getting you a new jacket and some extra thermal underpants." I would have grinned at that had it not hurt like a bitch. "Anything else you want? I know it must be heartbreaking for you that the one time we get an opportunity to go shopping, you're down for the count."

Without Red standing there, I would have prattled off a list of absolutely nonsensical items, but it was bad enough that anything I'd say would have to stand the test of Nate's judgment. I didn't need that from another asshole as well.

"Boots would be great," I offered, raising my right leg just enough so I could look down at the scuffed one I was wearing right now. "Sole's getting a little worn out."

Nate nodded, but hesitated as he turned to leave. "Size-wise…"

"Same as usual," I replied before he could say another word.

That earned him a frown from Burns. "Since when don't you know her size? You've been picking up clothes for her on the go for ages." Then a possible answer must have occurred to him and his attention skipped from my boots to my gloves before hovering near my face. I held it easily when our gazes met. My worries about not being able to properly hold a gun should have given it away, but apparently, that had taken some time to sink in. I didn't fault either of them that they were very quick to make an exit, leaving me sitting there with the packs, gear, and guns…

Smirking over at Red, I snorted. "You weren't afraid that he'd shoot you in the back of the head the second he got a loaded gun in his hands. You're here making sure I don't kill myself with one."

Red had the grace not to try to deny it, offering a small shrug instead. "I didn't believe that you'd be that stupid, but others disagree with me."

"About me being suicidal, or me being stupid?"

He wisely refrained from answering, but my guess was both. I really didn't like that he continued to prove himself a good judge of character. As much as I absolutely couldn't stand anyone associated with the bunch of lunatics that had, repeatedly, contributed to ruining my life, so far all of them had underestimated me, which had long since turned into a security blanket I had been basing a lot of my strategy on. Damnit. So much for that old adage about being careful what you wished for.

It took a while until the others returned, Gita and Tanner first, with Burns lagging behind. Nate dropped two already stuffed backpacks next to me before he turned to leave again, hesitating when I spoke up. "I want an ax. Like the one Minerva was carrying? Maybe two. If there's one advantage to being impervious to zombie bites and packing a little extra strength, it's being useful with edged weapons." I was surprised when Nate ended his brief consideration with a nod.

"Tactical tomahawk," Red said once Nate had left.

"Huh?"

"It's not an ax. It's called a tactical tomahawk," he insisted.

I couldn't help but snort. "Really? That's what you're wasting your breath on?"

"Proper designations are important. You're part of us now. Might as well behave like it."

I refrained from mentioning all the wonderful activities that came to mind at that statement. Raynor, burdened with a large bag, stalking toward us, her heels clicking loudly on the concrete floor, made that all the more easy. I couldn't help but tense—that woman just gave me the creeps, independent of what she'd done to me, but that sure didn't help—which in turn made me wince. Damn, but I couldn't wait for my body to heal up so I could do strenuous things like lounge around once more. She eyed me critically as she approached, dumping the bag unceremoniously beside my crate perch.

"In here is everything you will need to jump-start your GI tract," she explained without preamble. "Once you start, you need to keep to the exact schedule. Shouldn't be too hard, considering you will have nothing else to do for the next couple of days. I've added a list with the instructions, and recalculations should you be too much of an imbecile to keep to said schedule."

I could have come up with a million things to spew back at her, but kept it at a wry, "I won't." That must have annoyed her more, anyway.

Raynor gave a curt nod as she reached into the bag, pointing out various containers—and the shaker, complete with hand-drawn marks in what I presumed was her scrawl. "We need to reestablish your gut biome first, so it will be another four days until you can start on semi-solid foods. Until then you will have to subsist on this cocktail of vitamins, fatty acids, oligosaccharides, and amino acids. Remember, the exact number of scoops with the exact amount of water, spaced six hours apart."

"You do remember the part where I'm a scientist and used to following more complicated protocols than 'three scoops dissolved in sixty-four ounces of water,' right?"

I had to hand it to her, she smiled rather than scoffed, but that wasn't much better.

"Funny that you'd mention that." It wasn't. Reaching into the bag once more, she pulled out a thick wad of folders. "Here is the entire documentation on the serum project, as you like to refer to it. Including everything you brought us on that flash drive, with copies of your notes. I would be much obliged if you'd spend all that idle time you're facing looking this over and supplying me with the answers you promised in your grandstanding statement upon your arrival at our doorstep." I had seldom been less interested in anything scientific in my life, and that enthusiasm must have been plain on my face as a frown crossed Raynor's expression. "You do realize that this personally concerns you now? If not to hold up Raleigh Miller's legacy or save your husband's life, you have stakes in this yourself. The serum variant you were inoculated with comes with a lot less drawbacks than the old versions, but what you likely consider the underlying flaw—the absolute potential of conversion upon the expiration of the subject—is still a very active, central part of it. I'm ready to offer to develop an antidote for you and a select group of your choice, but for that you need to do the research first. If you don't, no one else will. It's entirely up to you."

I was surprised by her offer, but not stupid enough to believe that it wouldn't come with a catch—and there was still the testing of whether it worked or not. Finding subjects for that would be impossible, so the best she could offer me was hope to start with— and that was one resource I was not running very high on right now. I still inclined my head, mutely agreeing to her offer.

A nurse approaching with two liquid bags put an end to that discussion—one-sided as it had been—making Raynor snap an irritated, "Finally," to him before she nodded toward me. "Left arm, please. There's not much more I can do for you, but a dash of liquids and nutrients never hurt anyone. Because of the massive wound healing that your body is still concerned with, and the damage your left femur has sustained, another blood transfusion won't hurt, either." She paused when she realized that I still hadn't moved. "What are you waiting for? Scoot!"

I opened my mouth to explain to her that right now I lacked the fine motor skills to accommodate her request—if you could call it that—but Nate returning spared me that. It was comical to see her tense as she watched him approach, a pack slung over each shoulder, an ax—excuse me, tactical tomahawk—in each hand. Add to that the blank look on his face—turning his expression decidedly homicidal—and I could see where she might have gotten a little cautious. Sure, she had saved my life, but apparently her narcissism didn't go as far as to not realize how someone close to me might see that. And it wasn't like any of us believed her innocent where the fallout of their conditions, for lack of a better word, was concerned.

I would have loved to keep the staring match up that they had going on, but I sorely lacked the energy required. "Help me?" I asked, raising my left arm as I nodded toward the nurse, still holding the liquid bags. Without a word, Nate dropped his burden and set to extricating enough of my arm so they could reach the crook of my left elbow. Part of me was still wondering why they hadn't left a line in me to make this easier—at least until I caught a glance at my wrist, previously quite bruised from the multitude of needles they'd stuck into me there. The surface was completely healed, only the barest hint of a greenish cast underneath visible where the deepest of the bruises had been. Maybe that shouldn't have surprised me, considering how well my body was working with less than a day since it had been a slab of paralyzed meat on the operating room table, but it did.

"Start with the liquid nutrition in exactly six hours." Raynor's bark drew my attention back to her. Rather than ask what she was referring to, Nate quickly set an alarm on his watch before he accepted the bags from the nurse. Apparently those wheelie stands were overrated—or they were afraid one of us would use it as a blunt weapon. Considering the amount of ammo I was sitting on, that idea was hilarious—until I realized that it wouldn't be me doing that bashing, considering that my hands had about zero grip potential at the moment. Truly, a gift that kept on giving.

Raynor continued pointing out the next stages in my nutritional journey back to a working GI tract before she halted, something else occurring to her. "You are aware that you're running on borrowed fuel? Your body has barely enough energy on its own to sustain what's left of your muscles and reserves. If you key up now, you die." For once, she interpreted my deadpan stare as what it was—confusion. "Key up? Mobilize reserves only granted to you because of the metabolic changes due to the serum?" Raynor prompted. "You do that, you're toast. Also no overexertion of any kind. No running, no panic attacks. It will take a while for you to feel moderately human again, and until then you have to keep your metabolism as low as possible. If you can, don't even think." She said that like it wasn't something she thought I needed to concern myself with. "Your body will do its best to conserve energy. Don't do anything to antagonize it."

It was obvious that she considered her work done as Raynor turned to go, but me calling after her made her halt in her tracks. "Do you have any antiandrogens stocked here? As a personal favor to me."

Just to see surprise on that unshakable expression was worth the try. "I told you, you need low levels of testosterone for muscle regeneration—" she started, but cut off when I shook my head.

"Not for me. Her." I jerked my chin toward Gita. "But you do it as a favor to me. I won't let anyone else get caught up in this who doesn't have to. You want my full cooperation? Give me a reason to trust you." Raynor frowned, without a doubt gearing up to say something that would piss me off, but I forestalled her. "Yes, you saved my life, but that only goes so far. You're playing games. You want me to be an active participant rather than a pawn? Give me a reason." Talking so much in one go made me want to whimper with pain, but I did my best to ignore it. Getting confirmation for that guess in Raynor's eyes was worth it for sure.

She gave the idea some thought before she offered a brief nod, stepping up to Gita for a quick conversation. I didn't miss the torn look Gita sent me, but I ignored that as well. If I could have thought of anything else to get out of this damn deal, if you could call it that, I would have voiced it. Raynor stalked away and was back just as the nurse disconnected the clear nutrient bag and swapped it for the blood transfusion. She handed Gita two bottles of pills and a handwritten note, followed by what I was sure were equally asinine instructions as I'd gotten minutes before. She ended it with a succinct—and loud enough to carry to the rest of us—"If you decide you do want to go through with the operation, our facility is likely the last place on earth that is fully staffed and equipped for it. Even discounting that, if you grow tired of always being the weakest one of your friends, you know that we can remedy that, too."

Raynor was quick to leave after that, before I could change my mind regarding coming after her with the next best thing I could use to inflict blunt force trauma—lacking grip strength, any body part would do. I'd happily take the pain I'd inflict on myself that way. It was only then that I realized that if Raynor—like her entire staff— had also gotten inoculated with the serum, she could likely wipe the floor with me as it was. A sobering thought, but nothing worth dwelling on.

Gita was still frowning after Raynor, which thankfully made her miss the calculating look that crossed Tanner's face before he wiped it clean. My hostile stare catching his might have done the trick. It was none of my business, but I'd be damned if I kept my trap shut about that.

"If you do, make sure to only let them shoot you up with that shit after they're done with the rest, even if it holds the potential of being inefficient as you might very well die from the serum," I called over, getting Gita's attention.

Her brows rose in confusion. "If I'm stronger afterward, wouldn't it make sense to go the other way round?" she asked.

The very idea made me cringe hard enough that she saw me physically recoil, only increasing her bewilderment.

"Trust me, that's not something you want to be awake for," I grumbled. When that didn't do the trick, I snorted. "The serum turns your body immune to a lot of things, including painkillers and most anesthetics. So if you have a choice—use it. I didn't have one."

The expression of abject horror on Gita's face shouldn't have made me feel vindicated, but it did, a little. At least I'd made sure that she wouldn't run headfirst into her doom without anyone letting her read the fine print first. I knew I'd jeered too soon when the quality of her gaze changed.

"Wait. Does that mean that they did to you whatever they did to you while you were fully conscious?"

I avoided looking in Nate's direction—knowing that he knew was bad enough—but that got me a good look at the guys' faces. I really didn't care for the sympathy on Burns's, but at least he did a good job reining it in, knowing from experience that I didn't deal well with that. Tanner had definitely changed this stance toward Raynor's suggestion, yet didn't look that surprised. I was starting to feel that anyone associated with that damn serum program was quick to jump to the worst conclusions. Now, Jason and Charlie, freshly back from their radio call, looked like they dearly needed a hug themselves on top of those they wanted to dish out. I almost quipped at them whether they were ready to change their minds about helping Martinez, but it was too late for that, anyway. If it helped straighten out their expectations, that was fine with me. And maybe now they understood why Nate was so adamant about our medic getting his way, whatever he chose.

"Didn't have a choice," I repeated. No explanation because my jaw was giving me enough grief from all the talking I'd done. More to distract myself than because I was actually interested, I glanced at the transfusion bag. It was almost empty, making me frown. I had virtually no experience with things like that, but I remembered that normally it was a process that took hours rather than fifteen minutes. Neither that nor the nutrients before made me feel any different, but it was hard to say underneath the all-encompassing level of discomfort I was existing in. The nurse noticed my gaze but didn't explain. Considering that I had gotten the feeling that the staff here saw their patients more as subjects—as Raynor had repeatedly stressed herself—I figured he wasn't used to anyone wanting an explanation.

Ten minutes later, that business was concluded, and I was wrapped back up in my layers of winter clothes, still not breaking a sweat while the others had stripped off their jackets by now. Considering how warm the nurse's fingers had felt even through the latex gloves, I doubted that my body temperature was in the normal range. I couldn't find it in me to care. Right now, just continuing to breathe felt like a laborious task, yet the two times I deliberately stopped, my lungs expanded to draw in another breath about ten heartbeats later. It was somewhat comforting to realize that while my mind was going interesting places, my body did a good job running on autopilot.

I must have been staring off into space for at least twenty minutes, ignoring the bustling activity around us, when a sort of commotion running through our group drew my attention back to what was going on. Nate and Burns had been busy stowing away our gear in the large cargo crates that had been provided to us, but both halted now, staring toward the other side of the building. Nate was already turning away, but the light frown on Burns's forehead gave away the fact that something was indeed happening. I tried to make out what, but the only thing I saw was a bunch of soldiers lugging their packs and crates to the growing stack near the doors. It took two of them actively avoiding looking in our direction that I realized what this might be about.

"Someone you know?" I asked in their general direction, guessing that Nate would ignore me, anyway.

Burns continued to watch for a moment longer before he focused on me. "Know, yes. Those are Murdock and Davis. Haven't seen them since—" He stopped there, scratching his chin. I didn't miss the sidelong glance he cast Nate's way, who was industriously stowing things away now. "Any reason you keep avoiding 'em?"

"Nope," came the succinct answer from inside the crate, giving us quite the opposite message. When neither of us remarked anything—Burns because he was still musing, me because just sitting there was a chore of epic proportions—Nate stiffened, then turned to us. "I'm not avoiding anything. Like that's an option." His gaze briefly flitted in my direction but ended up trained on the soldiers. "They were part of my team. They chose to go with the other side. End of story."

The feeling must have been mutual, as virtually every other soldier joining the loading effort had done his fair share of staring our way. Those two didn't even glance in our general direction. That boded well. Because we didn't have any potential for conflict brewing so far, none whatsoever.

As if even vaguely thinking about his deeds had summoned him, Bucky Hamilton chose that moment to stride into the room. He had no avoidance issues whatsoever, but I was almost happy to see him gloating from the first second on, because that gave me the mental push to stop slouching and mobilize what little energy my body could muster to sit up straight. Red gave me something that might have been a warning glance—not that I gave a shit about that—before he joined the group of soldiers that came tagging along with Hamilton. I recognized a few of them—Aimes, the guy who had given us intel about the Colorado base was among them, together with the other four soldiers of his team. I was surprised to see the female soldier from back then along as well, but probably shouldn't have been. That cemented what I'd guessed after that all had been over—they hadn't snuck out. Someone had sent them to us, and if it hadn't been Hamilton himself, it had been whoever was in charge of him as well. So much for our grand victory. As if I needed something else to sour my already abysmal mood.

What I presumed was a quick status report followed, likely detailing what was obvious to anyone surveilling what was going on—we were about ready to depart. At Hamilton's loud whistle, all activity ceased, heads turning in his direction. Oh, was he basking in all that attention. His men saluted, some mighty giddy to get going.

I figured he would ignore us as long as he possibly could—likely until we arrived wherever we were headed to—but I was quickly proven wrong of that assessment when he started his speech.

"Ladies, gentlemen," he started, nodding in turn at the female soldier and one of the pilots, then the rest of the group in general. "Rejects in the back." Ah, so we didn't go unnoticed. How lovely. A few heads turned and the odd chuckle came up, but was quickly suppressed, like they were actually trying to be civil. The latter was likely due to Red donning a stark glower that would have even made me shut up had my trap been open. As much as Bucky was an asshole, at least his lieutenant had a firm hand, it seemed.

Hamilton barely spared a glance in our direction before he went on, but that still made the seething pool of aggression in my stomach skyrocket—which was considerable since I couldn't even hop off my crate right now.

"As you all know, reaching the objective of our mission is vital. Failure is not an option, and there is a good chance that not all of us will make it back. We are being sent into an unknown, possibly hostile, territory, and I expect every single one of you to do your best." I was waiting for another jeer in our direction, but Bucky disappointed me this time. He made eye contact with each of his men and women, skipping over us. "Use the two weeks we will be spending in transit for getting rid of the fat you've been collecting from sitting on your lazy asses, and make sure your hand-to-hand skills are up to par. We are taking as much ammo with us as we can carry, but you all know, Europe's not as full of trigger-happy assholes as the best country in the whole wide world." Some good-natured chuffing answered him. Bucky allowed himself a quick nod. "Time for one last gear check, then we move everything into the plane. Last chance to call home. We're leaving at 1700 sharp."

Acknowledgments were loud and enthusiastic. What rubbed me the wrong way was how downright fond his soldiers seemed of Hamilton. I wasn't sure why that surprised me—Taggard had been popular among his flunkies as well—but it grated. The soldiers jumped into action, loading the last crates and congregating into small clusters. Red was busy for a good five minutes before he joined us once more, not letting it show whether he was annoyed to still have to play liaison, or not.

"I presume you will want to let your people know what you're up to, although not all of you are coming with us?" he asked, first looking at me but then addressing Nate instead.

Would you believe that display of civility?

Nate was as surprised as I was, but didn't hesitate. "If you can get us a call through to Dispatch, we'd appreciate it."

Red's smile held a certain lopsided quality. "I can do you one better. Why not go directly to who you really want to get on the line? We have the open frequencies for New Angeles, and if they realize it's you calling, they'll let it go through, I'm sure."

I didn't mind not having to deal with Rita again, but his claim was a little disconcerting, if not that much of a surprise. They'd been quick enough to block us when Greene's people had been blasting out my speech, and as far as I knew, there had been no change on the open frequencies. As for the rest, Gita was likely the only one who knew more about that.

"Much obliged," Nate replied, his tone light enough that I almost believed it. The look he sent my way was cautious, making me roll my eyes at him. No, today of all days I wasn't going to pick a fight with Greene just to make myself feel better. I doubted that anything short of Bucky's head on a pike would accomplish that.

Red brought a small laptop over, handing it to Gita when she was the only one not looking stunned. There was minimal pointing and discussing involved, making me guess that they were using whatever satellite communications system was still operational that the Silo and Dispatch were also patched into. I used the time to rearrange myself on my crate in a way that made me think I looked slightly better than Burns's earlier assessment when we'd gone out to fetch them, but not sure why I bothered. We all had to crowd together to make it into the focus field of the camera as Gita set the laptop on another crate, then let the connection come alive. The video call window remained black while she rattled off a sequence that I was certain someone was taking notes of but would be useless after that one call, then turned on to a view of Greene plonking down in his chair, two of his usual hench people visible behind him. He did a quick head count but his eyes didn't remain trained on my and Nate's corner of the view.

"To what do I owe the pleasure of this unexpected call?" Greene asked, all relaxed as he leaned back in his chair. "You're all looking mighty cozy for having officially been labeled 'lost in the winter snowstorms.'"

Gita smiled. The others were mostly looking grim.

"Good to see you," I said when it became obvious that no one else was going to.

Greene took it in stride, his game face spot on. "And a very nice day to you, too," he answered with just enough of a teasing hint to sound like we were actually friends. "I presume you're no longer in the Silo? Seeing as they kicked you out a week ago and all that jazz." And again with the underhanded info dumping.

"Nope," I agreed with him. "We're in fucking Canada." No one seemed to be paying attention to us, but I had a certain feeling they wouldn't be happy if I blabbed about our coordinates.

"I see," Greene said. "Visiting old friends?"

I wondered if my deadpan stare had given that much away, but I did my best to nod ever so slightly in Nate's direction. Maybe Greene would get the hint, maybe not. It didn't really matter.

"Looks like we won't be home for Christmas," I went on. "All of us. Can you call our people, and Minerva up in Utah? Just so nobody gets sent out on a wild goose chase with no geese to actually, well, chase. Charlie and Jason got their own mission, and they already called their people, but the more people know, the better."

A brief smirk crossed Greene's face, but rather than regale himself by pointing out my less than stellar verbal dexterity, he cocked his head to the side. "Planning on going somewhere?"

I gave a quick nod. "East. And then East some more. As in, east across the pond. Got some things to do, places to be."

Greene's smile turned a little strained. "Can you possibly be any more vague?"

"Nope. It's all very hush, hush and need to know."

"And you don't," he stated rather than asked. I tried to grin, but it mostly turned into a wince as my still swollen cheek didn't quite cooperate.

"Something like that." I wondered how much to divulge, but as Red hadn't yet shot the laptop to scrap metal, I figured they weren't concerned with us sharing information—not that there was much else to share. "You might actually know more about possible destinations over there than we do. You know, something remote; romantic; completely overrun with something you need to send twenty super soldiers in to retrieve something."

Greene's face lit up like a small child that had just realized that he knew the possible answer to a riddle. "Oh, there's Guernsey," he mused. "But I think you'll be heading to either France or Germany. Or Croatia, but that's a stretch." He paused, waiting for a reaction from me, but as I didn't know anything, there was nothing I could contribute. "All lovely in the winter," Greene went on. "Well, thanks for the call. Send a postcard once you get there, will you?"

"We will," Gita replied before I could, making me guess that he meant for her to try to establish communications once we knew more. For the first time since dooming our friends to share our misery, I thought that having Gita—so very obviously the weakest link in our chain—along might just be a blessing in disguise, as she herself had insisted. That Bucky would vastly underestimate her was a given, but even Red had barely spent a moment judging her combat prowess and fitness. It wasn't without humor that with my recent change in immunological status, she'd kind of taken my usual place. Hopefully, she'd fare better than I had of late.

That about concluded the call, and ten minutes later we were getting ready to move our gear. That also meant saying goodbye to Jason and Charlie, both looking conflicted, more so than before. Nate spent a good five minutes firing off whispered instructions that were well received by nods only, until we parted ways after a series of back slaps and hugs. We watched as the two Chargers left, hopping into a waiting Humvee that they had all to themselves that, minutes later, left with two more in tow, presumably as an escort. With everything that we couldn't carry lost in our trashed cars below that crumbling bridge, we didn't even have anything to send with them on their way. And then it was time for us to leave as well.

The hangar, as it turned out, was beyond the huge doors so far having remained closed, likely so none of us could sneak over there and sabotage the—honest-to-God—plane being refueled right now. The crates were loaded inside using handcarts, stacks of them disappearing into the maw of the plane's body beyond the huge ramp. I'd only ever gotten close to commercial planes so seeing a different layout where the entire body of it—save for the tank, I figured—were open and accessible was strange. I couldn't really take inventory of it, seeing as hobbling over there, most of my weight on Nate's supporting arm and shoulder, took over the majority of my mental capacity. By the time he unloaded me into one of the seats on the left side of the hull of the cargo compartment, I was barely conscious and not much help as he strapped me into the belt harness. I had a brief moment of panic as he left, only to return with our packs, anchoring them to the crates still being loaded into the middle of the plane. They were stacked only one level high, leaving me a good view of where Red and Bucky strapped in opposite us.

Sure, with twenty people and what must have been over sixty seats easily, we had to end up exactly there. Burns noisily plonking into the seat on my other side thankfully drew my focus away.

"Ah, good old C-130," he remarked, rapping his knuckles against the hull behind his head. "Didn't think I'd get to fly with one of the old ladies again. You're in for a treat." My skeptical look made him burst out laughing, loud enough that Bucky looked over, clearly annoyed with the distraction. "No comforts whatsoever, and loud enough that you'd think they'd strapped you right onto the wings. What's not to love?" Just then, the engines of the plane came to life, proving Burns right where the noise level was concerned.

So many things came to mind, but sagging back against my seat was easier, so that's what I did. What the fuck had I gotten us into?

And, even more importantly: how the fuck would we survive this?

Chapter 2

The flight to the east coast came rather close to my new definition of hell, and considering my recent experiences, that was saying something. Under different circumstances, I was sure that I would have dozed off within minutes, terrible drone notwithstanding, but it just didn't happen. My body shut down all right, leaving me a sentient sack of meat slouched in the seat, barely capable of shifting to try to minimize my discomfort, utterly failing each and every time. Everything hurt, down to the roots of my hair. And there was nothing to distract myself with, giving my mind ample opportunity to get caught in mental loops and replays that did nothing to make me feel better. I soon gave up trying not to appear like I was a heap of misery, no longer giving a shit what Bucky or any of the others might think.

I didn't hear Nate's alarm go off, but when he unbuckled himself—ignoring whatever bullshit Bucky hollered across the crates in return, I didn't catch it—he went through the pack Raynor had packed for me until he resurfaced with a bottle of water, the shaker, and the white container, equally labeled with Raynor's exact instructions. Nate studied it for a moment before he unscrewed it, dumping five randomly filled scoops rather than three exact ones into the shaker and using at the most three quarters of the water indicated. He made sure to block Bucky's view of me as he shook the shaker long enough to dissolve everything, then held it to my lips so I could drink without even having to try to grab it myself. My mouth was parched from the dry air inside the plane, but swallowing hurt. It took me a little to realize that was not just because of spending way too long with that intubation tube rammed down my airways, but were likely the aftershocks of almost getting strangled. One more reminder I could have done without.

I didn't feel any better after downing the contents of the shaker, but nausea soon joined the myriad of other protests my body was lit up with. I managed to keep everything down, but that sapped what was left of my strength right out of me. I barely noticed as the aircraft touched down, although the absence of the droning noise was much appreciated. Nate pretty much dragged me out of my seat and onto the tarmac, the icy wind slicing across my face rousing me a little. It was dark outside, the lights indicating the location of the landing strip the only illumination besides the stars. They seemed dim compared to what I had gotten used to, but as Nate dumped me on a crate to get our packs, I had a moment to look at our surroundings. My eyesight was still weird, but I could definitely see quite well in the dark. I tried to remember if I'd mentioned that to Raynor, or anyone else around here for that matter, but came up blank. I'd have to see for myself—literally—if that was some advantage I'd managed to hide from the people thinking they were in charge of me now.

We'd landed on an airstrip belonging to a base similar to the one in Canada, only much smaller, and lacking the underground labs from what I could tell. There were some buildings, one hangar large enough to house the aircraft once it had been unloaded, but that was about it. It was cold but somewhat warmer than at the beginning of our journey. As I inhaled deeply, I thought I caught the scent of the ocean on the wind. It was anyone's guess where exactly we had touched down, not that it mattered.

There were some vehicles stationed at the base, but they were used for cargo hauling exclusively, leaving us to make the trek down to the nearby dock on foot. It was less than half a mile from what I could tell, but that was still way too far for me. From how they had handled getting on the plane, I'd figured that Nate and Burns were trying to make me appear stronger than I was, but that attempt died a quick death when I couldn't even manage to remain standing on my own for ten seconds, let alone walk twenty steps. Nate ended up carrying me in his arms like a small child, silently laboring under my weight. If anyone was making stupid remarks, I was too out of it to hear them. Nor did I care. Everything was god-awful, everything hurt, and it just didn't end.

The air grew warmer as light hit my half-closed eyes, a chemical smell replacing the cool ocean breeze. We must have entered the ship. The sound of unfamiliar voices, drowned out by my own near-silent whimper as Nate had to shift my body, the narrow walls around us necessitating that. Steps up, down, more corridors. A brief spell of vertigo as I was set down, hard, padded body being replaced by more fluffy sheets and a mattress. I thought I recognized Red's voice but deliberately blocked it out. I just couldn't go on anymore. It was all too much.

My mind, of course, had other ideas.

A loud thump—flesh meeting steel—followed by a low curse made me look up. All I could see of Nate was his back where he was standing in the cramped space by the end of the bunk bed. Judging from the tension in his shoulders and how he began shaking his left wrist, that had been his fist connecting to the steel wall.

"You done yet?" Burns remarked, uncharacteristically acerbic from next to him.

"Not by a long shot," Nate mumbled under his breath, his voice hard, laced with frustration.

"Well, feel free to resume once we're settled in. Until then, move it." It took my dear husband a good ten seconds to shake himself out of his stupor of rage, but pretending like he had neither conscience nor emotions wasn't new to him. I still saw the strain left around his eyes. Oh, he was livid, and I had a certain feeling that wouldn't change any time soon. Good.

Gita, just inside the door where she'd halted to give Nate and Burns room to move, cast a quizzical look at Tanner over her shoulder. Burns noticed, turning back to Nate. "Care to tell us what happened?"

I didn't miss Nate's passing glance in my direction. "That's not enough?"

"Enough to explain why you're frustrated as fuck, sure," Burns enthused. "But not wall-punching livid."

Someone else might have looked chagrined at that observation. Nate held Burns's gaze unflinchingly. "Nothing."

The short bark of laughter he got back wasn't very amused. "Same as her 'nothing' that ended up with us fighting our way through half the country?"

"Nothing that concerns you."

Nate's rebuke was sharp enough to hold a decidedly final note, but Burns shrugged it off without a care in the world.

"Have it your way," he drawled, then cocked his head to the side. "When's the last time you slept?"

"Sleep? Huh." Nate raked a hand through his hair, making it stand up at weird angles. He rolled his shoulders, as if that would help him think. "A week ago? The night before that snafu at the lake. When we still had cars."

"Healthy," Burns provided, but let his pack drop from his shoulder, no longer ready to keep Nate from smashing all the bones in his hand to powder.

Nate's ire, barely dissipated, came flaring right back to life. "You think I could sleep knowing that they're cutting up my wife, not knowing if she's going to survive and if I should even pray for that to happen? Or after they brought her back as a bloody, swollen, whimpering heap of misery? You tell me you could have acted any differently!"

Burns mutely raised his hands, signaling Nate to calm down. When he replied, his tone held a fake note of levity. "You might as well have. Nothing as simple as that will get her down. You know her better than that. Tenacious bitch won't bite it just to spite you." He got an answering snort for that, most of the tension dissipating once more.

The two of them then debated in hushed tones before they set to stowing away our gear. I turned my head, also so I wouldn't get lashed by whipping belts, ending up with my face mashed into a lumpy pillow. That made for a great view of the beige wall, the steel frame of the upper part of the bunk bed I was currently curled up in at the lower level, three more bunk beds lining the walls of the now terribly crowded cabinet of a room, and some lockers by the door. Every available surface—including some of the beds—was heaped with packs and gear as the others got comfortable, or as comfortable as possible. There was theoretically room for twelve, but the five of us did a great job filling the room. Gita did the smart thing and climbed up onto the upper bunk of the last bed at the opposite side, taking herself out of the equation of where to fit everything. I could only see one of her legs hanging down, but she kept joking with Burns as he kept unpacking. I was a little surprised that Nate had unloaded me onto the bed closest to the door rather than stashing me away in the back corner, but I certainly appreciated the fact that there was some more space around here to let the door open into the room. Sheesh, but whoever had furnished this room hadn't left an inch of extra space.

So far, I wasn't very impressed with this ship.

Things quieted down eventually, Tanner picking the upper bunk above Nate's while Burns took the lower one opposite—putting him where I planned to stash my feet, if behind the frame section—with all the middle bunks used for storage. That left Nate opposite me, not much of a surprise. Rather than plonk down on his bed, Nate leaned into the space occupied by my body—I wouldn't have called it having gotten comfortable as comfort was as far out of my reach as the sun. He scrutinized my face for a moment, his own expression pinched. He'd calmed down some, but the trepidation rising in his gaze didn't exactly make me feel better. I looked up at him with my one uncovered eye, not moving a muscle.

"Let's get you out of all that before you overheat," he mumbled, already reaching for me so he could reposition my body for easier access. I didn't try to help, too drained to attempt to bat his hands away.

It took him a good five minutes to peel me out of my jacket and the thick layer of fleece underneath, incidentally hurting me enough that I considered kicking him for real, not just accidentally. As soon as he let me go, I flopped over onto my stomach, trying to stifle my groan with the pillow. "Can't you just let me die instead?"

I thought I heard a sympathetic chuff from Burns's direction.

"Too late for that," Nate bit out between clenched teeth. When I made no move to do anything—expiring included, sadly—I heard him sigh. "Come on. I know it sucks, but sooner or later you'll have to get out of most of your clothes. And I have to check on your wounds."

That got me to crane my neck until I could give him a baleful stare. He held my gaze evenly, not backing down. Oh, well. I hadn't expected that to work, but it had been worth a try.

He was utterly careful as he unlaced my boots and slowly pulled them off, but even so I couldn't keep from wincing my way through every inch of it. Just before the left one came off, I turned my head away, staring at the horribly beige wall instead. The chorus of held breaths and sympathetic wincing was bad enough as it was, no need to join in myself. My throat closed down, but I was too exhausted to cry. Just as well.

Next were the thick tactical pants and warm leggings underneath, leaving me in the shorts that covered my underwear but left my thigh bare. I was pretty sure that the retching sound came from Gita's corner of the room but did my best to ignore it.

"What the fuck did they do to you?" Tanner asked, leaning forward so he could look around Burns. I used Nate pulling the clothes off my other leg to roll onto my side, again shifting the pressure off my back.

"What does it look like?" I tried to ask scathingly, but it sounded more like a weak moan. "They cut, and sliced, and scraped away everything that was dead to try to keep everything that might still return to proper function." I shut up when my gloves were next. I didn't look, but Gita did, immediately turning away once more. I wondered if she was already ruing her perch up there where she could get a good look at what was going on at the other side of the room. The thermal was next, until only the T-shirt and shorts were left. What little room there had still been on the floor by the door was now filled with my clothes.

"Where do you want to start?" Nate asked as he turned away to get some latex gloves, face mask, a scalpel, iodine solution, and the sterile suture needles from his pack.

"Bucky Hamilton's balls, cutting him right up to his teeth," I supplied. Maybe not the best topic to broach, but any filters that had survived the past year and a half were still offline.

Nate snorted as he kept rummaging. "You and me both," he muttered almost too low for me to catch, then louder as he turned back to me, "Thigh, abdomen, or back? That looks to be the worst. I don't think I have much to do elsewhere."

Wasn't that good news? I couldn't quite muster the strength to cheer.

"Leg," I offered. "Then I only have to turn over once."

I tried to steel myself as he swabbed the area with brownish iodine solution, the smears reaching pretty much from the old scars at my hip down to my knee, but to no avail. I tensed as the scalpel nicked a barely closed scar, white pus draining from the wound immediately. I wasn't sure what hurt worse, the cut or pressure he applied—not that it mattered.

"Why the fuck didn't you give her anything for the pain?" Gita squeaked from her perch, sounding the most like a squeamish girl as I'd ever seen her.

Nate didn't halt as he methodically wiped and cut, narrowly avoiding a small fountain as he opened the next swollen abscess. "Because virtually nothing works on her anymore, and the few things that do I don't have access to and wouldn't necessarily give her even if I did." He briefly glanced up at my face, whether to check my reaction or for reassurance, I couldn't tell. "Strong opioids still work, but not because they dull the pain. They just distract you by sending your mind on a bender. Can't really recommend it."

Right then, any little bit of distraction would have been welcome, particularly as the sudden, sharp pain did a great job bringing my mind to a clear state of high alert.

"Exactly how did you survive those first few days after you got speared by that rebar?" I pressed out between clenched teeth—that also hurt, thank you very much. "I thought you were high as a kite, but that's not quite true, is it?"

He snorted as he went back to draining the last filled lump on my thigh, then reached for the suture kit. "The immense, deep-seated pain of your fingers digging out the glue from the wound was decidedly a personal highlight. Making sense of the wave of zombies that came rolling toward us on that bridge and not keeling over, laughing hysterically, was another. I don't remember much else besides that you were less annoying than I'd feared."

"You say the sweetest things," I offered once I could breathe again, the first crooked suture done. I looked away when he started on the next, the tugging on my flesh decidedly worse than the pain. Turning my head to glance at Burns, I mouthed a silent, "Distract me!" at him. Rather than recounting any of the multitudes of anecdotes that I expected, he frowned.

"Are those strangulation marks on your neck?"

I couldn't help but hunch my shoulders ever so slightly, as if that would do anything to hide the dark bruises around my throat. "Wouldn't be the first time," I croaked, wincing slightly when the next time the needle went through my skin, Nate pulled a little too hard on the thread. Burns was obviously waiting for more, but I held my breath instead, staring at the steel frame of the bunk above me. There were a lot of things I could hardly deny, but if I could take that part to the grave with me, I would. Nate didn't volunteer an explanation, either. Let them guess. In the end, it was the truth that it was Hamilton's doing, one hundred percent.

"Roll over," Nate prompted when he was done, wiping the last drops of blood away from my leg.

Gritting my teeth—gently—I did, shimmying around so he could pull the shirt up to my shoulders. It stuck to my skin where wounds had started oozing in transit, making me wince as he pulled the fabric free. I did my best to ignore the muttering coming from the other side of the room—among other sounds. Nate quickly set to work, only that now it felt like he would have had an easier time just skinning me from tailbone to shoulder. It pretty much felt like he was already doing that.

"You seem a lot more lucid now than you were on the plane," Burns offered conversationally as he leaned closer, doing a good job keeping a straight face.

I glared at what I could see of him from where my face wasn't mashed into the pillow once more. "You think? I'm so absolutely thrilled about that. How does that even make sense? That my body shuts down when it only has to cope with existing, but gets me to hyper focus when additional pain is inflicted? Wouldn't it make more sense the other way round?"

Burns gave me a toothy smile but it was Nate who replied. "Think it through again. Right now you're barely existing so it might seem like that to you. But once you're back to full health, the ability to think clearly even through the haze of pain and be able to mobilize your reserves when you need them most is preferential to succumbing to numbness." He paused briefly as he had to cut deeper so he could press on what felt like my remaining kidney. "Welcome to our world."

"Can't wait to get some actual use out of that. Besides still being alive," I grumbled.

If my leg had been bad, my back was worse, the cleanup alone taking forever. And then there was another round of sutures. Nate only got to the second before he halted as Gita came vaulting down from her perch, still a little white in the face but looking rather determined. "Do you know a thing about sewing? Because unless you want to deliberately leave worse scars than she already has, you're doing a shit job," she observed as she inched closer. If it hadn't been my hide they were talking about, I would have started to laugh—it wasn't any day that someone could accuse Nate of anything short of perfection.

"And you could do a better job?" he griped, getting a curt jerk of the head from Gita.

"Sure can. I've been sewing and mending my own clothes way before that damn virus sent us back into the stone age," she replied, not without pride—but then hesitated. "Exactly how infectious is that pus?"

I thought about that for a moment, seeing as they seemed to be waiting for my expertise. "Have you cleaned the wounds with chlorhexidine yet?" Nate gave an affirmative grunt. "Should be okay. From what Raynor mentioned, by now the serum should have killed all bacteria in my body that don't belong, so it's mostly dead lymphocytes. Use two layers of gloves and make sure you don't puncture them, and you should be good." I waited until I felt her get to work—much gentler, and judging from the more even motions, more competent than Nate—before I added, "Thanks."

"You're welcome," came Gita's reply, muffled through her face mask. "I hope I'm not hurting you too much?"

"Don't worry about it," I mumbled, doing my best to relax. I really could have used a drink—not that I thought my body could handle it yet with my liver likely still in recovery mode, but the idea of it sounded good. Hell, a baseball bat to the face sounded great, if it'd just put me under.

The obvious air of awkward discomfort continued to hang between us, until I finally couldn't stand it anymore, using Gita's pause to get a new needle to turn around and look at the others. "Guys, this is hard enough on me as it is. Please don't make it worse. What is done, is done. I have a feeling that the next week is going to get worse. Right now my grip is shit and the best I can manage is an uneven hobble. I fucking have to relearn how to walk and run, and I don't exactly have a lot of time for either. I'm not trusting Hamilton or Richards as far as I can throw them, but I trust you. Fact is, I'm not doing particularly well right now, and I need to know that I can let my guard down in front of you. You all know that turning the other cheek isn't exactly my strong suit, and I might have slight problems concerning my ego sometimes…" I paused just long enough so Burns could get in a snicker. "For obvious reasons, I can't be weak out there. The moment I hop out that door, my head has to be held high, my back straight, and even if it kills me just to breathe, I need to be strong. But I can't keep that up around you. I feel like my sanity's hanging by a thread, and I don't get how my body is still going on because it should have given out hours ago, infusions or no infusions. Just—"

Tanner cleared his throat, effectively silencing me. I was grateful for that. "No need to explain. And no need for you to put on a brave face. You've proven—to all of us, time and time again—that you're one impossible nut to crack. You can let your guard down around us. We have your back."

He might have winced slightly at that last comment, I couldn't be sure, moving back over so Gita could continue. The tension in the room didn't quite dissipate, but Burns struck up a conversation with Tanner about destroyers—ships like the one we were on now, apparently—while Gita continued, Nate hovering beside her, ready to hand her whatever she'd need. I caught Tanner yawning hard enough to make his jaws crack, making me guess that the lot of them were damn tired and fighting to stay awake. It had been an impossibly long day for all of us.

When Gita was done with my back, I rolled over so they could work on my abdomen—Nate to clean, Gita to sew. Thankfully, there were only two scars that needed work there, most of the residual infection raging across my back. When Gita was finally through with me, she tried to hover, but Nate shooed her back to her cot with gentle insistence. I remained lying there as I was, trying to take a page out of Tanner's book, but I knew it was in vain when I felt Nate's hand on my shoulder. "We're not done yet," he reminded me. Weren't we ever.

Exhaling slowly, I let him help me into a sitting position at the edge of my bunk, my feet barely touching the ground. He sat down opposite of me and reached for my left leg, the suture marks standing angrily red and blue against my pale skin. My first impulse as he started to unwrap the bandages around my feet was to look away, but this time, I forced myself not to.

"Well, I never liked flip-flops, anyway," I tried to joke, the words getting stuck in my throat. I wouldn't have minded if he hadn't checked each individual stub, if there was even that much left. Yet rather than let go when he was done, Nate got a good hold on my heel with one hand, and dug the fingers of his other into the sole and middle part of my foot, making me gasp with pain—until some of it suddenly lessened.

"Your tendons are all cramped up," he offered as he continued to squeeze, but mostly rub, as if my foot was a piece of dough in dire need of a good kneading. "I'll ask around if anyone has a tennis ball on board that you can use to loosen them up more. Might not be the most comfortable thing to do, but it will help."

I did my best not to hiss when he moved further back. "I think Raynor packed up some things for me in that bag. At least I think I saw one of those stress ball thingies."

He didn't stop—it was definitely too early for me to do anything—but inclined his head. "We'll go through that tomorrow."

A few minutes later, he switched to my right foot. A little less pain there, but also fewer remaining toes. I idly wondered if that was connected, or mere coincidence. I couldn't have said with my hands. They both felt like useless claws, cramped and swollen, and hurting so much that I was tempted to slam them into the frame of my bunk over and over to make them go numb…

"It will take some time to get used to the changes in your body," Nate murmured, keeping his voice low now that Tanner and Gita were getting ready to tuck in, and only giving token responses to Burns.

"No shit," I huffed.

"I don't mean this," he stressed as he continued to work on my feet. "This you will get used to quicker than you think. Once the pain lessens and you regain function, with a little training your instincts will quickly override old reflexes and learn new ones. What I'm talking about are the metabolic changes. That you need to eat more; that you need to make sure not to run yourself ragged, because you can die if you do. That half of your body's natural defenses are either dulled or no longer work, like that you shy away from pain or get emotionally tired when you're near exhaustion."

I couldn't help but smirk. "You know, we've already had this conversation once. After I survived getting savaged, and we joined the gang once more." He shot me a long look, and it was exactly that what made me pause. "Wait. You knew already that I wasn't just like you, right?" I accused. "You realized that while my metabolism had shifted in that direction, it wasn't fully there."

I got an ambivalent shrug in return. "Doesn't change anything now, does it?"

"But you let me believe that I was one of you!" I keened, trying to pull back but he wouldn't let go. "Why did you do that?"

"Because in all aspects that counted, you were. Are," he corrected himself. "And considering how down you were, any pick-me-up I could think of was a good thing."

I wasn't ready to concede that point to him. "But I wasn't, and it almost killed me! I counted on being able to mobilize all the reserves left in my body when I fled from Taggard's compound and ran through day and night, trying to get away from those stashed undead fuckers!"

Nate's utter lack of an apology in his eyes made me want to throw something at him, but he moved on from my feet to my hands, so I very well couldn't. At least now I was mad enough that I didn't shy away quite as much from the scars where my fingers had been as I had with my toes.

"You survived, and that's what counts," he offered in a calm, measured tone that just added fuel to my flames. "Stop being such a drama queen. If you lose it like that in front of Bucky, he'll wipe the floor with you without even needing to get anywhere close to you. You're better than this."

The reprimand stung—but I knew that he was speaking the truth. "I know."

Neither of us said anything else as he continued working on my hands, then got more fresh bandages out and wrapped my cramping feet and hands up once more. I tried to stretch out and get comfortable in my bunk, but that was still far from possible. Nate turned off the overhead lights, casting us in relative darkness. Soft snores coming from all around us made me guess that we were about the only ones not drifting off.

I closed my eyes, trying to sleep, even though I knew it was in vain. After a while, I felt my body sink into that sedentary state again I'd spent most of the flight in—not quite asleep, but far from awake.

When my eyes drifted open once more, I moved my head to the side until I could glance over to Nate, expecting him to be soundly asleep by now, but found him staring, wide-eyed, at the bunk above his. He didn't move—I couldn't even see the rise and fall of his chest—except for his hand, closing to a fist, then opening again, over and over. I was tempted to ask what was going through his head right then, but refrained—if he'd wanted to let me know, he would have. Considering what we'd been though, I doubted there was anything he felt he couldn't tell me. And still—that physical distance between our bunks felt small compared to all the emotional space that was suddenly there when, until very recently, I'd been so sure that we'd made it past all that bullshit that drove other people apart. Realizing that, I knew I should have said something, but my mind was once more utterly blank, my body too exhausted to make up for that in a physical sense. So we stayed like that through the night, him staring straight up, oblivious of me, and me staring at him.

Chapter 3

Loud pounding on the door to our quarters drew my attention—calling it "rousing" me would have been an overstatement, as I barely managed to flip my head into an upright position, the rest of my body remaining unresponsive. My mind was sluggish enough that it took me a full ten seconds to recognize Red as he ducked into the room, almost having to squeeze through two of the lockers now overloaded with our winter gear.

"Breakfast is ready in the mess hall," he informed us. "If you don't want to eat with the crew, just inform one of the cooks in the galley so they know when to set something aside for you."

Nate had in the meantime heaved himself out of his bunk, not quite incidentally blocking the space between the bunk beds—and also the view of me.

"That won't be an issue," he told Red, his voice that mix between neutral and pleasant that usually set my teeth on edge because I knew that it was fake as hell. "Thank you for letting us know."

"If you want to, we can give you a tour of the ship," Red offered.

Nate was quick to deflect the offer. "Not my first time on a destroyer. I think we'll manage."

Red nodded, at least pretending to be a little at a loss for words. "They set apart the two unused helicopter hangars as training rooms for the marines, and everyone who thinks they need a little more space. I can have them block off a few hours for you if you prefer that. Midnight to four a.m. is usually quiet, I'm told."

I knew Nate was about to give another one of those answers, but I finally managed to heave my legs over the side of the bunk, the motion enough to draw his attention and make him pause for a second. Exhaling slowly, I forced my upper back to straighten so I could look at Red from around Nate's hip. "Why exactly do you think any of us want special treatment? That is, unless you and your flunkies don't want to associate with us."

I had to hand it to Richards, he was still unperturbed by my comments, just as before. "I don't think most of us give a crap either way," he replied, a little more succinct now. "But maybe you in particular would like not to invite unwanted attention."

My, wasn't that a loaded statement, but I knew how he meant it even before I realized that he was staring at the mess of scar tissue and swollen bruises that was my left thigh.

"Why, you checking me out?" I drawled, even managing a small smile.

"Wouldn't think of it," Red replied wryly, but then chose to ignore my needling in favor of finishing his conversation with Nate. "The crew of the ship would appreciate it if you stayed out of all operational areas. You're free to visit the mess hall, head, allotted recreational areas, and the hangars any time you like, but please check in with someone if you need to go out on deck. The sea can get mighty choppy in winter, and while they don't mind if we do target practice at the stern, they prefer not to get any of their human cargo swept into the ocean. Your crates are still stowed away, but we've set apart a rack in the armory for drills."

He hesitated after Nate's curt nod, then left, disappointingly chipper. I stared at the closed door for several seconds, trying to motivate my body to move. It didn't quite want to cooperate, but the fact that I got other input than agony from all over was a bonus. Actually, it was a tremendous step forward, but I was still in too much pain to appreciate it.

While the others dragged themselves out of their bunks and slowly got going, I did my best not to be in the way. I couldn't move fluidly enough yet to dress myself, but we found an easy solution for that. With everyone but me needing to troop to the bathrooms— sorry, the head, of course, as Nate tartly corrected me—it was easy to wait until it was just him and me, and he could rid me of the sweat- soaked, blood-and-pus stained clothes and get me into a new set. I knew I was feeling better when I got incredibly annoyed by how long it took him to get my socks and pants on. He noticed but didn't comment on it, instead fetching what counted for my nutrition these days while I hopped toward the door.

There was one huge advantage to the claustrophobic nightmare that were the corridors of the ship—it was impossible for me to face- plant, because whenever I lost my balance or staggered, there was a wall to hold on to or brace myself with. Nate tried to catch me once, but left it at a singular attempt when he made me howl with pain, and growl with frustration once I was on my own two feet again. I could tell that he was burning to offer a scathing remark along the lines of me being a lot quicker if I just let him carry me, but I would be damned if I let that happen. All the soldiers had seen of me was a feverish, weak waif, now turned into a cripple. Technically, watching me drag my sorry carcass around at snail speed wasn't much better—yet—but it helped put a damper on my grousing ego. I might not be strong enough for a normal, regular gait, but I could keep myself upright, and that was already huge progress over yesterday.

We met up with the others just outside the mess hall and strode in together, Burns and Nate first, then me, followed by the rest.

Nate stalked in like a bristling cat—or mountain lion, going by the mat of a beard that had taken over the lower half of his face, having grown quite considerably since he'd last shaved back in… Utah, my flagging memory provided. To someone unfamiliar with him, he might have seemed alert only, but I could read the extra tension in his shoulders easily enough. It seemed a little overkill to me, considering that it wasn't just us and Bucky's people in here, but I couldn't help but wonder if his apprehension was warranted. I was hoping not, as with me a clear liability, it didn't bode well for us if anyone was actually planning to come after us.

About three hobbling steps in, I forgot what I had been thinking about. I couldn't tell if anyone stared at me as it took my full concentration to keep going, using the wall to the right for support whenever needed. My left foot more dragged than moved properly as even the few yards from our quarters to the mess hall had overstrained my thigh muscles, but I forced myself to keep going. The entire mess hall was teeming with people, sailors and marines getting their breakfast, but two tables at the very back had been left empty. Red and one of the soldiers were just sitting down at one of them, so Burns headed for the other, two rows of seats over. I eased myself into the very first chair I reached, exhaling with real gratitude when the weight was off my thigh and feet. If I remained sitting very straight, I didn't even need to lean into the backrest. Perfect.

Between the others, something of a scuffle broke out as nobody wanted to sit with their backs to the room, and Nate wasn't the only one pulling the "I'm the most capable fucker around" card. It was hilarious enough to make me grin for a second, my cheek barely hurting anymore. I gingerly reached up and prodded my jaw, finding the swelling gone for good, and what pressure I could put on with my teeth only, with nothing to chew on, felt almost normal. So everything was ready for food except my intestines. And I was soon going to do something about that, too.

Gita and Tanner ended the ridiculous game of Chairs by taking the seats opposite me, leaving Nate to take the one to my right, and Burns pulled an extra chair over to the head of the table, to my left. Nate pushed the premixed shaker at me as they all got up once more to grab some coffee and chow from the lines at the opposite side of the room. I was sorely tempted to reach across the table and rearrange the many knickknacks they'd all brought to turn the seating order upside down once more, but that would have required a little too much motion than I felt capable of right now. Just as well—this way I had a few minutes to catch my breath and take a look around the room.

None of the crew seemed overly interested in us, although they were casting the odd curious glance at the bunch joining the food line. Me, they mostly ignored. I did my best to keep my bandaged hands in my lap, well out of sight. As I watched, the other table began to fill as the soldiers, already having gotten their chow, sat down one by one. Bucky wasn't among them, a tremendous relief—until I started to wonder where he'd ended up. I was notoriously bad with reading signs of rank on uniforms, but none of the crew that I could see seemed to be of higher rank. They probably had something like an officer's mess around—and I wasn't sure if it boded well if Bucky had the stage there to regale them all with tales of what a bunch of misfits he'd gotten stuck with. It stood to reason that Richards should have joined him, but I'd gotten the sense from Red that he was the kind of officer who'd rather hang around his men to integrate himself better in their midst, and, if necessary, be right there to resolve any conflict that might arise—pretty much playing it by Nate's book.

Burns had once tried to explain to me that officers were usually not supposed to mingle—that was their sergeant's job—but from what I could tell, this bunch here was as irregular as Nate's people had been.

Resolve conflicts, what a concept. As if I'd been tempted to start anything by throwing my shaker across the tables between ours and duck before anything could come back.

One after the other, my people returned, carrying trays heaped with surprisingly edible-looking food. Gita's eyes were a little wide when she saw the sheer amount of food Burns and Nate had accrued for themselves, and they resembled saucers by the time they dug in, decimating the eggs, bacon, beans, bread, granola, and cheese in record time. I felt my mouth water at the scents wafting over, not sure whether to be happy that at least part of my instincts had survived, or even more depressed that my own breakfast consisted of the contents of the plastic shaker right in front of me.

As soon as Nate's alarm went off, I hit the button on my watch to start the countdown, fumbling minimally as the first three fingers of my right hand were more or less functional, before I reached for the shaker—this time with my left—and threw that undefinable gray liquid down my gullet. And kept on going, swallow by swallow, as fast as my throat would work. That was a lot better than yesterday as well.

About halfway through the shaker I realized that both Tanner and Burns were staring at me. The same was true for two soldiers at the other table that quickly became the overwhelming majority of them until I was done. I set the shaker down with as much dexterity as I could muster—not a lot—and quickly pulled my hands underneath the table again. My cheeks should have heated up with embarrassment but my body didn't seem quite up for that yet, but squirm I could all right. That was, until Tanner cleared his throat, making me look at him instead of trying not to stare down the still-gawking soldiers.

"Damn, you really have guts of steel, girl." My bland look must have given away my confusion, because he laughed, shoveling some more eggs into his mouth. "All of us have been there, at least once. Drinking that shit to restart your digestion. Had the great honor twice, once after a couple of shots perforated half of my lower torso. That shit is about the vilest thing I've ever tasted, and I've lived two weeks off bugs while out in the middle of nowhere. Just seeing it sitting there on the table makes me want to hurl. How the fuck can you just chug it down like soda?"

I chanced a glance toward the soldiers, just to test my dawning theory. What I'd thought was them staring at my mutilated fingers was indeed a mix of awe and rather deep-seated horror—of exactly the kind Tanner had just described. I couldn't help but smirk a little, even if I wasn't yet done squirming—and now feeling ridiculous on top of that. But playing over that was something I was used to.

Gingerly leaning back in my seat, I crossed my arms over my chest and shrugged. "Seems like I'm just that much of a badass."

"That you are," Nate replied, low enough that I barely caught it. I cast him a sidelong glance but he pretended not to have said anything, further decimating his breakfast.

Raucous laughter coming from the soldiers' table let me guess that they'd found a more interesting topic to talk about, but I didn't miss the odd glances still coming my way. That I could deal with. As for the rest…

I didn't feel myself zone out as much as I realized that everything around me got hazy to the point where I had no idea what the others had been talking about for the past… five minutes? Ten? Judging from the fact that Nate had more food on his plate than before—a refill, probably—and Gita was done shredding her bread into pieces and eating them, each carefully smeared with butter or cream cheese, gave me some indicators. That the odd looks my way had taken on a different quality, as well.

"Just how much like a zombie am I staring into nothing?" I asked Nate, needing too damn long until my brain got the actual sentence out of my mouth.

"Only like a very fresh one. Two to three weeks, max," he replied, the corner of his mouth quirking up at the end. "Why, got an unexplainable hunger for brains?"

He and I were both staring at the other table now. "Not much food to find there," I quipped, still trying to shake myself out of my stupor. "Are you done soon? I think getting out of bed was only a temporarily good idea."

"Give me five more minutes." Part of me was miffed at that response, but just sitting there wasn't really pushing me. It wasn't comfortable, but compared to yesterday it was peanuts.

Once he was done, I managed to get up all by myself, but let Nate carry my shaker so I had both hands free to catch myself when I stumbled—and this time, I did plenty of that. The way back to our quarters wasn't long, but the last stretch I would have been ready to let him carry me had he offered—and it was a damn good thing that he didn't. Just as we were approaching the door, Bucky stepped into the corridor, turning our way. It damn near killed me to force my back to straighten and my left thigh to fully accept my weight, but I managed to walk the last five steps at almost normal speed, if of somewhat imperfect posture.

So much for motivation.

I didn't attempt to try to entertain myself with reading—least of all the heap of notes and folders Raynor had sent with me—but spent the next five hours and forty minutes just existing. Moving from one side to the other got easier with each time, and when I chanced lying on my back for a little while, it hurt, but not enough to draw my mind back into full focus. One more shaker of that terribly foul liquid, and I felt moderately up to sitting in my bunk, at least for a little while. That already felt like an improvement.

The others whiled away the day with reading, chatting, sleeping, and eating what Tanner dragged in when he went to hunt for lunch. In small groups of twos or threes they disappeared to take care of business or check out that makeshift gym Red had been talking about.

Nate remained plastered to my side, if trying to be unobtrusive about it. Just before dinner, I tried my luck with one of those squeeze balls to get my grip strength back, but had to stop after two frustration-filled minutes. I was getting better, but not quite that fast.

Dinner was a repeat of breakfast, only with different food. Again, Bucky was pointedly absent, but no one seemed to miss him. I certainly didn't as I amused myself with tearing a tissue into bits, rolling them into small balls and chasing them over the table top. It was a little early for the next stage of my nutritional journey—this time a shaker full of grayish-beige sludge rather than just gray—but I downed it while the others were digging into their chili abomination, anyway. I'd briefly looked over Raynor's notes while Nate had mixed up this batch. She'd presumed a completely sedentary lifestyle for me for a full four days. As that wasn't happening, I didn't see why I couldn't jump-start it all a little earlier. This time, the soldiers seemed to have been waiting, the entire lot—two tables full as they'd apparently all shown up at the same time—watching. I didn't disappoint them, but refrained from licking the rest from the rim of the shaker. It smelled bad enough, and the texture was… interesting. Tanner visibly shook himself as he watched me finish it, and more than one of the soldiers had a similar reaction. I gave them a two-fingered salute—all that was possible with my right hand—and went back to my tissue balls. The sailors and marines gave us all weird looks, apparently not having a clue what was going on.

Later that evening, we went through another fun round of "poke Bree with scalpels and needles," although this time both Nate and Gita were much quicker. Routine was only partly responsible for that. My thigh was still leaking, as were two of the worst scars on my back, but the rest had closed up over the last day. My skin still looked sallow wherever there wasn't any residual tan, and some of the bruises were fading much slower than the others. The night was just as bad as the last, if a little less painful—until the stomach cramps started.

This almost-dying thing really was a gift that kept on giving.

At just shy of four in the morning, it got bad enough that I decided I needed to use the bathroom, but when I tried to get up, the cramps got so bad that I quickly nixed that idea. As soon as he realized what the problem was, Nate bundled me up in his arms and carried me over to the next bathroom—that was thankfully empty— just in time managing to get my pants and underwear down. I spent what pretty much amounted to the most embarrassing fifteen minutes of my life with him there, that only got better when, halfway through, what hadn't yet been digested started coming up the other way. Nate took it all with a surprising dose of humor—and for once didn't even try to piss me off—as he called out to Burns, stationed outside the head, to please fetch us fresh clothes. As we were both in dire need of a shower, I decided that keeping the bandages dry made no sense whatsoever, and he helped me wash. At least now that the cramps had eased up, I managed to remain upright on my own, mostly needing him to clean the parts of my body that I couldn't easily reach.

Before getting dressed again, I made the mistake of glancing at the mirror above the sinks. It was partly fogged over and the lighting was dim enough to further obscure rather than enhance, but what I saw was enough to make me freeze. I almost didn't recognize my body, and not just because of the abundance of marks that hadn't been there last time I'd had a chance to look at myself in a mirror— several weeks ago. Pale and gaunt didn't even begin to describe it. I'd lost weight before—not having access to food will do that to you— but most of that had usually been fat, leaving me lean yet muscular. But that... thing that was staring back at me, eyes sunken, cheeks hollow, didn't look like it had enough muscles left to support itself. Suddenly, it made all the more sense that I couldn't walk, or even sit, without feeling drained—my body had literally started to eat itself up. A sob started deep inside my chest, building as it welled up, gaining strength. I knew that if I let it out, it would be the end of my composure, the end of what little strength and dignity I still clung to, doing my very best to ignore everything else—

Nate stepped up behind me, and for a moment, our gazes crossed in the mirror. It likely didn't take a mind reader to recognize what was going on inside of me, and seeing that look of pain on his features made my throat tighten up even more. This was something he hadn't managed to protect me from, and even though he was very much the reason why I was still alive, I knew that, on some level, he blamed himself for not having been able to do more. And that wasn't the only part where he'd failed me.

I more felt than saw him reach for me, yet before his fingers could lightly touch my shoulder, I stepped away, less from his grip and more from the insanity churning in my own mind. Grabbing for a towel, I did my best to pat myself dry, then had to remain standing still so he could reapply the bandages. I made sure to stay out of sight of the mirrors, preferring the stainless-steel appliances instead. Not folding in on myself and wailing like a banshee cost more energy than was still left in my body, but I forced my muscles to lock and keep me upright until Nate was done. I could tell from the tension in his shoulders that he read my reaction wrong, but I didn't have it in me to set him straight. Admitting how screwed up my head was right now would have made it all real, and then I'd have one more thing to deny—and that would be the straw that broke the camel's back.

As soon as I was dressed—if only in loose sweatpants and a tank top—I hauled myself over to the door, leaving Nate to deal with our soiled clothes and the questioning look on Burns's face. I more fell than climbed into my bunk, reaching for the powdered slush from Raynor's pack and mixed myself a new batch. Fuck her damn schedule, and fuck her exact amounts! With no way of knowing how much of the last shake my body had managed to absorb and how much had gone to waste, this was as far from science as it got. Besides, what could possibly go wrong? The only way this could get worse was me chewing off someone's face, so I might as well start building up strength to do that properly.

I was about to toss the contents of the shaker down as Nate and Burns returned, without their burden. Nate opened his mouth as if in protest, making me down the sludge with defiance burning in my eyes. He swallowed his words when he saw that I had Raynor's directions—which included a summary of what exactly was in each container she'd packed—open on the bed beside me. The remark to maybe let the one who could understand all that be the judge of how to use it lay heavy on my tongue, but I didn't say it, accepting his silent peace offering. This time, downing the sludge came with a hefty dose of trepidation. I could only guess at how much worse it must have been for everyone else subjected to this who could also taste the horrible concoction, not just smell it. Done, I dropped back into my pillow, for once welcoming the agony that ate up my lower back. As long as I was still feeling pain, I was still alive, and that was all that mattered. It might suck, and I had a very real idea that it would still get worse before it got better, but I'd be damned if I was going to give up.

Chapter 4

The next two days were full of the same, if with increasing mobility on my side that let me conduct the mad dashes down the corridor on my own. I found a new metric of overexerting myself: whenever I moved too much, or too fast, I usually hurled up more than could make it through my intestines, at express speed. It stood to reason that it might have been wiser to just rest and drink less, but with every moment of inactivity, that idea became less and less appealing. I could deal with the odd splatter of puke and going through my underwear a little too fast if that meant that a week from now, my metabolism might once more resemble that of a healthy, normal human. That, realistically, this would never again be the case I ignored.

Then day five rolled in, and finally a real challenge: semi-solid food. Raynor had advised a list of great things like mashed banana, mashed potatoes, or even, gasp, mashed apples. Rather than follow that, I dragged myself over to the line by the galley and accosted the first cook who was dense enough to stare at my hands as I put them down on the food line table.

"I need a blender."

He looked up at me as if he was actually surprised I could speak. He couldn't have been much past eighteen, his face still round and covered with pimples, and as he gaped, quite resembling a fish. One of his colleagues took pity on him, pushing him toward the back to fetch more food while he dealt with me.

"Miss, we're not a juice bar. If you want some smoothies, go two years back in time."

I stared at him, torn between correcting him of my marital status, and just plain tearing into him because he was annoying the fuck out of me. What I actually did was offer a small smile—or at least bared my teeth at him—as I responded in a calm, measured way.

"I need a blender. To blend actual food, not because I've decided to overdose on fructose. For reasons too complicated to explain now that are, without a doubt, well beyond your intellectual capacities in the first place, the only thing I can ingest right now are semi-solids. So either you give me a fucking blender right now so I can shred those fucking eggs and bacon into a mash I can ingest, or I'm going to come vaulting over there and beat you with one of those trays until I can use your empty skull cap to do the same."

Well, that was quite embarrassing—but it got me my blender, plus a connective cord, in under twenty seconds flat. Half of the marines and sailors were still staring at me as I took the soup bowl full of yellowish mush with brown flecks in it over to our table, sitting down hard in my chair. Burns was grinning from ear to ear but wisely kept his tongue, while Gita was in visibly high spirits. Only Tanner and Nate looked pensive, Tanner probably because he hadn't really gotten to see me in a temper yet, and Nate... well, the reason for him being Capt. Sourpuss this morning was anyone's guess. Maybe my incessant farting had kept him up all night. Who knew?

Part of me expected Red to come by to tear me a new one for that spectacle, but, if anything, the soldiers seemed mostly amused by my outburst. Maybe they'd had a betting pool going how long it would take for something like this to happen. Again, who knew?

After close to two weeks since I'd last eaten anything that had the consistency of food, the blended breakfast mush was surprisingly alien on my tongue, but I inhaled it all without much hesitation. I also stole a few sips of coffee from Nate's mug, but mostly kept it prisoner to inhale the heavenly scent.

I barely made it back to our quarters before Nate grabbed my shoulder—none too gently this time—and hauled me around to face him, his expression stony. "Care to explain what the fuck that was about?"

It didn't come as much of a surprise, but I was still miffed. "He didn't want to give me a blender. I made him. End of story."

Rather than reply, he made a grab for my arm—and pressed two of his fingers over the pulse point of my wrist, silently counting. I tried to pull myself free but to no avail; then frowned at him, his behavior not making any sense.

"Same question, different intonation," I prompted when he finally let go.

"Your pulse is steady and slow," he offered, in a surprised tone no less, as if that was an explanation.

"Duh. I didn't walk more than maybe eighty feet and I'm almost at the level of general discomfort where I'd stop classifying it as 'fucking painful' and just go with 'meh.' So, spill it. Why does me throwing a fit get your panties in a twist?"

Nate gave me the kind of look that made me guess he was seriously debating whether he should bother with answering at all, but Tanner stepped in, much to both our surprise.

"Let's just put it this way. A certain subgroup of the soldiers who got the serum had some anger management issues."

"And what's that got to do with me?" Maybe a dumb question, but considering how they were behaving, I couldn't hold back.

Nate's brows drew together in anger. "That you can fucking insta-convert if you flog yourself into a real rage fit! I am well aware of the fact that I didn't marry a very mild-mannered woman, but that was bad even for your temper." When I just kept staring back at him, Nate let out a weary sigh, scratching at his still-growing beard. "I guarantee you, those fuckers have a standing order to put you down if they have probable cause that it's happening, and we've always had a 'shoot first, check later' policy. Just… don't give them a reason."

I could see where he was coming from, but one little tidbit got me too hung up on it to concede that point to him. "'We?'" I echoed, not having to feign anger now. "What, it takes you all of a week to roll over and fall back in line?"

I knew I shouldn't have said that—salt and open wounds and all that jazz—but I never dealt well with my asshole moments being singled out. And, just maybe, there was more to his theory about anger management than I wanted to admit. The fact alone that this shit that was now coursing through my veins—and very likely still was the only thing that kept me alive—could alter my perception of the world and consequent reactions like this freaked me the fuck out.

The past few days, Nate had been behaving as even-tempered toward me as never before, to the point where I'd almost given up on expecting any different, but it was the glint of true rage that sparked in his eyes now. Oh, indeed, I hadn't just toed a line there, I'd waltzed right over it. But backing down had never been my strong suit, so all I did was turn my chin up and continue to glare at him, not doing a thing to tone down the challenge in my gaze.

"Yes, we," he bit out, enunciating each syllable precisely. "And that now also includes you, whether you like hearing it or not. All political and social differences aside, we are united in the fate we share, and the responsibility we have to keep the rest of the population safe from us. Don't worry—in the event of you completely losing it, it will be me who fires the bullet that puts an end to your illustrious existence, but it's reason that has them keep an eye on you, not just spite or whatever other ulterior motives you like to accuse everyone you meet of having. Get real, Bree. You're a potential weapon of mass destruction now, and you better learn to live with the consequences. You think you don't need my help and support? Then you better take my advice, or someone else will make you choke on it instead. Get a grip on your emotions and learn to focus them on what is important. You've had a year and a half of living your wild-child glory days that you never knew you wanted but were getting the most out of now that you did. That's over. So why don't you stop sulking right away and concentrate on getting better, without wasting needless attention on details that are neither important nor subject to your control?"

Guess I deserved that. Not that I was ready to admit it—which pretty much underlined that Nate was right—but in a sense, him chewing me out was a massive relief. Sure, I could have done without it, but besides delivering a lot of underhanded praise—like he expected better of me because he knew I was capable of it, and it was time I stopped selling myself below my worth—it also proved what I had been guessing for the past few hours: the worst was behind me, and my life was no longer hanging in the balance where he might feel he should treat me with kid gloves because any scathing remark he offered might very well become his greatest regret, as it was the last thing he'd ever say to me.

And something else I noticed—while my jaw was still clenched and my back ramrod straight, my body had overall started to relax, coming down from the brief high after the blender affair. While I'd never been prone to cry—and what little leanings there had been I'd quickly unlearned dealing with Nate on a daily basis—there wasn't that huge amount of frustration bottled up inside of me that our fights usually caused, enough to make me shake with tension. I wondered if that was an effect of the serum as well—or just the testosterone pills that Raynor had added to the heap of shit I was supposed to take to reverse my body's gradual degradation.

I was just about to voice those suspicions—with the odd barb thrown in there, because I'd rather die than give up on being petty—but a loud sob coming from Gita's perch on top of her bunk made us all turn her way. I hadn't even realized that she'd squeezed past us—and hadn't given a shit who else was listening in on our exchange—but there she was, white in the face, tears streaming down her face. "You can't just talk to her like that!" she wailed at Nate, anguish ringing from her every word.

I'd never seen my husband—and Burns, lurking behind him—look so flabbergasted and distraught before, making me burst out laughing. Yeah, I was an asshole, all right. Gita's—now decidedly hurt—gaze skipped to me, which made me laugh all the harder. Hard enough to pull the stitches at my back, but I didn't give a shit about that right now. Just plain out laughing like that felt too good—and had been so fucking overdue.

When I finally straightened, doing my best to wipe the stupid grin off my face—which was damn hard considering the confused expression on Nate's—before I turned to her. "Estrogen?" I guessed.

She nodded, trying hard to stop the tears running down her face. "It's turning me into an emotional mess! All that stuff your doc gave me is way stronger than anything I've been on before."

"Well, she doesn't half-ass anything," I offered, then turned to Nate, crossing my arms over my chest. "See what you did now? All your fault. You should be ashamed of yourself. Now apologize and go back to lurking around like a beaten puppy, waiting for the next time the newspaper comes for him."

Burns snorted as he made room for Tanner to step into the space between the bunks. As he pushed past me, he grunted, "You two really deserve each other," plainly aimed at Nate and me. At the last bunk, he climbed up next to Gita, slapping her back rather than offering the hug she might have needed right then, but I got the sense that, like me, she didn't exactly appreciate anyone underlining her vulnerable moments.

I turned my back on them, not just to lend them some privacy—or as much as our cramped space would allow—but so I could gloat into Nate's face. He'd done a great job calming down himself, once more offering that infuriating closed-off, neutral expression that would forever drive me insane. "A puppy?" he asked, faintly amused.

I gave an approximation of a shrug, damn glad that my body could move like that once more without agony exploding all through it. "Well, I'd make a stupid joke about doggy style now but my back and thigh are really not supporting such shenanigans yet, so want me to scratch you behind the ear instead? I could rub your belly, too, but that might escalate quickly, and not sure how much those curtains at the bunks really block out—"

Burns—gently—slapped my shoulder as he squeezed between us to get to his bunk. "Yeah, you do deserve each other. And take that outside. Ship's large enough that you'll find some other nook or cranny outside of this one."

Bless him, but Nate knew better than to cast a suggestive look my way. Instead, he nodded at where my bag of many poisons sat on the floor. "Continue to drink that shit. We'll get you some real food for lunch and dinner. Rest up during the day. And tonight, we'll see if you're up to more than just running your mouth at us."

I was still exhausted enough that the prospect of doing nothing all day long sounded enticing, but at the same time giddiness welled up from deep inside of me. Finally, I got to start on some exercise—even if it was just walking circles and some light stretching, realistically—so I could claw myself back out of the hole my body had sunk into. Something to look forward to.

Chapter 5

Dinner was a strangely somber affair. Nate sent me right over to the table, promising to take care of my food. For the first time, I sat down normally, without having to ease my body into the chair, but my triumph was short-lived. I didn't just imagine the borderline hostile stares I got from the crew taking their meal. Apparently, coming after their cooks was a no-go. All of a sudden, Nate's hint of chivalry took on an altogether different air, with me being told to go sit and wait, and then having my dinner sludge unceremoniously dumped in front of me. It was a good move, I had to hand it to him. To the crew, it probably looked like I'd gotten my proper chastisement off-screen and was now sulking in my embarrassment. The embarrassment part was true, if still less poignant than it likely should have been.

There was no jeering from the direction of the soldiers, which only made me all the more paranoid. The others hadn't mentioned any altercations from training, or otherwise running into them. Maybe I was just seeing things, but to me that felt like the other shoe was about to drop. That not even a single one of them was holding a grudge sounded damn near impossible. I was halfway through my sludge when I realized the likely reason for the seemingly existing truce—so far, they hadn't gotten much chance to come after the most likely target of their ire, who also happened to, right now, stand the least chance of defending herself. My, didn't that make me feel precious.

But it made sense—they would have done Nate a favor coming after him where he could drop that placid facade and deal out a lot of damage, venting all the frustration and rage bubbling a little too close to the surface for his own good. Like them, he could dish out as much as he could take, and they must have had orders not to incapacitate any of us. So why be that accommodating? But I was a different thing entirely. My, wouldn't hopping to the head, alone, in the middle of the night be fun. Then again, what could they actually gain from beating me to a bloody pulp? As it was, it stood to reason that I still wouldn't have fully recovered by the time we hit the road, so anyone adding extra days to that was a complete moron. Sadly, I had it on good authority that they weren't short on those. Only one way to find out.

Nate made me get some rest after dinner, which made a lot of sense, even if I insisted that it had been days since I hadn't managed to keep everything down. Bored out of my mind, I spent a good ten minutes staring at the wall before I leaned out of my bunk to get the thick folders Raynor had given me to look over.

It took me a disturbingly long time to read the first page, my mind constantly skipping away from the words, and even if not, half of them made less sense than they should. I was close to panicking when Nate bumping his foot into my knee pulled my frazzled attention to him. "Maybe you feel like you're rested, but you're not," he offered. "You haven't slept in over a week. You're only just starting to work on the huge nutritional deficit that your body has racked up. Your brain has enough energy to function and not let you career into obstacles, but likely not enough to make sense of scientific publications. That you don't realize all this is because one of the side effects of the serum is some degree of hyper focus ability for most. Give yourself a few more days." He paused to flash me a quick grin. "And if it doesn't get better, well. Then you'll have to slum it with us dumb grunts."

"Did you just admit that I'm smarter than you?" I preened, but let the folders drop back into the bag.

"Never."

One hour passed, then two, until Nate finally declared I had gotten enough downtime to digest. Judging from the roiling in my intestines, they were heavy at work, but I got what he meant. I briefly debated whether I should change into other clothes, but I'd spent most of my time in sweat pants, socks, a tank top to keep everything bouncy in place, and a thick thermal over it to keep me warm. I wasn't going to get any more comfortable, and all were clothes I could move in. They would do. I didn't bother with donning my boots. I wouldn't need them yet, and if I could spare my toes the ordeal, all the better. Besides, I'd seen how often the corridors were cleaned—our quarters were, without a doubt, the most unsanitary part of the ship, left to our care, which was next to non-existent, I was afraid.

I still hadn't figured out whether the ship was running on two twelve-hour or three eight-hour shifts, but by the time we left our cabin, the lights had been switched to red for the night cycle. The bright daylight illumination might no longer bother me as much as before, but I preferred the red light by a lot. While Nate squinted his way down the long corridors to the back portion of the ship—the stern, as Nate informed me what felt like the umpteenth time—I followed, for the first time getting somewhat of a tour of the ship. Burns had spent an entire breakfast raving about the Arleigh-Burke-class destroyer and how happy he was to be on one again, but so far his enthusiasm hadn't made much sense to me. It was all hard edges I bumbled into, gray and beige with some blue was as far as the color range would go, and everything was claustrophobia-inducing narrow. Yet as Nate led me through the different sections—and up one level—I started to get a little more appreciation for this fortress of the seas. It was certainly longer than I'd thought at first, but that wasn't hard, never having seen it from the outside, in broad daylight. I barely remembered anything of how I'd gotten here.

I hadn't known what to expect of the dismantled helicopter hangar-turned-gym, but it looked surprisingly like that Crossfit box thing Sam had dragged me to once—officially because she claimed getting fit would do us both some good, but I'd suspected because she was crushing hard on one of the trainers who she frequently ran into at one of the college coffee shops. The memory made me snort, a slightly rueful emotion spreading through my chest. One thing was sure—a month ago I could have easily wiped the floor with that certainly fit trainer. Now, not so much. Yet rather than despair, I forced myself to see the positive in this—I was still alive, and as Nate had reminded me with the guns already—I'd learned to be awesome once, I could do it again.

A bunch of marines were working out in the back corner of the hangar, pumping iron, and two of the soldiers were doing some exercises that made me tired just watching them, but otherwise we had the entire hangar to ourselves. Half of it was covered with thick mats, ideal for doing exercises on the ground or sparring. That's where Nate dropped to the floor, gesturing me to join him. Stretching first—or as much of that as I could muster.

It quickly became obvious just how sore and stiff I still was, the simplest stretch of any muscle in any direction turning into a chore. Rather than goad me on, Nate was patience personified, waiting for me to get there, often holding onto parts of my body to balance me, or gently push into the stretch, lending strength that I simply lacked myself. It probably looked like a really weird mix between physical therapy and a make-out session, but about two minutes in I'd forgotten that there was anyone else around, and cared about their opinion even less. Some parts hurt enough that my mind went white with pain, but I forced myself to pull through. Tendons stretched and joints popped, but by the time I got up once more, I felt like my body was a whole lot more limber.

Time for the next humbling instance: trying—and failing, quite spectacularly—to run.

Maybe it would have made more sense to start with boots on where the construction of the sole would have made it easier for me to propel myself forward more evenly, but the point of the exercise was for me to relearn how to use my feet, whatever the circumstances. To put it mildly, my frustration level soon reached an all-time high, but whenever I stumbled as I tried to walk up and down the edge of the mats, I forced myself to pause, calm down, and start again. By then, the soldiers had long since left, and the last of the marines gave up kissing his guns after my second spectacular fall, so it was just Nate and me to bear witness to my utter lack of coordination.

Up and down I walked, up and down. My left thigh started to pulse, then hurt constantly, followed by the scars on my stomach and back, but I kept going. With no immediate action to focus on, my mind kind of blanked out... until I realized I'd walked a good three rounds without stumbling—or even misstepping—once. Nate was watching me from where he was leaning against the wall, bundled up in a fleece jacket because heating wasn't really a thing here. I was sweating from concentration—and what amounted to exertion for me—but that didn't keep me from increasing my speed before hurling myself into a brief sprint. That was no straight line, but I kept my balance more or less, my calves quivering when I came to a halt at the other end of the mats. Partly, my spirits were soaring—progress, finally!—but I didn't dare turn around and grin triumphantly at Nate. I just knew that he'd have a comment ready that would bring me right down to reality, and I wasn't quite ready for that yet. So I started walking again, up and down, adding the odd skip or little jump to my routine.

The next morning, I walked into the mess hall without a hunch, wobble, or any need for support, sitting down without much care for what part of me landed on the hard plastic of the chair, and stretched my aching legs to ease my protesting muscles. Protesting from use, not from being cut apart and haphazardly sewn back together. I was tired as hell, but it was a good kind of exhaustion, already lessened by the three hours of downtime I'd gotten once we'd returned to our quarters.

Instead of the sludge I expected, Nate set down a plate heaped with scrambled eggs in front of me, followed by a cup of coffee from Burns. I hesitated, but then picked up the fork—needlessly cautious; I could easily hold it between my right thumb and index finger—and dug in. I still had some issues with keeping the tension up, so I tried to grab a knife with the left—bad idea. The knife went clattering to the floor within moments, underlined by a rather vile curse from yours truly that made heads turn all over—exactly what I needed right then. Smiling sweetly, I bent down to pick up the knife—with my right hand—and offered up the fakest, "Sorry, my bad," that I could manage. The fork would have to do. A hint of amusement crossed Red's face, but most of the other soldiers went back to ignoring me.

That sadly was no longer the case when I went for my next training session after dinner, and found almost all of them in the hangar, doing a lot of sweating and grunting. Bucky was missing, but so was Red, making my residual weariness return. Nate and Burns were with me, Burns to do some sweating and grunting himself, with Nate lurking around my general vicinity. Yesterday, he'd been relaxed, particularly once it was just us. Now he was tense as hell which translated awfully into his tone with me, giving me plenty to complain about in my head—a not quite welcome distraction. I did some stretches, then moved to the very back of the room to try some quick sprints. My body hadn't unlearned yesterday's progress, but I felt myself get distracted whenever I saw motion somewhere, and a lot was going on there, making me stumble and fall within moments. The mats were damn hard under my palms and knee when I caught myself, and I so didn't need the snickers piping up from somewhere to my side. I did my best to ignore them but couldn't quite keep my face from burning. Exhaling slowly, I pushed myself up once more—and ended up back on my stomach when my right foot gave out, toes that weren't there anymore incapable of pushing enough to propel me upward. Fuck.

I tried to roll over on my side and onto my knees to get up that way, but the scars in my lower abdomen hurt something awful, making me sag back onto the mat. I felt the light vibrations of footfalls approaching, but refused to look up. "Maybe start with something easy," I heard Nate remark—and then he dropped a jump rope next to me.

I first glared at the thing, then craned my neck so I could do the same to him.

"Exactly how's that supposed to be easy?"

He gave a nonchalant shrug. "Your balance is good, if not perfect yet, but that's not the reason you stumbled. You're simply lacking strength. So do something to build strength. Jump."

I was ready to tell him where to shove his advice, but instead crawled back onto my feet before I picked up the stupid thing. I'd never been the most coordinated person, and I still preferred to work out without any additional shit I could get all tangled up in, no less, but dutifully took the handles into both hands, brought the rope forward, and skipped over it—rather unenthusiastically. I fully expected to land back on the mat, flat on my ass, but while the muscles in my thigh protested, I managed to both keep my balance and hold on to the rope itself. Nate just kept looking at me blankly, silently urging me on, so I did another hop. And then another, and another, slowly increasing my pace until the rope continued to whir around me without coming to a halt on the mats behind my feet. I didn't exactly need my toes to jump, and after a few weird starts I managed to get the motion to work smoothly as well. My right palm soon protested from having to grip even something as light as the rope handle for so long, but that could only be a good sign. The squeeze balls could only do so much.

I was out of breath before my thigh threatened to give out so I allowed myself some rest, but as before, doing just a little seemed to affect me a lot. My body felt more alive, like a freshly greased machine, ready for more action. I tried to do a short sprint across the small side of the room again, this time managing to remain upright. And when I did fall on the way back, I was able to brace myself, coming down onto the mat in something between a push-up and a plank. That was mighty uncomfortable on my toes, but the supple mat gave me enough grip to keep it up. My hands did a surprisingly good job supporting my torso, so when finally the discomfort from my toes got too bad, I dropped to my knees but kept my body further suspended. So what if I did girl push-ups—I managed twenty before it was back to skipping rope, and that was twenty fucking push-ups more than I'd expected to do at all this week.

Once they saw that the comedic value of my performance had lessened, the soldiers concentrated on their own workouts, leaving me to fend for myself. Nate tried a few more things—like giving me a semi-heavy ball to throw, but I dropped that like a stone—but for now, I was happy with letting my body ease itself back into some good use. Once I was exhausted enough to call it quits, we joined Burns so I could sit around uselessly some more while Nate got to prove that he could bench press more than I probably weighed right now.

Easily. Repeatedly. Just not being crammed into that claustrophobic hellhole we called our home at the moment was a relief. I felt rather vindicated when my intestines produced quite the amount of gas, but hey, one doesn't get used to solid foods within the span of just one meal. Take that, you snickering idiots.

I'd hoped I would be able to sleep after that workout, but no. At least when I succumbed to that half-aware haze this time, I could occupy myself with counting the many small aches that flared up seemingly at random all over my body before they quieted down once more. When it was time to get up in the morning, I managed to crawl out of bed with barely any lag—until I realized we were the only ones. When I eyed Nate askance, he shrugged. "You want to take the shortcut, you have to put in the time. We do three training sessions from now on. One before breakfast, one after lunch, and the last at night. We'll try to get three full meals into you, and supplement the rest with protein shakes and whatever else Raynor packed for you." He paused, waiting for protest from me, but I wisely held my tongue. "Get dressed. We're just wasting time."

There was one advantage to trolling the hangar early—none of the soldiers were around, just marines and the odd sailor coming to train with them. They eyed us with a little curiosity, but when neither of us started doing something extraordinary, they focused on their own workout. After yesterday, I appreciated that more than ever.

Whatever had made Nate change his mind, I got to feel the full effect of it when he forced me through several rounds of drills mercilessly, barely leaving me enough time to catch my breath between exercises. He had me sprint, jump, squat, lunge, crunch, and whatever else he could think of—or so it felt to me. The worst of it was, he wasn't just standing there, barking at me, but doing it all along with me so that it was obvious whenever I started to flag. Part of me was angry that he'd expect me to keep up with him, battered and bruised as I still was, but my ego wouldn't let me drop down on my ass and insist that I had enough. So I huffed and puffed along, sweating through my clothes, feeling like the next breath would be the very last I'd manage—but there was still one more that I could draw.

It was only when he let me have thirty seconds of rest—that I spent lying flat on my stomach, all limbs splayed out—when I realized that it had been a good three cycles since I'd last fought for balance, or misplaced my step. My right side hurt, but less so from the scars and more because I simply couldn't get enough air into my lungs that my body needed. For the first time, my hands were noticeably warm as well, same as my feet. I felt awful, but at the very same time... alive.

"Are you going to stay down there for the rest of our training time? Because I'm not carrying you around anymore," came my husband's loving and encouraging statement.

Groaning, I pushed my hands underneath me, getting up in two quick hops. A brief spell of vertigo hit me, but I managed to shake it off without more than a little step to the side. Nate looked me over critically, then got the jump rope from the rack of paraphernalia and handed it to me. "Try to do double jumps if your calves are strong enough already." Still breathing heavily, I nodded, then started out slow like last time to get the hang of the motion once more. My palms protested, but I had a feeling that the abysmally bad grip of my right hand was just a little better.

When it was finally time for breakfast, I was ready to crawl over to the mess hall rather than walk, feeling like breathing was a chore rather than coming naturally. I still wasn't allowed to get my own food—which, all things considered, was a great idea as I would have just dropped the plate and spilled everything. While I waited for Nate to do so, I drank down an entire protein shake, and a water refill for good measure. The resulting burp made a few heads turn, and this time I didn't miss the snickers from the soldiers. Maybe they had been there all week and I'd only recently regained enough focus to notice. I didn't give a shit, and as soon as my eggs and veggies were set down in front of me, I pretty much inhaled them. I choked a few times before I slowed down and forced myself to properly chew, much to Gita and Tanner's amusement. I expected a few lewd comments, and when they didn't come, it reminded me awfully much of the fact that while I really liked them, they weren't my team. They weren't us. And still I'd dragged them into this. Damnit.

As soon as I was done, I took my sorry ass to bed, back for a few hours of mindless staring into space. I almost drifted off completely, but then it was time for lunch, and as soon as that was digested, more working out. Then dinner; more torment. Not-sleep. Workout and breakfast again. It all started to blur together, like in the first days because of the agony I'd been in. Now it was, more or less, mental boredom. Sure, Nate did a stellar job physically powering me out, but my mind didn't much appreciate that.

And then, finally, sleep. Three uninterrupted hours of real rest where my mind got to step away from it all into blissful nothingness. I didn't dream—at least not that I could remember—but when I became aware again, the world felt just a little more right. My morning workout went a lot smoother than the day before, to the point where, just for fun, I added another fifty push-ups without Nate having to badger me into them. He noticed, of course—and when we returned for our afternoon session, rather than walk over to the mats, he aimed straight for one of the punching bags hanging in front of what had once been one of the hangar doors.

"We need to work on your fighting skills," Nate remarked over his shoulder while he unrolled some tape, turning to look at me expectantly. I hesitated, then extended my hands toward him so he could tape them up. It felt weird as hell to feel the tape cross at different points now, particularly on my right hand, but Nate got it right on the first try. Of course he did. I had a certain feeling he'd put a lot of thought into this beforehand, to keep my self-doubt from roaring right back.

"So what are we up to now?" I asked.

He nodded toward the bag. "For obvious reasons, you can't do what you always do, which is to deliver over sixty percent of your attacks with a right hook or punch." Or maybe not. Then again, it wasn't like I hadn't been aware of that issue, but it still made my fingers contract into a fist involuntarily. I glanced down at my hand, then back up at his face.

"What do you suppose we do about that?"

"Make you get used to favoring your left," Nate offered. "And if your thigh supports it yet, a lot more kick and knee action. You're quick, and now more than ever, most of your strength comes from your hips. Use that. We'll work on agility tonight."

He cut off there, frowning at something behind my shoulder. I didn't need to turn to know what—or rather, who—it was. My shoulders tensed, and that punching bag wasn't all that enticing anymore to hit, compared to other possible targets.

"Yeah, those hips don't lie," Bucky drawled as he came sauntering over, Richards trailing after him. Judging from the sweat stains on their shirts, they must have been sparring over in the corner. Red gave me a curt nod of greeting that, once again, puzzled me. I might have even responded with a smile under different circumstances, but not now.

Nate resorted to glowering at Bucky, so I said what needed to be said. "Fuck off."

Bucky was all smiles as he kept staring at me—or, more precisely, at my taped-up hands. This once I would have preferred him to ogle my goods instead, but in baggy sweatpants and a still oversized thermal as I hadn't managed to fill out enough yet, I could see why that wasn't that appealing. And leave it to the asshole to zero in on what would make me the most uncomfortable.

"My, my, such language," Bucky drawled. "Normally, I'd venture a guess now what else you put that filthy mouth of yours to, but it's obvious that nothing's going on there." My right palm started to cramp with how much my fist tightened, but I kept my trap shut. Left hand, I told myself. I was so going to get my left hook up to speed, even if I spent the entire day punching my knuckles bloody.

Sadly, my fuming silence seemed just as satisfactory to Bucky as if I'd snapped at him.

"If you don't mind, we're not here to chat," Nate said, as perfectly neutral as Red was fighting to appear—both not quite managing.

Bucky was quick to make a grand, all-encompassing gesture. "Please, by all means, continue to amuse us with your clown show. With not much else on board as far as entertainment goes, watching you has become a favorite of many." At least he had the grace to walk away after that, but I didn't care for how he and the two soldiers he joined by the squat rack started to chuckle, the odd glance directed at us.

"I don't get why you always let him rile you up," Red remarked. Before I could reply, he went on. "We came over to check on your progress. The commander decided yesterday that he's extending his patrol route, so we get an extra four days on board. Do you think you'll be combat ready eight days from now?"

I offered up the sweetest pressed smile I could muster. "Why don't you keep your face right there and find out yourself?"

Nate's warning look kept me from falling into a fighting stance. There was the danger of Red taking me up on my offer, and then I'd look mighty old ten seconds later. "Easily," he answered Red's question.

"Good." Red nodded, ignoring my antics. "If you need anything, let me know."

At Nate's acquiescence, he turned around and left the hangar. I looked after him, still puzzled. "I just can't get a read on him."

Nate snorted. "Why? Because he's not as much of an asshole as you've come to expect from everyone?"

"Probably," I admitted. "So, left hook?"

"Start with some legwork first," Nate advised as he stepped behind the punching bag to keep it in place.

That, I did, soon working up quite a sweat. He was right, of course—the few times I tried to use my right hand, all I got for it was a lot of pain and little effect. Anything below the elbow was useless. My left hand still hurt aplenty as it was, particularly when I hit the stump of my index finger and the knuckle right adjacent to it, but it would do in a pinch. My left leg didn't do too well supporting me on a right kick, but sending both my left knee and heel into the bag worked well enough to make Nate stagger back on the fifth try. I allowed myself a small whoop of victory with some hopping in place, which earned me a chuff from him—and a small smile.

Small as these triumphs might have been, they motivated me a lot, just as Nate must have planned. I kept at it until sweat was dripping off me, to the point where I felt I was going to fall over from overexertion. I was halfway through Nate's water bottle—mine long since spent—when I gave up, and after a cautious look around, pulled off my thermal. There was no use in me keeling over due to a false sense of modesty. The sports bra I was wearing underneath covered more than what two of the female marines doing pull-ups over there were showing, and no one dared ogle them. I still felt a tad bit self-conscious as I glanced toward my reflection in the mirror by the free weights, but unlike a few days ago, what I saw didn't make me want to recoil anymore. Sure, I was still scrawny as hell, but my skin was back to a nicely flushed color, the dark ink of my tattoos standing out in contrast. I hadn't had a chance to check on how the 13 low on my back looked, but most of my scars were far enough away from it not to have distorted it too much. With my hair up in a now messed-up bun, the three X-shaped marks across my neck were visible as well. For the first time in a while—or maybe ever—I felt proud of them, no longer resenting but appreciating that they set me apart. The woman who was staring back at me was one thing above all else: proud to be who she was. I could live with that, I decided. Fuck the scars and missing appendages—nobody cared when they got my boot in their teeth.

With newly found vigor, I went after the bag, my body moving easier now that it wasn't sweating as if I was sitting in a sauna anymore. Elated, I started hopping in place more between attacks, loving how my muscles tensed and flexed, making it easy to ignore the residual discomfort. My thigh held when I grabbed the bag and sent my right knee into it three times before dancing back once more, same as with the kick that followed.

"Step away," I told Nate. "Gotta try something." As soon as he did, I tensed, then jumped forward, delivering a roundhouse kick with my left leg. And damn, that was a good one, making the bag swing hard enough that I had to duck and roll to avoid getting hit by it on the return swing.

I laughed as I came to my feet, immediately resuming an easy jog. Nate gave me a quick thumbs-up as he caught the bag and stabilized it again, resuming his place. I geared up for some left jabs next, but loud clapping from the other side of the hangar made me pause and look over. I knew I shouldn't—if I'd learned one thing over the past week, it was that I really shouldn't give a shit about anyone else but myself. But of course I did, because it was Bucky doing the mock applause, beaming a bright grin my way.

"Well done, Stumpy! Good for you, seeing as with those scars, you couldn't hack it as a stripper."

Anger, hot and so consuming that I felt my vision narrow at the edges, raced up my spine, making my entire body shake with it. Ever since walking into that base, it had never really left me, but the punishing amount of exercise Nate had put me through over the past days had done a lot to reduce it to low-simmering embers in the very back of my mind, easily ignored and almost forgotten. But now all that swung into reverse, fueled by my latent—and often quite prominent—frustration. I felt my already elevated pulse spike, my heart pumping furiously to get enough oxygen to my muscles so they could gear up—

The punching bag hit my hip just above my aching left thigh, forcing my attention to skip from Bucky to Nate—who was doing some bona fide glaring as well, yet not at the idiot over there, but at me. I could read him well enough to know that he wasn't actually angry with me, but frustrated with the entire situation. It was the warning in his gaze that got me to force myself to calm down. Right. Not losing it, not getting put down like a dog—that was what we were aiming for.

"Left jabs," Nate ground out, holding the bag securely now that he'd gotten my attention. "You need to hit harder, and faster."

That's exactly what I did. I poured all my anger, frustration, but also a whole lot of grief into each punch. What did words matter? They couldn't hurt me. Not if I didn't let them. And one day, very, very soon, I would be ready to retaliate, and Bucky could bet his stupid fucking grin that it wouldn't be with slander.

Chapter 6

Whether it was my newly rekindled anger, or the fact that I was more active, by evening that very day I had to admit that I wasn't getting enough calories into my body. Realistically, it seemed to be the latter—whatever it was about that damn serum that let those inoculated with it increase their metabolic rate to accomplish increased physical feats seemed to have kicked in, whether I'd tried to gear up or not. Or it was the simple fact that my body was recovering at beyond miraculous speed; considering the injuries it had sustained, I should barely be able to sit up on my own, not do workouts that could be considered as such. As I didn't feel hunger, I couldn't easily judge just how much my body was screaming for sustenance, but the fact that I felt weak rather than exhausted when I got up for dinner was telling. After raiding the protein and fat sections of the mess hall, I inhaled two more shakes once we got back to our quarters, and even that was barely enough to make me feel normal. That wasn't all of it, of course. While I understood why Nate was smart enough not to let Bucky bait him, I was also angry at him for not defending me—as if I would have wanted that, but still. So it was for the better that Burns asked me to tag along with him, giving Nate and me some much needed space and time away from each other.

I was looking forward to the training session with Burns—at least until I saw him chatting with some of the soldiers while I did my warmup, souring my mood drastically. They seemed to have a mighty fine time together, laughing and joking around. It didn't get better when rather than do drills or some other exercises, Burns signaled me to join him at the pull-up bars.

"Up with you," he suggested, going as far as offering his interlaced hands to boost me up.

Chuffing, I took a running start, easily propelling myself up to grab the bar—only to thump back down onto my feet when my right hand slipped right after my fingers closed around the bar, and my left really didn't have the strength yet to hold my entire weight.

Burns gave a knowing nod, reaching for the resistance bands hanging to the side—and to make things even worse, he selected the strongest one to tie it to the bar. I glared at him as I put my foot into the bottom loop of it, not suffering gracefully as he grabbed my rib cage from behind and—easily—pushed me toward the bar. I was tempted not to grab it, making him hold me there until we both felt stupid, but abandoned that plan after a moment. With Burns, I could never know; he'd likely laugh his ass off through ten minutes of not letting me down from there, turning the tables on me. Even more so,

I resented the fact that with the support of the band, enough of my weight was off my hands to let them retain their still weak grip.

"Sheesh, girl, take the ego out of it," Burns grumbled behind me as he let go, only stepping away once he'd made sure that I wouldn't plonk down once more. "You'd think that almost dying a second time and rebounding quicker than one of those battery bunnies would last longer, but no. You have to take the shittiest advice from our collective playbook, of course."

I glared at him, swinging forward and back slightly as I tried to distribute my weight better. My right hand was protesting vehemently, but I gritted my teeth and forced myself to push through the pain. The left was doing much better, particularly when I tensed more to attempt an actual pull-up. That wasn't happening, but just feeling that my arms, shoulders, and back were slowly regaining the strength to get there was balm on my soul.

Yeah, I might have had a slight problem with my ego, but far be it from me to admit it.

"You're one to talk," I groused. "You're not the collective butt-end of every joke around here."

Burns chortled, until he realized that I was serious. "Like fuck you are. Hamilton's an asshole, you know that. His people know that, too. Most may prefer him to Miller, but a lot of that is due to having gotten fed shit they couldn't refute, and mere habit. They sure don't have a clue where to shelve you, but you're doing a great job giving them the wrong ideas."

Annoyance made it just a little easier to continue holding on for another ten seconds. "And pray tell, what wrong ideas would that be?"

"That you're the spiteful shithead Hamilton says you are. Damn, do I really have to spell that out for you?"

My right hand finally gave, and I quickly untangled my crossed legs from the band so I could drop to my feet. My arms hurt almost as much as my hands, but a little shaking and swinging took care of that. The foul taste that Burns's words left in my mouth was harder to disband. There was challenge in his gaze when I met it, making me jut my chin out defiantly.

"Guess you do. Maybe he's right."

Bless him. Rather than take me seriously and continue to glower at me, Burns threw his head back and laughed, slapping my shoulder good-naturedly to make me stagger forward. "I've so missed this," he offered, a shit-eating grin on his face. "You're ten times more fun to be around when you're annoyed out of your mind. On the way up to the Silo I thought I'd never get to have this level of fun, seeing as you and your mister finally buried the hatchet, but now you make me almost happy to be in this shit show of a situation."

"Gee, always so happy to amuse you," I fake-whined, but then dropped the act. "Seriously, what did you mean with that? There's a good chance that at least some of them were at the base in Colorado. I must have shot someone they knew, or at least knew someone that did."

"As did I," Burns drawled, getting real. "And they won't let us forget that. But that doesn't mean that most of them aren't realistic enough to see that holding onto useless grudges won't benefit anyone. You pretty much rotting from the inside out went a long way toward smoothing over quite a lot of ruffled feathers. That, and the fact that you are an enemy worth having fought against, underlined now by how hard you're working on dragging yourself back out of your grave. They've all been there at one point or another, and they know how awful and hard it is. Strength—of character, not just sheer bull-neck brute force—is something they can all relate to, and admire. You've paid the piper, and now you start fresh with a clean slate. Sure, they'll rib you where they can, but you're used to worse from Martinez and me. Remember when I called you both pretty ladies when I was doing my push-ups with you both sitting on my back? You offered to find a parasol somewhere and some fancy petticoats to make the picture perfect."

Oh, I remembered, the memory making me smile. "That was pretty funny," I had to admit.

"And you barely managed fifteen push-ups at the time yourself, and looked ready to die after five rounds of sprints," he was quick to remind me. "So what's different now? That you actually have the strength, agility, and muscle memory to pull all that off without a hitch?"

"You know it's not that simple," I complained. "And it's different whether you laugh your ass off at me being weak as a kitten"—as he'd so lovingly remarked each and every time I'd landed face-first in the dirt on my push-ups—"or those assholes."

Burns snorted. "The difference is all in your head." When I just stared at him, he nodded toward the soldiers he'd been talking to before. "I've been on more missions with Hill than I can count. He's a good guy. Actually, the last time I was in the field with him, we were sneaking through your hometown, trying to extract you before the undead got to you." I couldn't hide my surprise at that revelation. "You know how that turned out," Burns went on talking as if he hadn't noticed my curiosity. "Without him, Hamilton, and some of the others, Martinez, Smith, Cho, and I would have been toast."

"Why did you come with Nate then?" I asked what had been puzzling me for just about as long as we'd known each other.

Burns gave a noncommittal grunt. "Gut feeling, for the most part. I knew about his discharge, but never tried to follow up on that with him, seeing as he dropped off the face of the earth after that. Figured, oh hell, another one jumping onto the crazy train. But seeing the old bunch of misfits back together, I realized that, misgivings or not, they were still the people I'd rather tough out the end of the world with than my comrades of many, many years. You're partly to blame for that, as well."

"Me?" I didn't have to feign surprise there.

Rather than reply, Burns nodded at the bar. "Up first, story time later." This time, it was enough for him to boost me up so I could hold on to the bar and get my feet into the band on my own. He poked my obliques hard to make me tense my core muscles to better support myself before he resumed his tale. "Call it instinct, if you will. Or being too much of an optimist. What Miller did— or at least the version they fed us—made me doubt both him and my own dedication to the cause. He's always been someone to play it fast and loose if he could, but he's a good leader who'd never needlessly endanger his men. Seeing a good ten of the old gang working with him reminded me of that once more. And then, there was you. When we set out to fetch whatever they wanted to grab from your old workplace, they had updated your info from scientist with useful skills to possible person of interest working with the forces we expected to oppose us. But I was there when they dragged your sick, raving girlfriend out of your home, and let's just say that I found it highly unlikely that someone who'd live with someone like her would be a bona fide bad guy. You were scared, and confused, and you had all the reasons in the world to let Hamilton whisk you away to safety and relative luxury. Yet you chose to stick it out with Miller and his people. Sure, I was convinced that you'd been actively plotting with him beforehand, which I now know you weren't, but it doesn't matter—somewhere along the way he convinced you that he was doing the right thing, and you trusted him to keep doing so. Call me a sentimental fool, but I wanted to believe that there was some good left in him. That something had either gone terribly wrong, or it all had been some even deeper undercover shit than we were already mired in. And I'm not the only one who's been holding on to that belief." He exhaled slowly, briefly checking on my progress. "Plus, most of them read the protocol of what he told you while they were getting ready to take you apart. Hearing it from him did a lot to make people second-guess what they thought they knew."

Huh. The fact that they'd also told Burns about that was telling—and a lot more impactful than I'd imagined. "He could have been lying," I pressed out between gritted teeth, trying to hold on just a little longer.

"Convinced that you were about to die? What use would that have been to him?"

I made a face but didn't continue to protest. He had a point there. "So exactly how do they see me?" I asked, this time for real.

"In short, a wild card," Burns explained. "They all know you're a super-smart scientist. They know Raynor wanted you up there, and the rumor is, so you can together tweak the serum to do away with the side effects we all so love." He offered up a brief, mirthless chuckle. "Nobody is comfortable knowing that they'll likely take a handful of their best friends with them if they die. A lot of them would give their lives to put an end to that, maybe even literally. That's why none of them ever tried to kill you, if you were wondering. Not at the factory, and certainly not at the base. From what I hear, your name's been in the VIP rosters of who to preserve pretty much since the shit hit the fan."

I didn't know how to react to that, so I chose to ignore it. "Do they also know that it was Bucky's idiocy that almost cost them that chance?"

"That has come up a time or two, usually in hushed tones, and quickly denied when someone else came in. Certainly rubbed a few people the wrong way. But you're here now, so no reason to keep complaining. Or ask for a black eye."

That vindicated me a little, but it was a very small victory compared to the ramifications. "What good that does me, really."

Burns didn't see it quite that glum, stepping away so I could drop down from the bar. He pointedly ignored my wince as I slowly opened and closed my fists to let the pain dissipate more quickly.

"It just might." When he caught my confused look, he laughed. "For you it's a shit change for your life, no kidding. But to them, it equalizes the playing field. You can't work in a lab anymore, but now you're one of them. There's a certain level of bonding that comes with shared fates. That's something they can understand, and commiserate with."

"And the fact that I led a bloodthirsty mob, out to kill them?"

"Depends on who you ask." He chuckled. "A few are holding a grudge. A few come close to understanding. Not everyone was happy with the kill order that went out last summer. Most don't really give a shit. They heard a lot about you that's too wild to believe, and they'd much rather see for themselves. Hint—this is where you need to change your attitude. A lot."

I had to admit, he might have a point there. "And how exactly should I accomplish that? And, just saying, them laughing at me whenever possible doesn't make it easy on me."

"Ego, girl. Leave it where it belongs—at the very bottom of your bag of tricks." He gave me a critical look. "You think you can hold on to a barbell?"

"If you spot me, why not?" What's the worst that could happen? A few more bruises that would heal in a day or two wouldn't kill me.

"Then how about we go over there and give it a try. And when Hill and Murdock start shooting the usual shit, don't turn into a prissy princess. Pretend they're Martinez and Romanoff. Or, better yet, Bates's twins. They both knew him, and if memory serves me, they got along really well." He would know, having been really tight with Bates himself.

I hesitated, but then inclined my head in agreement. What could possibly go wrong?

At first, nothing, which was bordering on anticlimactic. Burns secured one of the benches for us with a rack to put the bar on, then had me bench press that without any additional weights on to test my grip. It had been quite some time—since last winter, actually, in the bunker—since I'd done any weight training that didn't involve anything except my own body weight, and like with the pull-up bar, I needed a little to adjust to the fact that my right hand simply couldn't manage the same grip strength as my left. I'd never noticed just how much of that depended on the last two fingers of my hand, but it kind of made sense—now that I had the comparison punching me in the face, whatever I did.

"Okay, got it," I declared when I managed the second set of twenty without a hitch.

"Great. How much do you want to go for? Ten?" Burns suggested.

"And let you accuse me of lifting like a girl? Hit me with twenty," I shot back, grinning up at him. While I waited for him to fetch the weights, I pulled my knees to my chest, rounding my back to get some of the discomfort out of my scars. Hanging on the bar had strained the muscles of my lower back more than I'd thought at first—and I was sure that I'd do pretty much the same to my obliques and abdomen now. I was almost looking forward to having zombies snap at my face again—at least they left me the choice of what parts of my body to annihilate. I casually glanced over to the soldiers who were still diligently pumping iron, and while they were very focused on that, I didn't miss how they kept watching us just as I was watching them.

As Burns lugged the black weight plates over—quite casually, I had to admit—he paused behind them, eyeing their form critically. "Hill, you're an embarrassment to mankind, anyone tell you that lately? Next you'll have a hard time holding your plate up at the mess hall." Considering Hill was easily pressing dumbbells weighing more than I did—likely in addition to what I was working with—that statement made me snicker in earnest.

"You're one to laugh, zombie girl," Hill called over without missing a rep. "Haven't seen you fetch anything from the galley that you didn't threaten someone's life over."

I felt my cheeks heat up a little, but I didn't need Burns's warning glance to swallow the ire coming up inside of me. "Hell, I was hungry," I shot back. "I could have vaulted over that bar and gone right for that idiot's jugular, too, but then one of you pretty boys would have shit himself, and who'd want to clean up that mess?"

"Might have been an improvement on what they make us eat," the second soldier remarked dryly.

"True," Hill agreed.

"You really are a bunch of pussies," I pressed out as I took the—damn heavy—bar from Burns. He let go but kept his hands hovering right underneath it, ready to catch it should one of my hands or wrists flag. "We lived half the first summer off cat food. Anything that's not mouse-gut flavored tastes like chocolate now."

Hill laughed, like I'd cracked a really good joke, but the other guy—Murdock, I reminded myself, thinking I'd better start remembering their names, seeing as we were stuck together for a while—nodded slowly. "Yeah, I heard someone mention that before. Still better than bugs."

"Hey, don't knock beetles and centipedes," Burns offered. "Like crunchy meatballs with spaghetti."

"Ugh, you're disgusting!" I grumbled, doing my best to go for a seventh rep, but then gave up. The moment he saw me grimace, Burns grabbed the bar and heaved it onto the rack, relieving me of my burden. I remained lying there, panting heavily, then started massaging my wrists as soon as my hands stopped aching worse.

Murdock chuckled. "I'll drink to that!"

Burns ignored him, instead raising his brows at me. "You ready to do some actual lifting, or is your back still too sore for that?" My grip wasn't bad, but quite obviously, I'd have a much easier time working my arm and chest muscles doing push-ups.

"Only one way to find out, right?" I wasn't sure if I really wanted to do exercises that ended with me sticking my ass out, but then lying flat on my back, grunting like a madwoman, wasn't much better. Burns snatched the bar right off the rack as if it weighed nothing and put it on the floor for me. I hesitated for a second, but then threw caution to the wind and bent down to grab it for some deadlifts. The scars on my back complained, but that wasn't the reason why the bar slipped from my fingers on the fifth repetition. Cursing under my breath, I shook out my hands, biting the inside of my cheek not to cry out loud. Why pushing worked well but lifting not so much was beyond me, but there was definitively room for improvement.

"Here, try these." I looked up in surprise, finding Murdock standing next to me, holding out a pair of black wraps. "Wrist straps," he explained. "I use them to take some of the tension off my wrists. You wrap them around your wrists and the bar; creates a better connection. Not sure if that will make it harder or easier in your case, but doesn't hurt to try, right?"

I nodded slowly, hesitantly accepting the straps. Murdock bent over, showing me how exactly to get them around my wrists and the bar, helping me with the second. I couldn't quite keep from tensing as he touched me, but he kept it to a minimum, stepping away as soon as everything was in place. I tried again, this time making it to eight reps, and setting the barbell down with only somewhat of a "plunk."

"Works well enough," I admitted. "Thanks."

"You're welcome," he replied, even going as far as offering a small smile. Gee, we were getting downright chummy here.

"What happened to your wrists? They look fine to me. Repetitive stress injury from too much mission report write-ups?"

That made him laugh wholeheartedly. "Yeah, something like that." He hesitated, but then went on. "Got myself captured on an infiltration job. Turns out, they didn't joke about the sadistic bad guys being just that. When I wouldn't talk, they grabbed a hammer—you know the small ones that you use for really tiny nails? Doesn't look like much. Well, turns out, they're awesome for smashing all the bones of the hand into tiny bits as well." I couldn't help but wince, but he went right on, his left hand idly digging into the fleshy part of his right palm below the thumb. "Funny thing is, those healed up well enough, but the nerves went a little haywire. That's why I use the straps for lifting. You can keep those, I have plenty more." He paused, carefully studying my face for a moment. "It was your husband who got me out of there, and who was smart enough to tie compression bandages around my hands to keep everything together until they could get me to surgery. I won't ever forget that, whatever else went down."

I took that with the nod of acknowledgment he was clearly waiting for. "He sometimes has his moments. Don't worry, I won't tattle on you. His ego's already inflated enough." Right then, I was sure that Nate could have done with some positive reinforcement of his previous actions, but what was a white lie between barely-acquaintances?

"Thanks." Murdock laughed, then cast a quick look in Hill's direction, who was still busy working his tree-trunk arms. "Hey, I've noticed that your bunch are usually doing your sprints alone all through the day. Wanna race us? We do them at 2000 each evening. A little betting between friends never hurt anybody."

I was tempted to agree just to get the chance to annihilate some of them—I still wasn't close to my previous speed, but how fast could a lumbering hulk like Hill get?—but left it at an uneasy shrug. "Thanks for the offer, but I have a certain feeling that might end with knocked-out teeth and someone bleeding out on the floor. But I'm happy to race both of you any time. Just ask Burns how great it feels when a tiny woman makes you eat the dirt cloud she kicks up in her wake." I half-turned to grin at Burns, who shook his head at me.

"Nice tat, by the way," Murdock remarked, almost too casually. I couldn't help but stiffen, the need to pull down my tank top so that my lower back would be covered strong, but there really was no sense in that. Instead, I tried my best at a casual shrug.

"One of a kind. Well, one of twelve, really, but I'm the only one who got it down there." Unless they were blind, they already knew that both Nate and Burns had theirs higher up on their spines, just underneath their three Xs.

"Yeah, about that," Murdock started, briefly glancing at Burns but then going on to me. "Why Thirteen? So much more you could have done with Twelve. Like Dozen."

Burns's remark from back when he'd tortured me with the pull-up bar blazed red-hot across my mind, but I did my best not to appear too cautious as I gave a casual shrug. But why did this conversation have to slide into minefield territory like that? If that was even the case. I had a really hard time reading both Murdock and Hill, who'd stopped pretending to work out and was listening from his perch on the inclined weight bench next to Burns.

"Well, first off, it wasn't my idea," I offered. "They marked up our very special nutcases first, and back then that excluded me. Only got to sign on the dotted line when I did my dramatic 'thanks, but I'll stick with my guys rather than take over your snazzy lab bunker' stunt." The memory made me smile, as usual. "But it made sense, to all of us. Bates might not have been alive anymore, but none of us would have ever thought of not considering him part of our team. And considering how much of a countdown that turned into, it really doesn't matter in hindsight." That last part came out a little bitter, but I tried to hide that behind a small smile. I had no idea where the two soldiers had been during either of the clashes we'd had with their side.

Murdock gave a nod that was bordering on grave, making me wonder whether that was just about Bates, or the general loss of life—something I knew he had to be familiar with in that line of work.

"How did that happen, anyway?" Hill asked when the moment threatened to turn a little too heavy. "Bates, I mean. He could be quite the idiot, but he was a careful fucker, most of the time."

"He literally wasn't." Burns chortled, but at my hard look shut up. Some things really didn't need to be stressed—and better went forgotten if they weren't aware yet who Sadie's baby daddy was.

"He was stupid, all right," I said, trying to turn the conversation around. That part fit just as well to Burns's slip, even though I hated to have to recount it now. "He and I, we were out together. We were scouting that cannibal compound over in Illinois. Our quadrant was supposed to be too far out for us to get into any danger, or else Miller wouldn't have sent me with Bates. We were checking out a plateau below a ledge, and he must have heard something, because he left me there to go take a dump. When he didn't come back, I tried to check on him, but by then the sneaky fuckers already had him. They were too dumb to find me, and I managed to alert the others. But by then they'd already started taking him apart limb from limb. We had to wait until he bled out and turned because we needed that distraction to overcome their superior numbers. We killed every last fucker down there, for all the good that it did him. It was my shotgun slug that took him out in the end. That was the least that I owed him for saving my life."

Hill looked a little skeptical while Murdock nodded. Burns, of course, couldn't leave it at that. "You forgot the part where you hopped in the back of one of their trucks to get close enough for radio contact with us, jumped right off that when they got close to their compound, and did some damn fine sniping from a good distance when our distraction struck. My favorite part was when you went batshit crazy on the fuckers with your shotgun."

I couldn't help but sneer at him. "Yeah, you would know. You covered my back and let me do all the actual shooting." Burns's only response was a shit-eating grin, making me roll my eyes at him. Turning to the soldiers, I did my best at a neutral shrug. "What can I say. Must have done something right, or else that gang of misfits wouldn't have accepted me as their co-leader. Just if you were wondering, I didn't get that job just because I'm screwing the boss."

"Actually, for some that was a black mark on your ledger," Burns had to supply, chortling with mirth. "Cho was so fucking annoyed. I think it took him weeks to get over it."

That was news to me, and I didn't do a thing to hide that. "He didn't live much longer than a couple more weeks."

"Death's great for giving up grudges," Burns replied, his tone a little softer than before.

"Why didn't he ever say anything to me?" I had been wondering about their acceptance, of course, but seeing as leadership had always been an easily defined thing for us—Nate in all tactical situations, and the rest was usually unanimous—I'd never openly questioned it.

Burns huffed, then let out a soft laugh when I kept looking expectantly at him. "You're serious? And get chewed out by you in front of everyone? I'd rather try telling Zilinsky that she's a frail woman, and women can't fight—and then try to survive the fallout. Come to think of it, same counts for you. I think I'd prefer her beating me up. She's not such a damn resentful bitch."

I silently sneered at him for that, but left it uncommented. Turning back to Murdock, I tried myself at a casual shrug, but this time it was tense. We were kind of toeing a line there, and just because Burns had started it didn't mean I wouldn't get caught up in the fallout. Yet both Hill and Murdock took that statement with the stoic ignorance all of them had been showing me over the past week, for the most part.

"So she really settled down?" Hill wanted to know, taking the easy way out. "Never thought that would happen."

Murdock laughed. "Yeah, you also bet a bottle of damn fine tequila that Miller would never lose his head to a set of nice tits and a juicy ass, and yet here she is." He actually had the audacity to wink at me, so I didn't tell him what I thought of that assessment. That statement really could have come from Bates.

"Yeah, what can I say," I offered. "I'm such a catch." That made all three of them laugh, just as I'd intended—and nicely defused what was left of the residual tension. That sent our banter right into a lull, but it wasn't really awkward like before. Turning back to my barbell, I picked up Murdock's straps to get ready for another set. "Well, as much as I'd love to keep chatting, I have some actual work to do. Else, how will I keep juicy European shamblers from tearing off your pretty faces?" I got a round of chuckles for that, and both soldiers admitted that they were overdue to hit the showers. Burns sauntered over to me to give some more or less useful notes on my posture, but the slight smile on his face let me know that I'd done good.

Exhaling hard as I pulled the barbell up, I hoped that he was right. Maybe they weren't all assholes. Maybe I could trust Red with his attempt to build bridges where they had been burned. Maybe I could just grab one of these weight plates and smash it into Bucky's face hard enough to split open his skull, taking care of that problem once and for all.

Oh, a girl could dream.

Chapter 7

The next time we all congregated in the mess hall, I felt like something was different. Not a massive change, more like subtle currents slowly swaying in a different direction. I chalked it up to me seeing things—until I walked in on Burns and Tanner compiling a rather weird list. I'd hung back after lunch, hitting the head—and staying for an extended period of time; while my body was doing a great job burning a lot of energy, it also produced a lot of byproducts of that. When I finally made it to our quarters, I heard their voices through the partly open door, so I paused to listen for a few moments before entering.

"Murdock, Hill, and Carter are a go for the favorable list," Burns remarked. "Maybe Parker, too, but he's a tough nut to crack. Worked far too long with Hamilton to switch sides now."

Tanner grumbled something I didn't catch, then, "Aimes and Wu remain on the no-go list?"

"Stuck-up pricks," Burns agreed. "Or else they wouldn't have sent them to our camp back before Colorado."

"Gita said she talked to that Rodriguez woman who was with them. Says she's not quite such a hardliner."

"Put her down as maybe then," Burns advised. "How many does that make altogether?"

Tanner's reply came a few seconds later, as if he was counting. "If you factor us in, that's two more in favor of Hamilton. Odds could be worse."

That's when my curiosity got the better of me and I stepped inside, just in time to see Tanner make a crumpled paper disappear behind his back. "What's going on?" I asked, not even pretending like I hadn't been eavesdropping. "You should close the door if you're trying to be super stealthy."

Tanner laughed. "Nothing to do with stealth. Just trying to even the odds a little."

"What odds?" It was a warranted question.

"That someone sticks a knife in our ribs," Burns explained.

Way to bring my paranoia roaring back to life. "You think that's a real possibility? I wouldn't put it past Bucky to let us die if anything happens, but to have his people actively come for us makes no sense. Nate, sure. Me, maybe. But the rest of you?"

Tanner's grin was a real one. "We try to see us all as a package deal, you know? And to answer your question, no, we don't expect them to come after us. But if I've learned one thing over the past ten years, it's that someone who you've gotten chummy with is much less likely to watch you die than someone who can't stand you. That's why we've tried building a few bridges over the past days. It's not like we got anything else to do."

I couldn't quite refute that so I didn't try. It was obvious now what Burns had been doing with our workout session—besides giving me a one-on-more-than-one therapy session.

"Why didn't I notice any of that until now?" I muttered, mostly to myself, but Tanner still answered, giving me a somewhat uneasy look.

"You've been pretty out of it," he explained, tone careful. When I gave him a blank stare back, he scoffed. "Lewis, watching you for the first few days was pretty much a nightmare. You were just lying there, unmoving—and I mean like a statue, not just trying to lie still to avoid pain. People fidget. You didn't. And you were just staring straight ahead, without blinking. Not much difference when you were up and moving about. More than once I thought about asking one of the others to gently poke you to see if you were still alive."

I couldn't hold back a small laugh. "Oh, you know that you would have noticed it if I wasn't." This once, I was the only one who seemed to find that funny. "Guess I really was quite out of it."

Burns nodded. "Yeah, but you evidently needed that downtime. Now you're back to your pleasant, calm self."

I flipped him off—that I could do with both hands still—and turned around to crawl into my bunk. Yet before I was halfway in there, the door opened fully again, Nate stepping in.

"What are you doing here, lazing around with those idiots? I told you to meet me at the armory."

I tried to remember. He had said something, but I hadn't paid much attention, distracted by… not really anything. Damn, my mind still wasn't quite where it needed to be.

"Sure, was just grabbing my hoodie." Now, of course, I had to go through the laborious process of getting out of my thick thermal and into the sweat hoodie, all while crawling backward out of my bunk.

Nate gave me a hard look, letting me know that he knew exactly what was going on, but for once passed up the chance to chew me out. "Come on, you two as well. We all need some extra weapon drills."

"I don't," Burns complained, but at Nate's growl got back up from his own bunk and followed along.

I hadn't been to the forward sections of the ship yet, but it didn't really look that different—except that I already knew I would get turned around should I have to make my way back on my own. Nate never seemed to have any issues finding his way, something I hated him for a little bit. That sentiment didn't exactly lessen as we stepped into the designated armory—it seemed to have been something else before, judging from the paint of the stencil not quite fitting the others. Inside, two of the marines sat at a table, chatting casually—and a full ten of our fellow soldiers, busy oiling and polishing their gear. With a sinking feeling in my stomach I sat down at the empty smaller table in the corner when it became obvious that Nate wasn't just going to grab some weapons to take elsewhere. The next surprise wasn't too pleasant, either. Rather than hand me a pistol, he pulled one of the M16 assault rifles from the racks.

"You remember how to field-strip one of those?"

I glared daggers at him, my hands still folded on my lap underneath the table top. "I'm not a fucking imbecile."

"Then start," he taunted. "Ten times should be enough. We'll take it upstairs later if the sea remains calm enough that we can shoot on deck. Depending on how you handle it, you'll either take one of those, or one of the M4s."

"What's wrong with my carbine?" It had taken me long enough to get really comfortable with it over the shotguns. I didn't quite get why he needed me to switch again now.

"Because the M16 shoots farther, and I'm not sure how well you'll do with your sniper rifle—and the overall weight of the gear we'll have to carry."

"I did well enough last year, and that was before I actually learned how to fight."

Nate hesitated, briefly glancing at the soldiers, but they didn't even pretend not to listen in. "Bree, we had you carry a quarter of what everyone else was lugging around. Besides, we never had enough food for it to really weigh us down. Same for weapons and other gear. You have absolutely no idea what's waiting for you when we leave this ship."

That was a more sobering answer than I liked, making me drop my protest. And three seconds later, the M16, as my grip slipped spectacularly as I started taking it apart. Gee, didn't that start well?

A few minutes later, I knew why he had me start on the big, heavy things—there was a good chance I might have just chucked a pistol at him the tenth time I managed to fumble, or completely drop, the dastardly thing. It wasn't that the weapon was too heavy for me—with the exercises of the last few days, my grip had started to strengthen once more and was doing okay—but it was as if someone had exchanged my fingers for tree trunks, and clumsy ones at that. My right hand kept slipping whenever I held on to something, relying on the strength and stability of two fingers that weren't there anymore. My left was doing better on that account, but I'd seldom before realized how much my fine motor functions relied on my index finger.

It took me well over five minutes for the first round. As soon as everything snapped back together with a last push, I dropped the damn rifle and shoved it away from me with disgust, not caring any longer to suppress the curse that had been burning on my tongue for the entire time. Someone laughed at the other end of the room, but when my head snapped around and I glared at the lot of them, they were suspiciously silent, and mostly focused on their cleaning.

I closed my eyes and counted down from ten, then grabbed the M16 once more and started over. And over. And over again. On the tenth round, I was down to three minutes—abysmal time, but at least I hadn't lost any of the smaller parts this round. Nate nodded at the cleaning supplies in front of his perch opposite me, so I opened up the weapon one more time to—needlessly—take care of lint and signs of use that weren't there. Someone had already taken care of that in the days before, but that, of course, needed a lot more fine motor control that had me gritting my teeth again. At least those didn't hurt anymore, as small blessings went.

Nate consequently had me clean all the other weapons on the table as well, before he pushed my M24, still in its case, at me. I was more careful with that, deliberately slowing down my motions not to damage the sniper rifle we both had way too much emotional bonding going on with. I knew that it wasn't that delicate, but trading possible speed for accuracy made me fumble around less, and my ego needed that right now. When that was over and done, Nate pushed an entire heap of handguns at me. "Ten minutes. Go." And this time he kept the stopwatch in his hand, leaving me no chance to check on my progress.

Oh, there was fumbling involved. And cursing. Of course it had to be my Beretta of all things that went flying under the table, much to the amusement of the peanut gallery. And, just my luck, it had to happen just as Bucky came strolling into the armory, not missing a moment, including my scrambling around underneath the table. I knew a stupid comment was about to hit me in the face as soon as I resurfaced—very likely about what possible activities I could have conducted underneath there—but what he flung in my face was worse. "Stumpy, that's actually pathetic." Just four small words, without much inflection in his tone. Sexual innuendo might have made me mad, but that shit stuck. I dropped my gaze back to my Beretta, resuming where I'd had to stop, my cheeks burning, my throat tight.

Shit, but he was right.

Nate's utter lack of a reaction didn't help much. I could read the neutral look on his face well enough as he tried to pretend that Bucky didn't exist—on some level, he agreed with him, but he was smart enough not to mention that. He was also close to losing his composure over anyone demoralizing me like this when that was his designated job—to incentivize me to get better, not put me down.

But overwhelmingly, there was fear in his eyes that I was really trying, but this was about as good as I'd get. It was one thing to pick up the slack when I was still recovering and not quite back at fighting strength, but quite another when I'd always remain a liability from here on out. That thought sobered me enough that it got easier to ignore that idiot's taunting.

My spirit didn't exactly pick itself off the ground as we went topside after lunch, bundled up in enough layers that I felt like a giant fluffy ball. With three pairs of socks, I'd foregone padding the front of my boots, but I quickly realized that wasn't the way to go as I continued to slip inside my boots even when the grip of my soles on the ocean-sprayed deck was secure. I'd brought gloves—hating how the three empty finger parts flopped around—but took them off before getting my Beretta out. The cold bit mercilessly into my hands, but it was worst at the remaining stump of my right ring finger, making me grit my teeth before I'd even managed to fuck up anything. I'd wisely brought a full ten already loaded magazines to spare myself having to reload them out here, but the way Nate plonked the ammo box full of 9mm rounds at the table next to us didn't bode well for that. At least it was just the two of us, Hill, Red, and one of the soldiers whose name I still couldn't remember.

As soon as our "range" was cleared—the area in front of the already rather shoddy wooden targets empty after Red had tacked new paper targets onto them—the soldiers started their practice, while I went through switching my grip around for a good minute before I lined up the sights and fired. Thirty feet, and I didn't even hit the outer frame of the target, let alone the center of it. Exhaling slowly as I centered myself, I checked my stance, then fired again, this time pulling the trigger five times in quick succession—still not as fast as possible, but without giving my body too much time to jerk around. The muscle memory kicked in quickly, the last two shots finally getting close to the black center of the target. When I started a new sequence, the first shots again went wide.

Mentally steeling myself for his verdict, I looked at Nate once I'd emptied the magazine. "You don't need me to say it," was all he offered.

I sighed. "My grip is shit and I keep jerking every time I pull the trigger." Somewhat self-conscious, I looked over to the others—all hitting dead-center, of course, but none of them was paying me any direct attention as they reloaded the third or fourth time already—before going on. "It's not like I'm afraid. I just can't keep my hands steady."

None of the expected scorn showed on Nate's face as he held out a new magazine to me. "Then relearn how to."

As I continued wasting one magazine after the other, I realized that it wasn't just the lack of strength in my hands and resulting involuntary action. The problem was my entire body. Because of the scars on the right side of my torso, standing straight wasn't actually straight but a slight slouch to the right. Whenever I tensed in preparation of the recoil, my toes did funny things that further messed up my stance, and only after I incidentally switched my right foot for my left in the forward position did I realize that I was still trying to keep my weight off my left thigh. Shaking my entire body from time to time to try to do a reset helped, but only gradually. On the last two sets that I split the last magazine into I still had about a third of the shots go wide, but at least it only took three now to lock my body so that it was doing what it should have done from the start. Better, but still not good enough.

"Let's try again tomorrow," Nate suggested, awfully neutral—likely because I was gritting my teeth hard enough that the enamel should have made a cracking sound. As much as I hated the constant nagging he sometimes had going on, this was worse. Things were always bad when he started coddling me.

Even knowing all that, I was more than ready to throw in the towel, but when I saw Red reach for the M16 he'd brought along, I hesitated. "Mind if I give that a go?"

"Be my guest," he offered as he handed it over, without a doubt swallowing the taunt that it would be hard for me to miss at this distance. A good thing, because the spray I produced as I got a little too comfy with the trigger from the get-go was indeed embarrassing, but a little adjusting, and the next few—single, this time—shots were centered enough that if I'd been shooting at a shambler, their combined force would have at least made it stagger back. Not one of the juiced-up ones, but it was progress.

"Do a twenty-five meter zero," Hill advised, then waited until the other soldier had stopped shooting to be heard better, adaptive noise-cancelling headphones or not. "If you hit the target at that distance, the shot will be good at two hundred, too."

I knew he was just being helpful, but I wasn't in the mood to appreciate that. "Gee, think I would have managed such a stellar job shooting your asses out from under you before if I didn't know that?"

Hill laughed, but for once, Red wasn't so lenient with my jibes. "From what I heard, you didn't really do much of that in the few tousles you've had with our forces. What my guys told me, you hit shit-all at the factory, and shooting people in the back in zombie-overrun corridors doesn't really speak of stellar marksmanship."

I didn't need to hurl a "challenge accepted" in his face as I picked up the rifle from the table again and turned around to walk the distance to the next set of tables, right by the doors of the helicopter hangar. The left-most target was still pristine as Nate hadn't even picked up a gun and I'd done little enough damage that switching targets wasn't really worth the waste. With impatience I waited for the four of them to clear the shorter distance before I got ready, doing a few dry exercises before I loaded the magazine. I would show him marksmanship.

Because anger made me stupid, the first three shots barely hit the target in the left lower corner, but after some adjustments of my stance—and telling my ego to go fuck itself—I did much better. Much, much better than before, in fact; more than twenty of the thirty rounds hit the two innermost rings of the target, and virtually all of those clustered. When I lowered the assault rifle, I found Red giving a satisfied nod, while Hill and the other soldier had a good time laughing—for once with me, not at me. "Did you picture Richards's face there, or Hamilton's?" The third soldier called over, still grinning.

"Something a little lower, if you must know," I jeered back as I returned to them, handing Red his rifle. "Satisfied? Shall I get my sniper rifle out next? But you'll have to build us a floating target for that."

"This will do," Red replied wryly, accepting his weapon. "Have you decided whether you want to go for the assault rifle or the carbine?"

"It's not like I'll run into ammo issues if I switch," I joked, but only had a shrug to answer his question. "Let's see how I do with either in the next few days. My preference is still my shotgun, but seeing as you all think I'll just fumble and drop it, I won't even bother."

Hill had something to say to that, too. "The M16's stock is great for clobbering people over the head, if that's why you think you need a bird seed bomber. Go with it over the M4. You'll get used to the extra weight easily, and it will give you an advantage in the distance. For close-range, just let us do the cleanup and stand back. Less gore in your face to ruin your makeup, too."

I didn't have to force a laugh this time. "Gladly. It will do wonders to that goblin thing you've got going on. Who doesn't look prettier with gore splattered all over their mug?"

"She got you there," the other soldier sneered at Hill before picking his pistol back up. "Still got some shots to fire, so if you ladies would kindly put your ear protection back on. Or, better yet, take that inside to chat over tea and biscuits!"

Nate had already reloaded three of the pistol magazines, so after slapping my headphones back on, I slammed one of them into the Beretta and went back at it. And, wouldn't you know, I hit just a little better than before.

It was only once we were back below deck that I realized that Nate hadn't said a thing while I'd been shooting shit with the others. I was about to mention that to him, but dropped the point. "What do you think? Am I completely useless, or is there still hope?" So what if I was fishing for compliments a little? It happened seldom enough, and after how it all had started in the morning, I needed a little pick-me-up.

Nate's response was not what I'd been expecting. "You're certainly doing a great job performing tricks when the right people say 'jump.' Next, you'll be rolling on the floor, waiting for a belly scratch."

That made me halt in my tracks. Nate continued on, not even checking back on me.

"Well, thanks for nothing, asshole!" I called after him, shaking my head to myself. Whatever. I recognized the intersection, so rather than try to catch up to him, I turned left, cutting through two sections to head straight to our quarters rather than back to the armory. Burns was there, glancing up as I stomped in, dropping my Beretta on my bunk before peeling myself out of my many layers. Fuck regulations that I should keep it in the armory at all times outside training.

"Didn't go quite as expected, eh?" Burns ribbed me, but gently.

I paused, considering. "No, actually, it went exactly as I should have expected. I married an asshole, so why do I keep getting surprised when he's behaving like one?" Burns didn't reply, wisely keeping his opinion to himself, letting me stomp my way out of my clothes. I hit my left elbow and right knee on the bunks, which did wonders for my sunny disposition, but I forced myself to rein it in by the time I was back in my sweats and tank. "By the way, what's that guy's name with the longish black hair who's missing part of his left ear?"

"You mean Cole?"

I shrugged, momentarily hard-pressed to remember if I'd heard him mentioned before, but the ear part should be a good identifier.

Then I did remember; he'd been the one to sling around scorn right before we'd left the base as we'd picked up the others. There was some bad blood between him and Nate, no kidding, but he hadn't come after Burns, nor Tanner and Gita—or me, for that matter. "I think you can put him on the maybe list, too. He and Hill were having a good time cheering me on. Oh, and Red's got me all figured out. Just saying."

"Red?" Burns echoed, raising his brows at me.

"Richards," I corrected myself. "Damn fucker got me to hit a good twenty out of thirty on his M16 just by accusing me of hitting shit."

"Sounds familiar," Burns offered with a grin, then laughed when he saw me make a face. "Doesn't take much with you, really. But great job! Maybe you should swap him for Old McGrouch over there." He indicated Nate's bunk.

It was only then that it occurred to me what the reason for Nate's scathing remark could have been. I didn't know whether to laugh or cry at that.

"Maybe don't mention that possibility when he comes back," I offered. "Not that it is an actual possibility. Just saying."

The look I got for that was bordering on ridiculous, like me stressing that last part was something that upended Burns's view of the world.

"Is there something you wanna talk about, girl?"

I shook my head, kicking Raynor's bag to the side once I'd gotten my supplements out. "Nah, just idiots being idiots, is all." And that, ladies and gents, included me. At least I hoped it was just that. Because this wasn't something I was going to waste even a single thought on, considering what else was clamoring around in my head already. Nate suddenly, out of nowhere, getting jealous? As much as the idea made me want to laugh, it was mostly at myself. It made much more sense that with Hamilton being a problem in general but his second in command appearing the reasonable party, Nate was actively plotting to take Richards out to even the playing field. So far, provoking him had been hard; with him gone, Hamilton would be easy game for either of us. That posed the question exactly how uncomfortable thinking along these lines made me. The general level of ambivalence inside of me didn't exactly make me feel comfortable in my own skin. My, but weren't we on the fast track to devolving into grunting Neanderthals?

Chapter 8

By the time Nate returned—carrying his winter gear in his arms, his innermost layer dripping with sweat from what I figured had been an impromptu workout session—he was calm once more, and mostly ignored me. I'd gotten back to trying to make sense of Raynor's folders, but my thoughts kept running away from me, so I had given up quickly. Playing cards with the others was more fun, anyway. I'd also snacked my way through two packs of nuts liberated from the galley, putting my mind further at ease. Hunger I might not feel, but I could definitely tell when my body felt sated. Burns kept staring at Nate, waiting for an explanation, but eventually gave up as well. I hadn't asked whether that get-to-know-each-other program he and Tanner were running included Nate—I'd mostly assumed it did—but it didn't really matter, anyway. We were all slowly but surely going stir crazy, and now that my mental capacities were almost back to normal, I could tell that, too. Too little activity, too much tension, and no undead to take all that out on—not a good combination. I'd never expected I'd think that, but I was actually looking forward to the day when we were neck-deep in shamblers once more.

Dinner was a quiet affair as we were having meat—or at least something that the cooks claimed had once been some kind of animal or other—and everyone was too concerned with shoving as much of it into their faces as possible. Everyone at our table laughed when Gita let out a tremendous burp, and even Nate seemed to have gotten over whatever had irked him in the afternoon. Training after that was hard—but what else was new—yet satisfying, my body behaving a little more like it should. I slept like the dead that night, a full six hours, and only woke up when Nate shook my shoulder hard. My mind flipped from oblivion to full awareness within seconds, annoying the hell out of me. I'd never realized just how much of a physical advantage the serum had conferred on those inoculated with it. It also made me wonder exactly how much luck we'd had with our little chase-and-snatch action in Sioux Falls when we'd gotten us one of the juiced-up shamblers to dissect. I should have died ten times over that day alone. As scary as that thought was in hindsight, it did a lot to motivate me as soon as I stepped into our hangar gym. I still wasn't quite where I'd been before the damn virus had forced me to my knees, but I was getting closer, day by day. Considering all the downsides—and not just what would happen to me once I bit it—and the price I'd already paid, I would be damned if I didn't try to get the most out of this. So I ran faster, punched harder, ducked quicker, and did my very best to push myself beyond my limits. So what if someone snickered when I dropped down from the pull-up bar after only a minute, a twenty-pound plate between my knees? That still was sixty seconds of my grip holding strong with added weight it hadn't been able to handle only a week ago. Compared to the damage a zombie or wild animal could inflict, their stupid comments could only hurt so much. What Burns had told me before helped as well—if it had been him, or one of the other guys, I would have laughed in their faces and jumped back up. Now I had all the more motivation to make sure not to fail.

And then came the day when, just as we were finishing breakfast, Bucky—for once present—got up to address us all, with the odd snide remark thrown our way that we all ignored.

"Last day of lazing around on your fat asses. The commander tells me we'll arrive at our drop-off point at the ass-crack of dawn. You better get the best out of all the comforts we've been enjoying on board of this mighty fine destroyer, because starting tomorrow, you'll eat only what you can carry, and everything we meet will be out to chew your pretty faces off."

Cheers went up from the soldiers' tables. I didn't quite know how to react. Looking at the others, I was met with similarly mixed feelings plain on their faces.

"Well, at least now they have to tell us where we are going," I offered, trying to put a positive spin on this.

"Not until tomorrow morning, they don't," Nate provided, his ire quite obvious.

Burns, of course, had to chuckle. "We'll know soon enough when we see the street signs. I really don't need to know a moment sooner."

I was tempted to try to weasel some information out of Red, but seeing as Bucky sat down next to him, I decided that avoidance was the better part of valor. Last day—that meant I still had two training sessions in the gym, plus some time to frustrate myself to death in the armory. I decided that I had done enough of cleaning and disassembling, likely not needing to do much of either under pressure in the upcoming weeks. Simply handling my weapons would make a lot more sense.

Nate disagreed with me, making me do the very same drills over and over until I was ready to strangle him. My fingers hurt—and were reeking of weapon oil—as we quickly grabbed a bite to eat from the galley for lunch. Rather than relax, he had us all pack our packs in the early afternoon, tearing mine apart no less than five times until I'd finally stowed everything away in a manner that passed his inspection, if barely. The others were wisely keeping out of it, but to say that the tension ratcheting up between Nate and me was making the others uncomfortable was an understatement. I more fled than walked to the gym as soon as I was dismissed, but before I was even done with warmup, Nate was plastered to my side again, my backup Glock and one of the M16s in his hands. "You can do drills here as well," he bit out, pointing at a corner of the mats. "Plus some push-ups and crawling across the room. Your torso is still way too stiff, and it won't get better in full gear." And that in front of what felt like the entirety of the soldiers, including my favorite Capt. Asshole.

Rather than tell Nate where he could shove that M16, I dropped to the floor, trying to keep my face as neutral as possible. Just one more day, I kept telling myself. Things couldn't get much worse once we were out there. At least not between us. And no, my torso wasn't stiff like a statue's, and maybe he'd like me to demonstrate the strength of my grip by volunteering his throat?

As such things go, the angrier I got, the more I messed up, which in turn just made me even more frustrated—and angry. I must have been doing a shit-job trying to hide that because after the second time the Glock dropped from my fingers, none of the soldiers dared to laugh anymore. They weren't even looking at me as I dragged my sorry self across the mats, pretending I was working my way underneath some low obstacles while keeping my weapon up in both hands. On the other side, I jumped to my feet, then as high as I could, before I let myself drop into a push-up—rinse, repeat, over and over. Then back the entire way, and one more field strip. I was huffing hard enough that I barely got air into my lungs as I crouched over the weapon, trying to be both fast and precise—and fumbled both, the bolt not just sliding out of my fingers, but hitting the mats at a weird angle that made it roll away from me, too fast to grab when I reached for it. Just my luck that it came to a stop right in front of Bucky's left boot.

Reaching down to scoop it up, Hamilton flipped the bolt end over end in his hand, considering it. "My, my, how will you get anything done in the field when you can't even do the simplest things every recruit learns in the first week, Stumpy? Need me to lend a hand, seeing as yours don't get the job done?"

Everything inside of me screamed to come to my feet, my position on the floor too vulnerable—and at a really bad angle, with him towering over me. He was now tapping the bolt against his thigh right next to his crotch, forcing me not to look even in the general direction of it.

"Can I have that back, please?" I said in the sweetest tone—well, growl—I could muster, pretending like I was trying to kill him with kindness. Any method would do if successful, really.

"What? Oh, this?" He twirled the elusive part in his fingers. "I should make you crawl over here and beg on your knees for it, seeing as I constantly find you in this position, anyway. Or, better yet, send you out there without it. Maybe that will teach you."

I couldn't help but scoff, hard-pressed to remain in my more or less casual crouch as I stared up at him. "And waste a perfectly good weapon? That would make you even dumber than everyone already knows you are."

Bucky's eyes narrowed, but then he held out the bolt to me with a truly magnanimous gesture. "Here you are. I'm always happy to help." Yet as I reached up to grab the bolt, he didn't let go right away. "I can help you with other things as well. Judging from how you're reeking of frustration, I'd guess you're not getting enough attention at the moment. What a shame, really."

I put as much strength into pulling the bolt free as I could—which was considerable, as I'd been smart enough to use my left hand—yet Bucky let go a second later, making me fall flat on my ass. At least I didn't end up on my back with him jeering down at me, but it was close enough to make me want to ram that thing right up, preferably until he was choking on it. Russell, one of Bucky's flunkies, laughed wholeheartedly, drawing a few snickers from the others. My cheeks flamed up, forcing me to keep my face down so no one would see it as I quickly—and this time, flawlessly—reassembled the assault rifle. Bucky finally moved on, leaving me crouching there, vibrating with tension that I knew I just wouldn't be able to lose until I punched someone in the face. Exactly what I needed right now.

"Up for a round of sparring?"

My head shot up, my eyes first fixating on Nate's face, then the extended hand he was offering to pull me up. After how he'd snapped at me first, I wasn't keen on giving him a chance to wipe the floor with me now, but it was impossible to read the anger blazing in his eyes for anything but what it was. I wrapped my fingers around his, letting him do the work—and, unlike the last time we'd done this, didn't go right into a swing. Had it really been that long since last we'd sparred for real? My tongue, unbidden, danced back to the perfectly formed dental implant crown now sitting where the tooth had been that he'd knocked out—the very first sign that something was wrong with me that I hadn't been able to ignore any longer. So much had happened since then—but one thing would always remain the same.

I barely waited until he'd fallen into a neutral stance before I attacked, not bothering with great technique for a start. He was right—my first instinct was to go for a jab with my right hand. Rather than prove Nate right that this wasn't the best idea, I used it to feign, quickly moving out of his reach when he attempted to block a swing that never came. My foot went up, only lightly brushing his hand as he quickly evaded me, but it was a first contact. I danced back, regaining my balance just in time to block his punch with my lower arm. His foot shot out, hooking around my calf, making me stagger, but not fall. So we weren't just pretending. Good.

Of course, I'd gone through all of the motions I now used over and over during the past weeks, but it was different to use them in combination now. It took me a good five minutes to score the first real hit, the heel of my foot hitting his obliques perfectly. He'd been right—again—when he'd torn into me as we'd come here today; I was still stiff, but this was a great way to limber up. Nate staggered back and I came right after him, dipping deep into my reserves to jump as far as I could—and slammed my left hook square under his jaw as he was still trying to evade me. Pain exploded across my knuckles, but it was a familiar, acute kind of pain, not that damn lingering agony that had been my life for far too long.

It felt liberating. It felt good. I smiled.

Until both of his feet landed square in the middle of my abdomen and he kicked me off him, my body flying a good two yards through the air until I came down hard on the mats, too stunned to roll. Yeah, that hurt, too.

We scrambled to our feet at the same time, only that he hesitated while I didn't. Using brute strength, I bull-rushed him, slamming my shoulder into his stomach while my arms went around his torso. He hadn't expected the move and hadn't braced enough, ending with me managing to drag him down. Letting go, I reared up to go for his face once more, but now he was ready, blocking each punch. I made ready to use my elbow next, but he saw that coming, rearing up to topple me over backward. I ended up on my back with him looming over me, our legs still tangled. Rather than repay my favor from before, he pushed away, letting me roll over and come to my feet.

I was just about to start the next attack when Bucky's rasp, coming from somewhere behind me, made me remain bounding on the balls of my feet instead.

"Oh, it's so cute to watch you two lovebirds cuddle with each other. You're not pretending that's a real fight, are you?"

Nate's face was completely void of emotion as I glanced at him for guidance, giving me nothing. Turning around to face Hamilton, I tried for the same, but panting with exertion—and just a little high from my endorphins kicking in—I knew the best I could aim for was a jeer, so that's what I went with. "Just having a little friendly tousle there. You should try it. Might get that stick out of your ass that you've got permanently crammed up there." In the past, I'd wondered why my mouth always had to run in the wrong direction. He'd ultimately cured me of that notion. Why shouldn't I be deliberately goading him on? What did I have left to lose?

Bucky kept that superior smirk right in place, but I didn't miss the hint of real anger in his eyes. Oh, he was annoyed with me, all right. How dare I speak to him like that after he'd so properly cowed me in the past? At least I hoped that was what was going through his head. I took a momentary mental pause to ask myself, did I actually want to provoke him? My body had gotten stronger, yes—but not that strong. And while Nate hadn't deliberately let me get through his defenses, I was aware that he hadn't gone into full offense with me yet. Then again, bruise each other up we might do, but not go for any real damage. While all my attacks were for real, of course I always held back a little.

With Bucky, I wouldn't have to. And I really, really didn't want to.

"Think you can do better?" I called out to him, stopping my hopping to spread my arms wide in invitation. "It's so damn easy to come for a woman when she doesn't even have the strength to sit up straight anymore. Too afraid to try now when you'd meet with some actual opposition?"

I knew it was stupid. I knew that I would lose—and very likely end up hurting a lot worse than over the past week. I didn't find it in me to give a shit. The anger churning in my gut would get me through the worst, I knew that. I wouldn't go down without a fight, and I'd damn well cause some damage in return, and that was all that I cared about. Besides, I would have to test my limits sooner or later, and it wasn't smart to do that in the field.

It was obvious that the same thoughts—at least about me not being up to besting him—went through Hamilton's head, but he only hesitated for a moment before he pushed the notepad he'd been carrying at the flunky by his side. If he thought he was intimidating me as he pulled his fleece jacket off, revealing quite the amount of muscles barely contained by his T-shirt underneath, he was betting on the wrong horse. He didn't make a move to take his boots off, but I wasn't afraid that he would stomp on my bare toes. I would have donned mine had they been around, but they still sat under my bunk, and my discarded, stinking socks weren't really worth the hassle. I caught Nate's gaze as he stepped off the mat to make room. Oh, there was enough caution—and scorn—there to fill an entire book, but also a hint of satisfaction. Neither of us was delusional about my condition, but unlike Bucky, he knew that my punches could hurt—and if it helped take the edge off my frustration, why not have at it? I just hoped he wouldn't get all "I told you so" over my ass when he was patching me up later. At the last moment before I turned away, I caught the hint of a smile crossing his features. Whether that was in anticipation of me socking Bucky a good one, or watching my usual confidence snap into place, I couldn't tell, but it was neat to see Nate do something other than glower.

It took everyone else in the hangar about twenty seconds to realize that something was about to go down that was more interesting than their current preoccupation, the entire lot of them coming closer, building a loose ring around the mats. Part of me wanted to step closer to where Nate and Tanner were lurking, but I trusted the rest not to kick me in the knees while I wasn't looking. As I waited for Bucky to be ready, I rolled my shoulders and tried to get the last few kinks out of my muscles. I considered getting wraps for my hands, but my knuckles would survive either way, and the scar tissue would hurt like hell, so it was just the same. A hint of nerves got my pulse kicking up a notch, but I latched on to the resulting spike of adrenaline rather than tried to quench it—I'd need that, and much, much more.

"You ready?" I called out across the mats when Hamilton was finally done. He kept his knife strapped to his thigh, as if it wasn't worth the time unbuckling that.

"So eager to be put in your place, Stumpy?" Bucky jeered back—and attacked.

I hadn't expected him to take the initiative like that, but it was easy to avoid his bull rush. I danced out of his reach, idly kicking for his thigh, just to see whether he would evade me or take it. He did neither, twisting around lightning fast and made a grab for my ankle. Oops. I narrowly avoided him twisting it by letting myself drop, gravity wrenching my foot out of his loose hold. Rolling over my left shoulder, I was up in time to meet his kick toward my torso with the fleshy part of my thigh, throwing a punch as he stumbled into my reach. The knuckles of my right hand hit him square in the eye, even though he tried to pull his head back in time. I had to pay for that hit, though, when his left hook rammed straight into the scars on my abdomen, making pain explode all through my torso.

We both stepped back to catch a breath, me ending up right next to Nate. "You were right," I wheezed out when my lungs finally started to work again. "Right hand's useless."

"Might still end up as a black eye," Nate offered as he watched Bucky gingerly touch his upper cheek. "But I told you so."

I flashed Nate a quick grin before I got ready for the next attack. One thing I had to hand to Hamilton, he was quick, particularly for a guy packing that amount of muscle on a somewhat compact frame. I knew I could be quicker—but not when he was waiting for me like that. I feigned left, then right, before I kicked toward his knee, ready for him to deflect. He did, but not in a way I'd expected. He sidestepped and kicked at my leg, only to pivot the second he came down for another kick. I narrowly avoided that, immediately lunging for him to go at him with my left elbow. I missed his head, the blow glancing off his shoulder. I tried to disengage quickly, but his left hook hit me by surprise—literally—smashing right into my nose. It didn't even hurt that bad, but blood gushed from it, forcing me to step farther away to be able to wipe if off my face.

"Had enough already, Stumpy?" Bucky jeered across the mats, giving me a brilliant smile.

"Oh, you mean because of this?" I said, spitting some of the blood out that had gotten into my mouth. "'Tis but a scratch!"

I was surprised to get several cheers from all around, not just from Gita, who was whooping at the top of her lungs. Yeah, Burns had been doing a stellar job watering down the lines.

Feeling even more motivated than before, I came after Bucky, going all in with a sequence of kicks. Two landed; the third was too slow and he managed to move in as I came down, his arms closing around me like a vise. I knew what was coming but it still hurt like hell as he flung me over his shoulder and came right down on me as I crashed onto my back. His elbow hit me in the right side of the abdomen, like his previous attack, making me howl with pain. I knew he was going to follow that up with a few punches, and to save my face, I rolled, giving him a great opportunity to hit my lower right back as well. Of course he went for it, making my scars and still tender tissues underneath light up with pain.

Bingo.

Rather than disappear in a haze of pain, my mind kicked into overdrive, my body following a moment later. Instead of using my momentum to come to my feet, I forced myself to slow down to lure him into another punch. He fell for it, yet before it could land, I reared up with my hips, wrapping both legs around his torso and neck. He lost his balance, falling over backward in his attempt to shake me, which pulled me on top of him. Right out of our roll, I started pummeling his face and torso, hitting as fast and hard as possible with my left fist, finishing with a slam of my left elbow at his throat with my entire weight behind it. I felt him tense underneath me, knowing he was gearing up to flip us over once more, and quickly let myself fall back into a roll—and this time I came to my feet, a good two yards away from him. I was right across the ring from my people, but that didn't matter. I was sure that the whoop to my left came from Murdock.

Grinning down at Bucky, blood still dripping from my nose, I made a "come hither" gesture with both hands raised in front of my body. "How's that for enough?"

I knew he could have jumped right to his feet—my punches had landed, but I hadn't been able to hit that hard unaided—yet Bucky got up slowly, his eyes skimming over my body, watching my every motion, likely for the first time actually paying attention to what I could do, not how he could land a low blow. I shouldn't have welcomed that so much. After all, it killed my last chance to win this fight. But as I waited for his move, I realized that I wasn't even so much doing that to vent my own frustration, but simply to prove to myself—and everyone around—that I could. He could call me names up and down, all day long, as long as he wanted, but I'd watched him spar with Red and Hill a couple of times. Neither of them had landed more than a few punches, while I had made him bleed. That alone was worth it. No more ignoring me now.

Getting a good feeling for how my body felt when it was starting to slide from all green right toward the danger zone was another.

I hurt, no shit, but I was holding up better than I'd expected. When Bucky came for me, I knew that wouldn't be the case much longer, but really, he was a head taller than me and almost twice as heavy. The fact that I wasn't lying on the mat yet, unconscious, was a feat.

My assessment had been right—he was done playing, and while I fought with everything I had, we both knew that I was losing. I still got a few good jabs with my knee in and the odd punch, but then he threw me again, and this time I could tell he wouldn't let me turn things around on him anymore. It was when I realized that his plan was to sit on me and choke me with his arm pressed against my windpipe that I knew I had to do something about that. I wouldn't have minded either that much, but I caught that glint in his eyes just as he came down on me to keep me pinned, and I knew I had to act. So I did the only thing I could still do, with my right hand, because he already caught my left—the one I'd done the most damage with—and wrenched it onto the mat, in a way that when I tried to rear up, my shoulder gave a weird, painful twinge. Then his other arm pressed against my trachea, making me go as tense as possible to keep him from cutting off my airways.

And of course, he had to go for the lowest asshole drawer in the shelf as he leaned heavily enough on my left thigh to force me to pull it away to the side, thus landing between my somewhat spread legs. Jerking his hips forward—yup, he definitely liked beating me up—he leaned down until his breath was all over my face as he asked, "Feel that?" and repeated the motion, pretty much laying down on me—until he froze

I didn't need to force a smile onto my face. It came all naturally. "Feel that?" I echoed—and shoved his knife just a little farther up, making sure that it not just pressed against his shirt but cut right into the outer layers of his skin. "That's yours, if you're wondering. Should have pinned both of my hands. Rest assured, even with only three and a half fingers, my grip is still strong enough to stick you like a pig. Now, get off me."

Of course he didn't, but I could deal with his almost dead weight on me as long as his crotch was nowhere near mine—and he'd been smart enough to pull back once he'd realized what was going on. Too bad, really.

"Would have been too much to expect a fair fight from the likes of you," he growled right in my face.

I didn't bat an eyelash. "I hate to break this to you, but no physical fight between you and me will ever be fair, and that's not my fault. Besides, I thought this was something you subscribed to as well. Who cares about a fair fight when all that counts is coming up ahead?" I raised my brows at him. He didn't react. "Seeing as you're not going to move, let's use this occasion for a nice little chat, shall we?" I proposed. "I would be much obliged if you took your arm off my trachea. Unless you want me to get a cramp in my right hand that makes it jerk upward, uncontrolled, repeatedly."

I could tell from his considering look that he was calculating whether he could incapacitate me before I got to that, either try to suffocate me or slam my head into the mats until I was unconscious, but seemed to realize neither was possible. He didn't remove his arm but eased up until I could breathe more or less freely again. It was enough.

"I have no idea what we would have to talk about," he sneered.

Just for fun, I poked a little harder, making him wince. Great abs training for him, I was sure, but didn't expect any thanks.

"Oh, I can think of a few things," I suggested, trying to get a little more comfortable. "How about you stop being such a dickturd? You and I both know that you have zero interest in touching me, let alone fucking me. So drop that crap. Just because some imbecile wrote a psych eval about me based on what happened in Taggard's little underground bunker doesn't mean that will get you anywhere. Might have worked last year, but not now. I do greatly prefer not to be raped, but do you really think that's worse than what's happened to me so far? Don't be so fucking naive." Raising my head up as much as his hold on me would let me, I aimed for a sweet smile. "I will bend, but I won't break. Not from anything you can say or do. But if that's too hard for you, I can be nice and rid you of those shriveled raisins that you call your balls, right here, right now. What do you say?"

I only got a grunt in return—or maybe that was because I pushed the knife in just a little farther—but I could see in the way he glared at me that the message was received. Might as well deliver the rest, seeing as neither of us was going anywhere.

"Speaking of which, as you're already reorienting your view of the world at large… I'm not my husband's weakness—I'm his strength.

All you do by trying to get to him through me is piss me off, and you really won't like me when I'm angry." Damnit, even that little reference was making his eyes narrow, but I was wise enough not to exploit that—yet. "Let's talk shop here, shall we? You're neither as bulletproof as you think, nor as untouchable. I should probably not tell you this, but why not. Raynor has it out for you. She's fed up with your continuing incompetence. You couldn't even fetch me when she was asking for that, who knows where else you have failed her? She'd much rather see Miller take your place—or me. Why not both of us, seeing as we come as a package deal? You might have guessed that already, but that's the real reason I'm here. I'm sure that in your orders there's another explanation, but we both know that it's bullshit. Tell you what? I have absolutely no interest in working for that bitch, and whoever's above her in the hierarchy of your little organization there. You can be top dog all you want, as long as you leave me and my people the fuck alone. But I swear to you, if you give me even a hint of a reason why I should change my mind, I will. And I will come out on top, and you will wish that I had eviscerated you today. Are we clear on that?"

Bucky snorted dismissively, but I knew that he wasn't that stupid. "Are you done talking trash?" he wanted to know. "Not that I've ever heard anything else from you."

"You're the one who's still lying on me," I pointed out.

"I can't move up unless you withdraw the knife."

"Oh, you mean this one?" I said—and rather than retract it, I shoved it another inch up into him, making sure to cut deep. I doubted I'd get lucky and perforate his intestines, and right then, I didn't care whether I did or not. "Do we have an agreement? I need you to say the words. And I need everyone to hear them." I jerked my chin toward our bystanders, who were, to a man, undecided what to do with the situation.

Hamilton's face had turned into a grimace, but he still let me wait a full ten seconds before he finally gave the smallest of nods. "We do."

"Good," I said cheerfully, rearing up once more so that my lips were almost touching his ear. "And never forget—the only reason why I didn't castrate you today was because I simply didn't want to."

I pulled the knife out with a jerk that was hard enough to make the hilt slam into my abdominal scars, but I didn't give a fuck about that now. Bucky launched himself off me the same moment I scrambled back, both of us ending in a ready stance at the different ends of the circle. Never one to risk a hard-earned victory, I relaxed first, giving a dismissive flick with the knife to get some of the blood off it. It wasn't much, but enough to be easily visible, covering parts of the blade. "I will keep this as a sweet souvenir," I told him, offering him another fake smile. "I hope you don't object."

"Keep it," Bucky offered, ignoring the small pool of blood that was spreading on his T-shirt. "It's a worthless piece of trash. Fits you." He paused, then added, just as I was about to turn around, "Stumpy."

I considered not reacting, but since we were already being so chatty…

Turning back to face him, I grinned. "Yeah, you say that like it's demeaning, for me. Right after defeating you, with the hand that took the brunt of it. Exactly what do they feed you? Because I'd add a little more carbs in the mix. Your brain doesn't have enough energy to work right." I could do that dramatic pause, too. "Besides, Bucky… two can play that game. I guarantee you, I will have the last laugh in this, you petty, little fool."

There were no outright cheers, but some good-natured if suppressed laughter going on. The two soldiers closest to the door— Cole and Aimes—stepped away to make room for me to pass as I aimed for them, both offering me a small nod. I did my best to keep a straight face, but it got harder from second to second. Yeah, I could maybe bullshit them all, but that didn't mean I was as relaxed as I pretended to be. If I'd been smart, I would have lost the fight and let him have that little triumph. But I'd had a chance, so I took it, and I didn't really find it in me to regret it. And only feeling a little beat-up with a possibly broken nose was better than being dragged the whole nine yards.

I was almost to the door, trusting that Nate and the others would pick up my discarded clothes on the way, when two of the marines stepped in my way, blocking my exit. I still had the bloody knife in my hand, but did my best to make that none too obvious, next to my thigh.

"Can I help you with something, gentlemen?" I asked, rather than the, "Get the fuck out of my way!" that I wanted to hurl at them. See, I could be a pinnacle of diplomacy if I wanted. I was still panting with exertion and pain, so the words came out slightly breathless, yet my tone was calm enough.

They didn't exactly exchange glances, but the one to my left fidgeted a bit, until the other responded. They were both in gym clothes, so I couldn't even guess at their rank, or whatever. "You need to come with us. To the brig."

I didn't need Burns or Nate to translate that for me. "Absolutely not." Then, "Why would I?"

Now they did exchange glances, and the one that had spoken eyed my hand with the knife uneasily. "Ma'am, you just attacked your commanding officer with an edged weapon—"

My pulse, already refusing to slow down after what had happened, spiked. It was almost comical to feel the world around me snap into perfect clarity, down to me seeing a bead of sweat make its way down the marine's forehead. My muscles tensed without my conscious doing, gearing up for another fight. Sheer surprise was probably the only reason why my left fist wasn't already flying toward his face.

"You got to be shitting me," I grumbled, briefly glancing to the side to get my bearings. The others were coming but still half a room away. Murdock and Hill were the closest soldiers, chatting with Aimes and Cole. I couldn't see Red anywhere, but that didn't matter. He'd been here before so he was likely over there by the weights. Focusing back on the marines, I cocked my head to the side, then crossed my arms over my chest, this time no longer hiding the knife—but I did rotate my grip so that the blade was flat across my wrist and pointing toward my elbow on the inside of my arm. "He's a lot of things, but he sure as hell isn't my anything."

"But you're—" The other marine finally found his voice, only to be cut off by me immediately.

"I am an independent technical advisor," I lied—or maybe even said the truth. Nobody had defined my role in this shindig. "I haven't even vowed to my husband to obey him when I married him. I'm certainly not letting that idiotic buffoon order me around. I hope this resolves things?"

Rather than wait for a reply, I stepped forward, intent on simply pushing through them, but they didn't budge, pushing me back immediately.

"Ma'am, I insist—" the first marine tried once more, but looked a lot less authoritative than moments before now that I was literally standing face to face with him.

"You insist on what?" I asked. "Being imbeciles who can't differentiate between a good-natured tussle"—my ass—"and an attack? Or being accomplices to a repeat sexual offender and are now holding his not-quite helpless victim accountable for defending herself? Pick one." I knew it was a low blow, but one thing I'd learned in the past year and a half—the good guys usually got incredibly uncomfortable whenever rape was mentioned, and if I could use that sentiment to put an end to this before I gave anyone an actual reason to throw me in the brig—or right over the side of the ship into the freezing-cold ocean—I would always play that card.

The marine whose face I was staring at grimaced while the other donned the expected horrified expression. "Ma'am, we certainly didn't mean to imply—"

"Move out of my way," I bit out, making them both jerk slightly from the steel in my voice. "Don't you think that if any of them had some issues with what I did that they'd take care of that?" I glanced over to the soldiers, who were only paying us so much attention. "I'm getting tired of this. If you insist on behaving like despicable human scum, why don't you take me to your CO? Let's see what he has to say about this. No? Then what are we still doing here?"

"Is there a problem?" Nate asked from right behind me, his voice that homicidal kind of neutral that was impossible to take for anything else.

The marines squirmed for a few more moments before they stepped to the side. As soon as the way was clear, I rushed ahead, adrenaline flooding my veins anew. How I made it to our quarters, I couldn't say; it certainly didn't happen with me choosing turns deliberately. I stormed right to the very back of the bunks, mostly to let the others in behind me, but also because I just couldn't stop yet. Every fiber of my being was vibrating with tension, too-long suppressed frustration bubbling over right into blinding-hot rage. It barely registered when Tanner pulled the door shut behind him, but that shoved the lid right off my barely-contained self-control.

Dropping the knife, I balled both hands to fists, trying for another second to hold it all in—but to no avail. Throwing my head back, I screamed—and then, there was no holding it all in anymore. All that pain and grief, fear and frustration, came roaring to the forefront of my mind, no longer content to hide in the dark recesses where I'd tried to stow it all away indefinitely. Everything that had happened since fall—and a lot before that—crashed through my head, a maelstrom of emotions that I simply wasn't equipped to cope with. I screamed until I was all out of air, then took a noisy, sharp inhale and continued, my voice so loud that it hurt in my own ears. And when that simply wasn't enough, I slammed my fists into the steel wall in front of me, first once, then over and over and over again—

Somewhere, almost buried underneath all of what needed out, alarm bells started going off in my head, and I forced myself to stop, then bend over when even something as simple as inhaling almost got unbearably hard to do. Panting, I tried to get a grip on myself, but

I simply couldn't. My left hand was bleeding but I couldn't even feel it, my body was too keyed up for that.

Fuck. Fuckfuckfuckfuck—

Turning my head to the side, I looked up at the others, finding Nate and Burns pretty much shielding Gita from me, the lot of them wedged into what little open space there was by the door. Burns was looking mildly concerned, while Nate was squinting at me, trying hard to get a good reading.

"How do I fucking stop this?" I pressed out between clenched jaws, forcing my fingers to dig into my thighs to keep myself for going for the wall again. It would serve absolutely no one if I broke my hands for good. "I can't... calm down. I just can't! How do I fucking stop this!" The last words left me as more of a shout than anything else, my control slipping again.

Nate was there, gripping me from behind, pinning my arms to my sides. I tried to buck against him, but his embrace was tight as a vise, unmoving whatever I did. I fought, then gave up, screaming as he held me until my throat was raw and my ears were ringing.

I didn't feel better once my scream cut off, ending in more heavy panting. I felt worse, much, much worse. Whatever had set it in motion, that breakdown had pulled aside the curtains, forcing me to stare reality straight in the face. And damn, I really didn't like what I was seeing. I felt like a broken, bleeding shell of my former self, stripped down to the bare bones, everything raw and exposed.

I inhaled shakily, ready to say something—what, I had no idea—but a loud knock at the door made us all pause. The others looked mighty welcoming of the distraction as it was. Honestly, I was surprised that it had taken Red this long to come after us—or it could be the firing squad, ready to finish what the marines had started.

Nate hesitated, but the fact that I'd gone as limp as a noodle seemed to communicate that I was done losing it, so he let go and stepped away, giving me some much-needed space. At his nod,

Tanner pulled open the door. It wasn't Red, nor the firing squad, but a tall, thin Asian woman—one of the Navy officers.

"Lieutenant Commander Nekanda," she introduced herself, peeking into the room cautiously. "Commander Parr would like me to extend his sincerest apologies to you, and ask you all to join him for dinner tonight." Her eyes skipped across the lot of us until they landed on me. "Sergeant Buehler also asks your forgiveness and understanding for the misunderstanding that has happened between you and her men. She has set actions to punish them."

That was so not the news I'd expected. I had to thoroughly clear my throat to get it to work once more, but tried to sound relaxed— not ready to keel over—as I replied. "Nobody needs to be court-martialed because of me. I have a very good idea who put them up to this. And he and his ego already got what they deserve." Not really, but it was a start.

The officer kept her face perfectly neutral, so it was hard to judge whether she considered me an utter imbecile, or smart. It didn't really matter. It was only when the silence turned awkward that I realized that she was still waiting for an answer.

I glanced at Nate. He was still trying to gauge my reaction, but at catching my gaze, he directed his attention to Nekanda. "Please tell the commander that we will gladly accept his offer," he told her quite pleasantly, as if he wasn't still on the verge of making a grab for me once more.

She inclined her head. "I will come fetch you at 1900." She hesitated, clearly at odds with herself. "You should maybe swing by the med bay and get that fixed." It took me way too long to realize she was talking about my nose. It was then that I realized that the lower half of my face was caked in dried blood, and quite a few rivulets had made it across my cheeks while I'd been lying on my back as well. It looked bad enough in the tiny wall mirror that had miraculously survived my attack of its general surroundings. Reaching up, I gingerly touched my nose, but while there was a little swelling and some discomfort, nothing was broken. My quick nod was enough, making the officer scurry off as she closed the door behind her.

"Well, that was unexpected," I croaked out, quickly clearing my throat once more. "Now, anyone care to tell me why you're all looking so glum?"

Gita gave the guffaw that I'd expected from Burns. "Think they have steak? I could do with some steak." She grinned brightly. I flashed her one in return, not caring how grizzly that must have looked.

Nate, Burns, and Tanner were still awfully quiet. I was burning to ask, but dropped the point. I had a feeling it would come out sooner rather than later. "So what exactly does one wear to a dinner with the captain of a ship?" Looking over at my pack and the few things not yet stowed away, I shrugged. "I have ratty old thermals and slightly less ratty newer thermals. Black's always a good idea, right?"

Nate shook his head as he turned away, muttering something under his breath that I was sure I didn't need to hear. Oh, this was going to be so much fun, I just knew it!

Chapter 9

Three hours later, Nekanda was back, waiting for us to file out of the claustrophobic quarters into the slightly less claustrophobic corridor. Her eyes lingered a moment on my hair, but she didn't comment. I felt like asking her whether she approved of seeing that same dried-blood color missing from my chin that had finally replaced the patchy blondish pink that the decontamination shower in Raynor's lair had left me with. I wouldn't have gone with such a dark, muted color myself, but the hair color that Red had dropped off that day together with my Beretta was the only one I'd had at hand—and it certainly fit my mood. In all fairness, it made a lot more sense than the riot-red I'd gone for last summer before setting out on our crusade. Back then, painting a target on my head had seemed like a wise idea. Now? Not so much. And as Gita had noted as she'd helped me work it into my curls, both of us sitting on the bathroom floor—it went great with the bloodshot in my eyes.

And yes, I was wearing a black thermal with my dark gray cargo pants and boots, not giving a shit whether that was appropriate or not. It wasn't like I'd packed any other clothes—or at least not any that weren't much worse.

Judging from the sense I was getting from Nate, we were walking to our execution rather than dinner, but I hadn't gotten a chance to rib him about that yet. I was way more concerned about what the fuck that serum was doing to me to care about his finer sensibilities right now. The others weren't quite so glum, although Tanner was a close second. Gita still seemed mostly excited, so for once I chose to latch on to her example. It couldn't really get much worse, now, could it?

I knew I was wrong when we entered the officer's mess, and the tension increased about tenfold. I had no idea who the officers present were since I had next to no recollection of how I'd gotten onto this boat, but I could tell that there must have been some kind of exchange, as not only Nate glowered all the way over to his seat beside me, but also Burns and Tanner remained rather tense.

It was a single table that had been set in the middle of the room, not exactly fancy, but miles above anything I'd sat down at long since the shit had hit the fan. The salt-and-pepper-haired trim guy standing at the head of the table must have been the captain, Commander Parr. Next to the officer who had fetched us, there was only a single other female officer present—the Marines' top dog, Sergeant Buehler. I couldn't remember having seen any of them, or the other two men waiting to the side of the table that hadn't been allocated to us—the ship's XO, Commander Leary, and Higgs, the chief engineer. After the bitching about who was going to sit where in the mess hall, I half expected there to be a squabble now, but with all of us in single file order and no seat better defensible than the rest, it was—from captain to empty end of the table—Nate, me, Burns, Gita, with Tanner bringing up the rear. The difference between the officers—all standing ramrod straight—and Higgs with his perpetual slouch was telling, making it easy to guess that he was the head of one of the many stations on the ship, and less prone to becoming a pain in the ass.

"Thank you for joining us for dinner tonight," Parr finally said after a pause that was long enough to make my two remaining toenails curl up.

I waited for Nate to say something, but he and Parr had already started a glowering match, so I took it upon myself to be the chatty head of our delegation. "Thank you so much for the very unexpected invitation." Didn't mean I had to even pretend to be diplomatic.

Parr nodded, which somehow was a signal for everyone to take their seats. The guy opposite me—Leary, sitting between the captain and Nekanda—tried to start the same bullshit with me as Nate had going on with Parr, but I gave him a pleasant, slightly insipid smile. Buehler was frowning, but when she caught that smile, she snorted under her breath, quickly trying to hide it under a pretend coughing fit. That made me remember that I had, in fact, seen her working out in the hangar a couple of times. She'd even helped me get one of the heavy weight plates onto the bar when my right hand had been acting up. For what must have been the millionth time I cursed Bucky for being such an asshole. The last two weeks could have gone down a lot smoother otherwise.

While I had been busy studying the lineup, most of them had started browsing the small paper slips placed at their designated places, so I picked up mine. There were what amounted to three meal options printed on each. "You circle the one you want," Burns whispered as he leaned closer.

"Yeah, I figured that," I murmured back. "Seeing as that's what all of them are doing now."

That got me a snort—and unlike the marine sergeant, Burns didn't try to hide it, which was a small relief. Buehler herself had a hard time keeping a straight face. She struck me as the kind of woman who would inappropriately roar with laughter, and be great to gets drinks with afterward. I'd come here with the full intention of repeating to her what I'd already told Nekanda—to let her marines off easily—but I decided to renege on that. It would likely have offended her, unlike anything else I could have flung in her face. And if it had happened because of her wrong judgment, I was sure that the two imbeciles had slinked away with a mere slap on the wrists.

After one of the young sailors had collected the menu slips, Parr returned to scrutinizing us, beginning with Nate. "I hope that besides a few minor misunderstandings, your stay with us has been pleasant, Capt. Miller?"

And that's when I finally figured out where the latent animosity among my guys came from. I hadn't even thought for a moment how being among members—officers, no less—of other branches of the military could turn out to be for us. Except for looking at Nate as our leader, I'd never seen any of the guys act as anything but equals—and Pia, of course, his undisputed second in command. Rationally, I'd been aware that they were a mixed bunch, but I still hadn't quite figured out how the hierarchy should have been, which had long since turned inconsequential, anyway. Now, maybe not so much.

Nate gave Parr a rather stern look. "As you are, without a doubt, aware, Commander, I have been dishonorably discharged and stripped of my rank. And even if that hadn't been the case, bearing in mind our recent history, I wouldn't use it anymore."

Parr took that without any kind of reaction, his attention skipping right over me. "And you, Sergeant Burns—"

He got a tight, fake grin for that. "Same difference, although you'd likely have to call me a deserter. Don't care about my rank, either.

Would just complicate things otherwise because technically, that would set me up as the leader of our illustrious bunch, and as that's the farthest thing from what I want, thanks, but no thanks."

Before Parr could ask, Tanner offered, "Those three are our top dogs. Don't look to me for answers. I wasn't in active duty at the time, and the rest is history."

Unexpectedly, Buehler spoke up at that. "How come you weren't? From what we've heard, the Army mobilized overnight, starting said Tuesday, and besides us and the Navy, they've had surprisingly high report rates." Her gaze briefly flickered to Tanner's left hand where a similar mark was inked like the three across his neck. "Or maybe not that surprising for some."

Tanner's answering grimace was a painful one. "Because I was doing time, and until they realized that they might have used me as an asset, civilization as we know it was no longer existing."

Now wasn't that an interesting tidbit? Leaning to Nate, I whispered, "I'm starting to think I'm the only one sitting here who's got nothing for the shit being flung around to stick to."

Nate did not deign to answer to that. A wise choice.

Tanner's smile had turned a little more jovial by the time he continued. "It wasn't the worst place to hunker down and wait until the situation cleared up, and the guards had weapons aplenty that they didn't need anymore. Me and a few others likely had an easier time surviving the first months than a lot of those caught outside. After we'd had to do a thorough cleanup of our cell block, of course." If anything, his tale got him an admiring nod from Buehler. Tanner glanced at his seat neighbor next. "And our girl Gita here did a great job turning from city girl to survivalist all on her own." It was then that I realized that I'd never asked her for her surname, wondering now if she even used one.

That explained, Parr's attention turned to me, and I could tell that he hadn't skipped over me to snub me, but because he had a really hard time placing me in context to the others. "May I presume that at least you, Dr. Lewis, still use your academic title?"

I wondered for a moment whether he was trying to bait me, but his tone was too pleasant for that. My fingers twitched involuntarily, my desire to hide my hands under the table top strong once more, but I forced them to remain where they were, right there in plain sight.

"Actually, I pretty much stopped seeing myself as a scientist the day I got my marks. When I joined my fellow scavengers, out there, exiled to the roads." And gee, wasn't I being romantic tonight. Turning serious, I went on. "And I'm sure Capt. Hamilton has already informed you about my recent history, and how our paths have a tendency to cross in not quite peaceful ways. You'd better forget most of what he might have told you about us as it's as much heavily biased as very likely completely untrue."

Oh, Bucky must have told quite the tales, judging from how Buehler once more struggled to remain neutral, while the other officers—except for Higgs—did some communal glowering. Parr did the best job appearing unaffected.

"I think his exact words to describe you were that you are an exceptionally intelligent woman prone to making exceptionally stupid choices."

Against my better judgment, that assessment made me snort. "Yeah, he'd think so, I'm sure. I'm also sure he neglected to explain his own idiocy and insubordination while heavily layering on ours. Don't get me started on that man's shortcomings."

Once more, Buehler spoke up, and judging from how the officer next to the captain grimaced, she wasn't expected to. "He told us that you were all under his command, with absolutely no mention that you were, in fact, not part of the army any longer, or never had been. I only found out about that last week when I had a chat with your communications specialist at the gym. It's probably a moot question, but how exactly did you come to be here?"

"He's not our commanding officer," I repeated what I'd already told her marines.

Nate cleared his throat next to me, making me shoot him a sidelong glance. "Technically, he is. You were there when you agreed to follow his orders."

I had to think hard, trying to make sense of that. "Oh, you mean at that meeting with Raynor and that buffoon of a general, or whatever he was?"

Nekanda and Leary looked scandalized at that, while Buehler and the chief were mostly amused.

"Yes, that meeting," Nate pressed out.

"And you think I actually remember anything from there, except that I was fucking glad I only lost three fingers, a bunch of toes, however many non-vital organs, and the fucking bacteria didn't eat off half of my face?" I had a good recollection still of how Raynor had baited me into agreeing, but that was beside the point.

Nate's expression was unreadable, but I got the vague sense that he was rather amused by the reactions my words drew from the other side of the table. The captain still remained impartial, but Buehler was itching to ask, I could tell. And since we were still waiting for the soup—if there would be any, I had no stinking clue—I was only too happy to regale her with the tale.

"You see, my beef with Hamilton is many-fold, but the part that is likely most pertinent for you is that he has a history of disobeying orders where I am concerned. I'm not one hundred percent sure, but I think that every single time we met, he had a standing order to bring me in, and he never really tried. Well, once, at that factory, he did, but considering that they had set a trap with a good two hundred zombies locked away that they unleashed on us, I don't think the plan was for any of us to survive. The powers that be wanted me on their side for the help I could have given, but he let his ego get in the way every single time. You likely heard about us going to war against him, which culminated in us forcing a truce on him?"

Buehler inclined her head. "His version of the event was slightly different." The way she stressed that made it obvious exactly how much our stories diverged.

"I'm sure it was. Fact is, by then the lead scientist of his faction knew that I wasn't immune to the zombie virus—and even less so the massive bacterial infection the bite of our undead scourge comes with—and she sent him out to invite me to come to her so she could keep me from rotting from the inside out. He must have neglected that small detail, which, in hindsight, looks to be the only real reason he was sent there with orders to agree to our terms, as they could have just as easily fought us until everyone on both sides would have turned into zombie fodder. That scientist is now so pissed off at him that she has managed to convince their military strategists that it would be wiser to let me and my husband do his job instead. If you thought we were along as technical advisors, think again. We're both here as a test run to see what we can accomplish, and how their soldiers handle having us in charge. That is what is actually happening, and that is also the reason for the altercation that so utterly confused your men earlier today. Hamilton is a limp-dick asshole who is watching everything he has ever been fighting for slip right through his fingers, and only because he was a fucking idiot over and over again. I'm not even sure if he still knows why he is holding the grudge that set all this in motion, but we sure don't want to be a part of this. So, in the light of all that information, whose version of the story do you believe?"

"Neither," Parr answered, making me turn my attention back to him. "But then I have the luxury of not having to take sides. You are all guests on my ship, and as far as I'm concerned, I'm happy to have you off tomorrow morning." He offered that with a hint of a smile that made me realize that, indeed, he was joking, but only so much.

I tried my best at an appeasing smile. "I think I speak for my people when I say that we thank you for offering us your hospitality, and that you and your crew have treated us well. We'd love to catch a ride back home, though, from wherever you're kicking us out."

"France," Leary, next to the captain, provided. "And we are to check back in exactly one week for a few hours, then return for final pickup in a month. If you're not there after three days, we have to resume our route back to the States."

That was the most information anyone had given me so far, and I was surprised to get it from them, now. He seemed to be waiting for something in return from me, but all I could do was shrug.

"You know more than we do," Nate explained, finally relaxing. "How much sense that makes I don't need to explain to you. As my wife has already mentioned, our reasons not to accept Hamilton's authority are many, and all of them directly relate to the fact that he's not a good leader."

"And still you chose to come along with him," Nekanda protested. "Why?"

I wisely kept my trap shut, leaving it up to Nate to answer that. He hesitated, considering, and went with the truth. "The others had a choice. Not so much Bree and me. The options they gave us were to either fall in line, or watch them slaughter our friends. I don't have to explain that this wasn't a hard choice to make."

None of the others reacted, so Nate must have filled them in before. I couldn't remember; maybe I'd been the one to spill the beans. The first few days of my recovery were like one hazy acid trip.

"Doesn't mean that we won't do our best to make this mission a success," I offered. "Whatever said mission will turn out to be. Hamilton might be an ass, but his lieutenant knows how to handle his men, and he has done his very best to turn us all into one fighting team." Several of the officers nodded, Buehler the obvious exception, but judging from how she was suddenly studying her blunt, short fingernails, I had a certain feeling that she and Red had gotten along exceptionally well. Good for them.

Perfectly on cue, our meals arrived, serving as a welcome distraction. Conversation turned to food and other related anecdotes, what still lingered of the previous tension soon forgotten. Chief Higgs was almost as bad as Burns with his vivid recollections of what sailors did once they were off their destroyers, and the others easily kept the ball rolling. There was only one slightly awkward moment when, over dessert, Parr asked Nate how it had come that the army had kicked him out, but Nate's reply was a surprisingly self-reflective one. "I swore an oath to protect my country. Then I put my ego above that. I had no place among their ranks anymore, and they were justified in doing so." Parr and Leary gave curt yet almost admirable nods. That made me wonder if, maybe, Red had run interference for us, correcting a few assessments Bucky's lies might have put in place.

All in all, it was an almost pleasant evening with a few hitches along the road. The food was a bonus, even if I could only really enjoy the scent of it. Not having to sit where Bucky or his flunkies could gloat at me was nice. We parted as, if not quite friends, more or less respectful comrades fighting on the same side of a battle none of us had chosen. Knowing that they wouldn't leave us stranded in France out of spite was a relief. Knowing that we might get stuck there for at least half a year if our rendezvous didn't work out, not so much. But Parr explained that their job was to patrol the northern Atlantic, including most of the European coasts this side of the Strait of Gibraltar. That was also why they had the marines with them— something I was told wasn't ordinary—as a recon and salvage team. I could tell that Buehler was itching to come with us, but her mission was a different one.

On our way back to our quarters—sated, and in Gita's case, slightly inebriated—I felt a little better about our lot for the very first time. Working with the likes of Bucky was hell for me, and I knew I wasn't alone in that. But people like Parr or Buehler—and in a sense, Red as well—let me see a light at the end of the tunnel. Their dedication to a job that had pretty much become obsolete as the zombies had overrun the cities spoke of dedication and duty that I'd found sorely lacking from a lot of people in the recent months. The likes of Bucky, I didn't trust to uphold our truce come spring. But someone like Parr wouldn't even have let things escalate this far.

It stood to reason that the events of the last year and a half had made many reflect on what duty meant for them. The fact that Parr, Leary, and their crew all still serving on the destroyer, far away from any families—if they had survived—was telling. I still couldn't relate, not on a personal level, but I could respect that—same as I was, if much more grudgingly, starting to respect it in Red and the other soldiers. Hamilton wasn't an asswipe because he was in the army, but because he was the human representation of fecal matter. There was hoping I wasn't completely wrong, but if that was the case, I had the feeling I'd only get a few minutes, at best, to regret it.

Yet it was that exact thought that made a different kind of unease well up inside of me. Whoever was giving orders to Bucky and his lot must have different goals than Parr and Buehler, who clearly saw it as their mission to uphold what standards of civilization there still were, and help rebuild by using what dwindling resources they still had available. But, like them, the soldiers had initially helped the settlements, and were still adamant about that whenever asked. So what the fuck had gone wrong?

I had the sinking feeling that I'd very soon get an answer for that, and it likely lay in France.

Chapter 10

I was exhausted by the time we returned to our quarters, but not quite tired enough to tuck in yet. So when Nate suggested to do one last check on the few bandages I was still wearing, I followed him to the head without question, not quite sure what to expect. That he didn't have any nefarious intentions was obvious from his mood—quiet, bordering on glum—that he no longer tried to hide as soon as it was just the two of us. I hopped up onto the bank of sinks once I was down to my underwear to make it easier on him to check my thigh and toes. He pretended to poke around some, but we both knew that it was a moot point. All of my wounds had closed up for good a few days ago, and while there was still some residual bruising, there was no need to reapply any of the bandages.

I was a second away from asking him what this was about when he looked up from my thigh, both hands now set on the steel frame I was sitting on, as he looked me dead in the face.

"Thank you for not spilling the beans on exactly why you came so close to eviscerating Hamilton today."

Something deep inside of my chest seized up, and it was easier to joke than acknowledge it.

"It's such a nice word. Eviscerate. So underused in everyday language."

Nate snorted, and I knew he was about to call me his little homicidal maniac again, but for once passed up that chance. Instead, he exhaled slowly, and it was only then that I realized he was shaking slightly with tension. No, emotion, I corrected myself. Holy shit—Nate was about to have a nervous breakdown. Swallowing became incredibly hard for me, frustration hailing from not knowing what to do—or say, or how to react and make it all better—made me reach for him, but he turned his head away, no longer able to look me in the eyes.

"I'm so fucking sorry for what I did to you," he whispered, his voice a low croak full of emotion and a world of regret. "Not just what that fucked-up mind control shit made me do. Everything. None of this would have happened if I hadn't chatted you up in that park. If I hadn't selected you from that three-page long roster of possible choices who could help me down in the hot labs. Shit, I didn't even really need any help; I could have just gone in there without any protection. We made sure to scrub it all well in advance."

"It doesn't matter—" I tried, but he cut me off with a jerk of his head.

"It does. If I'd just let you go like most of the other scientists, none of this would have happened."

No, it wouldn't. In that, he was right. "I likely wouldn't have made it back home to Sam."

"You would have," he insisted. "It wasn't that bad on Friday afternoon. Else, we would have realized what was going on and hadn't gone ahead with the mission."

That, I was certain, was a lie. Maybe they would have done it differently, but Nate had been too fixated on getting confirmation—and revenge for his brother's death—to back down.

"I would have died," I offered next.

Again, he shook his head. "No, you wouldn't have. Bucky and his men would have collected you. Did Burns ever tell you that he and the others who came from Bucky to join me were out there that night, helping along? Maybe if they'd found you, someone would have set them to making sure you'd remain in one piece. Hell, without you missing, maybe they would never have sent anyone to look for you at your workplace."

"I doubt I was anywhere near important enough to warrant that." I chuckled wryly. "Besides, it doesn't matter. I would have been dead by then without you."

He continued with that senseless recount of would-have-beens as if I hadn't spoken up. "Chances are, you would have been working with Raynor from the start. You being there might have made the difference for Taggard going elsewhere to look for the serum."

"We still don't know exactly how that went down," I objected. And likely never would. Just because we assumed that Alders and what remained of his army of demented eco warriors had tried to further corrupt the inoculated soldiers didn't mean that Raynor's people hadn't known about that. Didn't make much sense, but they'd been awfully quick about developing that mind-control component of the newest version that they'd shot me up with—if that had even been the truth and not just a lie they'd sold us. I had absolutely no way of verifying any of that. I'd checked. That wasn't part of the documentation she'd sent with me, and likely for a very good reason.

So many things I didn't know. So many things I didn't give a shit about.

"Doesn't matter," Nate echoed my sentiment. "Hell, maybe we would have ended up in this exact spot anyway. Only that I wouldn't have dragged you through hell and back several times over. And you'd still have a choice to do something else than become a blunt instrument."

That made me snort. "Yeah, and do you know what would happen tomorrow? I'd die. Or if not tomorrow, then the day after."

"They would have inoculated you with the serum. You'd have been immune for over a year already."

"Doesn't help me one bit if I'd never learned how to fight," I stressed. "Besides, you're not listening to me. That entire point is moot. I wouldn't have lived long enough for Bucky—or Burns—to find me. You're the only reason I'm still alive."

He still wouldn't look me in the eyes but raised his head to study my chin. "Explain."

Me and my big, fat mouth. Sighing with exasperation, I tried to avoid having to do that. "Don't make me spell that out, please."

"I have no fucking clue what you are talking about, so you don't have a choice."

Crossing my arms in front of my chest, I tried not to feel too stupid. "Really? Don't you remember how this all started between you and me? You, that fit, muscular, tattooed, ex-military guy, and me, pudgy little lab rat?"

I'd expected him to laugh in my face. That mix between a frown and a smile wasn't much better.

"I still remember that after our little stay in that motel, you were walking funny when you left," he drawled.

Rolling my eyes, I playfully punched his arm—none too gently.

"You know exactly what I'm talking about, and it wasn't that."

Surprisingly, he took me seriously for once—exactly when I really could have done without.

"Did I complain? No. Did I ever make you feel like I didn't appreciate having something to grab and hold on to? I'm rather sure the answer is still no."

Grimacing, I tried to find the right words to make him see my point. "That's a situation where that whole 'it's not you, it's me,' thing applies. You didn't need to say anything, because, like all women, I have a mean cunt in the back of my head that does nothing but demoralize me. Or had. The apocalypse did a lot to set my priorities straight. But my point is, I cared, and I hated that I cared, and the easiest solution was to go on a kind of crash salad diet thing that I managed to keep up for about ten hours or so. But even failing that, I tried to make a few healthy choices. Like drinking my coffee black, and not inhaling a whole bucket of chicken nuggets on my way home."

It was funny to see the consequences of that dawn on him. "So what you are saying is that I saved your life because fucking you made you so self-conscious that you didn't pig out and consequently missed all the contaminated shit in the first place."

"Not necessarily self-conscious," I griped, trying to defend myself. "But we had a fun thing going there. I figured I might do something to keep it going a while longer? But yes, that's exactly my point."

"Sheesh, and there I always thought you meant me teaching you how to fight when you kept insisting that I saved you."

"Well, that, too," I conceded. "But none of that would have happened if I'd continued to guzzle foamy atrocities."

He shrugged that right off. "See, and I'm right again."

"With what exactly?"

Nate laughed softly. "You've always saved yourself. Back then. Now. You don't need me. But all of the shit you've inevitably gotten drawn into is something I stirred up."

"You didn't hold a gun to Bucky's head and force him to turn into a despicable asshole," I protested. "And even if you had, that's no excuse for what he did. To both of us. Not just to me. You know that I'm not holding any of that against you? I can be a damn resentful bitch, you know that. But I know where to put the blame. And it's not on you."

His soft laugh was a harsh one. "Not even for insisting on coming with you? That's one 'I told you so' that I can't reason away."

I pursed my lips as if to consider that point, but ended up shaking my head rather quickly. "Could I have survived that night after without you? Yes. But I'm damn glad I didn't have to. Would that asshole have found a different way to try to play us against each other? Hell, yeah, and I don't want to consider how far that might have gone. Stop blaming yourself, because I don't. You always accuse me of chasing rabbits in my head that I can't catch? Well, how about you take a page from that book, too. We got this far, and we will make it through this. Together. Now we have to, because what I did today was irrevocably hammer down that I'm someone who will not be disregarded or underestimated, so that better be worth something. I refuse to let anything Bucky did define me. You should do the same."

Nate nodded, then finally looked—really looked—at me again, still conflicted.

"Sometimes I wonder what I did to deserve you."

I flashed him a bright grin. "You're an insufferable asshole that no other woman in the world can stand. Congrats. I'm such a catch."

"That you are," he replied—but rather than kiss me, he moved back to lift my right leg so he could get a better look at my toes. Leaning back, I let him, trying very hard to internalize the grumbling I wanted to do so very loudly. Ah well. It was probably for the best. A week ago I hadn't been able to properly run, and while I felt a lot better, I was sure that, come tomorrow, I would very soon get to test my limits, and how easy it was to get there still. What I needed now was rest, because there was no telling when would be the next time I got some, and what was waiting for us in Europe.

Fucking France. That had been one of Greene's guesses when we'd chatted with him before leaving on that plane. I still remembered that. It was great to have some details, finally, but getting that confirmation meant one thing, really: whatever they had sent us here to fetch or do, it was something that Greene was aware of, so likely it had to do with the serum and the zombie virus. And considering how things had gone so far, it could only get so much worse than any of us had expected, that morning, when Bucky and his guys had gone one way, and the lot of us turned the other.

Chapter 11

Bucky came swaggering into the cargo hold, Red by his side, Cole and Russell hot on his heels. They were in full gear but not yet the overwhites to make them virtually undetectable in snowy terrain. "Think we should wake the rejects up yet?" he asked the soldiers trudging along behind him. "Or wait until they have to scramble like a poked ant hill?" His flunkies cackled dutifully. Red's expression remained as stony as they came—even when he was the first to glance over to the cargo crates and found us—also in full gear, perched on our packs—sitting there.

"You'll have to try harder to get me scurrying," I called over to our idiot-in-charge, making him turn around slowly. I grinned brightly and waved, quite happy with how my glove modifications had worked out. No more flopping going on now.

Bucky's eyes narrowed, but he didn't do more than give us a passing glance. Red parted from the group as they ambled to get their own gear ready, while he walked up to us. "I presume you packed enough rations and ammo for five weeks?"

"I presume the Commander told you that he let it slip what his pickup plan is for us?" I shot right back.

Red shrugged as if that was beside the point. "Leary and I have been working out a few times together. Might have slipped out that I found it a shit-awful idea to leave you in the dark until we're all on the beach and the landing boats have returned to the ship."

"So you're going to give us a proper briefing now?" I hazarded a guess.

Red hesitated, but silently shook his head. Too bad.

Within the next ten minutes, the other members of our team filed into the cargo hold, getting ready for departure. More than one of them eyed me surprisingly uneasily, making the fake grin on my face more real by the minute. I bet I could have picked out exactly which of them had been along in Colorado. Those lingering glances gave it away. At least I hadn't wasted that hour it had taken me to braid my hair as I'd worn it all summer long, making sure that no wisp of it could escape and distract me at the wrong time. Now, of course, it would be hidden away under a nice, fleece-lined wool cap—that also did away with Nate's penchant for dropping mud on my less-than-stealthy red tresses—but until we left the relative warmth of the ship, my war 'do was in full view. And damn, it did a thing or two for my confidence as well.

It was barely getting light outside—not that I could make out anything past the ship in the heavy fog—when we loaded into the rigid-hulled inflatable boats that would bring us from the destroyer over to whatever shore we were supposed to land on. Between us, our gear, and the weapons, there wasn't much room left, but even in the choppy sea, the boat felt surprisingly steady. They'd been smart enough not to split our group, and neither Bucky nor Red was in the same boat as us, so I couldn't try to see if my prediction was true that if any of us fell overboard, they'd sink like a stone and drown. It did make me wonder what that would mean if whoever that was insta-converted—would he spend the rest of his undead days in the shallow waters, trapped? My, what an afterlife to subject dear Bucky to…

Vague shapes appeared ahead of us, turning into a sandy beach and dunes behind it. It was mostly empty, with some debris strewn around that might have come from boats or houses that were still hidden by the fog. With the wind slicing across what little of my face was exposed, I wasn't too disappointed not to have to jump right into the thick of a zombie mob, but I was kind of disappointed to find France so… empty. And rather unremarkable so far. I knew those thoughts would come to bite me eventually, but it was a pleasant surprise.

Exiting the boats proved to be a laborious and not altogether dry affair, but the weight—and size—of my pack gave me more grief than the ocean surf and treacherously soft sand. Yesterday I'd felt like I was almost back to full strength, but even before we'd all rallied around Bucky and watched the RHIBs disappear into the fog above the sea, I had to admit that I'd maybe overestimated my stamina a little bit. And by that I meant I really wanted to crawl back into my claustrophobic bunk and forget about anything and everything for a few more days. But seeing as that wasn't going to happen, I might as well focus on Bucky, while Red and two of the soldiers whose names I still didn't know were securing the beach.

"Welcome to France!" Bucky hollered way too loudly, but the wet air swallowed up the sound better than I expected. Most of our people were looking at Bucky while Nate and Burns did their own study of our surroundings. For once, I trusted them to do their job so I could focus on Bucky instead. I had a certain feeling that interacting with him—and Red—was going to become my job. Oh joy.

A few cheers went up but mostly grunts. There was tension in the air, of the kind I knew all too well. The unknown was often worse than the nightmare we'd all gotten used to staring down. And with visibility down to below three hundred feet, there was a damn lot of unknown going on. All there was to see was sand, dunes, and some washed-up debris and driftwood. Not very exciting.

"Gee, and not even any baguettes or fancy cheese waiting for us," Tanner called out from where he was standing at the very back with Gita. He got a few laughs for that, and a lot of agreeable nods. Was I the only one left who didn't really want to do that much socializing?

Even Hamilton allowed himself a small smile. "We might just find us some of that later. Situation is this. We're at the beach in northern Normandy, a few miles outside of Cabourg. First thing we do is establish that we're in the right place, and find a good place to set up camp if we can't make it into town today. I expect that we will have cleared it by noon. Command has virtually no information about how shit went down in Europe, so while finding out more isn't our main objective, it's an opportunity we shouldn't lightly pass up. The LT will collect any hard data you find—newspaper articles, video hardcopies, you name it. Cole and Parker have video cameras along to document anything we can't take with us." He paused, his eyes flitting to me and staying there. I was just waiting for the first of so many slurs to come, but instead he added, "And if you find anything even remotely science-y, call in Lewis. There's a reason we brought her along."

Well, that was unexpected, and almost friendly. Nobody needed an explanation who he was referring to—but then again, all our snazzy new jackets had come with name tags on velcro strips, so it stood to reason that if they could read, they could find me. As if I was so hard to pick out.

Red took over then, calling out names for teams, with Bucky apparently content to leave us stewing knowing little more than what he'd just dropped on us. Before Richards even got to calling out our names, Nate was giving orders, using the new hand signals we'd taught each other in the past few days. I couldn't do half of them, really, but in a pinch they would do. The whole exercise was one of futility, anyway, and mostly designed to annoy Bucky—which it immediately did.

"You think that shit's gonna fly around here?" Hamilton barked at Nate, who only gave him the side-eye while telling Tanner to make sure nothing—dead or alive—got close to Gita, and me and Burns to stick with him.

Only when he was done did he turn to fully face Bucky, his face emotionless. "I don't think so. I know so," he retorted, not quite levelly but with less heat than I'd expected. "I've always done a better job than you at everything. Don't see why that should change now."

I had not expected that. Nate thinking it, sure. But saying so out loud? Bucky turned stiff as a statue at his words. A few of the soldiers snickered, not quite taking Nate seriously—but also not ignoring him completely. Or maybe they knew he was telling the truth. I was so not going to sleep—at all—expecting a knife in my remaining kidney any hour now. Awesome. Nate could have at least waited until I'd had time to test my strength.

"Mic check, everyone," Red called in over the open frequency from where he had wandered off, standing away from the bulk of us, close to where beach turned into dunes. "Every group, report in at fifteen-minute intervals, or when you find something of interest. That includes all kinds of predators, bipedal or not. You can all be heroes later, but for today, let's try to keep the casualties to zero."

I wondered just how annoyed Red was that he'd have to play babysitter and mediator on top of his other duties, but his voice was even. We quickly checked in, then split up in the designated groups. We got the westernmost sectors, down the beach toward the town

Bucky had mentioned. Not having had a clue where we would land, we hadn't been able to study any maps, and as far as I knew, we didn't even have any to start with. So good old checking street signs it would be, until we found some.

There was minimal radio chatter, making me grumble inwardly at how professional this whole operation appeared to be, with Bucky the only exception so far—and maybe Nate's posturing, but I'd gotten the sense that had been overdue, likely for years. While Tanner and Gita remained at the beach near the waterline, Nate, Burns, and I hoofed it up to the top of the dunes so we could catch a glimpse of what lay beyond. More fog, although it seemed to lighten inland. Sand, turning to grass-covered soil. And lots and lots more of that as soon as we topped the rise. To the west, a few houses were barely visible, with a road running parallel to the dunes about a mile inland. More debris, the odd broken-down car, but nobody—dead or not-quite-yet—in sight. I inhaled deeply, but the scent of the ocean was still too strong here to get more than a hint of anything else. Moving helped keep the weird sensation of the world swaying underneath my feet at bay, making me hope that my body would soon get accustomed to being on land once more.

The first round of sign-ins went over the coms, Burns reporting in for us. "Nothing so far. We're heading toward the houses to the west of our sector."

I looked down the slope to the beach. "Should we take the others with us?"

Nate shook his head. "I doubt things would be so quiet here if there are squatters hiding over there. They can always join us at the village once you've cleared a few houses."

It took me a good three minutes toward the road to understand what he meant. I made sure that my com was still switched to receiving only. "What you're actually saying is that you want me not to have an audience when I face-plant my way into a possible trap."

Looking back from where he was walking slightly ahead of me, Nate snorted. "Something like that. I'd ask how you're doing, but you're tense as hell and still favoring your right leg, so the answer is rather obvious."

"I'm fine," I bit out, pretty much underlining his suspicion that I was, indeed, not. Or not entirely. Not yet.

Burns clearly wouldn't have any of our squabbling. "It's not enough that you survived what most others wouldn't have, let alone wanted to? You have to rebound into immediate superhero form?"

"Did you expect anything less from me?" I asked but couldn't help being a little mollified. I knew where Nate was coming from— and while I hated to admit it, I was glad that he was giving me space and time to get my bearings. "Just sucks, you know? Ever since I woke up from not dying in that damn beige motel room, I've been waiting to be just as super as the lot of you are. They even shot me up with the newest, presumably refined version of the serum. And what do I have to show for it? A limp, a weak thigh, and I'm lugging around my weight in ammo that I'm not entirely sure I can hit something with. Sure, sounds like a win to me."

"So it's a minor setback," Burns admitted. "You're not here to win any awards with your awesomeness. That you can carry your own ammo and defend yourself is a bonus, not a requirement."

"What's that supposed to mean?" I complained, then actually thought through his words. "What aren't you telling us?"

Burns shrugged while he continued to scan our surroundings, kicking a small heap of rags for good measure. "Know for sure? No more than you do. But it's obvious, isn't it? They couldn't expect you to rebound like you did and turn into Crossfit Barbie. The only thing they could have relied on was you being fit enough to move—and do whatever it is you can do when you can't shoot or run. So you're here not because they expect you to perform at a hundred and fifty percent physically, but because of that overinflated brain of yours. I'm surprised Bucky even let you out of his sight."

Nate had an answer for that. "He did because he knows the two of us would never let anything happen to her. He'd just get in the way."

This was getting better and better. "Gee, I'm so happy that you all have such high esteem for my capabilities."

"Just being realistic, is all," Burns offered, flashing me a bright grin. "Plus, nothing like getting you all annoyed to make you go off in those undead fuckers' faces. If a little ribbing keeps me from having to do the actual work, you'll feel the burn all the way through Europe and back to the States."

We were close enough to the single house set apart from the others in the distance that I didn't need to reply. Rather, I let Burns bust in the front door and waited until Nate gave me the clear from inside to enter. We spent a good five minutes securing the two stories before Burns reported in that we'd found the property deserted—but not empty.

There were differences to what I was used to from buildings like this—for one thing, the French had a thing for building more resilient houses. I had no idea how old this one was but from the creaking floorboards I would have guessed well over a hundred years, and it looked sturdy as hell. A few of the glass panes of the windows were broken, letting in rain and leaves, but it was mostly undisturbed. No shamblers, but also no signs of anyone hastily evacuating the premises. There were preserves in the pantry, and we wisely steered clear of the fridge. A newspaper lay discarded on the kitchen table, the pages crinkled and yellowed after a year and a half of sun exposure. I couldn't understand the words, of course, but the pictures on the front page were telling their own stories—overfilled hospitals, evacuation camps, and riots. Nothing new there.

"It's dated from a week after the shit hit the fan in the States," I observed as I continued scanning it. "Looks like they had a little more time than us, whatever good that did them."

Nate glanced at the paper over my shoulder, then picked it up and shoved it between some of the straps on the outside of my pack. "Let's move on. Nothing interesting to see here."

I nodded, following him to the door, but I lingered a moment longer at the threshold. "There are no signs of looting here," I observed.

"Your point is?" Nate asked from the outside, a little annoyed with my delay.

"It's a perfect house for looting," I pointed out. "Far enough back from the town that it's easily accessible—and defensible—even if the town's overrun. There's a road right there for cars to drive up to the door so you can more easily drag things out without risking exposure. At the very least, people should have come here to get blankets, coats, and food that doesn't spoil."

Nate continued to look at me, willing me to say it. Sighing, I finally stepped outside, closing the door behind me. "This house should have been looted," I insisted.

"We found lots of properties in Montana that were still sealed up," Burns reminded me.

"Yeah, Montana. I'm sometimes surprised they even realized that there was an outbreak in the rest of the country," I griped. "France is smack in the middle of the continent. They had a much higher population density than we did."

"Exactly," Nate replied. When I glared at him, he offered up a wry grin. "You just answered your own question. More people. More people who died or got infected. Means a much lower chance of anyone else making it." He looked around, nodding toward the single broken-down car in the distance. "I'm sure the larger towns were just as much epicenters of slaughter as we've seen with ours. If we're stupid enough—and you know Hamilton well enough to make that almost a certainty—we'll get there to see for ourselves. But here? Few people around, and everyone getting sick must have kept the tourists away. So they either died, or must have long ago wandered off inland, where there's food and water aplenty." His eyes narrowed. "But you know all that. So what's with the questions?"

I pretended to do a quick sweep of the back of the house as it got into view. "Wishful thinking, maybe," I admitted. "Would have been nice to land and run straight into survivors, you know?" Thankfully, the radio squawked before I could admit that getting a chance to check how steady my shooting was might have been great, too. Nate was still eyeing me way too cautiously for my own good.

"Anyone find anything remarkable yet?" Bucky asked.

All the other groups reported in negative, so it was up to Burns to break the news. "We got a house here, intact. From what we can see of the town over there, it looks just as empty."

Bucky took that without a snarky retort. "All groups, head down the beach toward Cabourg. We'll do a quick sweep of the outlying houses, then head into the town center. Hill, try to set up a communications hub and scan to see if you get any frequencies."

It didn't take long for the other groups to close up to us, with the countryside deserted and no obstacles in the way that would have warranted extra care. I remained close to Nate and Burns, figuring it made the most sense to stay in clusters rather than spread out completely. Being on high alert in the obviously deserted stretch of the countryside made me feel vaguely stupid, but I remembered enough of last year not to let the apparent lack of shamblers lull me into a false sense of complacency. Besides, it wasn't just the zombies possibly hiding in ditches that had my brain wanting to jump at nothing.

"Stop it," Nate grunted in my direction, making me halt in glaring at the two soldiers advancing to my right. When I eyed him askance, he gave me a level look. "I get that you neither trust them nor feel comfortable relying on them, but you'll get eaten if you keep needlessly diverting your focus like that. Be wary when we set up camp, if you must, but not out here in the open. Nobody's gonna jump you while their own hides are on the line."

I wasn't quite sure if that last statement should have comforted me, but the hint of scorn lacing Nate's words was enough to annoy me—and, as he had planned, take him seriously enough to shove my latent suspicions aside for more active ones.

"If you say so," I grumbled as I paused at a lump of rags—but, like before, it was only that, discarded clothes, not the remains of whoever they had belonged to.

"I don't like this," Burns voiced exactly what was going through my head. "It's all wrong here. Too much debris for an actually deserted place, but nothing in sight."

"If they are still around, they're likely hiding closer to the town center," Nate suggested, nodding down the road we were ambling toward and the houses slowly taking shape in the distance. "Right now it's not cold enough for snow here, but we've known for a while that some of them are smart enough to nest inside. Just because one house was deserted doesn't mean the others are."

I was tempted to tell Captain Obvious that we weren't complete rookies here, but instead turned on my mic when I saw Nate fiddle with his com unit. It was one thing to keep conversations just between the three of us if we needed a moment of privacy, but quite another when calling for backup might depend on a working connection. I didn't need Nate's silent hand signal to know to zip it. Even if I had given a shit about appearing unprofessional by entertaining everyone with my constant rambling—and I kind of did, I had to admit, grudgingly—I knew that it was damn distracting, and that was the last thing we'd need if there was anything lurking in the town ahead. One last suspicious glance to the side revealed that neither of the soldiers was glancing in my direction, let alone keeping track of what I was doing.

Then the last soft hills evened out, the town of Cabourg spreading out before us. There were maybe three hundred buildings, half of them still hidden in the fog, with plenty of barricades and broken-down cars everywhere. As quiet and deserted as the countryside just a mile out had appeared, this looked a lot more like I'd expected. Still no remains anywhere in sight, but if I remembered from our early spring venture into Casper, undead presence often came with a great cleanup effort.

"Williams, Russell, Rodriguez, follow me. We take point checking out the main street," Bucky commanded as the last of the stragglers caught up. "The rest, spread out, but be smart about it. Always make sure to stay in sight of the next team, and try to keep track of possible evacuation routes. If all hell breaks loose, we meet at the beach, eastern direction."

I watched as the three men and the female soldier who'd been with Aimes back when they'd given us the intel on the Colorado base broke away from our disorganized line, slowly making their way along the road toward the first houses. None of them looked extra jumpy, but Rodriguez kept glancing over her shoulder a few times, slightly distracted. At first, I thought it might be inexperience that had her on edge, but then the wind turned and I got a full face of death and decay—sure signs that we were not alone. It was hard to judge the direction, but it seemed to come from the landward half of town—exactly where her attention had been straying to.

It was only when I realized that Nate wasn't crinkling his nose that I decided to speak up. "Getting some mighty foul smell from south by southwest," I reported.

Someone laughed over the com, and I thought it was Hill who offered a good-natured, "Sorry, my bad."

Part of me wanted to gnash my teeth, but instead I kept repeating Burns's advice to myself—treat them as if they were part of our team.

"I'm not contending that you smell like a pig," I retorted. "But if there's someone here who knows what a decaying slab of meat smells like, it's me. Trust me, we're not alone."

Rodriguez piped up before anyone else could offer up a few choice remarks, her voice slightly strained. "She's right, I smell it, too. Not even you can stink up the head like that, Hill."

Bucky gave a signal, making the other three with him halt as he eyed the surrounding buildings more closely. "Richards, take three teams to the southwestern edge of town. The rest, follow me."

I didn't know what to make of it when Red called Nate and Tanner to follow him, along with the three soldiers assigned to him. Part of me wanted to protest that taking Gita straight to where we guessed the thick of the fray might be lurking was premeditated murder, but I respected her too much to do that to her. Tanner would take care of her, I was sure. That left Nate, Burns and me free to do what we knew to do best, with the others as great backup.

We split away from the other half, now under Bucky's direct control, walking a slow circle through high grass and weeds of what used to be backyards and fields until we reached the next large road leading from the town center into the countryside, roughly to the south of it. The fog still obscured the sun, but the ambient light was bright enough to make me guess that any minute now it would break through, giving us a better view of our surroundings. The urban sprawl of the town was stronger here, away from the beach, but that mostly meant more sheds and still-erect fences to obscure our sight.

"Miller, check the western half," Red whispered into his com. "Munez, Davis, Murdock, you're with me. We take the eastern. Tanner, remain in the middle and split to whatever side makes contact first. We're about three hundred meters out from where the other teams will come to the main square by the church, so if you see movement that far ahead, don't necessarily shoot first and ask later."

Was that a joke? I was still puzzling about that when Nate signaled me to follow him, with Burns bringing up the rear. My left thigh gave a twinge as I ran along the road, crouching between cars where I could, but I did my best to ignore that. Nate paused at the first house, peering between what remained of the fence into the yard beyond, but then signaled me to head over to the next. Red mirrored our advance on the other side of the road, two of his guys taking a quick detour into a side road before they joined him once more.

It was at the third house that the stink resurfaced. I didn't need a college degree to put two and two together when I saw the half-eaten carcass of a deer, swarming with flies, on what used to be the front steps leading up to the house. "We have possible contact here," I reported in, keeping my voice low.

"We got movement in the backyard," one of Red's men said. "Some bones, and what I think used to be a raccoon."

Burns caught up to me, hunkering down behind the same car I was hugging. While he was still looking over the carcass, I picked up a stone from the curb and threw it against the wall of the house, jerking at the sudden sound of it clattering onto the front stoop.

Nothing, then repetitive banging coming from the inside, as if something had suddenly roused and gotten caught on furniture— the cadence familiar enough to make it obvious what was going on. My fingers tightened on my M16, but after a second I shoved it back on its sling, grabbing for my tomahawks instead. Only one way to find out if my grip was any good on those, I figured.

Pointing at my chest, then at the house, I silently told Burns that I was heading over to check it out. He squinted at me, not entirely happy, but gave me a nod of acknowledgment. Nate joined him just as I stepped from the curb through the open gate, careful not to make a sound as I eased through the dead leaves beside the carcass. From up close, I could see that it had been wrenched apart completely, literally torn limb from limb, the long bones cracked where something had tried to suck out the marrow. I lacked the proper knowledge of bugs to tell how long it had been there, but considering it wasn't yet stinking too badly, I figured the remains were from last night.

The front door was closed—and considering the bumping I'd heard inside had originated from the front of the house, I aimed to keep it that way—so I eased myself along the wall toward the back, hoping to find easier access through a terrace door. The fence, covered by vines now brown and mostly leafless, had partly caved in, forcing me to slowly crawl through it to make it to the backyard. I paused as soon as I could glance around the corner of the house, trying to look at everything at once. There was a shed and what used to be a small pool, the once-blue tarps a crumpled heap piled against the side of the rickety structure. I doubted anything larger than a mouse was lurking in there, but made a mental note not to rely on that. Chairs and a table were reduced to splintered wood, the bits and pieces strewn all across the deck. And there it was, a three-part, ground-to-ceiling window array, the middle pane open into the room beyond. Undefined stains covered the frame, blood and feces if I had to take a guess. The reek was much stronger here, as if I'd needed more confirmation.

The hedge rustled behind me, spilling out Nate as I ascended the three steps to the deck. He gave me the "move back" signal as soon as he caught my attention, but I ignored him, instead ambling toward the door. What was the worst that could happen to me, that I got infected again? Fat chance.

His curse was low enough that I barely caught it, but all the more vehement for it. I was a step away from the glass when he grabbed my arm and pulled me back. "What the fu—"

I didn't bother with answering, instead used his hold on my right arm to swing around and hack at the zombie that was suddenly right there in the face. Dramatic move, but not a smart one, as the sharp ax blade sheared off its nose before it got stuck in the lower jaw. Maybe I should have stuck with blunt weapons after all.

Realizing what was going on, Nate immediately let go of me to come at the second undead pushing out onto the deck with his sledgehammer. My zombie let out a near-silent scream as it tried to reach me, never mind the ax stuck in its jaw. Gritting my teeth, I brought down the other tomahawk, hoping that my right hand would hold up. It did, but I only managed another glancing blow to its head. Thankfully, the momentum of the swing let me wrench the other tomahawk free, and the next swing hit home. Nate dispatched the third shambler crowding through the door, leaving us both panting from the brief spurt of exertion.

"Well, that was anticlimactic," I noted, nudging my downed shambler over onto its back. It didn't come as much of a surprise that it looked like hundreds of other undead—not that I had expected anything different. They'd been smart enough to seek shelter, but not much beyond that. Glancing into the house, I found the room beyond the deck in disarray, more remains of animal carcasses mixed with what used to be furniture. One corner in particular was covered in fecal matter, swarms of flies buzzing over it. Absolutely no need to venture inside.

Nate finished his own cursory examination of the corpses before he gave me a nasty look, jerking his chin back the way we had come. I spread my arms wide and gave him the universal "who cares?" look before I followed his order, slinking back to the main road.

"Three undead, nothing out of the ordinary," Nate reported in as he followed me. How he managed to put a note of accusation in the last part that was pointing like a blinking neon arrow at me, I didn't know, nor did I care. It wasn't just my imagination, I realized, when I found Burns grinning from ear to ear as we joined him.

The other parties had busted down a few more doors, Tanner getting two busts while Red's guys were covered in enough gore to warrant a good scrubbing already. Oh well. If I'd ever had worries that we wouldn't fit right in, that put them to rest. We met up in the middle of the first larger intersection, Nate and Red briefly coordinating before we split up once more. Ten more houses followed, with mixed results. There were shamblers around aplenty, but they seemed disorganized at best, and even though they must have heard us bust down doors down the road, none of them ventured onto the streets to investigate. They were all well-fed, and we found plenty more animal remains to account for that. Considering the state their lairs were in, my guess was that most of them had been former residents that, after snacking on the family pets, had learned that there was game aplenty to be had not far from town. They also seemed to prefer a semi-solitary state, five or six the most we found at one single place. They provided a great workout but not much of a challenge. Nate kept eyeing me critically, but so far my body was performing well enough that I wasn't about to become a burden.

At the next checkpoint, Red hung back, giving me a similarly judging look.

"I'm not about to keel over quite yet," I told him, not bothering with keeping the latent ire out of my voice.

"Wasn't implying that you were," he replied. "And I'm sure you will let me know if you get there."

I stared after him for a second before following Burns further down the road. Apparently, I wasn't the only snarky one around.

What else I might have observed about his mannerisms went unnoted as a gunshot ringing loudly through the foggy morning made us all halt in our tracks, looking toward the source. It had come from deeper inside town, where our scheduled meeting point with the others must have been. A staccato sequence of an M16— presumably—going off followed, laying to rest the question whether it was just an accident, or first signs of heavy opposition.

Red was already giving us the go-ahead when Bucky's voice grated over the main frequency. "Cole, you dumb fuck!" followed by, "Meeting heavy opposition, two streets east of the town square. All groups, merge on my position!" I really didn't like that my mind had run along the same lines. Couldn't he have been as incompetent as he was despicable?

Thanks to the ongoing shooting it wasn't hard to guess where we were headed, but I was happy to let Red take point, hanging back with Gita instead after Nate signaled me to lay low. He and Burns went right after Red, taking point after we crossed another intersection. I would have complained about being left out, but my thigh was hurting, and that damn pack seemed to be weighing half again as much as it had when we'd landed on the beach, so I didn't protest. Besides, someone had to protect our rear as well; I didn't miss the shadows moving behind closed windows all through the town.

The din from the rifles going off only increased as we drew closer, making me guess that they'd met with more shamblers than they'd expected, or they'd have avoided them altogether. Since stealth was no longer a necessity, I chose to use my assault rifle over the tomahawks, a decision my hands, in particular, were very happy with.

We were just outside of the hot zone when Nate stopped to fire down a side street, putting an end to our comfortable stroll. I flattened myself against the next wall, Gita beside me, her eyes darting around nervously. "Stay behind me," I whispered to her. "Need someone to keep them off my back if we get surrounded." Fat chance of that, but Tanner seemed relieved to be off babysitting duty for a while.

What had been a single disoriented shambler that Nate had gunned down quickly turned into a small mob, a good fifteen of them coming toward us. They were surprisingly silent, only the odd moan or grunt coming from them. While their clothes were reduced to rags, all of them looked decidedly healthy—as far as that could be said for the undead. I squeezed off a few rounds but held back, relying on Nate, Burns, and Red's people to take out most of them. My aim was good if not stellar, and I didn't like the answering twinges flaming up all over my body that the recoil of the weapon brought on. I'd do in a pinch, but I was a far cry from where I'd been last summer. Not good. So not good.

Red gave the signal to move on, all of us following in groups of twos and threes. Nate lingered a moment to check on the downed shamblers, using that as an excuse to plaster himself to my side. I didn't need to see the look of concern crossing his face to know that I was projecting my misery outward at gigawatt strength, but there wasn't much I could do. I gave him a quick thumbs-up before I ignored him. I didn't need to tell him that the best he could do for me was clear the path up ahead so any shortcomings of mine wouldn't come to bear. He and Burns quickly caught up with Red once more, leaving me trailing behind.

We only ran into one other, much smaller group of the undead before we reached the broad street that supposedly had served as the main route for the others, as evidenced by heaps of dead bodies, clustered together. At a glance, I estimated them at well over fifty, a lot more than the shots had indicated, making me guess that they'd only blown their cover of silence once the thick of the fray had become unmanageable otherwise. Two of Bucky's people were waiting for us there, Rodriguez and Williams, seamlessly falling in with Red once he gave them the signal. Red split us into two groups, us and them, signaling for us to remain on the southern side while they took the northern sectors. Together, we advanced further west toward the town center. An eerie silence had fallen over the street, every creak of wood and rustling of leaves setting my teeth on edge. From how the beach and the lone house we'd checked had been empty, I'd presumed there weren't a lot of the undead around, but that theory was obviously wrong.

A sequence of dull thuds coming from the other side of the street told me that Red's people had made contact, presumably in another small street branching off to the side as Rodriguez, on the main street, was still moving forward at a cautious pace. Nate gave the others the signal to disperse, until it was only me and Gita who were mirroring her. Gita looked vaguely pissed at being left out, but one glance in my direction and she abandoned her apparent protest. Rodriguez hadn't missed our silent exchange, smirking slightly, but a loud thud coming from up ahead had all three of us alert and ready.

Three houses further down the road, an open door was creaking in the light breeze as it swung open and closed slowly. I tried to remember if I'd noticed it when we'd stepped out onto the street, but it was impossible to ignore now. Rodriguez paused, pointing first at herself, then at us. I gave her a quick nod, signaling Gita to hang back as I sprinted forward to check. There was no debris in the doorway so the door had been opened very recently. I inhaled deeply as I crept closer, trying to catch any lingering scents of decay that might alert me to the presence of the undead, but the entire street kind of reeked, so that didn't give me anything. Pausing below a window a few feet away from the door, I eased myself up until I could try to peer inside, but only caught my reflection in the dirty window. Ducking, I crossed the distance to the door, making sure that the street was still clear before glancing inside. Furniture, in light disarray but without the omnipresent scat covering everything—one of the hallmarks of having stumbled into a zombie lair. Reaching for the door, I eased it closed, then signaled the others to proceed as I stepped toward the corner of the house.

I had a split second to notice movement at the very edge of my peripheral vision, then the zombie was on me. It had once been a slight girl, late teens, but it barreled into me with the force of a linebacker from where it had been crouching behind a stack of crates. Twisting, I managed to get my rifle up between us before it could snap its teeth at my face, but even though I braced myself, it forced me into the middle of the intersection. My instincts told me to wrench the weapon free and use the stock to bash its face in, but my grip wasn't holding up well, and while I felt muscles in my arms and back ready for some action, I didn't dare move my aching fingers even a little. Fuck awesome timing, really—

Rodriguez was there, coming up from my left, determination on her face. She pushed the muzzle of her assault rifle right into the zombie's temple and pulled the trigger, a single shot all it took for the girl to go slack. I stepped away, letting the corpse drop to the ground, waiting for Rodriguez to admonish me—but all she did was look at my face to check that I was okay before she sprinted for cover. I kicked the shambler for good measure, then checked out its hidey-hole to make sure nothing else was waiting there for us. I'd seen a bunch of them pull sneaky moves, but usually, it was luck that let them get the drop on us, not active hiding maneuvers. The others must have passed through the intersection, and there was no way it could have snuck along from the other street where I saw a few more shapes run for cover. I filed that information away for later. At the very least, I would have to discuss this with Nate.

About fifty yards down the road, someone opened fire, making us pause just in time for a string of undead to come bursting through what remained of a glass door, tumbling into the street in their attempt to follow the gunshots. Rodriguez and I did a good job decimating them before they knew what was coming, with Gita getting a few well-aimed shots in between us. Tanner had done well prepping her for this, even though she still looked about as scared of her rifle as the undead we'd just reduced to a heap of rags and decayed flesh. The trip up to Colorado had taught her a lot, but I remembered all too well that it had taken me more than just a handful of encounters to feel at ease with my weapons.

Signaling Gita to secure the road, I followed Rodriguez into the house, quickly clearing the lower floor. There were signs of habitation here, but a lot less than the ten zombies we'd just mowed down would have produced had they been in here for more than a week. The frown clearly visible on Rodriguez's face made me guess that she was about as happy as I was to realize that the shamblers had learned stealth tactics over here.

Back out on the street, I caught a first glimpse of the town square up ahead, maybe two hundred yards away. Even from here I could see the barricades erected of cars, furniture, and everything else that had been available. Someone had tried to make a last stand there and lost, if I had to take a guess. Rodriguez took point, but halted at the next house when more gunshots from the northern side kept going on for a good thirty seconds.

"LT, what is going on over there in your quadrant?" she asked into her com.

Nobody answered, until Nate's voice came over the line. "Southern quadrant is cleared. We only found a handful. I'd say we move north and check what has the others pinned down." Not quite an order, but the kind of suggestion that would make it easy for Rodriguez and the others to follow.

"Negative," Rodriguez shot back, momentarily eyeing Gita and me. "Move on to the other side of the square. I'm taking Lewis north with me. If they need more backup than we can provide, we'll radio in. Better to know you've cleared our fall back route if we have to rely on that."

"Roger that," Nate replied with sarcasm heavily lacing his voice. Rodriguez let out a silent sneer but jerked her chin toward the next intersection, taking point herself. I followed, but not before giving a scowling Gita a nudge with my elbow.

"We're a package deal. Don't mind them."

We paused at the intersection, but when nothing moved up ahead in the square, we took the turn right and headed north. Corpses littered the street, not all of them recent, and most eviscerated and dismembered. Several of the doors up ahead were open, with drag marks visible on the ground. A look inside the first revealed a heap of more recently deceased, making me guess that whoever had cleared the street minutes ago had disposed of the shamblers that way to keep the street somewhat clear.

Shots up ahead made us pause. Rodriguez tried hailing Red again, and this time, she got a response. "We ran into heavy opposition," came the lieutenant's response over the com, barely audible over the shots we heard both over the line and in real time. "Keep an exit route clear to the south!"

"Miller and Burns are already on it," Rodriguez replied, not quite disobeying his order. "We're joining your six in five."

Part of me wanted to harp that there was no need for her to be exceptionally cryptic, but maybe she wasn't. The meaning was obvious, and at her nod, I joined her sprinting toward the next good cover.

A broader road opened before us around the corner, and it became obvious why there was so much going on here. Whether they'd been hiding in the houses or not, the road up ahead ended at the northern part of the town square, where the sturdy barricades seemed to have held through the outbreak—but were severely overrun now. Corpses already littered the street and every available obstacle that had held them back, but still more were coming, getting decimated by the soldiers at a good rate, but not good enough to push back the tide.

At least it looked like they had already lost ground and were still retreating, if at a slow pace. The barricades and layout of the street turned the mouth of it into a kill chute so it was a bit like shooting fish in a barrel, but those were piranhas rather than cod. Parker was kneeling at a downed soldier's side who had been dragged out of the thick of the fray, proving that we weren't as impenetrable a force as most of us loved to think.

The three of us joined the fight without requiring extra orders, a couple of soldiers gladly ducking for cover to reload or catch their breaths as we took their places. To be fair, Gita was doing a slightly better job than me, particularly when it came to reloading, but I told myself—through gritted teeth—that a dead zombie was a dead zombie, whether it took me three shots or one to bring it down. Seeing as nobody else was concerned about conserving ammo, I chewed through three full magazines quickly before I ducked into one of the open doors, signaling Cole to take my place instead. Hill and Murdoch were busy reloading inside, Hill obviously having abandoned his attempt to get the radio gear going. With something akin to awe, they watched me stow away the empty magazines that hadn't made a real dent in what I had easily accessible outside of the pack on my back.

"My, someone's a little paranoid," Hill observed with a grin, then had the gall to laugh at his two extra spares.

Rolling my eyes, I threw two of my spare spares at him that he caught easily. "You'd be the first to complain. Besides, there was that one time where I almost died because I ran out of ammo because some shitheads ambushed us. That will never happen again."

Murdoch didn't look particularly happy about the reminder of what had happened at the factory—making me guess he had been a part of that—while Hill smirked.

"Well, it's not like you didn't pay us back for that," he called across the room. "You didn't have to mow scores of us down with that deathtrap on four wheels once you got there."

"Actually, I did," I shot back, making sure everything was secure and I had enough ammo at hand not to have to fumble for more any time soon. "And felt damn good, too."

Hill laughed. "Yeah, guess we had that coming. Damn fine driving you did, considering you were high as a kite." When he caught my frown, he gave me a superior smile. "We have a file on you, missy, that distinctively noted your performance rating. Good thinking, numbing yourself with the booster to stay alert until your system crashed. It's decision making like this that made the brass take you seriously in the end. They wouldn't have let Raynor take you apart and put you back together if they didn't think you'd come in handy in a tight spot."

I would have loved to wring his neck for more information, but Hill ducked outside, taking his former place at the crates once more. Murdock followed, running across the street to a post one house closer to the barricade. I allowed myself a few more seconds to relax, then did the same.

Even with twelve people already in place, the addition of the three of us had made a difference. Within the next ten minutes, the stream of undead turned into a trickle, allowing us to make it over the barricade and into the northern end of the square. As we disposed of the last remaining shamblers, Bucky so happened to wander into my sight, in perfect timing turning around to look squarely at me. I would have been lying if I'd claimed that my trigger finger wasn't itching like hell, but I lowered my M16 a little and concentrated on checking the broadening perimeter that was quickly established. Shooting him was too easy; way, way too easy. Besides, all joking aside, I was sure that Hill wouldn't have a single qualm executing me if I tried. Well, the perfect time and place would come, I was sure of that.

As we secured the square, Nate and the others joined us, making us fall back into the previous small groups. We were set to guarding the southern exit while Bucky, Red, and three others busted down the door to what must have been the town's bank. Their behavior downright puzzled me until they emerged ten minutes later, Red stowing something away in his pack while Bucky walked over to Aimes, who had a portable sat nav unit ready. I was surprised that still worked, but then we'd had a lot of satellites up there and apparently not all had become space junk yet. Bucky prattled off an address that he double-checked from a piece of paper in his hand, making me guess that they'd retrieved it from a safety deposit box inside. Why it had been there—and how they'd known about it, and gotten to it, no less—I had no clue, and as before, our esteemed leader wasn't about to divulge any extra intel to us grunts. Nate was quick to take the address down and check the map he must have liberated from one of the houses, showing the location to me. It was a good fifty miles inland, somewhere to the northwest of Paris.

"Three to four days, if things don't get worse than they were here," he noted grimly.

I nodded absently, instead trying to discern what Hill was reporting in, now that he had had time to get his gear up and running. The wind was picking up, finally chasing the fog away, but also making it impossible to hear what was going on over there as Bucky discussed it in hushed tones. My gaze skipped over the houses nearby, snagging on some words spray-painted there in faded red, accompanied by arrows and other signs.

"Directions," Gita noted as she joined us. "It says that they are rallying near Ajou. Whoever still has a pulse is welcome."

I gave her a sidelong glance. "You speak French?"

She gave a half-hearted shrug, but I would have had to be blind not to see the pride shining behind her eyes. "Four years in school, plus had a thing for a Canadian guy who joined my class junior year. Did you know that the French have over a hundred vegetable-related words for dick?"

"I'm sure that piece of information will help us immensely," I enthused, but gave her a pat on the back. "Good job."

I waited for Nate to offer any additional comment, but when he was still busy staring balefully in Bucky's direction, I decided it would fall to me to break the good news—and keep the part about how to possibly enhance my vocabulary to myself.

Bucky shut up as I got close enough to legit eavesdrop on them, for once passing up the chance to tear me down. No fun at all when he was acting professional.

"I take it that Ajou is our next stop, after we've picked up whatever you need to get at that location you just retrieved from inside the bank?"

A look of surprise crossed Bucky's face, making me want to applaud myself. Ha! It was gone after a moment, replaced by a scowl. He opened his mouth, but before he could bark at me, Hill interrupted him, looking excited.

"Where did you get that from? I just managed to find a frequency with an automated recording on repeat, mentioning that village over and over again."

I was tempted to screw with him, but if Bucky was acting professional, I couldn't very well behave like an ass.

"See those scrawls on the wall? Says that the resistance is meeting in Ajou. Or was, when whoever left the directions gave up on their last stand and fled."

Red gave a small nod. "I've seen similar markings all over town. Just couldn't translate them." He turned to me. "You speak French?"

Bucky looked ready to give me a cause to try to beat his face to a bloody pulp, so I quickly forestalled him. "Doesn't take a genius to decipher it. It's the only word in caps in that sentence. Just look it up on the maps."

Hiding the small, triumphant smile that wanted to creep onto my face, I left them standing there, returning to Nate's side. Bucky looked ready to chew through steel, and Nate's answering glower wasn't much better. Red, as usual, saved the situation as he turned to the assembled soldiers.

"We've got what we came here for. We're heading south. Aimes, Wu, Rodriguez, you take point. Call in for reinforcements the second you see anything so we can do some proper recon. The rest, get ready. We're moving out in five."

Chapter 12

It took us about twenty minutes, heading south by southeast, to realize just how damn lucky we'd been with picking our entry vector—or that was how long it took for our luck to run out. Maybe the shit-ton of ammo we'd had to waste to clear Cabourg should have given it away, but I'd chalked that up to a fluke. The beach had been empty, after all. But when we kept running into groups of undead, whether we stuck to the roads or tracked across the fields, one thing soon became obvious.

France—and extrapolating from that, Europe—was a zombie-infested hellhole.

And it wasn't like shooting one group took care of the problem.

It was noon by the time that Cabourg and most of the coast line disappeared from view behind us, cutting our progress down to less than a mile an hour. Over the last hours, Richards had tried to establish a routine tactic—let recon try to deal with any stragglers they couldn't avoid after sneaking around larger groups—but even to me, it was obvious that this wasn't going to cut it. Next time we were all gathered in a loose bunch, Nate left his post at my side and strode through the soldiers to where Red and Bucky were trying to look like they knew what they were doing. I was sure they did—or thought they did—but considering that this situation much more resembled our MO of how to survive the apocalypse than what they had to deal with, it only made sense to share tactics. Neither of them looked surprised as Nate stepped up to them, but their closed-off expressions were far from inviting.

"You know that this will only get us all killed if you keep it up much longer?" Nate spoke loudly enough that he was easily heard by everyone around, another change from the quiet decision-making process of before.

Bucky, already gearing up for a fight, wasn't impressed by Nate's statement.

"You're the one who has two girls along who wouldn't have passed our standards for field deployment," he offered, his voice equally carrying back to us. I felt my teeth grate against each other before I'd willfully started gritting them, but Nate shrugged off Bucky's taunt without a single muscle moving in his face.

"And yet they both survived that first summer without having a hint of combat expertise or could hide behind secure walls. I'm not afraid for them—besides the fact that we'd have their backs if needed. It's the rest of us I'm concerned about. Three people at random rotations aren't enough."

While Hamilton was still thinking of the next insult he could hurl in my general direction, Red jumped into the breach. His entire demeanor was that he was talking to Nate at eye-level, not down from above like the idiot-in-charge. "Fire teams of three to four people, two out, thirty to sixty minute rotations?"

Nate gave a nod that seemed equally leveled, like it was the smart and obvious solution.

"That gives everyone plenty of time to rest, and I'm sure we can secure our own backs. If we get more intel from up ahead, we can avoid most obstacles and it will be faster and less tiring for all of us."

"Good thinking," Red agreed. The sidelong glance he cast at Hamilton wasn't exactly a warning—outright insubordination wasn't his thing—but even to me it was clear that had Bucky protested now, he'd simply have looked like a petulant child screaming at the smart decision the adults had just reached. Hamilton gave the barest hint of a nod, then wasted a good ten seconds in a glaring duel with Nate— who stared right back, not giving an inch.

"How is it that suddenly I'm the mature one?" I asked Burns, who had a hearty laugh for me but wisely no retort. "Didn't take him long to flip back into leader mode."

"This again?" Burns grumbled, not giving me the time of day for my glare. "Come on. You knew this was going to happen sooner or later. And considering the alternative, do you want to be the one in charge? We both know that you're not the most diplomatic person."

Looking at where their glaring match was still going on, I shook my head.

"No, I really don't want to. And I'm glad that he found his backbone. It just…" I trailed off there, not knowing how to finish that sentence.

"Rankles that you're back to common grunt?" Burns teased.

He wasn't wrong there. "Kinda."

"You'll get over it," Burns was quick to assure me, his hearty slap on my shoulder proving that no, I wasn't quite there yet.

Red was quick to split us up into fire teams, thankfully leaving it to Nate where the five of us were concerned, and volunteered to act as third party in our second team. It made the most sense for Nate, Burns, and me to form one team, leaving Gita and Tanner with Red as the other. I doubted that, had Nate known just how overrun the European continent seemed to be, he would have let me out of his sight even for a second back in Cabourg. That was a thing of the past now. The soldiers split into two teams of four and two teams of three, making up a grand total of six teams. Firearms were switched for anything that could—silently—exact blunt force trauma, and rather than send out single recon troops, Red had two fire teams advancing, with the others hanging back, on a thirty-minute rotation, just as he'd suggested. As the first seven were sprinting ahead, we resumed our trek. I kept studying the soldiers, trying to judge their reception of Nate stepping up from his previous role as the exiled recluse. There was doubt and open anger on some faces, but most—predominantly from those who I'd had a chance to talk to before—pretty much ignored what was happening. The command hierarchy was still in place, and that seemed to be enough for them. For the first time I wondered exactly what all their ranks—and history—were. I was sure Burns would know but as he didn't volunteer the information, I didn't ask. Just being cold, miserable, and tired was taking up enough of my concentration as it was.

"Why are there so many shamblers around here?" I mused an hour later, after we'd fallen back from the forward position. "I know that Europe had some large cities, but nothing really comparing to New York City or Los Angeles."

Nate gave me a sharp look. "You do realize that, discounting Russia, Europe had twice the population we did? There's a reason we set up the bunker in Wyoming, and why most of our solo tours have run through the Midwest."

That wasn't exactly news to me, but also something I hadn't really considered. "So there are, what, possibly up to twenty million shamblers hanging around here?"

"Likely closer to fifty," Red interjected from where he was walking slightly ahead of us, not looking back. "We can't know for sure as we haven't yet managed to set up communications with anyone from around here, but considering the outbreak in central Europe was mostly propagated by the virus directly, not via contaminated food sources, we estimate that the conversion rate was higher." He paused, and now he did look back at me. "Didn't you notice that there were a lot of corpses left on the East Coast when this shit all started, but not that many as soon as you got into the previously already borderline deserted stretches of land?"

I hated to admit it, but he was right. I still remembered wondering about coming to the same—back then puzzling—conclusion when we'd switched from hoofing it to acquiring cars. Virtually everyone in that damn town where we'd picked up the Rover had converted, with barely any permanently dead around.

Unlike me, Gita got hung up on something else than conversion statistics. "Fifty million zombies? Just in France? Are you fucking kidding me?"

Red shrugged, his attention strafing forward once more. "The plan is to avoid most of them. Might get a little hairy the farther inland we get, but we just need to find the right tactics to avoid them. I doubt the weather will remain as mild as it is now. Give us some good snowstorms, and the roads will likely be as deserted as they should be."

Silently shaking my head, I tried not to let my spirit drop at the very idea of that. I was freezing to the point of my body giving involuntary shivers every few seconds, and the cold was making my joints ache, particularly on my hands. To say I was physically miserable was an understatement, and that was discounting the pain my still not-quite recovered body was lighting up with whenever I moved. I knew that there was no way around that, so I gritted my teeth and tried to tough it out—which went well for another forward rotation, but when it was time to get ready for the next, I found myself trundling through a stretch of forest, and the last time I'd actively paid attention to my surroundings had been crossing a small access road between fields.

Fuck.

I forced my senses to focus—which worked well enough, now that I tried—but I hadn't yet made up my mind how to deal with this when I realized that just following the bobbing motion of Nate's pack before me was lulling me into stasis once more.

"I think I'm slipping."

Nate halted immediately, turning around to scrutinize my face. Burns caught up to us, making sure to keep watch so we could let our guard down for a bit. The three of us stopping immediately drew more attention than I'd ever wanted—or needed, right then—with Hill and Aimes wandering over.

"Found anything?" Hill asked while he and Aimes joined Burns in momentarily securing the location.

"Nope, just a little maintenance required," Nate muttered as he motioned me to turn around so he could start rooting around in the top of my pack for the last few portions of Raynor's protein sludge.

"I'm neither hungry nor malnourished," I complained as he thrust the pre-mixed thermos at me. Just considering downing that without-a-doubt ice-cold shit gave me hives—and made me shiver hard enough for my teeth to clatter, but that likely came from standing still for over a minute now.

"You're exhausted," Hill observed before I could do more then take a first gulp. Yup, it was as bad as I'd imagined. Not just to humor him but also to distract myself from what I was doing, I raised my brows at him. That was all it took for the beefy soldier to chuckle and jerk his chin at me. "I know you tried to build up strength and stamina on the trip over, but there's no way your body has recovered fully after what you've been through. Several hours of physically taxing march, plus that pack of yours, and it doesn't take a medic to guess why you're all white in the face and shaking."

"It's cold," I supplied, trying for rational but mostly sounding petulant.

"Which means your body is burning through even more fuel," Hill replied, then turned to Nate. "How many boxes of ammo do you have her carrying? Don't even think about denying it. I ran into her back in town and got to see firsthand that she's an ammo packrat. Makes sense for a fight, but she won't get to reload all of the magazines if she falls over and dies within the first day." He gave a low chuckle. "Besides, would likely take a good bunch of what I'm carrying to take her down, and I'd like to hang on to that until we get to some obstacles that can't be avoided. Stop being such pansies about this. She's not up to fighting strength yet, so don't treat her like she is. She deserves better than that."

I didn't need to turn to Nate to hear him gnash his teeth, but cut off what I knew would be not the friendliest answer possible.

"Excuse me? I think I can estimate better than anyone else here what I can carry, and what's too heavy."

A hard jerk coming from my back made me stagger, Nate starting to dig through my pack in many ways undermining what I'd just said. Hill didn't even try to suppress a wide grin as he watched my dear supporting husband and Burns distribute the heavy containers full of cartridges between them. I glared at them silently, but felt so fucking relieved with the weight off my back that it was hard not to cry—ignoring that I wasn't prone to doing that, except when I was… damn exhausted.

"What's the holdup?" Red must have given the others the order to halt before he came over, a slightly guarded look on his face as he found us standing there with Hill still playing Cheshire Cat.

"Just got a little hungry, is all," I offered, saluting him with the sludge. "And apparently everyone else is so bored out of their minds that they found that entertaining enough to stop and watch."

I could tell that he knew that I was bullshitting him, but since no one else spoke up, Red left it at a small nod. "Not a bad idea. Wu, Williams, get some hot beans started. Forward teams, take five to grab a snack or two, you'll get the leftovers later. We'll make camp two hours from now, maybe three, depending on the terrain up ahead. We'll have to deviate from the direct route, Munez just found a larger group of undead clogging the plateau beyond the woods." He lingered for a moment longer, trying to read more off my face than I was happy to give, but then trudged back the way he had come, the dry, high grass at the edge of the clearing rustling with his every motion.

Rather than get a fire going, Wu broke out a camping burner, Williams helping him dump cans of beans into a larger pot to streamline the process. Crackers and bread were pooled and redistributed, and our recon teams were just about getting ready to defend the perimeter when Wu came over, pushing two steaming aluminum cups full of beans at Nate and me. I was more than happy to wrap my fingers around the mug, gloves and all, while Nate grimaced.

"Something wrong with the beans?" I asked belatedly as I was already chewing on the first spoonful. The others got their cups in turn, no one hesitating—but it was then that I noticed that more than one smirk was beamed in Nate's direction. He actually waited until the very last ration was portioned off before he dug in, ignoring my curious looks. "What the fuck is that all about?" I asked Burns instead, hoping he'd answer me. "I'm obviously missing something." I didn't need to catch a snort from Cole to underline that.

Burns—who had gotten his cup after Gita and Tanner, and several of the other soldiers as well—was amused by my question, but for once did his own staring at the smirkers. "Nothing important, really. Nothing that concerns you," he quickly amended after getting a glare from Nate that was shy of baleful. Only the worst of our combined shenanigans had ever earned us such looks, and usually delivered by the Ice Queen. Remembering that made me miss her even more. I was sure that she would have cut right through any stupid games going on, as there so obviously were. I just didn't know the rules.

"Oh, come on. Now you have to tell me," I needled Burns.

He was still reluctant, but Nate finally tore himself out of his glower, ladling beans into his mouth with abandon. "It's Army tradition that the men eat first, officers last. It's an officer's obligation that those under his command are strong enough to fight, and it's a sign of their respect for him if they then share their parts if rations are running low."

I stared at him, meditatively chewing my beans, feeling a little like a cow chewing cud.

"So, basically, they snubbed you." He nodded. "And you're making it so much worse because now you're glaring at everyone like a hurt little baby."

I definitely deserved Nate's—bordering on warning—glare, but Cole's guffaw and Aimes trying not to choke on his beans was well worth that. I couldn't keep a smile from spreading across my face, hoping that my good-natured snort might smooth a few ruffled feathers. "That's just ridiculous. Plus, we are each carrying pounds of food in addition to what we have along for communal distribution. They couldn't starve you even if you were the most respected guy in charge ever."

That whole intermission made me think. Had we ever done shit like that? I honestly couldn't remember. More days than not that first summer, I'd been so exhausted that I'd been useless for preparing food, and I'd literally eaten everything anyone had pushed at me, not caring for anything else until it was all gone and the dregs licked up. And this year, with thirteen going on ten, then only four people left, it had usually been a matter of who opened a can first and handed it off later in regards to any kind of order in which we'd eaten.

Hill, also still loitering near us, turned to Burns. "You kept her along for the entertainment value, right?" Burns wisely kept his opinion to himself, but even that didn't break Nate's brooding.

I should have been able to relate—after all, it was only hours since I'd whined to Burns that I felt left out—but it wasn't like he had a right to expect them to treat him any other way, as he himself sometimes reminded me. Come to think of it, it was kind of a surprising gesture as most seemed to think his opinion at least valid, but therein likely lay the very reason for the action. Going toe to toe with Bucky and hashing things out with Red had left more of an impression than I had guessed at first, and now it was time to put Nate in his place, and more so, remind everyone else of where he belonged.

Damn, but sometimes I was glad not to have to get caught in all that bullshit.

Raising my cup in Wu's direction—and by extension, Bucky's near him—I grinned brightly. "Please keep feeding me first! I need the sustenance, and any gesture short of punching me in the face will go unnoticed, I guarantee that." And I was more than happy to receive the wave of good-natured chuckles that earned me—doing a lot to disband the latent tension and gloating. Even Nate allowed himself a small smile as he pumped his knee against mine. I didn't miss Bucky's expression souring. So easy. So worth it.

I finished my sludge while everyone else was digging into their beans, grudgingly accepting the remainder of a pack of nuts from Nate when he foisted it at me. I so didn't care for being babied like that—even if the small voice at the back of my mind reminded me that I likely needed it. Way to hijack my victory. My pack sure felt a lot lighter as we moved out once more when everyone was done stuffing their faces. When Burns caught my scowl, he had an easy grin for me but kept the inevitable reaming that I knew I had coming to himself. That didn't keep me from noticing that a few of the soldiers were smirking as well, killing what little levity had managed to sneak into my thoughts. So much for letting my guard down. But at least I wasn't about to fall asleep while walking anymore.

We weren't more than ten minutes into the next leg of our journey when Red had us halt, briefly discussing something with Bucky—and, much to that asshole's dismay, signaled Nate to join them. I was tempted to trudge along but remained where I was standing next to Burns, perfectly hating how Nate had turned his back on us so I couldn't read any emotion off his face. Even bundled up as we all were, it was impossible to miss the tension in the men's postures, and for once I didn't think that it was due to the latent animosity between them. Playing games over lunch was one thing; ignoring danger, quite another.

"Now that looks promising," Hill enthused from behind me. I shot him a curious look which he shrugged off. "If I've learned one thing from all my years in the army, it's that you never want the brass all whispering like blushing school girls."

Aimes, still too gloaty for his own good about how I kept shifting my pack this way and that, nodded. "Yeah, particularly if it happens moments after a patrol comes back." He cast a sidelong glance at Hill. "Bet you a pack of nuts that we have to either backtrack half the way to the coast, or walk well until after dark till we make camp."

Hill considered for a moment. "Walnuts or almonds?"

"Trail mix. No raisins."

After weighing that in his mind, Hill snorted. "No deal. I didn't buy the LT's bullshit yesterday when he claimed that they wouldn't work us to the bone long before we got to—" He broke off there, giving Aimes a particularly overdone conspiratorial look.

"Like I give a shit where we're going," I grumbled—but the fact that they seemed to know more than I did grated.

Surprising me, Aimes—so far never one of my fans—chuckled under his breath. "You're such an asshole." He turned to me. "None of us have a clue where exactly we're headed. He's just fucking with you."

"And you're all okay with that?"

My question seemed to puzzle them, but rather than respond, Aimes turned to Burns. "She always like that?"

Burns grinned brightly. "You should have seen how she used to glower before they included her in the command decisions. I'm still not sure if Zilinsky didn't force Miller to offer her co-leadership so she wouldn't have to deal with that any longer." He ignored the scathing stare he earned from me, but it sure cracked Hill and Aimes up.

"I bet," Aimes responded, surprisingly cheerful. "Takes a special kind of stupid to actively want to be involved in that shit."

I refrained from explaining to him in minute detail what I thought of his assessment. It wasn't my fault that I thought myself beyond the likes of simple-minded knuckle-draggers. Glancing over to Nate once again, I sighed, telling myself that not being the one who gave orders this once was not going to be the end of me. Hell, it had been such a relief on the journey up to the Silo not to have that kind of responsibility riding on my shoulders. Why did it have to grate that much only hours into our mission?

Because I didn't trust who was in charge, that's why, I answered my own question as Nate came back to us, his face carefully closed off, which in and of itself told me a lot. The fact that he didn't look ready to whip around and go straight for Bucky's throat wasn't very comforting.

"Change of course," he told Burns and me, and the others by extension where they were hovering close by. "There's a group up ahead that's moving along the ravine we were planning to cross. Mid-streak size, maybe five hundred strong. If we head northeast for a few miles before cutting south we should get around them." He paused briefly, his eyes flitting to Aimes and Hill, making me guess he'd caught their earlier remarks. "No way we'll reach our set camp area before dusk, but we'll try to get there before full dark. That's unless we come across anything suitable before that."

Aimes elbowed Hill, both of them smirking. I didn't quite see the humor in having to extend today's march, but far be it from me to comment on that. Or anything else for that matter, seeing as there wasn't anything important to say.

Even changing course, we happened upon a few stragglers almost immediately, making me guess that it had been sheer luck—and maybe the holdup caused by my much-needed break—that had kept us from running right into the undead horde. Not a single shot was fired, keeping most of the zombies unaware of our presence, but progress was slow going in sprints only a few hundred feet at a time before we had to wait for the signal that the way ahead was clear. I was damn glad for that when it was time for us to take over scouting duty, but at least I got to get a better feel for my tactical tomahawks. The fact that Nate seemed to be everywhere—both playing vanguard and finishing off every shambler that I couldn't dispatch within ten seconds—wasn't lost on me, but far be it from me to protest. I didn't need to see the concerned look in his eyes to know that my reaction times were shit, my movements sluggish even in combat. Oh well. At least the end would be quick if I bit it this way.

Lo and behold, I didn't, but soon wished a zombie would get too close as the day dragged on. I was barely capable of doing more than put one foot in front of the other when we reached a clearing in a patch of forest, opening up around a derelict two-story building. It looked like it had seen better days—in World War II. Everything was overgrown, the path leading through the rusty, unhinged iron gate long fallen into disrepair. Red was quick to send three teams to secure the building, but they were back in under ten minutes. All that grass and brambles that we had to fight through to get here had served as a natural barrier for the zombies, leaving the site virtually untouched by the apocalypse. I could see why that made it a prime location to set up camp, but wondered how Bucky and Red had known where to find it—and what the contingency plan looked like if it had been overrun as well.

Watch schedules were set up before anyone even got a fire started for hot water, Red once more conferring with Nate for a few moments. When Nate told the others who was up and when, leaving me conveniently out of the conversation, I noisily cleared my throat. "I'm not ditching my duty."

"Of course you're not," he told me as he dropped his pack onto the ground. "You're up for watch right now. Richards will fill you in on the perimeter setup."

I was about to start grumbling—to myself only, but still—as I made my way back out of the drafty building, until I realized that, just maybe, getting first watch was a good thing. It relieved me of camp setup duty, and by the time I'd be done, I would have a warm meal waiting for me. I didn't miss the significance of it also leaving an undisturbed seven or eight hours of sleep for me, something I knew my body was needing more than food and water right now. Well, maybe not food, but close.

I was just in time to listen to Red explain to Parker and Munez how far out he wanted to extend the perimeter so I didn't even need any special briefing treatment. If either of the soldiers felt like protesting that they were on duty with me, they didn't show it. Stepping out into the cold wind cutting right through my layers of functional wear wasn't pleasant, but I forced myself not to flinch as I gripped my assault rifle more firmly. It was only for ninety minutes, two hours tops if anything happened. I could get through this easily. A little quiet and solitude wouldn't kill me.

As it turned out, I didn't need to fend for myself, as maybe ten minutes into slowly walking through the hip-high brown grass, Nate materialized next to me, brandishing a thermos in the hand that wasn't pawing his weapon. "Thought you might want some company."

I stared mutely at him until he pushed the thermos at me a second time, and waited for him to take over watch for me before opening it. The hot tea inside—laced with protein powder, if I wasn't completely wrong—certainly went down easily, even if it burned the tip of my tongue a little.

"Not expecting me to be up to holding my own yet, huh?" I jeered around a second cup, stomping my feet for warmth that I knew wouldn't come.

"I know you can," Nate offered. "Doesn't mean you have to."

"And Red didn't protest you throwing a wrench into his watch schedule?"

Nate's lips curved up into a quick smile, likely at the moniker. "He didn't mind me volunteering to pull a double, if that's what you're concerned about."

I considered griping about special treatment, but dropped it. Fact was, if a bunch of zombies broke through the brambles and came directly for me, I'd be damn glad to have Nate hanging around. Maybe tomorrow would be different, but today I really wasn't quite there yet.

We continued along the set track in silence until we reached the end of the sector, about a hundred yards outside the gate. "How's the mood in camp?" I asked, glancing toward the building, the hint of a fire visible in one of the rooms only because I knew what to look for, and my eyes continued to work well in the dark. "Just how much on my toes do I need to be? Figuratively speaking, of course. We both know that literally won't work that well anymore."

I expected Nate to roll his eyes at the jibe, but he ignored it. "Calm enough," he offered. "I think Aimes is just hanging around to find something to rub my face in, but Hill and Murdock seem to be genuinely interested in Burns's BS. Not saying you can completely let your guard down, but I don't think anyone will try anything stupid until we're way farther inland. They must be expecting us to expect something. Let's give them a few days. Then we'll see. I made my point today. Hamilton made his. Until I actively escalate things, he'll give us a few days to lull us into a false sense of complacency."

Not exactly the most comforting assessment, but I wouldn't have believed him had he told me I was just being paranoid. There wasn't anything else to say so we left it at that. I certainly was grateful for his company, and not just because being out here in the darkness, alone, wasn't the most comforting thing to do.

Time passed immeasurably slowly, and it felt like forever until Munez waited to meet us at the edge of the gate, signaling me that my watch was over. I acknowledged that with a nod, but waited until he was back at the building before I turned to Nate. "I presume this is your shift now?" He nodded. "Guess I should get some chow."

Another nod. "Fill up with anything hot you can get," he told me. "And then catch some sleep. Don't try to stay up, don't watch your back. Trust that we will do that for you. You need some rest, more than anything else."

My first impulse was to protest, but instead I inclined my head. He was mirroring my own thoughts from earlier after all. "Considering I'm a minute away from falling asleep standing up, I think that's a good idea."

I kind of waited for him to add anything else—or, you know, kiss me goodnight. Stranger things had happened between husband and wife in the past—but when a raise of his brows was all I got, I turned around and made my way back to camp, not needing to check over my shoulder to know that he was watching me until I got there safely. The camp itself had been split up into three parts so our huddle around the fire didn't look as segregated as I'd feared—or hoped for. Burns was quick to fill up my thermos with hot water and a teabag dropped in, while Tanner pushed a steaming bowl of rice at me. "Which one do you prefer?" He held up two bags. It took me a moment to realize that those were the MREs they'd sent with us on the plane out of the Esterhazy base.

"Give me whichever you guys like the least," I offered as I went over to grab my sleeping bag from my pack—and, in afterthought, got Nate's as well, wrapping both layers of insulation around myself as I flopped down next to Burns.

"They're all equally bad," Burns proclaimed, not even stopping to chew as he was shoveling the contents of his own Meal, Ready-to-Eat into his mouth.

Tanner snickered. "And not the kind we got back in my reserve days. Still tastes like cardboard, even if it's full of protein and fat. Here, take the Chili with beans. The texture is a little better than the beef stew."

It was only then that something occurred to me. "You don't know that I can't taste any of that shit." Tanner gave me a weird look, making me laugh. Well, snicker. Laughter would have required more energy than I felt like I had left to spend. "Virus fried my taste buds when I got infected, or something like that. I really can't taste it. Hand over the one you like less. Fuck texture. I can't exactly feel hunger anymore, either, but those weird shakes I'm having are not just from the cold."

I didn't even check what he ended up giving me as I dug into the rice, supplementing it with the surprisingly warm bits of meat from the bag. I was tempted to let Burns have the contents of the other small bags, but decided that nibbling on some crackers and sucking sauce straight from the package went really well with the rest of Raynor's sludge. It wasn't exactly the feast of kings, but a lot better than what we'd been having for most of the year, out on the road. I couldn't quite quell the creeping suspicion that the quantity and quality of the food—obviously better than the guys' joking indicated—was what had Burns more enthusiastic about our present company than I'd expected.

I didn't need a reminder to heed Nate's advice. As soon as I'd polished off my dinner, I rolled up in my sleeping bag, fully clothed with my M16 right next to me. As Nate's shift wasn't up yet, I used his sleeping bag as an additional blanket, hoping it would stave off the cold. It didn't, but I was fast asleep long before he could recover it for his own purposes.

Chapter 13

I woke up with Nate gently shaking my shoulder, the strength of his grip indicating that it had taken some considerable patience on his part to rouse me. I stupidly blinked into the light of early dawn as it filtered into the building. "Here, got you something to drink," he told me once he was sure I wasn't going to doze off again. It came inside a steaming, open thermos, but the smell alone told me that it wasn't tea. Electrolyte solution, if I wasn't completely wrong, and judging from the sticky residue it left on my lips, way too sweet for me to drink had I been able to taste it. I didn't remember packing any electrolyte powder, even less some laced with added sugar—presumably of the non-toxic kind—but my brain wasn't yet up to discussing that. I drank it down without much thought, waiting for my body to stop aching so I could get up and put it to good use once more. Since that didn't happen, I had to make do with the cards I was dealt, but what else was new?

Breakfast was a somber affair, beans on bread and crackers getting munched on with some tea or coffee to wash it all down. The harsh morning air did nothing to disband my brain fog, but I did my best to fake alertness as we broke camp and got ready for the day's march. Nothing had broken through our perimeter at night, but I didn't miss a few heaps of rags and rotting meat by the side of the now well-trodden path we used to get back out of the forest. Visibility was a little better than yesterday morning, the fog only minimal, but that didn't mean that the weather was good. There was hardly any sunshine, and the few stray rays that made it through the heavy cloud cover did nothing to warm me up. We kept heading roughly southeast, but had to backtrack and change course twice before midday. Red kept up a rapport with the forward fire teams whenever he wasn't part of the advance himself, his maps out as he did his best to chart a new path with every obstacle that we hit. And obstacles there were aplenty, including some deliberately detonated bridges and erected barriers swarming with the undead. Nothing looked recently abandoned, but wherever there was some cover, something lurked in the shadows. More than once, he and Nate conferred for a while before a new course was charted, particularly where architectural obstacles were concerned—with surprisingly little resistance from Hamilton. That made me realize that I knew next to nothing about his qualifications except for his lacking moral compass, making me guess that, unlike Nate, he wasn't so fond of blowing things up or judging if they were still structurally sound enough to be trusted.

Noon came and went without a longer break, until we got close to a small village in the early afternoon. It was pretty much just four houses, two barns—cute, small, wooden buildings, nothing like the behemoths from home that I was used to—and some rusting vehicle husks by the side of the road. Red and Bucky debated briefly, but I didn't quite see why we shouldn't go in and try to raid what provisions there might be found. Sure, we had those MREs, but they were a rather limited resource, and it didn't hurt to stock up when the opportunity presented itself. I must have muttered parts of that out loud as Hill—again lurking by my side as we waited—gave a low guffaw.

"You always that ready to get a face full of undead?" he jeered.

"I'm always ready to get a face full of food," I snarked back. His stomach rumbled in response, making me crack a smile. "And sounds like I'm not the only one."

"Scavengers," Aimes huffed, giving me a disdainful look when I didn't make a move to appear chagrined. At least that was the reaction I presumed he was waiting for. "Always ready to take what isn't theirs."

I couldn't help but snort. "Exactly who are we robbing blind if there's no living soul left to feel the loss? We all have to eat, and seeing as most people didn't get the chance to hunker down in a cozy little base, that means taking food wherever they can get it from."

At first, I'd thought that Aimes was just being an ass, but when Bucky gave the order to move in and clear the houses—as stealthily as possible—more than one soldier looked uncomfortable. That we encountered minimal resistance—just a few squatters in one of the buildings, and a family of foxes that quickly ran off in the southern barn—seemed to make it all worse for them. Pickings were slim, the pantries and cupboards looking like they'd been first raided by the former inhabitants, then by the shamblers, but we came up with about five pounds of pasta and some boxes of rice—gourmet menu of the apocalypse. I snatched up some extra pairs of socks and underwear from the remnants of the bedroom of what had likely been an old lady's house, making sure that no one saw what I let disappear into my pack. Now was not the time to let the next stage of the ongoing battle of the most ridiculous panties that Burns and I had been waging since forever flare up. Even inside, I was fucking cold, and some extra fabric to pad my gear with wouldn't hurt.

Back outside, I found Red studying his maps again, half his attention on what else the others dragged out of the houses—mostly blankets and tools for cutting, slashing, and bashing in heads. He looked up when I cleared my throat. "Where exactly do you guys get off acting all abashed now, after you've spent half the summer dragging everything useful out of every house you passed in Montana and North Dakota?"

He didn't even try to refute the accusation in my voice, but then that was the logical conclusion where all the things in their storage warehouse had come from.

"That was different," he claimed.

"Because whatever you were carrying off, we couldn't get our grubby little hands on?" I ventured a snarky guess. I so didn't care for the deadpan stare I got in return. "Seriously? That's just screwed up. Forget I asked."

"So to you it's okay to take dead people's possessions?" Red asked, a hint of bewilderment in his voice.

Could this conversation get any more unreal? "Well, first, they're dead," I stated, glancing at the soldiers who were drawing closer to listen in on us bickering. "I'm not sure it really constitutes anything immoral then. Second, even if they were still alive, they won't be coming back any time soon, and by then all the food would have spoiled, anyway. Already most of what we find comes with some extra protein content unless you want to spend hours picking it all clean. Give it a year or two, and there won't be enough left to steal. And third, I'm alive and I'd like to stay that way. So unless there's someone around I can ask—nicely—to share their food with me, I'll take it. I need to keep breathing to be able to have a guilty conscience." Red didn't look impressed by my diatribe, so I paused to scowl at him. "And stop with the fucking hypocrisy. We've run into troops of yours that came to raid a mall of all things, fully equipped with vehicles to haul off whatever you need. That wasn't just a handful of people happening upon a cache. That was planned. Get off your high horse."

Before Red could answer, one of the soldiers milling around did. Cole, of course. The fact that I knew his name—and remembered him to be one of Bucky's closest flunkies—said a lot. I still kept forgetting the names of those that mostly left me to my own devices. "But that's exactly the difference between us, and scum like you," he pointed out, sounding very self-satisfied. "We go out there and get what people will need—not just now, but next year, and a decade from now. Designated areas, with designated items to fetch. We store the surplus, and distribute what's needed at the moment. Do you really think you can meet the needs of a settlement with over five hundred people, as a group that's, what? Ten people and four cars? Please. Stop deluding yourself."

He had somewhat of a point, but not one I was willing to concede. I skipped over the part where what he described was pretty much what Minerva, head of the Utah settlement Jason and his people were from, had proposed for us to do. "Yeah, speaking of help. Where were you assholes when Harristown was almost overrun? Oh, right. You were busy razing that other Missouri settlement in the Ozarks because they wouldn't bow to your will. And why waste all those pulse-vests you put on the shamblers to do the dirty work for you on just one mission, if you could send them north and threaten the next town over into compliance? I think nobody bemoans not having a boxspring bed if they're not besieged by a flood of zombies."

Cole had the audacity to snort, but Red was far less amused by my accusations.

"That wasn't us," he ground out, sounding like I'd actually gotten under his skin. A sore spot maybe? Interesting.

"Maybe not you personally—" I started, but he cut me off before I could get any further.

"The army didn't raze any settlements, independent of their acceptance of our help, nor did we sic the undead on anyone," he stressed, his gaze as adamant as his tone. "We only used the beacons to anchor larger groups of the undead to keep them away from our installations, but never as a weapon." He paused. "And we only started that in the summer, which was weeks after you pulled that stunt near Harristown."

"You sure about that?" I harped. "Because we didn't just run into them once, but several times over, states away from your little Colorado base. Just a thought—could it be possible that the left hand doesn't know that the right hand's trapped in the cookie jar?"

Red continued to glower while Cole laughed, quickly shutting up when his lieutenant's ire turned on him. Rather than back down, Cole shrugged. "She's not entirely wrong about that, LT. There's a good chance that she and her misfits ran into a few more surprises than we managed to clean up." Cole's smirk returned to me. "Too bad that you had to waltz in and shoot Taggard before anyone could compare notes to ask him about the parts that you couldn't both verify. When they dragged him along to the base, I thought someone higher up in command had lost their mind, but turns out, they knew they could rely on a stupid bitch being stupid."

At Red's glare, he shut up—the frown on Red's face promising some extra duties in store for that idiot later—but Cole kept gleefully smirking to himself. I felt my cheeks turn warm, for once happy about the cold to mask the whisper of embarrassment making it up my spine. Then again, I could take some—deserved—reaming when it also gave me confirmation that I might otherwise never have gotten. If I wasn't reading Red's anger wrong, he wasn't annoyed that Cole had insulted me, but rather that he'd blabbed too much. I still couldn't find it in me to gloat. The consequences of my actions kept me in too much pain for that.

"We all know that I did you a favor," I huffed when I got my emotions back in check, the words coming out carefully neutral. "And trust me, that's not a can of worms you want to open with me."

"Don't I now?" Cole jeered, again ignoring Red's glare. "Why, because you'll steamroll me with your rightful indignation? Exactly how many times has that worked for you?" Two of the other soldiers gave some supportive chuffs. I could have used some of that myself, but it seemed my people were still very busy looting. Maybe that should have given me some pause, but it really didn't.

Spreading my arms to my sides, I did my best to make my grin a real one. "I'm still alive. I'd say that's as good a definition of 'working' as any. And no regrets whatsoever about that." Cole's eyes narrowed, making that fake grimace on my face just a little easier to hold. "I mean, I'm not the one who keeps losing people left and right in traps they set themselves and were too incapable of springing properly. You can jeer at me all you want, but you won't kick me off my soapbox that easily."

"Nah, you're doing a stellar job of that yourself," Bucky's voice came from behind me, immediately setting my teeth on edge. I couldn't keep myself from stiffening, but did my best not to impulsively turn around. After all, I had my M16 in my hands; it wasn't like I couldn't shoot him in under five seconds flat if he gave me a reason to. New reason, I amended. When I did turn around, it was with casual, slow motions, doing my best to keep Bucky, Cole, and Red all in my field of vision. Of course the asshole was grinning, making me wonder if there'd been a shared memo before we set out on this shit storm of a mission: annoy the bitch by constantly flashing your coffee- and tobacco-stained teeth at her.

"I have my moments," I conceded, not trying to tone down the anger rising in my voice. "But, looking back, my scoreboard looks mighty fine, if I may say so. Haven't raped anyone, haven't shot innocent civilians nor doomed them to get eaten. Haven't eaten any, either. Cannibalism notwithstanding, can you say the same for you and your people?"

Too late I remembered that damn mayor of Harristown and how me infecting him had wreaked havoc at the Silo, but Bucky refrained from using reason to get back at me. Indeed, he refrained from answering altogether, as Cole effortlessly kept the ball rolling for him. "Makes me think—don't you regret not coming with us at that intersection after we dragged your sorry ass out of the ruins of that biotech company, back when this all started? One wrong decision that sent you down a path that led to a lot of awful situations for you. It's way too late now to change that, but don't you ever wonder what you could have spared yourself if you'd decided differently?"

Shifting my focus from Bucky to Cole, I tried to remember if I'd seen him back then, but my memories of that morning were way too clouded to say. I barely remembered the faces of the people who'd stayed with us a while longer and had died as we'd fled from the zombies pouring out of the city. Not only compared to that, finding an answer to Cole's question was easy.

"No." I didn't appreciate that look of surprise that crossed Red's face. The other idiots remained impassive, but that was enough to force me to explain. "Never regretted that decision, or any other that ended with me coming in contact with any of you. I don't regret becoming part of the Lucky Thirteen, and I certainly don't regret raising an army to show you condescending assholes that half of the country isn't ready to roll over and die." Of course, Bucky and Cole had to get smirky at that—because of the consequences that had for me, I was sure—so I couldn't leave it at that. "If anything, the only thing I regret is that when we tried to decide what to do earlier this year in spring, that I didn't bring up the idea to just pack our gear, find a nice, quiet spot somewhere with game aplenty—say, Alaska—and say fuck you to civilization. We wouldn't have had to deal with people who only had scorn for us. We wouldn't have lost someone every time we tried to actively help and do the right thing. So yeah, maybe you do have a point with that scorn of yours about us risking our necks to bring generators, electronics, or medicine from out there to the people in the settlements. Never got us anything but trouble." I snorted at my own words, not having to stress that I didn't really believe that. "Oh, right. I forgot. Virtually all that bullshit happened because you either didn't do your jobs, like taking out those cannibals before we had to, or you were directly responsible for our people's deaths, like at that factory. You can try selling that bullshit to the townies at the settlements, but not to us. Sure, push it all at Taggard now, claim he was to blame for every single thing that went wrong because all you ever wanted was peace. If that was true, you had so many opportunities to avoid bloodshed, and you missed every single one of them."

Rather than do me the favor of insisting that I didn't just call him a hypocrite, Bucky snorted. "And you're any different? Once they realized you were still alive, everyone counted on you to make a difference."

Holding his gaze evenly, I smirked. "That old tale? Aimes already tried getting under my skin with that bullshit, back in Colorado. Didn't buy it then, sure as hell don't buy it now."

I didn't like the way Bucky's face lit up. Never a good sign. My fingers tightened a little around my rifle, try as I might to remain relaxed. Where was everyone else? It was very unlike Nate to leave me alone like this. Casting around, I realized that Hill and Murdock were still inside the buildings as well, making this feel a lot like… a setup? But for what? I had a feeling that I was about to find out when Bucky turned to Red. "Tell her. She won't believe me, seeing as she's convinced that I'm a scheming asshole—"

"As you've gone out of your way to reaffirm, time and time again," I interjected.

Bucky ignored me as he went on. "And I doubt she'll take it from Cole, either." A pause followed that I answered with a grimace, no need for fakery there. "But for whatever reason, she seems to trust you, Richards. So, please, enlighten Miss Lewis here why no one has yet wrung her neck like she deserves." Of course he had to deliver that with a smile, that one genuine. "Oh, my bad. I forgot."

I did my very best not to react, even if everything inside of me was screaming to slam the butt of my rifle into his face until all that remained was a bloody, caved-in ruin. For maximum effect, he turned away and walked toward the eastern end of the town, nodding at Cole in passing to join him. That left Red and me standing there. Judging from Red's frown, he wasn't overly impressed with Bucky's antics, either, but when he caught my gaze, he obliged. Or rather, followed an order, I reminded myself. Weren't they all playing it by the book? I didn't trust that behavior any more than I trusted Hamilton himself.

"He's right," Red offered, managing to sound neutral, even if his face betrayed him. "Except for a few bits of news weeks after the outbreak, that was the one event that got command scurrying. I haven't seen Emily that excited since Raleigh Miller joined the project."

"Emily?" It was hard not to pick up on that. "That sounds oddly familiar." Not for the first time I wondered if he and Raynor were a thing— at least passingly. I wasn't sure that sociopath of a woman was capable of normal human interaction required for any kind of relationship.

Red ignored me. "Before that, she didn't have much cause for celebrations. We had less than twenty virologists left once we managed to organize who had survived, and the only other two besides her that had any firsthand knowledge died under suspicious circumstances early on."

His pause there was screaming for a guess, and I was only too happy to oblige him. "Alders and his eco warrior flunkies?"

I got a curt nod in reply. "It took us over a year to find out the cause for that, but that's beside the point. When Brandon Stone called in that you of all people had popped up at his very doorstep, the excitement that caused was almost enough to make people ignore who you'd been traveling with."

"Almost," I echoed, snorting.

Red conceded with a shrug. "At that point, the powers that be wouldn't have been happy to see Miller still around, but they would have been happy to accept you two as a package deal. Communication was still patchy in spring, so it took days to get command to settle on a decision, what offer exactly to extend to you—"

"And by then I already had the mark tattooed across my neck, and was happily disappearing into the wilderness once more," I finished for him.

Another nod. "Of course we could easily track you thanks to the trade network—"

"Gee, so nice of you to admit that," I harped—and got ignored yet again.

"But we didn't manage to get any of our agents anywhere near you in time," he went on explaining. "We had people in Dispatch, of course, but no way to easily approach you without raising suspicions. There was talk of kidnapping you then, but you were gone before we could enact that plan."

That made me chuckle. "You people really are incompetent fucks." At his raised brows, I elaborated, only too happy to rub that in his face. "I was wandering through Dispatch, all on my own, for over an hour when we got there. And spent some quality time, drunk, on the dance floor. Except for when we were getting the tattoos and stuffing our faces, I was never around more than two or three people at a time." Thinking back, it was hard to remember feeling so careless and free— except that it wasn't. California had felt like that, too. That made me wonder how long it would be until I got to feel like that again.

Red wasn't very impressed by my scorn. "It wasn't that easy to reach all parties involved and coordinate them, and while you can pretend like your husband let you prance around that cesspool teeming with misfits, you weren't as unobserved as you may remember." Now wasn't that a little tidbit to chew on later? "Either way, you were off to the Silo before anyone could snatch you up, so command decided to approach you at a neutral meeting point."

"The factory," I hazarded an informed guess. "Very neutral, with all those zombies locked away to unleash on us, should we refuse to cooperate."

Red gave me a weird look, and it took me a few seconds to realize that it was surprise again, even if he tried to cover it up quickly.

"We were lying in wait for you there, yes," he acknowledged. "But we found the facility already teeming with stashed-away undead. Hamilton decided that they would work well as an incentive to make you more agreeable, but they were never to be released. That was a knee-jerk reaction based on the fact that your people seemed ready to fight to the death at a moment's notice."

"Wait." None of that made any sense. "How do you accidentally unleash a zombie mob that kills way more of your people than we ever could have?" Not to forget, "And if not you, who stashed them there?"

Disappointment crossed Red's face, as if I should have been able to answer my own question, at least the latter one. "We never got confirmation, but our working theory is that the facility was used as one of the locations to produce the virus-activated syrup. The zombies likely used to be the plant workers, including the better part of the nearby town's residents."

The implications made my heart sink. "So they were a test run of sorts?"

"That's anyone's guess," Red conceded. "Fact is, we could have handled the situation better, I agree with your assessment of that." So Aimes had tattled on what I'd hurled at his face when he'd tried to make me feel guilty about that, back at our base camp for the Colorado assault mission. "By then, everyone knew that command figured you were the next best thing to our salvation. It might have taken days to coordinate for them to reach a decision, but only hours for the news to spread among the men and women who were doing their very best to stabilize the country and work tirelessly on providing security and whatever else the settlements needed."

I cut him off with a raised hand. "No need to try to sell me on that bullshit. Still not buying it."

Red chuckled softly. "I don't need to sell anything. I know that you're lying, but I get it. You might have been high as a kite at those negotiations, but I could tell that you meant it when you said you were there to avoid further bloodshed. You have your quarrels with some elements"—no need for him to glance over his shoulder to where Bucky was joking around with Cole and Parker—"and a lot of that might even be warranted. You're wary of us as a united front for that very reason, but once you can ignore your own platitudes, you know where to place the blame, and that it doesn't lie with the bulk of us—or the settlements. You were awfully quick to throw your lot in with Greene and accept his offer to settle down right at his doorstep. You believe in our vision of a better, stronger, united nation, or else you wouldn't be here."

"I'm here because I didn't want you to murder my friends in cold blood," I pressed out, more annoyed with the sense of agreement his words caused in me than anything else.

"You could have continued to negotiate," Red insisted. "Your word to continue to work with us—particularly in the lab—once we all returned would have been enough for Raynor to make Morris accept any deal coming from you. You were quick to accept because you were afraid to be stuck with us without backup, that's why you caved so easily." I had nothing to refute that claim with, so I remained silent. At least he didn't gloat in my face as he went on. "Fact is, a lot of people were disappointed when we returned from the factory without you, and a good third of our people dead. We lost track of you then, and could only verify that you were, in fact, even still alive after interviewing some of the people from that settlement you washed up in, and from what the marines at the Silo were ready to share of their own investigations. A week later came that grand speech of yours, and I don't think I need to elaborate on the rest. People held up hopes that you would come to your senses until you hit the base, but that negated all the goodwill most were still extending to you. There are still those that believe you can be put to good use, but they don't exactly rely on you being intelligent enough to see reason."

I so didn't care for that narrative, but I could see where he was coming from—and it explained so much, certainly how the soldiers treated me. This morning, I'd been kind of surprised that no one had tried to jump any of us yet, but Red's words underlined why—they didn't see us as enough of a threat to take any of us out, and while they sure seemed to hate not just Nate's guts for what he had done but also extended that very same courtesy to me, it still wasn't enough for them to go against their orders. In short, I'd become too insignificant to warrant getting shot in the back of the head for insubordination. Maybe that should have eased my rampant paranoia, but it didn't. Not completely.

"Why tell me all that? Besides that ass ordering you to."

"Because you deserve to know," Red insisted. "You deserve to know that you could have been their savior, and you let them all down. Maybe think of that next time you wield blanket statements like an ax, ready to cleave through a zombie skull. You made them your enemies, and yet, they are ready to see beyond that."

"Because command isn't done with me yet."

"Because Emily Raynor isn't done with you yet," Red amended. He held my gaze for a full five seconds, then turned away with an exasperated sigh. Clearly, I had been dismissed. He then stuck two fingers in his mouth and gave a sharp whistle, making heads all around us turn. "We move out in five," he called, pausing when his gaze returned to me. He didn't add anything, but the way he kept looking at me made me guess that he was trying to convey a message—and my mind was too locked in its own hamster wheel circles to grasp it. Shit.

I was still mulling that over when Nate and Burns joined me, trudging out of the house they'd been searching with Hill, while the others followed Murdock out of another. So they had waited for a moment to single me out and get me away from my people—and while it was easy to attribute that to Bucky, I didn't buy it. Yup, that didn't really sound like him—he would have just snatched me up, dragged me behind one of the barns, and delivered his message after adding to my half-healed collection of bruises. At least with that, it would have been easy to guess what he was playing at. With Red, all I could tell was that he was still trying to play me, but I didn't get why he bothered to make things so complicated—and that made it hard to guess why he was doing it in the first place. I so didn't like that.

"Any reason why you're scowling like that?" Burns asked, but the way he and Nate kept glaring in Bucky's direction made me guess that I could easily get away with a lie—if it even was one.

"Found some sexy panties for you," I quipped instead. "Might keep them, though. Not sure you deserve them."

Burns's raucous laughter was balm on my soul, and I told myself to just forget about what had happened. Nothing I could do about it now, and it wasn't like I had the time or opportunity to hash out the details with Nate. Not that I particularly wanted to, I had to admit. There was one part about it all that Red hadn't stressed—not even mentioned, I realized—but that stood out like a red-hot spike in my side: it had been Nate's order that had made Bailey eat that damn tainted chocolate bar to make himself insta-convert, bringing an end to negotiations at the factory by escalating things before any kind of agreement or deal could have been struck. Wilkes—and probably every single soldier here, and back home—thought that Nate was the mastermind behind our crusade, using me as a figurehead only. In fact, that was also a very good explanation why no one but Bucky had tried any funny stuff with me—they didn't think I made a worthy target. I trusted Nate with my very life, but it was impossible to forget how everything between us had started—with him manipulating me. If not to fall for him, then to join him, and later, to learn to survive without going crazy with fear first.

Staring after Red as he sent the first fire team forward, I couldn't quell the resentment toward him that was welling up inside of me. I was not going to let anyone make me doubt Nate—but I also wasn't naive enough to ignore the fact that he was still very happy to lean back in his proverbial seat and let me drive when it was convenient for him.

When it was time for us to take the lead, I was only too happy to bash in some shambler skulls that got in our way. That part of my life had always been so simple. When had everything else gotten so fucking complicated?

Chapter 14

As the day dragged on, the weather soon got worse, light snow falling between icy gusts of wind slicing across the few exposed parts of my face. One might have figured that with visibility dropping as the conditions worsened, the shamblers would have called it a day, but the opposite was true. The early darkness seemed to trigger their nocturnal roaming behavior—as Red liked to call it—ending with us encountering way more than I felt the lot of us was equipped to handle without using firearms, which would have likely called down several hundreds more on us. So sneaking around and backtracking it was, until even Bucky seemed to have had enough of making me suffer and called for an early night, a good five miles short of where we should have made camp. By then I was tired and miserable enough to stop caring about the emotional malaise my conversation with Red had thrown me into, but I all too soon was reminded of that when it was first watch shift for me again, and I had no additional cause for paranoia than the predators possibly lurking beyond the few feet I could see.

The third time my perimeter round made me cross paths with Hill, I paused, waiting for him to catch up with me. "What's up?" he asked, sounding about as enthusiastic as I felt.

"Got a question for you, if you have a minute."

He chuckled softly as he checked his watch. "Still seventy-two more left. Ask away. Anything beats staring into the darkness."

Considering that a bunch of shamblers could have danced right by us and we wouldn't have seen them, that sounded less like a security hazard than it probably was. I wondered how to approach the topic, but Hill didn't really strike me as someone who would appreciate me pussy-footing around it for long. "It's about something Richards said to me earlier today." I cast him a sidelong glance, waiting for some reaction that would indicate that I was right in guessing that Red had made sure to get me alone, but Hill gave me nothing except for a brief shudder when the wind hurled yet more sleet in our faces. "He said that, back in the spring when we popped up on the radar, everyone got very excited about me still being alive."

I'd expected to have to explain in more detail, but Hill's low laughter spared me that. "Ah, I see. He tried to butter you up with that tale about you being our savior, or something like that?"

I couldn't hold back a snort. "More like, guilt-trip me. But yes, that."

"And now you want me to tell you that he was bullshitting you? Because I'm so much more trustworthy than the brass," he surmised. I paused and looked away, pretending to peer into the darkness, but there was nothing to see.

"So far, you haven't lied to me."

"Got no cause whatsoever to," Hill responded, faintly amused. "Tell you what, girl, I'm the wrong one to ask about that. Haven't needed a savior myself in over fifteen years, and that's not going to change any time soon."

"But you were there," I insisted, biting my lip as I hoped I wasn't making a fool of myself. "I'm terrible with names but a lot better with faces. I think I remember you from that damn intersection, when I went with Miller and what remained of his guys while the rest of the scientists went with Hamilton and the lot of you."

"Good catch," he admitted. "Ever second-guessed that decision?"

I hesitated, but then shook my head. It was only fair that I gave a little myself. "No. I'm aware that everyone thinks I should, but I haven't."

"Good." When he saw the surprise on my face, he snorted. "If you doom yourself, you should do it with conviction and without looking back. Yeah, I was there. I was at that factory as well, and before that, I would have been part of the group to bring you up to Raynor's fortress. What's the part that has your panties all in a twist? Why none of us is planning on going against our orders and taking any perceived or real misgivings out on you now?"

"Honestly, yes, but that's not what I was wondering about. Just checking how much bullshit Richards is trying to feed me."

Hill kicked at some rocks in our way, the smaller ones not even skipping as they landed in the thickening blanket of snow on the ground. "Was there some excitement about them finding you again? Yes, but the LT likely exaggerated that in favor of, how did you put it? Guilt-tripping you. We'd lost so many smart people by then that anyone popping back up on the radar was good news, but what's all that to grunts like us? Just more work to either guard or play fetch. The part he likely left out was that who else was still living and breathing caused way more of a stir. After running the show for over seven months, Hamilton had been sure there wouldn't be a contender for top dog around anymore who'd be able to go toe to toe with him. And not only did your husband survive, but also his two favorite attack dogs, and a whole bunch of other very capable people. How to approach them was what held up command before they settled on sending us out to meet you all head-on. Raynor wanted you, and from what I hear, some of the brass was ready to extend a really sweet deal to the rest of your people to immediately double our strike team capabilities. Strangely enough, it was a kill order that we got the day we set up shop in that factory. So either some messages had gotten mixed up, or..."

He trailed off there, giving me a bright grin. I could easily fill in the blanks.

"Or someone expected to meet too much opposition to be able to fulfill their orders," I finished for him. Which was exactly what had happened—predictably so.

"We still would have done our best to keep you alive," he offered, as if in afterthought. "But not because they thought you were their savior."

The heavy layers of my gear weren't enough to stave off the chills that statement sent down my spine. "So what changed? Because if I'm honest, I'm only moderately concerned that one of you might shiv me as I take a dump, but that's about it."

Hill gave me a look that told me I should already know the answer. "You kicked our asses, that's what. The brass might be so very fond of all those fancy words, but the grunts only care about one thing."

"Getting fed?"

That got me a loud laugh. Something rustled in the bushes, making us both tense and wait for it to come hurling at us, but it must have been some small animal, scurrying off.

"That, too," Hill said. "Two things then. Showing strength is always a good shortcut. The likes of Richards and Hamilton would never admit it, but a lot of us gave you props for that stunt you successfully pulled. Or Miller pulled and you did a good job pretending like it was you, who cares. Not everyone was on board with the shit that started up over the summer, least of all kidnapping women but also slaughtering the lot of you scavengers on sight, without even offering you a chance to join us. And while many might hate your guts because your crusade got friends of theirs killed, it was the type of show of strength that also gets you some admiration, like an enemy that you know is worth fighting, and maybe even losing to. You were the antithesis to everything, good same as bad. That's why we've had a small problem with deserters since the summer, and also why Wilkes over at his Silo has his hands full with extra mouths to feed. He might not want that job, but he's shown that he's more of a mediator than contender. After getting their teeth kicked in, some people like to be cautious and wait out the storm until it blows over." He paused, then asked, "Want some advice?"

"Sure, hit me with it." I was certain I wouldn't like what he was about to tell me, but it wasn't like I could back down now.

"Stop being such a judgmental bitch, and things will blow over."

Yup, I'd been right with my assessment, but that didn't mean Hill didn't surprise me there. "Judgmental like what? You really need to be specific there."

He chuckled under his breath. "Ain't that the truth. All of it, or as much as you can manage. Could every single one of us be holding a general, and more recently, personal grudge against you? Hell, yes, but that doesn't mean all of us are, generally and personally, out to get you, or turn into murdering, lying, raping bastards. You are burning more bridges with your behavior right now than when you led your misfits to Colorado. Just let it go. Water under the bridge, can't change what has already happened. You're stuck with us, and we're stuck with you. Not two sides, two opposing forces and ideology, but all of us, as in people. Start dealing with what happened and how people are treating you rather than resenting what may or may not have happened. You don't have to like us, and we sure as hell won't easily like you. You probably won't have to deal with any of us ever again once this is over. But until then, you don't have a choice, so make the best of it."

"Gee, that sounds cheerful," I grumbled when nothing else came to mind. Hill seemed mighty proud of himself and the blow he must've known he'd just delivered, but at least he didn't jeer in my face. Maybe there was some good advice in there. Maybe not.

"Just a thought," he proposed.

We trudged on through the snow that was falling heavier now without a sign that it would let up soon. It was a good place to end this travesty of a conversation, but as I had him talking with his heart on his sleeve, I might as well get a smidgen more insight before my prejudiced bitch behavior had a chance to burn that bridge for good.

"I've been wondering for a while now..." I started, trailing off when words failed me.

"It's too cold for me to whip my dick out, if that's why you're hedging. You'll have to contain your curiosity until much later."

That remark, as expected, made me laugh. "No, thanks. Absolutely no curiosity there. What do you and your people think of how this all started? I mean, you all know about Alders and his eco warrior would-be terrorists."

Hill gave a condescending huff. "Heard? Yes. Believe? Not a chance."

Another surprise. "But we all know that the sugar's contaminated, and even after almost wiping us off the face of the earth, Alders continued fucking with us, giving Taggard that tweaked version of the serum that would slowly turn everyone into zombies."

"And? You yourself should know best that a single person can wreak a lot of havoc. Doesn't mean they started the apocalypse."

"So at least that part is true?" I just had to get confirmation. "That Alders managed to somehow infiltrate your illustrious organization and work on eroding the very pillars of your foundation?"

I got another laugh for that, if toned-down enough not to carry very far. That one scare had been enough. "Not saying he's single-handedly responsible for all the shit that's happened, but we lost a good thousand people to that. And it was effective in stirring up enough shit to bring you down on us, no sense denying that. You know he's a scapegoat. Both of them were. And Hamilton got you to take them out for him within a single day to tie everything up with a neat, tidy bow. Now there's no one left to prove otherwise. Convenient, wouldn't you say?"

And it was that last comment, after the jeering that I deserved, that made me pause.

"You don't believe it," I stressed, maybe needlessly.

Hill shrugged. "It's all the same to me, really. I'm just a grunt. What do I care? What does anyone else care about my opinion? Maybe you should take a page from that book as well. I'm sure someone way higher up than me—and your personal friend Hamilton—knows, and knows how to pull the strings." He grinned. "Or maybe I'm just a dumb fuck who likes to amuse himself with conspiracy theories. Who knows? Get back to your watch. Besides, why are you even that paranoid? Sure, you stirred up some shit, but you couldn't have killed more than five, maybe seven people on our base. We lose more while cleaning weapons in a good week."

I was about to turn away and do what he'd told me to—get back to perimeter watch—but halted. Yet when I looked back, Hill's silhouette was already disappearing into the dark of night. What the fuck had that been about?

I was still mulling that over by the time I reached the other side of my sector, finding Nate waiting for me, thermos in hand. I accepted it wordlessly but oh, so very grateful to have some hot liquid to help thaw me, or at least make my shift a little easier. For once, I was almost happy that the weather made it impossible to read the look on my face, and maybe the residual tension in my shoulders as well. It was fucking cold, so of course I was miserable, no surprise there. And by the time my shift was over, I was too numb to give a shit about Hill's misguided comments anymore. Some hot chow, then more shivering in my sleeping bag until sleep finally overwhelmed me.

So far, France really wasn't shaping up to become my new favorite place on earth.

Chapter 15

I t was still snowing when I woke up again, but now it was less of a white hell and more winter wonderland out there, the world cast in a thick layer of fluff. After a little detour west, we continued on our southeast path, now twice as treacherous with the ground hidden by snow and slippery with ice. That we didn't end up with a slew of broken bones before noon was pure dumb luck. Even my lighter pack was soon perilously heavy, and when I went down the third time and landed on my ass hard enough to bruise, I didn't really feel like getting up again. Nate didn't leave me that option, grabbing my wrist and dragging me back onto my feet, but that didn't help much. The day didn't get much better after that.

The only thing that brightened my mood—if one could call it that—was the fact that no one singled me out, neither for altercations nor talks that left my skin crawling. What was going on between us was a very long shot from camaraderie, but at least no one was out to ambush the other party. That had to count for something.

One more night of cold and snow, and another day that made me wonder if it had been for the best that I'd made it out of the hell of that operating room. My entire world seemed to consist of cold, with harsh breaks of yet more cold. I dreaded having to step out behind a tree not because of the possible embarrassment, but because that required me to take off my gloves and pull down my pants, exposing way too much of my body to the elements. And it wasn't like I wasn't wearing enough layers—underneath it all, my skin was clammy, my underthings sticking to me like the sweaty rags they were turning into. My scars felt stiffer every day, particularly the nightmare landscape that had once been my left thigh, and what remained of my toes and fingers. Fingers mostly as I hadn't pulled off my boots since back on the ship. I would have killed to spend just one hour in a cozy, warm room, but sadly, nobody gave me that choice. At least I was too numb to give a shit about what Red and Hill had told me. Screw them. Screw all of them, trying to fuck with my mind. I knew what I'd done—the good and the bad. Nothing was going to change that.

The cold front passed, bringing more fog, but compared to the icy sleet that was downright balmy. We passed two more villages but had to stay clear of them, their overrun state obvious from over a mile out. We were lucky when a bridge that we had to cross was still intact, if needing an hour of cleanup to get across the barricades. It got a little better as we went on, a few rays of sunshine breaking through the clouds. This wasn't so bad, now, was it?

I could tell something was up when Red took our two teams off the rotation, sending a few of the fastest runners ahead instead. I could see a town to the south but that didn't look very menacing. Besides that, it was flat land with some trees clustered together here and there, car wrecks peacefully rusting in the white-speckled, mostly brown countryside. A signpost nearby proclaimed that the towns in the other directions were even further away, so there shouldn't have been much cause for alarm.

When Wu and Rodriguez returned, both out of breath but not looking scared, I figured we'd soon find out what was going on. Shit, but I hated being in the dark.

"Road looks clear," Rodriguez explained after she'd managed to stop panting. "The gate's a bust, but electricity is out so we can easily scale the wall. Munez and Davis are checking the grounds inside. Should be clear; they haven't sent up a flare yet."

"Or something ate their faces," Wu supplied, grinning. "Doubt it, though. Unless there's a surprise waiting for us inside."

"I sure hope there is," Bucky drawled as he had us head in the direction the others had just returned from. Nate didn't look particularly happy about not knowing any more than I did, but for once didn't pull Red back. I figured if this was important, they'd sooner or later tell us. Hopefully.

Maybe two miles later, we hit a winding cobblestone path, barely broad enough for two cars to pass, splitting from the main road that we'd been following since after the bridge. There were no signs, but the underbrush looked overgrown enough to make me guess that whoever had planted the hedges there had valued their privacy.

The gate Rodriguez had referred to came into sight soon after, barred with heavy, criss-crossed struts over the already sturdy-looking, cast-iron fence. Davis was standing on the stone wall that started on both sides of the gate, Munez below him, his eyes roaming over the vegetation outside of the wall just as Davis did the same for inside.

Bucky had barely stopped when Nate got up in his face, not quite confrontational, but a long shot from calm. "Are you finally going to stop bullshitting us and tell us what we're here for? We can't find anything that we don't know we're looking for."

Hamilton's disdainful gaze said quite plainly that he thought that was very well still an option, but he surprised me by giving a different answer. "We're here looking for a safe. It's likely located in one of the offices in the main building. But to get there, we'll have to clear the grounds first."

Nate took that without blinking, just as if he hadn't expected anything else from Bucky. "What kind of opposition are we expecting? This doesn't really look like a place that was teeming with people to begin with, and the lack of additional barricades suggests that it wasn't used as a last refuge." I wondered what he thought the reinforced struts at the gate were, but he was kind of right. In Cabourg, same as at the bridge earlier, there'd been a lot of cars, sand bags, and other heavy materials, now rotting in the desolate landscape, to still work as an actual hindrance. Someone had made sure the gate was impossible to bust through with anything short of a tank, but that was it.

Rather than reply right away, Bucky exchanged his assault rifle for a shotgun. That wasn't buckshot he carried as extra ammo. "Only one way to find out, right? After all, this is a scavenger hunt. We might get to hunt us some scavengers."

Nate had a rather bland look for that pun; the others didn't react. I tried to but couldn't help but scowl. There was some residual grinning going on from Russell and Cole, but they kept it on the down low for once. Red seemed exasperated at best, and, surprise, surprise, it was that which got Hamilton to wise up for once.

"Frankly, we have no fucking clue. We only have a location, that's it."

"That you got from the bank vault?" I asked, just to make sure nobody forgot how smart I was.

Hamilton barely acknowledged my presence with a glance. "Bingo. And yes, we need what's inside that safe. There should have been some guards posted back in the day, but I doubt they felt the need to hold down the fort when everything went to hell. Might just be an easy walk in the park for us."

I didn't seem to be the only one skeptical of that, judging from the amount of grenades I saw people put where they were readily accessible.

"What kind of place was this, anyway?" I asked. "In the middle of nowhere, seventeenth-century architecture, lots of old trees? Looks a bit large for anyone's private residence."

"It's a conservatory," Bucky offered, still feeling talkative. "I hear they specialized in orchids."

"Orchids? As in flowers?" I didn't have to face my incredulity.

Hamilton snorted. "And they send you to college for that? What a waste of everything."

I bared my teeth in a silent sneer at him, but Nate's quick shake of the head got me to shut up. Orchids, really. What could orchids have to do with anything that could possibly be of interest to whoever had sent us on this wild goose chase? And why was the address to this place hidden in a bank vault in the middle of a small town in Normandy?

Gita cleared her throat, drawing my attention to her that way. "It makes sense to hide something you want to keep hidden somewhere no one would think to look," she suggested. "Like keeping your porn stash hidden in your underwear drawer."

I was tempted to ask her how old she thought I was that I'd had anything to hide that wasn't already in digital format, but swallowed that remark. "I'm sure mothers all over the world loved to burst that bubble."

Gita wasn't deterred. "Bad example, maybe, but the principle holds true. Just as you said, who'd think to look for anything worthwhile to survival at a place that's likely full of books and dried flowers? Who knows what's lurking in the cellar?" She suddenly looked vaguely ill. "And botanists have labs, too, right?"

I could tell that Bucky was having the time of his life listening to us speculate, but at my questioning look, he snorted. "Nothing as fancy as that. We're just looking for the next piece we need. That's what we came here for. You want me to spell out your task? Clear the grounds, make sure nobody gets jumped by anything, and within a couple of hours we should be on our way once more. Think you can do that?"

"Easily," I retorted.

He flashed his teeth in a smile. "Then shut your useless trap and get to work. We're burning daylight."

I'd honestly expected more of this. The more I learned about this mission, the less I felt I needed to know. Maybe they really had just wanted a few more grunts along who could hold a gun. I wasn't buying it, but that didn't change our current situation.

I wasn't very enthusiastic about having to scale that wall, but Burns boosted me up before I could protest, and dropping down the other side wasn't that bad, thanks to a heap of leaves that the wind seemed to have blown into that corner. Inside, a sprawling garden scape welcomed us, in clear neglect but lacking most of the signs of destruction that seemed to be everywhere around. The front part, from the gate to the first of the buildings, was easily as large as five football fields. Securing this would take longer than just a few minutes.

"Secure the garden first, then the ground floor inside," Red instructed us, quickly dividing the fire teams among sectors. As before, he would go with Tanner and Gita, leaving me to roam with Burns and Nate. "Once we've established the perimeter, hold your positions. We won't be staying long, and it would be a shame to find the undead hordes waiting for us outside. So be quiet if you can." I was hard-pressed not to yell at him that, sure, after almost a week of running and sneaking my first action would be to shoot at everything to attract maximum attention, but by the time the words were on my tongue, Nate, Burns, and I were the last remaining by the wall, the guys waiting for me to take point. Sighing, I resigned myself to my fate, heading through the overgrown garden for the back of the house.

As much as I'd been happy to squabble with Bucky, paranoia was quick to whisper up my spine, making me jump at every crunch of a leaf from behind me—and up ahead where Cole and Parker were following after Russell. Exhaling slowly, I forced my nerves to calm down. I'd done shit like this so many times, I'd forgotten to count… and that was before we'd set out this spring. Just a routine cleanup, with raccoons and other smaller critters our likely foes. The air smelled fresh and the rime-covered leaves were undisturbed except where members of our team had trodden before, making this scene much more undisturbed than most of our camping sites had been. Just a house with a garden, that was it.

Mansion, really, or maybe villa would have been more accurate. I was sure that my high school had taken up less ground than this building—plus its two outbuildings, or whatever those were—did. And there were still two greenhouses that I could see, with likely more beyond the main structures. "Does anyone actually live in a place like this?"

"I don't think it was anyone's home," Nate interjected as he kept scanning the trees over by the wall. "Workplace, maybe, or other representative place later used for something else. Look at the size of that parking lot. You wouldn't park your Bentley out where rain could leave unseemly smudges all over the glossy paint job."

He had a point there. "So, left greenhouse first?"

"Looks a little large for orchids," Burns, closer to the outbuilding, mused. "But there's too much snow on the roof to see inside."

"We should check it out. Maybe they have zombie orchids. Could be fun." I got no response, which wasn't much of a surprise. "Might also be a good place and time if you want to stage a coup. Just saying."

Nate glanced over to Burns, who, if anything, was amused by my suggestion. "Last year would have been so much more of a pain in the ass if you'd already known how to handle a gun when the shit hit the fan," my dear husband surmised.

"No idea what you're talking about."

"You like to stir up shit when you're frustrated," Nate pointed out, but rather than ignore my suggestion—at least the first part of it—he turned toward the greenhouse. "Let's do this. If it's empty, we should be out in under ten minutes."

"What, the coup?" I asked hopefully.

"The greenhouse," Nate deadpanned. Spoilsport.

I was only too happy to let him take point. My hands might have been steady, but my icy fingers were still acting up. Add to that the adrenaline now freshly flowing in my blood, and I wasn't too sure just how much use I would be with that rifle. That thought alone irked me enough to want to meet some heavy opposition, well aware of the inherent idiocy of said thoughts.

We paused a few yards away from one of the doors to the greenhouse, listening. It was near silent, our presence having scared away what small critters and birds might have been around before. Our boots crunched softly on the gravel, and coming the main building, I heard someone curse softly, but that was it.

I didn't like dead silence. It usually meant there were shamblers around, and considering how sneaky some of them had been in the past, I didn't really like our odds. The greenhouse was one of those elaborate ones that you'd see in a botanical garden, not just a single-story cover for salad. Anything could be lurking in there.

Nate first cleared away what snow and rime covered the glass panes of the door, waiting for something to smack against the other side. When all remained silent, he broke the lock before easing the door open. I'd expected the greenhouse to be warm inside—or, at least warmer than the outside—but somewhere, parts of the ceiling or windows must have been broken because a cool draft met us, carrying only a hint of musty air along. I'd smelled worse in the thicker parts of the forests. The natural decay of plants was enough to mask what else might be rotting inside, making the back of my neck itch. Maybe not my brightest idea to go inside, I had to admit.

Nate went in first, then Burns, with me bringing up the rear. I hesitated, then closed the door behind me. The guys were starting to fan out so I followed, distracted by the crunching of dead leaves under my soles. Despite the cold, it smelled dank and dark inside, like we'd stepped through a portal into a nightmare fantasy landscape.

Burns's guess proved to be surprisingly accurate. Most of the plants inside the building either grew up to the struts that held the glass panes high above our heads, or covered the ground, a lot of them dead since the specially preserved climate inside was a thing of the past as well, as was whoever had been the caretaker. There were no signs of animals inside, not even nests or tufts of fur that hinted of them having found refuge in months past. The light snow cover on the outside cast the interior into shadows, making me the only one who could easily see unaided—what I could actually see, with dying greenery everywhere.

It was too quiet in here, making me antsy. "We could make a break for it, you know?" I proposed. "Just grab the others and hoof it back to the coast. Wait for the ship to pick us up again, and count on the rest to bite it because they're lacking several skilled team members."

Burns snorted, but Nate seemed less enthusiastic about my suggestions. "And you don't think they have a contingency plan for that possibility?"

I could see where he was going with that. "Yeah, but we're all together. We have weapons. And compared to last time, I can fight now."

"I'm sure that the captain has orders to leave us stranded if we're the only ones who make it back." Nate exhaled slowly as he kept studying the palm fronds lightly swaying in the cold air currents. "Besides, I gave my word. As did you, as I have to keep reminding you."

"You don't," I snapped. "And what is an oath worth that's been forced at gunpoint?"

"We're not having this conversation now," Nate bit back, real anger visible in his eyes. "Or ever. Let's secure this building, then get over to the main one. We have a job to do."

Resentment welled up inside of me, hot and impossible to suppress, so I whipped around to stalk in the opposite direction lest I do something that ended with me on the floor, on my ass, and not in a fun way—and found myself face to face with a zombie. Rather, what was left of its face, the left side looking like it had taken the brunt of a shotgun blast, and not one loaded with pellets. The left eye, most of the nose, and parts of the skull were gone, the jaw slightly unhinged. The sheer fact that it had—obviously—been shadowing my movements for a while and only now got ready to pounce told me that it must be a smart one. When I realized that the rags it wore looked like a dress shirt and suit, on a still rather muscular frame, I figured it had likely been a security guard rather than desk jockey.

I knew I had to act—raise my weapon, shout to alarm the others, drop so I wouldn't make a prime target—but I couldn't. My pulse increased, my heart pounding almost painfully fast in my chest... but then it started to slow down, leaving me sluggish and slow rather than alert. It was as if someone had leeched the very adrenaline from my veins—and the fucking shambler, cocking its head to the side as it slowly opened and closed its ruin of a mouth, seemed to feel that instinctively. Crap.

Just as I managed to get my M16 up, it came at me. Not in a running start like I'd expected, but it instead hurled itself into the air, faster and stronger than should have been possible. Its trajectory was a near perfect curve, with me at the landing point. I had a moment of clarity when I realized that all I needed to do was take a step back and start shooting at where I'd previously been standing, but by the time that thought turned into action, the zombie came crashing down on me.

Well, at least the painful yelp that tore itself from my chest would make the others notice that something was wrong.

It was luck more than reflexes that made the M16 and my left arm end up between me and the snapping jaws as the impact made me topple over onto the ground, my pack forcing my body to bend in interesting—but not pleasant—ways. The zombie weighed a shit-ton, making breathing all but impossible as I strained to keep it as far away from me as possible. That only worked for its teeth. It had no problem whatsoever pounding at me, hitting my right side—of course—right next to the protection of my pack several times. My vision went white with agony. Finally, my instincts kicked in, making me push hard, then roll over my left side, hoping to somehow not end up trapped. The shambler tried to keep its grip on my arm and shoulder, but that actually helped me heave myself onto my feet, my lack of height for once helping. That move, of course, brought my head way too close to the zombie's, but nothing I could do about that now.

Leaves rustled as something came rushing toward us. The zombie hesitated, which was all I needed. I hated letting go of my weapon with my right—weaker—hand but this once, not following Nate's advice to punch with my left sounded like a good idea, seeing as the zombie was still gripping that arm. I drove my right fist up into its jaw just as Burns swung his heavy sledgehammer, hitting what was left of the zombie's skull. I felt the impact translate through bone and flesh into my hand, making my fingers explode with pain twice in as many seconds, but I didn't give a shit about that. The zombie went slack for a moment, and a kick to its thigh made it stagger away from me, finally letting go. I quickly stepped back, raising my M16, but Burns already brought his hammer back around, this time aiming for the ruin of what was left of the shambler's face. Bits of bone and gray matter sprayed everywhere. The shambler went down, taking another hit that smashed what remained of its jaw. One final blow, and there wasn't much left above its neck, the thing going still for good.

Panting, I stared down at it, my body still not quite recovered from the shock. Burns kicked the now dead-for-good carcass before he looked at me, a little out of breath himself. "You okay?"

I nodded, although that was as far from the truth as it got. I definitely did not feel okay. Breathing hurt. Just standing still and existing hurt. "Yeah. Just… surprised me. Did you see that pounce?"

"Was hard to miss," Nate offered as he joined us, only passingly glancing at the corpse, his eyes flitting over everything at once. "Question is, how did you?"

What I thought was my remaining kidney was throbbing in too much pain for me to mouth off to him, but I did my best at a flippant response. "I was distracted." No shit. "I thought I saw something moving over there, and must have missed it." That, of course, sent both of them into high alert once more, making me bite the inside of my cheek. So much for me being a competent liar. "It was nothing. Just light playing along some palm fronds weirdly."

Nate still insisted on checking out that corner of the greenhouse. Nothing, except more dead or dying plants. Not even zombie feces. Standing there, looking around, I almost wished something would jump us, just to break the tension. Maybe it was the dusky light created by the layer of snow covering the greenhouse, but the atmosphere was eerie bordering on surreal, and that wasn't something that made me feel comfortable staying here.

"Maybe it snuck in after us," I proposed when, five minutes later, we still hadn't found any sign of habitation except for the corpse remaining on the floor where Burns had felled it.

"Door's still closed," Burns noted. "I doubt it could have eased it open without us hearing it."

"Or feeling the additional draft," Nate added, casting around almost as nervously as I felt. "We still need to check that other wing over there."

I followed him as he set out in the indicated direction. We passed a row of tables—not overturned—covered in neat lines of pots, the dried-up stems of orchids all that was left of the flowers. I doubted I could have walked past those tables ten times without disturbing them. Where had that damn shambler come from?

We reached the very end of the wing where there was a shallow pool let into the tiled floor, murky with algae and decayed plant matter. Still, neither of us was stupid enough to get too close, lest something reach out to draw us under the surface. Leaves crunching behind us, making all of us jerk around, but it was just a palm frond dropping to the ground, the dead husks of its neighbors rustling softly.

"Let's get out of here. We don't need a repeat performance of that," Nate murmured, his voice soft, as if the thought of disturbing the air around us further was bordering on sacrilegious.

I wasn't sure what exactly he was referring to—me freezing up, us getting attacked by a circus freak-level undead, or collectively jumping at shadows—but far be it from me to protest. We left the body back by the entrance, only making sure to bar the door we'd come in through after we exited. Relief flooded me as the wan sunlight outside greeted us. I let out a breath I felt I had been holding forever. Nate took the lead while Burns signaled me that he would bring up the rear. None of the other teams were visible in the garden, but it only took us about a minute to cross footprints in the grass besides the gravel path that lead toward the main building.

We briefly paused at the edge of the parking lot. Five cars and a small tractor were rusting away, haphazardly placed across the open space. They looked like ordinary cars, no reinforcements to weather the apocalypse, nor higher-priced models that might have hinted at belonging to someone important. They could have been sitting in any random supermarket parking lot as well—likely having belonged to employees that had gotten too sick to drive themselves home, or preferred to catch a ride with friends not to be caught out there alone in the ever-escalating chaos. Because we were already here, we briefly checked for habitation, coming up blank. I couldn't say why, but the light, airy scarf I saw wrapped around a headrest through a hazed-over window made me feel weirdly melancholic. It all looked so normal, but that wasn't the "normal" I was used to any longer. Normal was getting jumped by the undead, not keeping fancy accessories in your car.

"Main buildings next?" I suggested when the somber mood stretching between us got beyond uncomfortable. Nate inclined his head, taking point once more.

As we neared the main entrance of the building closest to us, elevated at the top of a sprawling set of stairs, I could just see Davis standing outside the lower level side entrance, watching us as much as the sprawling gardens around us. Nate gave him a casual nod before heading for the stairs, the three sets of footprints in the snow covering them letting us know we weren't the first. The door—gate, really—at the top remained open yet unguarded, Nate signaling us to halt while he did a preliminary check before we ventured inside.

The room we entered was huge, easily taking up the entire width of the building. Furniture was scarce, and most of that had been covered in white sheets that were billowing in the breeze, same as what remained of the curtains, most still attached to their rods. There was dirt on the floor, muddy bootprints and the odd leaf, but most looked so recent that it must have come from the team that had entered before us. Our steps echoed where not dampened by carpet, making a different kind of unease creep up my spine. Maybe it was due to the soldiers' weird reactions to looting that small village, but I felt incredibly unwelcome here. Unwelcome, and very out of place.

My radio crackled as Munez's voice came on, reporting in that the gardens and ground floor were secured. Bucky answered, and I could hear him call out from the next room over where another massive staircase sat. As we drew closer, several of the others came up from the lower floor, more than one pair of eyes casting around restlessly. So it wasn't just me who was weirded out. I waited for Nate to report the incident with the zombie, but except for looking tense as hell, he didn't give a sign that anything was wrong. That Burns and I both had zombie head shrapnel bits clinging to us caused less of a stir than I'd expected, but then I realized that there were a few heaps of rags near the central stairwell the first team had used to enter the building. Just your garden variety zombies, nothing alarming about that. The thought was strangely comforting.

Red had the five of us secure the level while the others cleared the floors above, not suspicious in the least. I did my best to remain alert, but my focus kept slipping. Maybe I was burning too much energy again, I told myself, but now was not the time to stock up on some fat and protein. At least the unease and rampant paranoia ceased, ebbing away into dull comfort, but that only made me feel weirder. Going toe to toe with that shambler had left me twitchy as hell, so at least that lizard part of my brain was online and functioning once more, no further freezing incidents. My right hand kept twinging with every heartbeat, but I did my best to ignore that as I switched the assault rifle for my axes. Burns was giving me a few cautious looks whenever he thought I didn't notice, but Nate seemed entirely unconcerned.

Maybe I was just overreacting.

Yeah, right. Because freezing up in the middle of an attack was what had kept me alive until now.

"All clear," Red reported over the radio. "Keep securing the main entrance and lower side gate. I'm sending Murdock, Aimes, and Wu down as reinforcements." A brief pause, as if he was debating with someone while switching his mic off. Then, "Lewis, come up here. Second floor, third door down the right corridor. You can't miss it."

Now Nate did send me a somewhat concerned glance, one I ignored as I made for the stairs. Anything to give my mind something to focus on that it wouldn't slip away from, or so I hoped. None of the others made a move to follow me, although Gita seemed anxious.

Hell, that made two of us, or would have, if my screwed-up mind had been capable of that. If this was a side-effect of the serum, I really didn't much care for it.

I passed the three soldiers on their way down, then followed the stairs up to the top level. Rodriguez and Davis were standing guard, motioning me in the direction Red had indicated. There was some minimal damage up here, a few overturned and broken pieces of furniture told of a fight—or an overzealous former security guy having some anger management issues. Only one door in the corridor was open, leading into a large room that was dominated by a huge mahogany desk. Fancy bookshelves lined the walls, except for the picture window opening into the garden. What marred the majestic office air were the soldiers milling around with their muddy boots and streaks of gore across their gear. Bucky and Red were busy leafing through stacks of papers, everything they deemed inconsequential ending up on the floor. Next to them, a section of a shelf had been removed, revealing a huge safe built into the wall behind—apparently the origin of the papers they were perusing.

I had a distinct feeling that we'd arrived at the address they'd retrieved from the bank at Cabourg.

Question was, what were they searching for?

"Got it!" Cole let out a whoop from where he was standing, hunched over a keyboard, at the desk, ignoring the racket the portable generator was making that had been plugged into the computer—and presumably, his laptop as well that I hadn't seen him use before. I hadn't even known they were lugging either around with them.

Bucky turned around, a slight grin crossing his face. "The files?"

"Uh, I got it to boot up," Cole amended.

Bucky grumbled something hostile under his breath but turned back to throwing papers this way and that. Red briefly scowled at him before he noticed me, idling just inside the door. Signaling me over, he nodded at a pile of papers set to the side, next to an antique-looking globe inside the bookshelf. "Here, look through that."

I glanced at the stack. At least it was in English, some kind of report. "Might help if you tell me what I'm looking for."

Hamilton snorted but at least held his tongue. Irritation crossed Red's features, and for once I was sure I wasn't the source of that. "Anything you recognize," he finally offered after weighing his words for way too long. "You'll know when you see it."

It was easier to just ignore exactly how stupid this entire situation was so I let it slide, instead dropping my axes on the shelf and grabbing a chunk off the top of the stack. Senseless, really. How could I possibly find anything if I had not the faintest clue—

My eyes snagged on a three-letter abbreviation, recurring, with numbers behind it. XLC. The damn virus. Or serum, more likely. I'd long forgotten what numbers it had been on those vials I got out of cold storage in the hot lab to destroy, with a torn glove, while Nate had likely been kicking the shit out of the decontamination shower walls I'd locked him in. Or the numbers Alders had been ranting about, of the original serum strains and the weaponized virus it had later been turned into. But I was a hundred percent certain that it had been two-digit numbers, all of them, with variations of them in the appendix. All these had three, some even four digits.

Looking at the very top of the page, I quickly scanned the text, but it was next to useless gibberish. I checked the next few where yet more version numbers were listed, but this barely held up for an inventory, no explanations whatsoever.

"Why does someone in a super fancy office in an orchid conservatory have documentation about the serum project?" I asked, glancing at Red and Bucky but also keeping an eye on reaction from the others. No one looked surprised, confirming that really, we were the only ones not knowing what this was all about. Maybe another late-night talk with Hill would help with that. From the bland stare I got from Bucky, I knew he wouldn't be the source of information.

Red glanced at the papers in my hands. "What did you find?"

"Nonsense," I offered, shoving the stack at him. "It's all nonsense."

"Yeah, that's what science shit looks like to the rest of us," Cole grumbled from where he was bashing away on his laptop, obviously frustrated.

"Usually. Helps to have a degree or two," I quipped in his direction, but turned serious at Red's frown. "Is it possible that this is written in some kind of code? Because this looks like an email that wants to sell me penis enhancement pills, in particularly bad grammar."

I heard Rodriguez snicker in the background—maybe she was finally warming up to my charms. Red continued to stare at me for another second, then shook his head. "It actually is."

"Trying to sell—" I started, but he cut me off before I could get any further. Really, did no one have a sense of humor left?

"All the printouts are encrypted," he explained. "And it sure as hell doesn't look like the cypher will be in any of these books."

"Basic-level text replacement," Cole chimed in. "If I can get inside this fucking system, find the right files, and run the cypher app on them, we should get the original text."

Red dropped the papers, obviously agreeing, so I didn't bother with the rest of them. Bucky did the same, glaring at the safe one last time before slamming the door shut. "Then why is it that you incompetent asshole are still talking, and not getting the job done?"

"I'm trying," Cole muttered, never taking his eyes off the screen, his fingers flying over the keys. "But it would take me a good ten minutes to explain to you what I'm working with here. Ten minutes I'd rather concentrate on getting in."

Bucky didn't look abashed at his outburst, but also not like he gave a shit that Cole gave as good as he got. For a while, the only sounds in the room came from people carefully shifting from one foot to the other, and the incessant clicking of the keyboard.

Someone cleared their throat behind us. When I turned, I found Gita hesitating by the door, looking both eager and terribly apprehensive. Before Hamilton or Red could bark at her, I asked, "What's up?"

"Maybe I can help with that," she offered, her eyes dancing from me to the setup at the desk.

Hamilton gave a derisive snort that was usually reserved for me, but Cole paused, glancing at her. "This is a little above writing apps in Java or Objective-C."

Gita beamed a smile at him that was full of derision, but said nothing. Cole hesitated, then motioned her over as he stepped aside, launching into an explanation that sounded about as cohesive as what had been printed on the papers. Gita listened for a few moments, then started spewing gibberish of her own as she usurped the laptop and began typing without missing a beat.

Glancing at Red, I found him returning my gaze with a slightly bemused smile. "It's like listening to little baby birds chirping in their nest, isn't it?" I wisely provided, earning myself a good-natured snort for once.

Seeing as there wasn't anything for me at the moment to do, I dug through the pockets of my pants until I found some pre-packaged jerky, almost spilling a bunch of magazines on the floor in my attempt to get there. Hill laughed at what I guessed was my ammo packrat habit, but cut off when Red gave him an admonishing stare. "Now that the generator's already running, why don't you do something useful and try the radio frequencies again? You said you almost got something in last night?"

Hill dutifully dropped his—enormous, once it hit the ground next to his equally large frame—pack, getting out his equipment. Cole ignored him as Hill dropped it all on the remaining free space of the desk next to the generator and set to work. Watching him scan frequencies was only so interesting as I meditatively chewed my jerky. Everyone else seemed to be content to be inside a room that was, for once, not cold enough that rime covered everything, paying just enough attention not to be caught off-guard should anything undead come barging through the guards outside and into the room.

"What is this about, anyway?" I asked Red while pretending that Hamilton wasn't in the room. I could do that for five more minutes, no biggie. Red ignored me, but I could see a muscle in his cheek jump. "You know, contrary to what some people believe, I'm not stupid. I can put two and two together. Eventually, I'll figure it all out, and then the big reveal won't really be much of a surprise anymore." Still no reaction, but that didn't keep me from prattling on. "We ran into a security guard in the greenhouse outside." Now he did look over, but his lips remained sealed. I beamed a bright smile at him. "Judging from the fact that he was missing half his head but was still moving, I think it's safe to assume that he wasn't a normal shambler. Oh, and he had some freaky jumping action going on." Still nothing. "A guard, at a site that has garbled papers referring to the serum project. Come on, give me something to work with here. Or all you get from me once you decipher those files is a nod that yes, I can read that, but I won't tell you what it really says."

As expected, that got his attention, but also that of the idiot in charge. "You will talk," Hamilton said with the kind of conviction that was begging for a punch in the face.

"I might be lying," I offered rather than the claim that I wouldn't, which would have just given him an opening to explain exactly how he would facilitate his part of the deal. "You have no way of checking if what I tell you is true, unless one of your grunts has unexpected previous life experience. Which I know they don't, or else you wouldn't be stuck with me."

Gita let out a triumphant whoop, she and Cole high-fiving each other, which put a halt on my attempt to weasel more information— or any, really—out of those recalcitrant assholes. "We're in!" she proclaimed, a little out of breath with excitement. "What files do you need decrypted?"

"Well, isn't that the question," I grumbled while Red walked over to them so he could look at the screen. He seemed to have more of a clue than the printouts let on, seeing as it took them all of a minute to find something to be printed—only that the ink in the printer had dried up, nobody had brought a replacement, and there were no other cartridges to be found.

"Copy all that to your laptop and on some external drives for backup," Red ordered, still scanning the screen.

"You know, there's a good chance you're missing out on so many possibilities with that idiotic strategy of yours," I remarked, waiting for Red to bite. He didn't. "I mean, I get it. The bitch had to be put in her place first. But sawing your own arm off just to spite me won't really do you much good." When I still got no reaction, I turned to Hamilton. "Or did you get a gag order? Blink twice, or stare at the left upper corner if you can't confirm it verbally." Bucky's gaze kept boring into mine, not even a single eyelash quivering. "Need me to elaborate? You didn't know that she's a hacker." Well, neither did I, but I didn't need to admit that. "And back when you were all, let's kill 'em all if you don't cooperate, you didn't know that Tanner's one of you. No need to deny that, I saw Richards's reaction when he noticed that he had the three marks across his neck. Trying to execute them would have ended with several casualties for your people. We're in this together, whether you like it, or I like it, or whoever the fuck came up with this plan likes it. Let's pool resources. Exactly what do you have to lose?"·

Sadly—but not surprisingly—my vote for rational thinking went ignored. All Hamilton had for me was one of those sleazy smiles. "Then I wouldn't get to see you squirm all the time with indignation and frustration, and trust me, that's the biggest satisfaction I'll ever get from anything."

I was tempted to snark at him that he really must be needing to get laid, but I was not going there. So I let my silence—relaxed, and as far from indignant and frustrated as I could make it, which likely wasn't working—be my answer.

"Lewis, take a look at this," Red said once Cole was done feeding no less than four flash drives to his laptop. I didn't miss that Gita let something disappear up the sleeve of her jacket, her attention seemingly wandering to the view of the garden but I didn't buy the disinterested act. I absolutely felt like refusing, or at the very least stomping over there like a petulant child, but that would have negated my demonstrated willingness to cooperate, so I was stuck with doing so willingly.

Gita and Cole moved to the side as Red indicated me to park my ass in the desk chair previously pushed to the side. "We have about another thirty minutes until we need to move on," he explained. "See if you can make any sense of anything on here."

I glared at the stupid dainty computer mouse but decided that making a fuss that would cause me to backtrack would be even worse than going straight for the kill and trying to swallow my dignity. Using my teeth, I pulled my gloves off, dropping them next to the keyboard. Yup, using the mouse with a three-fingered hand was about as awful as I'd expected; it worked, scrolling and all, until I forgot that I was missing the fingers that stabilized it, and the first time I made a stronger motion to the side, it went flying off the desk, landing on the papers littering the floor. Someone snickered but I didn't catch who. By the time I was about to heave myself out of the chair—which was painful enough thanks to where the zombie in the greenhouse had pummeled my side—Gita had already picked it up and was putting it back on the mouse pad. Swallowing thickly, I told myself to get a grip and resumed. Random scrolling didn't lead to much so I went for searching the text. Yet when I tried to open the search window with the usual keyboard shortcut, I missed three times—not because I would have needed my left index finger for that which wasn't available anymore, but because I had absolutely no sensation in the fingertip of the middle finger next to it. Well, that was promising. Pretending like nothing had happened, I used the mouse to navigate the menu to accomplish the job, but at the back of my mind my paranoia screamed. Forcing myself to concentrate on the text helped only so much.

"It looks like a proposal for new trial runs," I muttered a few minutes later. "Clearly written by someone who expected the reader to be up to date with the proceedings. There are a lot of references to previous discussions and alternative shit. It's almost like they didn't want anyone not in the know to be able to make any sense of this."

Red ignored my sarcastic remark. "But it is about the serum project?"

"Presumably. You know, a smidgen of context—"

"Not going to happen," Hamilton interjected, not that Red had appeared in the mood to volunteer anything. "Are you done? Because there's no need to waste any more time if you're just uselessly sitting on your ass."

I clicked over to the folder view and checked a few more files, but it was about the same. One contained experiment conditions and ingredient lists, but it wasn't like I could just read that and find some hidden clues in there. Just to annoy Bucky, I tried to spend as much time as I could looking preoccupied—which wasn't hard, as no one was actually paying me any attention—but eventually had to give up. This wasn't like Raleigh Miller's data on that flash drive that Nate had been hogging all through the apocalypse, full of information, carefully vetted, set up to be read by someone else. This looked more like a backup data dump, only to be later checked on for one specific detail or another by someone who was very familiar with the overall concept.

As soon as I pushed away from the desk, Bucky ordered the others to pack up so we could get going. I narrowly avoided getting plowed over as the room exploded into activity. After grabbing my pack where I'd left it by the shelf, I pulled on my gloves and retrieved my weapons, without a further word slinking outside to join Nate and the others downstairs. Gita was still busy filling them in, adding a lot more details that, even with her explanations, still made no sense to me. I shook my head at Nate's questioning look in my direction. Nothing new, except shit he already knew himself.

I fully expected that Red would keep us in the dark about where we were headed next, yet once we were all assembled at the foot of the central staircase, he turned to us at large. "We're heading south next, toward Ajou." I remembered that this was the name of the town Gita had found spelled out all over Cabourg as the place for the resistance to meet. "Hill's still getting a repeating message in several languages on one of the frequencies. We have no clue if we will find anyone alive there, but they need to have some kind of setup to power their radio station, so that likely means a secure shelter at the very least. Depending on what we find there, we will decide on how to proceed. We shouldn't meet with much more opposition than before until we get there, but try to conserve your energy. The next leg of the journey after that won't be quite such a walk in the park."

The way his gaze lingered on me, I knew he was waiting for me to ask about details—or where, at all, we were ultimately headed—but I kept my trap shut. This was getting old—and if they didn't want my input, why bother? Yet until we were back outside the wall, and even for the next two hours of marching, I couldn't help but glance over my shoulder repeatedly. Of course that could have been a fluke— one security guard, certainly a beefcake before he turned, getting the jump on me. I sure wasn't in the best shape of my life, and Burns had taken care of the issue quickly enough. But it hadn't been the first zombie I'd encountered after not dying on that operating table, or even the fiftieth. Something about this was very, very wrong, and if I'd learned anything in the past year, it was that consequences always came back to bite me.

Chapter 16

S omething was indeed very, very wrong, but not with anything lurking in the shadows. I was barely lucid from exhaustion by the time we shacked up in a small farm house and adjacent barn, and expecting me to actually stand guard was an idiotic undertaking. For once, Nate didn't shadow me as Red seemed to have him tied up with yet another important meeting I wasn't a part of, and by the time he came to relieve me, I only nodded at him in passing as I dragged my sorry ass over to the house to force some chow into my body so I could curl up in my sleeping bag. I was dozing off as soon as I had zipped it up to my chin, trying to get comfortable—yet instead of actually falling asleep, my body froze. It wasn't exactly like with the zombie attack—looking back, that had felt more like a stalling engine—and only took me one sluggish minute to work out what was going on: my body had reverted to falling into a coma rather than real sleep, like at the very beginning of this damn mission. Panic started clawing at my mind, powerful enough that my pulse should have skyrocketed—but it didn't reach beyond my racing thoughts, and even those disappeared like dandelion seeds ripped from the flower's stem in a storm, every few seconds. It felt as if I was locked inside a meat suit, with a heavy damper on my brain on top of not having control of my body. Fucking hell. Add to that more than just a dash of delirium—that I barely recognized as such—and I would have been tempted to go for my Beretta to put an end to this had I been able to move, or even blink.

Burns and Tanner were sitting closest to me, and when Burns remarked that I'd been really quick to fall asleep tonight, looking over his shoulder to me as he said it, my hopes went up that he'd realize what was going on with me. Yet I was barely able to blink, let alone move or croak out something, simple breathing a Herculean task. Tanner muttered something I didn't get, making Burns laugh and glance back once more, as if to make sure I hadn't caught it. Our gazes crossed and he winked, as if to make the fact that I had presumably caught Tanner's derogatory reply our secret, but he was facing forward by the time I managed to close my eyes a second time. Damnit!

More chatting, more soft laughter, until Burns suddenly went quiet. I managed to pry my eyes open, but it took me forever. He was looking my way, only now with a frown creasing his forehead. "You doing all right there, Lewis?" I tried to blink, but even that didn't work anymore. My breaths evened out, turning shallow enough that the edge of my vision blurred, then went dark. It was hard to focus. It was hard to keep breathing. It…

"Bree?" Burns, now coming from much closer. A large hand enveloping my shoulder, shaking me softly, then not so softly. The motion got my head to snap to the side, my eyes flying wide open and remaining that way. Burns leaned over me, his gaze skipping over my face until it landed on my eyes. "Shit," he muttered, tearing off the glove of his free hand so he could check my temperature on my forehead. As soon as his skin came in contact with mine, he shied back, then checked more thoroughly, his hand almost ice cold against my skin. "You're burning up."

Tanner's head appeared next to mine. He looked as concerned as Burns sounded. "She's running a fever?"

"Not just that, I think." He leaned closer, snapping his fingers right next to my ear. I wasn't sure what that should have accomplished but it seemed to make sense to him. "Girl, wake up," he said, shaking me a little more. I tried to tell him to stop, but only got as far as opening my mouth. Nothing came out.

Letting go, Burns looked around, thinking for a second. "Gita, your watch shift is up next, right? Good. Go fetch Miller. Tell him to hurry. Make sure you're easily heard when you explain, loudly, that you changed your mind and want to trade watch with him. Now, go."

He then went back to trying to rouse me, but to no avail. I managed to keep myself from slipping further so I could at least retain my ability to think and handle what sensory input my useless body managed to receive, but that was about the extent of it. Nate dropped to one knee beside me a few minutes later, his eyes skipping from Burns to me. "She's unresponsive?" he guessed even before he checked my temperature.

"I think she's right in there, but she can't move," Burns explained.

"Shit," Nate muttered, perfectly in agreement with me for once. After confirming that I was hot as a pizza oven, his eyes skipped over my entire body, as if he'd suddenly gotten X-ray vision and could see through the sleeping bag and my gear. He and Burns looked at each other without exchanging words. When Burns didn't bring up anything, Nate exhaled slowly, coming to a decision. "Tanner, go fetch Parker and Richards. Don't tell them what's going on. For now, we're keeping this on the down-low. The last thing we need is Hamilton getting nosy. If we can keep this quiet and between as few outside people as possible, the better. I know you can bullshit your way through this."

Tanner cleared his throat. "Easy, seeing as I have no fucking clue what's going on." He paused, likely looking my way. I couldn't tell, he was standing too far away. "I'll be right back. Gimme five."

Nate looked after him for a moment, then his gaze dropped to my face. "Don't worry. We got this."

Worry wasn't exactly what was tightening around my heart like an iron fist. Worry was wondering whether I'd get hot tea in the morning, or whether a sudden incursion of shamblers would force us to break camp before anyone could get tea started. This? This was way beyond that. The fact that my body didn't respond to the abject horror that I was feeling made it so much worse. The few times I'd fallen into this state on the destroyer hadn't been that bad, more like an absence of top-level consciousness while some of my senses had still been working, with my mind tuned down to basic function. This now? This felt exactly like it had been on that operating table, only that my mind was sluggish rather than focused on all that pain. And more pain. And still more…

I realized that I was losing myself in chasing that memory, but it was hard to focus on anything else instead. Nate and Burns were talking in hushed tones, but it was all just noise to me. Trying to take stock of my body was definitely the wrong thing to do as it seemed like the fast-track to crazy town.

Silence fell as Tanner returned, Red and Parker in tow. Parker was muttering under his breath about needing sleep or else, but shut up as soon as he saw me lying there. "Ah, hell, no," he muttered. "I'm not getting close enough to that so it can chew my face off."

It was a token of how concerned all of them were that nobody laughed at his assessment. It took me a moment to realize that he thought they'd called him in to verify that I was dead.

"She's just paralyzed," Nate explained. "Lucid, at least to a point, but we can't rouse her completely. I think she was about to fall asleep when her body shut down. And she's running a high fever."

Red hunkered down next to me but didn't make a move to verify that last bit. "Since when?"

"No clue," Nate admitted. "I didn't know anything was wrong until they got me from my watch shift. She did hers without mentioning anything."

Burns grunted. "She was sluggish this afternoon, when that undead fucker came for us in the greenhouse. I thought she was just clumsy because, you know. Probably wasn't."

Nate grimaced but nodded reluctantly. "She's been quiet since we left that conservatory. That's not her usual MO."

Oh, the nice things people say about you when you can't defend yourself.

Parker listened to it all, then took a knee opposite Red and reached for my forehead, then checked the lymph nodes at the side of my neck. My eyes and throat were next, twice as unnerving as usual as I couldn't even squint against the glare of the flashlight. "Any new injuries? Not just superficial cuts. It would have to be something deep enough to reach a blood vessel for her to get an infection from it. Or some serious deep tissue bruising perhaps? Any broken bones?"

Nate's eyes had been watching my face carefully while the medic assessed me, but at that they zoomed up to Parker's. "Do I look like I'm psychic?"

He got a flat stare back for that. "You're her husband."

"But not her keeper. What's that got to do with anything?"

I was sure I heard someone snicker in the background—Burns, probably—and Parker did some bona fide squirming as he explained. "If anyone's seen her naked, that would be you. When, you know…"

I wouldn't have put it past Nate to make him finish that sentence, but his sigh of exasperation let me know that he was worried for real rather than just annoyed. "Really? When exactly would we have been getting it on when we're all practically living on top of each other, it's freezing cold even when the sun is out, oh, and let's not forget that the entire continent is teeming with the undead. And even if we didn't give a shit about all that, I sure as hell wouldn't let her strip naked if all we needed was to peel away the layers from a very limited area." He chuckled at Parker's abashed look. "You're just as bad as she is, sometimes."

I would have snorted if my throat would have let me.

Nate's gaze dropped to my eyes. The hint of a smile crossed his features as he looked back up to Red. "She's definitely lucid."

"How can you tell?" Red peered into my face, puzzled.

"Because that was the look in her eyes that she gets when she's ribbing me." He focused on Parker. "Give her something to break the coma's lock on her. Then you can ask her yourself."

Red nodded, but Parker was still hesitating. "You know what happens if I pump her full of adrenaline. I can't just put her under again once she's back in control of her body. It looks like she has an infection, and that means I'll have to cut into her. You don't want her fully responsive for that."

Anything was better than this hell. I sure wasn't the only one thinking that, as before I could even try to relate that thought to Nate, he was already voicing it. "Without knowing where the infection might be coming from, it's not like you have any choice. Besides, you don't get it. You've never been in that state. I have. Get that adrenaline shot. I'll take full responsibility."

"Do it," Red affirmed, drawing a hostile stare from Nate for that.

I would have laughed, but just then Parker rammed a needle into the side of my neck, and ten increasingly less sluggish heartbeats later, I sat up with a loud gasp, first feeling alive, then like my heart was coming right out of my chest.

"Easy there," Parker crooned, pushing at my shoulder, but I was so not going to lie back down.

"Lie down," Nate insisted, a lot less gentle than Parker as he shoved my other shoulder backward. Looked like I was going to lie back down after all. My pulse was still galloping as I stared at the ceiling above me, the dancing shadows of the fire nearby twisting my mind this way and that. Or maybe that was the adrenaline continuing to mess with me.

"What the—" I panted, barely finding the energy to speak. Roused I might be, but not quite over that shit.

Before I could do more, Nate was leaning in, making it impossible for Parker to do the same. "You heard all that? Just nod, that's quicker." I gave a light jerk with my head. "Good. Your take on that? Falling into that half-coma can be a sign of exhaustion as well, but today wasn't that bad, and you've been eating enough. Enough extra to put on some weight. Do you agree with me on that?"

I nodded.

"Any injuries you're aware of?"

That was much harder to answer, and it took me a good ten seconds to order the thought fragments zipping through my mind to form a coherent sentence. "I'm a little banged up, but nothing serious." But that wasn't true. Breathing out slowly—which really was a series of shallow pants—I did my best to steel myself. "My left middle finger's acting up. I think Raynor was a little too optimistic about just clipping off the very top and removing the nail."

Nate glanced at Parker, but the medic shook his head. "Might become an issue if it turns color, but not enough to cause a fever that high. With the serum working full-strength for weeks, her entire hand would have had to rot away to cause sepsis on a level to kickstart a systemic response."

And right there we had the likely cause. Talking was hard enough that I waited for them to figure it out. They were smart guys. Eventually, they would.

Red was the one to go for it first. "You think she still has a latent infection from before?"

Parker shrugged but didn't look doubtful at all. "It makes the most sense."

"But why now?" Nate interjected. "I've spent the better part of a week cleaning her wounds until not a single one was swollen or warm, with no pus leaking out for more than a day."

"Something deeper," I croaked out, drawing their attention back to me. Easily ignored I wouldn't be, even though I could so have done without all this. "Raynor said she expected my immune system to take care of it all. Must have missed something. Had weeks to fester and spread." And my, wasn't that a lovely thought. Suddenly, lying still was getting increasingly harder, my fingers itching to grab the next available knife and cut into myself until I could get it all out!

Nate's fingers wrapped around my left hand, partly hidden from view by how our bodies were aligned toward each other, and squeezed. It wasn't much—and made me all the more aware that I wasn't feeling part of my middle finger anymore—but it helped a lot to center and calm me down. Breathe. I just needed to breathe, and it would be all right.

"Anything still sore?" Parker asked, rather unhelpfully. "If it's infected enough to cause fever, you should be feeling it, at least as a diffuse ache."

I stared at him as if he'd gone mad. "Want to ask me the scale question?" He frowned, so I explained. "On a scale from one to ten, how much I hurt? Twenty, on a good day. Thirty, in the mornings. After an entire day of running, hiding, and fighting? Fifty going on infinity. But if I had to take a guess, somewhere on my right side, likely toward the back. That's where the worst of the damage was." I swallowed thickly. "Maybe my left thigh, but while that's flaring up several times a day, it's not a constant, diffuse ache, as you so succinctly put it."

Red snorted while Parker was hard-pressed to decide between being pissed off or just plain taken aback. Annoyed with their continuing inaction, I started peeling myself first out of the sleeping bag, then the layers on my upper body until I was in just the thick thermal that I could push up to my shoulders as I hunched over. "Take your pick."

Parker needed exactly five seconds and two prods to make me howl with agony. Bingo. "There's some light subcutaneous bruising," he noted as he squinted at my skin. I wondered if bruises could even show with all the scar tissue present around there. He had me lie back and prodded the side of my abdomen next. If before it had been bad, this was so much worse.

"Liver or kidney," Parker mused as he pulled back.

"Don't have a kidney there anymore, and half my liver's gone. I think," I helpfully supplied between clenched teeth.

Red sounded surprisingly chipper when he surmised, "Only one way to find out." He got a hostile glare from me for that, but he met it with an even one. "Or do you have a better idea?"

I shook my head.

When I looked at him, I found Parker chewing his bottom lip, clearly apprehensive. "I'm not a trained surgeon," he offered when the guys noticed his hesitation as well. "Not that it matters much. The way your body works now, you either die, or whatever I do is, at best, helping just a little. And there's only so much I can do in the first place."

Nate's smirk wasn't a friendly one. "Let me guess. The part that has you all twisted up isn't that you're afraid of not being able to do the job, but doing it without anesthetics, painkillers, or even a good old paralytic."

This just kept getting better and better. Parker shrugged. "I don't have anything strong enough to knock her out. And Hamilton has the only two doses of paralytic. I presume you don't want to go over and ask him for it?"

I was sure that it was a waste of time, so before they could continue to hedge around, I put a stop to this. "Just do it. I don't care. Either it's something you can fix now, or I'll likely be dead tomorrow." That realization didn't even shock me anymore. Everything becomes normal when it happens often enough. And it wasn't like I'd said anything that everyone present hadn't been thinking.

"Where?" Nate asked Parker, briefly casting around. We were in the barn, out of sight of the others, who were bunking inside the farm house. It was as far from sterile as anything could get, barring me rolling in animal feces.

Parker seemed to come to the same conclusion. "Over there. Spread a tarp over the packed dirt. If that keeps her from splitting her skull open as she thrashes, all the better. I'm not keen on spending the entire night on this."

Nate uttered a sound low in his throat that came close to a growl, but rather than go after Parker, he helped me get up. I didn't expect a pep talk from him—after over a year and a half together, I knew him well enough to be aware that he didn't believe in postponing the inevitable—but as I was half-standing, half-hanging on him, he pulled me closer, his lips briefly touching my temple. "You'll get through this," he whispered, low enough that only I could hear him. "It will be hell, but a long shot from everything you've already been through. Don't forget that."

I was hard-pressed not to laugh in his face—maybe it was for the better that he didn't do pep talks more often—but my throat closed up with emotion... and something else. So all I did was nod. By the time I lay down on the tarp, my middle bared, the skin from my ribs down to the partly covered crease of my hip smeared with iodine solution, the warm, fuzzy feeling was gone, leaving only fear. Parker did a last round of prodding, also to make sure that no other parts of me drew the same level of reaction, thankfully coming up blank.

"How do you want to do this?" Red asked Nate, surprising me a little that he seemed ready to defer rather than insist on knowing better. Burns and Tanner were waiting nearby, none of them looking very excited but trying hard to hide it. Nate considered, weighing his options—probably literally.

"Burns, you take her thighs and hips where you don't get in Parker's way. Those are her strongest muscles, and you have the most mass to keep her down. Richards and I will try to keep her head and upper torso down. Tanner, take her lower legs." His gaze skipped to Parker, then back up my body, still calculating. "Stay sharp." When he caught my curious look, he shrugged. "Depending on how exhausted your body is, it might not happen, but I give you a fifty percent chance that you'll kick into overdrive, and then it will take the four of us everything we got to hold you down. Welcome to the joys of doing field surgery on the invincible."

I didn't feel very invincible right then, but did my best to relax as I gave Parker the go-ahead. Nate put his left forearm across my upper chest, his fingers grabbing one shoulder while he leaned on the other, making it hard to breathe for a second. He also kept me from seeing anything except him or the rafters above. His other hand wrapped around the fingers of my left, waiting for me to squeeze back. It took them a little to get ready, and when Parker simply poked the marked part of my anatomy, making agony flare up and me, consequently, buck, it proved to be more than necessary to do some coordinating. Parker's remarks about me smashing my own skull open echoed through my mind, the folded sleeping bag underneath my head suddenly feeling way too thin to cushion any impacts. Exhaling, I closed my eyes, waiting as my heart raced inside my chest. Trying to prep myself once for something like this had been bad enough. A second time? Impossible.

Something touched my free hand—Burns, I realized, belatedly. If he wanted me to try to crush his fingers, I was only too happy to oblige him.

"Let's do this," Parker muttered—and a second later, I felt the sharp bite of his scalpel. Try as I might, I couldn't keep a whimper from escaping me. Everyone froze, including Parker, my panting the only sound.

"Keep your hand over her mouth," Nate told Richards. "If she bites off one of your fingers, you're doing it wrong."

"Har har," Red remarked, but did as he was told. I might have appreciated that under different circumstances, but Parker resuming made that pretty much impossible.

I'd hated that paralytic that had turned me into a dead slab of meat on Raynor's operating table with the kind of vengeance only reserved for very few people and even fewer things, but now I missed it. Enough that, less than a minute in, I was ready to plead with them to go ask Hamilton. Even if I had to crawl on my hands and knees myself to get it, that would be okay. But I couldn't, because not only did Red's iron grip on my jaw make sure that only very muffled sounds escaped me, no. It was impossible for me to plead with anyone or anything.

So all I could do was try to push through the pain, and draw the next, inadequate breath through my nose. Breathe. Just breathe.

Parker was quick, taking less than thirty minutes, which, all things considered, was bordering on a miracle. That was still a billion minutes too many for me. It was probably my saving grace that my heartbeat remained strong enough to keep me in a state of constant panic rather than drop and send me into shock or cardiac arrest, but it didn't feel like that. Twice, I bucked hard enough that I almost threw Burns off, and Nate's grip would have slipped had Red not pushed hard into both of us; but somehow, they managed to keep me mostly restrained. Parker's near constant cursing told me that it wasn't easy on him, but I had a certain feeling that he wasn't quite the stranger to such circumstances. He'd sure been quick enough to switch to impersonal pronouns when he'd thought I'd already died.

The pain didn't lessen once the sutures were done and a bandage applied. It might even have increased as they let go of me, stepping away so I could curl up into a ball, trying but failing to lessen the strain on my abdomen and everything right through my body to my very spine. Shit, but that hurt. So. Fucking. Much.

"Uh, what the fuck is going on here?" I heard Hill's voice from somewhere near the barn door. "Guys, don't give me a reason to beat you up. You know what the LT said…" He trailed off there as he stepped inside where he could see more. "LT? What are you doing in here?" Everyone was staring at Hill, motionless, except for Parker, who was busy pulling off the surgical gown and gloves, both appropriately bloody.

If I hadn't been one giant mass of agony, I would have started to laugh. Oh, the irony. Hill of all people, coming to my rescue.

Nate and Red traded glances, the warning on Nate's face clear. Richards looked down at me once more, likely to make sure that I was, after all, going to make it, before he turned to Hill. "Some post-surgery complications. You know how it is. Would be much obliged if you didn't go around camp, telling everyone about this."

"Telling everyone about what?" Hill stammered, still reeling a little.

"Exactly," Nate answered for Red.

Hill's gaze dropped to me but I couldn't read his expression, upside down and with my vision blurry with tears. "She going to make it?"

Parker, finally done, nodded. "As things are, she was lucky. The infection was mostly in the interstitial space, no previously unaffected organ directly affected. Her liver's somewhat inflamed but should be okay in a few days, now that there's no necrotic tissue covering parts of it. She was right. It was likely some residual bacterial necrosis from the initial infection. It's a surprise Raynor and her team managed to clean her up as much as they did. Lucky you."

Lucky wasn't what I was feeling right then. Quite the opposite, really. As if almost rotting away once wasn't enough. No, it had to come in stages. Rationally, I knew that this was likely the last I'd ever see of that, but with my body still hurting all over with every breath I took, it was hard to fight down the paranoia and panic. Although, right now, not having someone cut me up was already a huge improvement. Then again, I hadn't really felt that lucky after Bates had died, cut to pieces by the cannibals, and we'd officially given our merry band of misfits a name—the Lucky Thirteen. I hadn't been sure whether Nate had meant that in a sarcastic way or not. The same was still true now. Lucky me, indeed.

Hill disappeared after making a zipping motion over his mouth. Everyone else seemed ready to give me some space, but Nate remained by my side, conflicted. I could read that pinched look on his face even with serious distraction.

"If that's all—" Parker started, but Nate held him back immediately.

"Check her hand."

Ah, right. Part of me wished he hadn't snatched up that tidbit, but I only put up minimal protest when Nate reached for my left arm and pulled it away from my stomach. Parker scrutinized it for a moment before he started touching the affected finger, first prodding, then getting out a fresh, sealed scalpel and lightly nicking the pad.

"Not feeling anything there, huh?" he murmured more to himself than me. I shook my head. He did a few more nicks toward the knuckle, until I flinched. He continued to consider, turning my hand this way and that under his flashlight. "Might just be some residual bruising," he offered eventually. "I lack the skill and knowledge. You felt your other fingers go numb before. You can probably better tell what's going on than I ever could."

He didn't need to tell me this. I also didn't need a recount of what might happen if I ignored it for too long. Maybe.

"Cut it off. Right to where the nerve damage has progressed. Still got the middle finger on my other hand to flip you morons off." I didn't even care anymore that my voice was shaking so hard I was surprised anyone could understand.

Parker hesitated, but then got a fresh pair of gloves and wiped off the blade and my finger. "I could be wrong—"

"Do it!" I screamed, way too loud for our damn undercover operation, making everyone jerk. Outside, I heard a flock of birds take flight, adding extra drama that I so didn't need. Exhaling shakily,

I caught Parker's gaze, making sure that there was no doubt left on my face, even if my gut felt like it was sinking right into the ground underneath me. "Do it," I repeated, calmer and more measured now. "I don't have time to keep screwing with this. My body needs to heal, and it can't heal if it has to fight infection over infection over infection. The loss of sensation is recent. I remember bumping the scars at the tip while training in the hangar, and it still hurt like hell. That was maybe two weeks ago. Now I can't feel anything past the middle part. As much as I hate losing even a quarter of an inch from that finger, that's still better than the entire finger, or more. Don't make this any harder on me than it already is. Please."

Parker inclined his head, whether to avoid having to continue to look in my face or to focus on his task, I couldn't say. He tore open a sterile pack of gauze and spread it out on the tarp. "Put your hand there. Splay your fingers. I'll try to make it quick."

I watched as he fashioned a tourniquet, but then looked away as Nate reached around me and grabbed my hand just below my wrist, making it impossible for me to jerk back. He held my gaze evenly, a sure, "You can do this," if I'd ever seen one. But at the last moment, I cast my eyes down, forcing myself to watch. Maybe that was the fever talking, but if they had to continue to cut me limb from limb, the least I would do was watch. It hurt like hell, but what else was new? Certainly not that sensation. Or what followed afterward, and Parker didn't have Raynor's iron-steady hand, nor her skill. I told myself it would be all right, but didn't find the conviction inside of me to believe my own lies. How much worse could it get?

But then I realized, if the shit with Taggard's trap hadn't happened, it likely would have been Martinez's job to do this, and suddenly, I was glad to be stuck with people I couldn't stand in a country that, so far, had only been desolate and hostile. I knew that it must have been bad enough for the guys to hold me down while Parker did his job. Actively inflict pain and damage that could never be undone? That was a different circle of hell entirely. I knew that, but still it didn't change a thing. Because it was my damage, my hand.

As soon as Parker was done, I dragged my sorry self over to my sleeping bag, having to wait for Nate to get it ready and help me bundle myself up so I wouldn't freeze to death during the night. My body temperature regulation was shot, making me shiver with exhaustion and cold while I was still burning up. Spending so long with a substantial part of my core exposed didn't help. Neither did the heat quickly building up do a thing to lessen the pain in my abdomen; on the contrary. Damned if you do, damned if you don't. So I curled in around myself, my aching hand inches from my cut-up stomach, and, quite honestly, prayed that I'd die.

Chapter 17

Nate and Red shared a few words before he and Parker left. I didn't follow their exchange, but it didn't sound very amicable. Neither the part where Red accused, "How could you let it get this far?" to what Nate bit back, "This is all your fault! She should still be in a hospital, not hauling her way too scrawny ass across Europe!"

Oh, the confidence they had in me.

Sometimes it was better for people not to tell me to my face what they thought of me.

Burns made sure to clean up everything that my blood might have come in contact with, while Tanner went out to relieve Gita of her watch duty. It was well past midnight now and everyone should have been asleep, but I heard their murmurs over at the other side of the barn continue for a while yet, likely the guys updating Gita on what she'd missed.

Nate joined me a little while later, ignoring my hostile grunt as he molded his body against my back, but he was careful not to connect with me other than my shoulders and below my hips, or reach around me and touch the war zone that my torso had morphed into once more. I couldn't even say why I wanted to be left alone. Probably because that way, no one could have intruded in my wallowing. A few painful breaths later I gave in and let him offer his arm as a cushion for my head, pulling me closer where I could stand it. And when he reached up and gently touched my cheek, I started to cry, for once not feeling like keeping all that pain and frustration penned up inside of me. It wasn't even the physical aspect that brought me to my knees, although that certainly didn't help.

"We'll get through this," Nate repeated that mantra that had lost any spark of hope it had ever been able to ignite inside of me. "You will get through this."

I shook my head. Even that small motion made my torn abdominal muscles flare up. As did taking the next breath. If I could just stop doing that…

"You will," he insisted, as if that would do anything for me.

"Maybe I don't want to," I mumbled, not caring whether he understood or not. "There's always something worse coming up. Like, I'll never be able to catch a break. It's just not worth it anymore."

There was only one way Nate ever reacted to me going on like this—and I probably uttered those words because I needed him to bark at me and tell me to stop being such a baby—but instead, he hugged me closer, his free hand lightly digging into my shoulder as he buried his face in my hair. Rather than comfort me, his show of silent support and affection made me cry all the harder, turning me into a sobbing, useless mess.

Weeks ago, the wave of mental exhaustion that swept through me should have been enough to physically pull me under, but that fucking serum was doing its job for once, keeping me awake and laser focused with every pinch and ache rolling through my body. I realized that sleep wasn't just a long way from coming but likely impossible, maybe even for the next few nights. Perfect. That was exactly what I needed.

"Maybe I'll just burn out," I continued to sob into my sleeping bag. "Or there'll always be a next infection, and eventually, there won't be enough of me left. Once my GI tract is gone, it's over. Unless you keep me hooked up to infusion bags that keep me alive, with nutrients going straight into my bloodstream. You'd do that to me, wouldn't you? Make me suffer till my absolute last, agonizing breath."

Nate remained quiet for a while, but eventually answered with a sigh that held a welcome exasperated note. "It's more fun when you're physically venting. That usually ends with both of us getting off, not just sounding like petulant children."

My answering burst of laughter hurt like hell, but it actually felt good. "Why won't you let me give up? At some point this year I must have surpassed the point where I'm still worth the trouble."

Ever the bastard I so loved to accuse him of being, Nate took his sweet time to reply, but did it with a soft laugh himself. "I guess that says more about me than you."

"Yup." No sense in not agreeing.

"Guess I'm a lost cause, too. Like a honey badger. I'll never let go once I've sunk my teeth into something."

That made me snort. "You really are a catch. Insulting me, dehumanizing me—"

"Oh, shut up," he grumbled. "Go ahead. Go look for someone else who's willing to put up with you. And who manages to keep you the right amount of crazy so you're motivated but don't get any weird ideas."

"You really think you're doing that?"

"I know so," he insisted. For whatever reason, that gave me a mental pause. People, motivating me... not quite something I wanted to think about right now. Yet now that my subconscious was starting to drag up things, it was hard to put the lid back on.

My silence must have gone on for too long as Nate prodded gently, "Why, would you want me to stop?"

"I don't think you could," I pointed out. "Because then you would get bored and stir shit up, and you much prefer to lean back and watch me do it instead." I paused. "That's what you have been doing the entire time."

He didn't answer right away. "You say that like it's a bad thing."

I gave that some thought, although my initial reaction was to snap that yes, it sure as hell was. I settled on saying, "It tends to add to my list of grievances," instead.

I felt him tense behind me, sure that he would have rolled me onto my back so he could stare into my face if that wouldn't cause me immeasurable pain.

"Would you really prefer to return to how things were when you spent your entire time throwing hissy fits behind my back because you felt ignored?"

It was a valid question, and one that was surprisingly easy to answer. "No."

"Then what are you complaining about?"

"It's just that I thought we were in this together," I complained— more softly than I wanted, realizing that it was real disappointment that made my heart clench as I uttered the words. "As equals. Both signing at the same dotted line. Yes, I want to be part of the decision-making process, I want to shoulder part of the blame when it all goes to shit. But I don't appreciate you setting me up as a scapegoat."

And there I'd gone and done it again. That was real anger and heat in his voice as he responded. "You know me better than that."

"Do I?" Now I was the one who needed to see the look on his face, and while it cost me a lot to turn over, I managed, somehow. His features were closed off, a stony mask not even I could read, but Nate was incapable of keeping emotions out of his eyes—yet rather than anger, it was pain that I saw there. Not what I'd expected, and that left me at a loss of what to say.

He gave a loud chuff as if to shake himself out of his funk, cocking his head to the side as he, in turn, took in every line of my face. Considering how dark it was inside the barn, he couldn't really be able to see much. "Bree, what's going on? You know that I don't mind being your punching bag, emotional or physical, and I make you repay the favor more often than you likely signed up for, but this isn't you. You have to give me something to work with. Not shut up, almost mid-sentence, and close me out."

Easier said than done. "I don't know," I confessed. "Some of it is just pure and simple frustration. And I'm scared shitless, that's not helping. But there are some things that people said—"

"What people?"

Assholes, the lot of them, but that wasn't specific enough. "Mostly Richards and Hill."

"Fraternizing with the enemy, huh?" he teased.

"That's Burns. I just seem to have a sign over my head that says, 'randomly accost me to screw with my head.' At least with Hill I'm sure he's not doing it deliberately. Red? Very much so. Makes it less effective, but might still be working."

"Why, what has your granny panties in a twist?"

I couldn't help but smile. "Ah, you noticed."

"Like anyone could miss that," he chortled.

"Room enough inside for both of us, if you ever get tempted," I snarked, but forced myself to stop getting sidetracked. "It was something that Hill said... I don't know, yesterday? The day before? Shit, it's all blurring together. Fucking fever." At least I hoped it was that, because if the next festering abscess turned out to be in my brain, that was it for me. I was a little surprised that this aspect made me mad rather than that it presented a welcome alternative.

"Bree?"

"Thinking." My hand shot up as if to raise an admonishing finger, but the motion was enough to send pain racing down to my elbow, making me remember. Right. "I'm not even sure what it was, but something he said tipped me off. And it wasn't that part about not believing how Alders and his flunkies kicked off the apocalypse."

Nate's mouth twisted up, as usual when his closer-than-comfortable involvement with that turned into a conversation point. "He's not the only one. I've talked with a few of the guys, also the sailors and marines on the destroyer. It's too farfetched for most to believe, and absolute nonsense for the rest."

"But we all know that the sugar is contaminated, and nobody's stupid enough to deny that the serum and virus originated from the same source."

"Still doesn't explain how one insane scientist and a bunch of vegan hippies managed to pull off what every terrorist organization out there couldn't."

"You don't believe it?" I didn't have to feign surprise there. We'd never actually discussed the point, mostly because I didn't want to prod that figurative sore wound in his side, but I'd assumed we agreed on this.

Nate shrugged, softly enough not to disturb me. "Not saying that. But I can see where someone with Hill's intellectual horizon would dispute it."

"Oh, such a fancy way of calling him stupid. I've missed that, you know?"

He flashed me his teeth in an approximation of a smile. "Do you believe it?"

I closed my mouth when the answer didn't come right away. Had I mulled the possibility over? Of course; many, many times. "It doesn't matter. We have no way of verifying any of it, and the last two people that we knew were connected to that are dead now." There still was my old co-worker, but her mind had been too far gone to make sense of much anymore. I doubted that she could have provided any answers, even if she'd known anything, and I sincerely doubted that to begin with.

"That's not what I asked," Nate remarked. "Do you believe that they did it? How they supposedly did it?"

I debated with myself what to say, but didn't come to a conclusion. "I want to deny the possibility more than anything, but that's the only part we can't deny. It all happened, and it keeps happening. It would help if we knew how they contaminated the syrup. And how they managed the distribution logistics. The only actual detail that we have is that your brother, for whatever reason, was working with a weaponized version of the serum, the activated version. I'm sure that, by now, I've read a huge chunk of his research, and I still have no clue about the why. They spent decades putting shackles on the virus to ensure that the serum was stable until after the demise of the subject. I have no freaking clue why he undid that, and what he was up to with the new ideas that he was waiting to implement until he could work on them with me. I'm likely missing something there. Or maybe it was all sanctioned from higher up. Who knows?"

"Emily Raynor likely does," Nate offered.

"Probably." It would explain her lack of excitement about Raleigh's new data that we'd brought her. Not because it wasn't news, but because she was sitting on a time bomb that had already exploded, and adding anything extra to that like new, explosive revelations wasn't in her best interest.

"I've missed that look."

"What look?" I asked, perplexed.

"That look you get when you really need to know something that's far out of your reach, and you know you have to sacrifice something dear to get it. You had that same look on your face at Stone's lab in Aurora, when they offered you to run it. I'm still surprised you chose me over that."

"I chose you all over that," I clarified. "You alone wouldn't have been enough to sway me."

I loved the lopsided smile that gained me. "Well, you gave it up, either way. The important question is, will you do it again?"

That confused me. "No offers on the table, far as I know."

Nate snorted. "Come on, you know that Raynor will ask you to join her when we get back. And you're not stupid enough not to expect her to have the stick waiting as soon as she whips out the carrot."

That was true, even if I hadn't had the mental capacity to consider that yet. Constant agony will do that to you.

"I could ask you the very same question. Whether Hamilton survives or not, if you don't mess up to the point of deliberately sabotaging the mission—which you swore you wouldn't, and aren't you Mr. Honorable of late?—they will want you to work with them again." Nate's silence told me that I wasn't going to get an answer, but that in and of itself provided one. And it was that silence that made me realize something else. "That's the reason why you've been pretending to let me steal the show, isn't it? So nobody gets any stupid ideas and tries to reinstate your former rank, to make the grunts actually want to follow you! You're such a damn coward!"

I crowed that last bit loud enough that someone at the other end of the barn stirred, which Nate used as an excuse not to reply for a moment. When he did, he looked surprisingly defeated. "Maybe?"

"Do you really have to turn that into a question if you already know that I know the answer?"

He laughed softly. "I see you're feeling better already."

I shook my head. "Nope. But my head's clearing up, and I can't help being a smart-ass."

"Truer words have seldom been spoken."

I didn't know what to make of that admission. Did it surprise me? Yes, a lot, but at the same time, not so much. If I considered our friends back in California, Nate wanting to rejoin the Army screamed of betrayal. I was sure that some of them would understand—likely those in the same boat with him, and it wouldn't have surprised me that if he ever chose to go for that option, he would negotiate a general amnesty for them if they wanted to follow—but others, not so much. Sadie would hate him for that decision, and I myself wasn't exactly delighted by that idea, either. But I could see where it was a tempting scenario for him, to return to what was familiar. Just the mention of a lab had the same siren call for me. And would it be so bad? Considering Raynor's dislike for Bucky, I could see her lobbying to have Nate as the chief of security of her base instead. It wouldn't be much different for either of us whether we'd stay there or return to California, only that if we stayed, we'd both be back to working in our respective chosen fields where we were the cream of the crop rather than two random troublemakers with a penchant for maneuvering ourselves into the focal point of conflict. And I sure as hell could have found a way to get out of anything physically taxing like late night watch shifts and hauling my weight in ammo around. It was tempting, no shit—but we could have had that easier if we'd wanted it in the past, and we had burned a lot of bridges along the way. Raynor's influence might be enough to protect us from possible ramifications, but the very idea that I was living in comfort thanks only to someone else's grace was making me want to hurl. I hadn't started that crusade just to end a conflict prematurely that might have cost more lives than we could lose—no, I'd meant it when I'd said that I wanted to be free. And while Nate might be missing the camaraderie of the old days, I knew that he felt the same.

Silence fell, both of us feigning trying to get some sleep. With him, it was likely sheer willpower that kept him awake. Until…

"You never told me what Hill said that got under your skin," Nate prompted.

Damn. I considered pretending to have forgotten—or plain out lying—but I knew it was no good.

"He asked me why I thought they'd all be out for vengeance. For the base in Colorado, you know?"

He nodded. "What about that?"

"He made me sound like a fucking imposter," I grumbled. "Like I just waltzed in there after the lot of you had cleared the corridors, and all I did was talk. And shoot Taggard. At least that's something nobody disputes."

It was only when I got a weird look from Nate that unease started creeping up my spine. "What?"

"Bree, they actually don't have that much of a cause to come after you," he explained, his voice uncharacteristically soft.

"But I killed scores of soldiers! That whole base was full of them, and the incursion of shamblers—"

I cut off when Nate glanced away from me and over to the other side of the barn where I knew Burns was sleeping—who'd been with me as I'd made my way through the ducts first, then the detour to the labs, and after that the corridors to the cafeteria where we'd had our grand stand-off.

"Shit," Nate muttered. "I thought you were exaggerating before, but I didn't think you'd actually believe that."

"Believe what?" If my voice got a little hysterical, that was only natural. "Nate, what the fuck are you talking about?"

He shook his head as if to disband his own thoughts, then actually reached for the side of my face to keep me from turning my head away. "Bree, you were tripping balls when we assaulted that base. The booster shot I gave you was way too strong for your mind to handle. It was set up for someone my weight, whose metabolism was running at the speed yours is at now, but certainly wasn't back then."

I really didn't like the sound of that. "What are you saying? That it was all in my head?"

I could have done without him hesitating. "Not everything," Nate said, way too cautiously. "It was quite the ride, and you did end up totaling the Rover. Shit," he repeated, shaking his head. "I should have realized that when you told Sadie how we'd collapsed the slope to get into the base and beyond their primary defenses.

I thought you were just making fun when you exaggerated that much."

"That doesn't make any sense," I muttered—but fact was, if what he said was true, a lot of inconsistencies suddenly did. "I know what I did—"

"What you think you did," he corrected.

"I blew through all of the magazines I'd packed," I protested, if feebly.

"Yeah, when we cleaned up the base of the well over thousand zombies that ended up being drawn there. And from what Collins told me, some before you got to the cafeteria as well."

"But the soldiers—"

"You didn't shoot," Nate clarified. "Burns said you ran into a bunch, but after shouting some obscenities at each other, they went down another corridor while you continued forward. The only place where there was an actual firefight human against human was outside, by the armory, when a few of the soldiers chose to make a stand rather than surrender before it became obvious that we weren't the incursion they needed to be afraid of. I think overall, less than fifty people died of gunshot wounds. On both sides," he stressed.

This couldn't be true. None of that.

"But I know what I saw. What I did. Same as with the factory. I…" I trailed off there, frowning at him. "Was that all in my head, too? I mowed down at least fifteen soldiers when I sprung you, Pia, and the others."

"That's all true."

"Then why did the booster affect me differently the second time?"

I got a helpless gesture from Nate. "Maybe because the virus screwing with your system changed things? Maybe because it was a higher dosage? Or maybe it got worse as time passed? You were actively dying the first time hours after the injection, which coincides with when we hit the base the second time. And you were definitely hallucinating then, as well."

"I can't fucking believe this," I muttered, finally jerking free of his soft hold. This time, I welcomed the resulting pain. I wasn't exactly confused, although my mind was definitely riling. "This just—"

"Changes nothing," Nate offered.

"Changes everything!" I insisted. "That's why none of them take me seriously! They really do think that I'm just a delusional imposter!"

"Nobody thinks that. And you do have reason enough to be paranoid. You heard what Hill said when he came in, right? He thought he had a reason for that. But just, maybe, you're not as much of a deranged serial murderer as you like to pretend."

"I wasn't pretending anything," I protested, hating how petulant I sounded—until Nate's words before that sunk in. Quite the thought to drag me back down to reality. "Shit."

"That seems to, as usual, perfectly sum up our situation," Nate observed, not without mirth. "Come on, shake yourself out of it. Yes, you were high, and maybe you didn't quite pull the stunts you imagined you did—"

"It all looked very dramatic to me."

Nate laughed. "That should have tipped you off in the first place. Doesn't change a thing. You made a difference. You're responsible for giving hundreds, if not thousands, of scavengers and traders a chance to make it through the winter, and ending that conflict before it could actually escalate also saved a lot of soldiers. So what, you didn't Rambo your way through that base. You still kept your wits about you, and you accomplished what you came for. Maybe your ego takes a bit of a beating for that, but you must be used to that by now."

"I married you. Forgot about that already?"

He grinned at my jibe before he turned serious again. "I have a feeling that, before this mission here is over, you will have more blood on your hands, and regrets that you cannot explain away this easily. Trust me, sooner or later, your biggest fears always catch up to you. Be glad that hasn't happened yet."

"You think that's my biggest fear?" I asked. "That I kill someone who, if not innocent, didn't have to die?"

"That you sent someone to die who didn't have to," he amended. "But I'm sure that's a close second. And yes, I am speaking from experience." There was nothing I could say to that so I held my tongue. Nate looked away, a wave of sadness crossing his features. "I don't know what I'll do once this is over," he went on saying, unexpectedly giving me an answer to that question after all. "Part of me wants to take any offer I can get. To redeem myself. I can't wash my hands clean, but I can change things." He sighed. "Of course I'll never know, but I could, maybe, have done things differently; influenced decisions, kept some of the worse shit from happening, if I'd swallowed my pride and come with Bucky and his people when I realized that we were on the cusp of fighting a battle we'd all, one by one, eventually lose. But I was still angry, I was too proud." He grimaced. "And I was high on the booster Martinez jacked me up with once he'd staunched the bleeding because otherwise, I would have collapsed. That shit can really make you do a lot of stupid things."

"Still no excuse for why we got hitched," I provided dryly.

"It's a chance for both of us to make up for the path not taken," Nate insisted, but he didn't sound as enthusiastic about it anymore. It didn't take a genius to guess why.

"We don't owe them shit," I spoke his thoughts for him—and found myself agreeing, maybe now that I'd learned about the side-effects of the booster a little more than before. "Maybe we could have made a difference if we'd both come with them. Maybe we wouldn't have made it through that day. We'll never know."

"Do you want to?" he asked. "Work with Raynor, I mean? Tear apart what my brother was working on, see what else you'll get out of her or whoever else is in charge of what used to be the serum project, and maybe be the one who makes a difference?"

I still didn't have an answer for that, and I wasn't sure that would change until the very last minute I'd have to prevent having to make up my mind. But that question reminded me of something else. "Not sure if Gita told you, but the files she helped decrypt at that conservatory? They were full of references to the serum project. Different virus strains, but some of that might have been artifacts from the encryption. Bucky and Richards only needed confirmation that they were on the right track. They didn't really care about the contents."

Nate took that with less surprise than I'd expected. "Well, they waited to launch this mission until they could drag you with them," he pointed out. "Makes sense it's about this."

"So that means I'm already helping Raynor, right? And not exactly out of the goodness of my heart. I feel like if I agree, I'll never be able to walk away from this shit." Glancing toward where I couldn't see my aching hand, I sighed. "Not sure I can, anyway. But hey, I get now why you were so damn apprehensive to get involved with this all over again. You can walk out but you can never leave, right?"

He snorted at my very bad quoting habits, but didn't answer. That was okay. We'd both shared enough for more than one night, and probably had enough to consider for a decade. All bickering aside, I couldn't help but relax as I cozied up to Nate, waiting for his breathing to even out as he fell asleep. It didn't happen, of course, but that was kind of a relief as well. When the adrenaline shot eventually wore off—or rather, the shitload of adrenaline that my body had produced because of Parker cutting me up; I doubted that anything from the injection was still flowing through my veins—I felt myself slip again, but it happened gradually this time, closer to a light slumber than the waking coma of before. It didn't scare me that much, and when I tried, I easily managed to rouse myself. So I let myself go, drifting off, wondering what new and enticing disaster the world had in store for me tomorrow. Maybe by the time I had to make up my mind, something might have happened that made it easier to accept—or impossible not to.

Chapter 18

I refused to get up when Nate did, figuring that, if yesterday's shit show had any advantages, it was me getting out of some early morning chores. It wasn't like I was any use. I had a hard time using a shovel to fill the latrine or bury the ashes of the fire pits. My grip still slipped sometimes so I couldn't be trusted with the hot water or dishing out breakfast. My fingers were so stiff in the mornings that I couldn't even open the packages of the MREs without using a knife, and often not even then. And today, quite frankly, I really didn't feel like laughing my disabilities in the face and pretending like I was okay.

It took Bucky about five minutes to notice once I was overdue. That was as much of a respite as I got before he came waltzing into the barn, heading straight for where I was still bundled up in my sleeping bag but had wisely already unzipped it. I braced myself, counting down the seconds. At least him storming in here made me guess that Parker, Red, and Hill had all kept their traps shut.

"Wakey, wakey. Eggs and—" Hamilton sing-songed, swinging his right foot forward for a well-aimed kick.

I moved at the very last moment, executing something between a roll and a scramble, miraculously ending up on my feet. I did my best to grin at Hamilton as I straightened, because really, it took all my strength not to scream my head off with how much moving hurt.

Bucky seemed disappointed that he hadn't gotten to kick me out of my makeshift bed, but only so much. "Already slacking off, cunt?"

I let my breath escape between clenched teeth, blinking once to try to center my swimming vision. It really didn't get any better when I saw two or three versions of that asshole at once. But at least my mind was working, which was a nice improvement over yesterday. I quickly weighed how to handle this, but decided that acting like the recalcitrant bitch that everyone apparently thought I was would work quite nicely.

"I was hoping you'd come and wake me up with your dulcet tones," I retorted, maybe a little late, but thankfully not as out of breath as I should have been.

"We're moving out in ten. So slap your makeup and smile on so we can get going."

I was tempted to flip him the bird, but considering that only worked well with my right hand anymore, I refrained. Instead, I grabbed my sleeping bag and left. My pack was missing; I figured Nate had taken it outside with him after removing everything I didn't absolutely have to carry to make the day a little easier on me. The ice cold air hit me square in the face, the first rays of sunshine blinding my eyes for a second. I slouched as I waited for my senses to reorient themselves, allowing myself the slightest of whimpers to try to deal with the agony radiating up from my abdomen.

My vision cleared, and that's when my breath caught in my throat—and not just from the discomfort radiating through my body.

The air was clear; so clear that I could see each individual small snowflake dance in front of my face that the wind swept up from the ground and trees. The sky was mostly overcast but let a few beams of sunshine through like the fingers of God. I could easily see the low hill at the other end of the soft valley we were in, a good four or five miles away. But it wasn't just the absence of fog that was to blame for this—up close, every pebble on the ground, every rime-covered blade of grass, every groove of a boot print in the mud that had frozen solid over night was in stark focus. Moss on stones, dirt smeared across the underside of a pack, fingerprints on a gun from last night's cleaning. And it wasn't limited to visuals. I could smell the hot beans that Cole was shoveling into his mouth as if I was holding the cup right under my nose. The scents of ash and smoke lay heavy over the camp—and yes, over there was the latrine pit. We'd been out in the field long enough to add a note of old sweat and unwashed bodies to that as well. I bent over, my left hand pressed into my right side—which did not help—waiting to hurl up the last thing I'd eaten, but the sense of nausea disappeared quickly—as did most of the sharp pain. Oh, I still felt sore as hell, but everything was just a little duller than a moment ago, when I had been concentrating on… everything. The brain fog was gone, leaving my thoughts sharp and clear, if a little overwhelmed at the moment.

Something behind and to my side drew my attention, as if instead of currents of air it was water rippling all around me, giving me a vague physical sense of… something. I stepped aside, my body moving before my brain could even give the command. Bucky plowed through where I had just been standing, my quick motions making him narrowly avoid hitting my shoulder and hip in passing. Rather than anger, confusion rose inside of me.

What the hell was going on with me?

Hamilton ignored me as he sauntered on. My senses continued to assault me with useless information as I followed his path with my eyes, simply letting it all wash over me. My gaze slipped to Parker when Hamilton passed by him, but the medic was doing everything in his power not to look in my direction. He was tense and twitchy, a sure sign that something was wrong—or he was avoiding something. Someone.

I turned my head to find my bunch all grouped together a few feet away from the barn. It was easy to catch the small tufts of hazy air steaming up from Gita's tea cup. She saw me standing there just then, her eyes creasing with worry. She was about as bad as Parker containing her unease. Burns was better in pretending that it was just a casual glance he cast my way, but I still noticed how tense his shoulders were. When Nate did a similarly bad job keeping concern off his face, I knew that something really was going on—but I didn't think with them.

Walking was weird. I hadn't felt it as I'd staggered out of the barn, pain dominating over all other sensual input. My balance was off, my right foot having a slightly harder time than my left, which kind of balanced out the fact that my left thigh was stiff, the muscles needing a few cycles of tensing and relaxing to start working properly. The strain on my abdomen was screwing with me as well, but as I squared my shoulders and forced my torso to stretch, it worked surprisingly well, if one was to ignore the pain. Dulled or not, that fucking hurt.

I paused next to Nate, my mouth already open to say something—what, I wasn't quite sure, but that I should let him know that something was off was a given—when a loud crack at the other side of camp drew my attention. Munez, snapping the branch he'd been using to check for dying embers in the fire pit. To me, it had been almost as loud as a gunshot. When I turned back to Nate, I found him scrutinizing my face.

"You look like you've seen a ghost," he murmured.

"I'm not hallucinating," I said, just a tad bit defensive. Our conversation about what that damn booster had done to me was still fresh on my mind. "But something's going on."

Any further discussion was cut short when Bucky barked at us to get going. I still had to take care of business—which I did, unabashedly, after scurrying behind a tree—and get my pack. That turned out to weigh next to nothing as Nate seemed to have retrieved everything from it except for our few spare clothes, his, and now also my sleeping bag. The pack itself likely made up for most of the weight. It felt weird and too light as I shrugged it on, but even so it put enough pressure on my fresh wound to increase the level of discomfort. Gritting my teeth, I closed the hip belt across my stomach, hoping that the constant pressure would eventually be a good, distracting thing rather than the reason I bit it today.

As we set out, I shamelessly let Nate hand me food that didn't exactly count for a breakfast of champions, but as long as it provided fuel for my body, I didn't care. They'd let me sleep in longer than I'd thought. "Sleep" was of course the wrong word, and I had been aware of them stepping outside one by one, yet without a clear sense of how time was passing. Now? Now my pulse pounding in my ears was like a constant, loud clock, ticking away precise increments of time without fail.

Nate kept watching me like a hawk, paying very little attention to our surroundings—or was he really? I jumped a few times as a flock of birds took flight or something cracked in the underbrush as we passed, and every time I noticed him react. Not as much as I did, maybe not even on a conscious level, but his attention turned this way or that, his head cocked ever so slightly to the side. Subtle shifts—like what someone did who had the same level of awareness as I'd woken up with, but had had years to fine-tune his reactions.

I got the feeling that, somehow, Parker's actions from last night had loosened some kind of safety lock on my system. That very idea was creepy as hell.

My suspicion that this was exactly what was going on strengthened when it was our turn to do forward recon, and I gave the guys a good run for their money. Nate had looked borderline mutinous when Red called us forward, but even if I had been dragging myself on with my teeth, what else should he have done to keep everyone else from being suspicious? I held back until we were out of sight of the main group, then set a pace that felt more like what my body wanted to do. My whole body was singing with the need to move, pain or no pain. Going faster made my life hell, but rather than dull from the agony, my senses seemed to sharpen further. Ducking behind cover was the worst part, forcing my torso muscles to work, but as long as I was running or walking I could handle it. Of course, Nate and Burns both noticed that rather than hang back, I took point even when Nate tried to hold me back.

Moving was one thing. Fighting quite another. I didn't want to test that theory so I did my best to stay away whenever I saw anything about that could have been a shambler, or caught that distinct note of rot and decay in the air. We avoided all but one nest, two shamblers hiding in a ditch by a small access road, but Nate and Burns took care of that without needing any help from me. As we returned to the others, Red was watching my every motion cautiously, and he seemed to come to the same conclusion as Nate and Burns had: I was functioning, so no need to draw any more unwanted attention to me.

Even so, I really needed a break at noon, spending the entire time sitting on my pack and shoving food down my gullet. My body was close to shaking with exhaustion, but the last few days—before the fever had set in—had taught me that some of that was due to not enough energy to burn. So refueling was what I did, until my stomach ached but my muscles stopped spasming at weird intervals. No longer did I need Nate's reminders to keep a close eye on my fuel gauge. I didn't miss the partly satisfied look reaching that very conclusion painted on his face. I chose to see that as a good sign. If my behavior was something both he and Red were obviously familiar with, I must be on the right track.

We were up and moving for thirty minutes again when I realized that I hadn't taken any of the supplements that Raynor had packed for me. I considered getting them from my pack on the move, but didn't when that sense of hyperfocus continued to last into the day. In the morning, I'd had the sneaking suspicion that the pain had somehow forced me into dipping into reserves that the serum helped access, but I knew not just from Nate's tales that it was impossible to keep that up for that long—or without a lot of willpower and determination. I wasn't doing anything except maybe trying to mute my senses, certainly not enhance them, so it couldn't have been a temporary effect. I was starting to see why Nate hadn't been that heartbroken in the end for me to get shot up with the serum, all immunity effects aside. This was kind of awesome.

We ended up making camp in the thick of a forest, some kind of wooden deer stand structure the only real cover we found, so that and some tarps turned into makeshift tents would have to do. I asked Gita to switch watch shift with me, then tracked down Nate before he could disappear with Red for their nightly powwow. "I need to talk to Parker."

Nate didn't ask, just nodded. Ten minutes later, the medic got up to relieve himself, presenting us with the perfect opportunity.

We waited until he was done with the actual part of it, then Nate came after him, grabbing him so he could slam Parker's back against a thick oak tree, a hand over his mouth immediately stifling his cry of surprise. I listened for anyone coming from the camp, but couldn't hear anything from that direction. Parker had been stupid enough to pick a part of the perimeter that would be empty of patrols for the next five to ten minutes, more than enough time for me to do what I had in mind.

Coming to a halt behind and a little to the side of Nate where Parker could see me as he was still trying—in vain—to break Nate's hold on him, I pulled out the plastic baggie I'd retrieved from the bottom of my pack. Holding it up to Parker's face, I shook it, making the pills inside dance. "I'll make this quick. Just answer my questions and you can be back with your buddies in no time, and still able to function." Maybe that last bit was overkill, but considering that tonight was the first time in fucking forever that I was feeling remotely like myself, I had a reason to be pissed off. Parker gave one last push, then went slack against the tree, blinking once to show that he understood. "Good. We'll let you talk in a sec. What exactly is this shit that I'm supposed to take every single day? And please be so kind to point out the psychotropic mood stabilizers so I can skip them from here on out."

Nate had been staring at Parker the entire time—likely what intimidated the medic more than finding me stalking toward him like a hissing cat—but that last bit made his head whip around, his eyes intently searching my face. I did my best to give him nothing. With luck, Parker would provide a better response than I could have in the first place. It was relief to see Nate's surprise was genuine, although I hadn't expected a different outcome. I knew that some things he could reason with keeping from me, but actively screwing with my mind was a little above even him.

Our exchange happened in less than a second, and when he glared back at Parker, Nate was his usual stoic self. "Don't scream. Just answer her questions, and you're good to go." He then carefully removed the hand covering Parker's mouth, but not the arm that was still pressed across his upper torso and windpipe.

Parker inhaled noisily, but thought better of the shout he was evidently gearing up for. It took him a little too long for my liking to tear his nervous gaze away from Nate to focus on me instead, but nothing I could do about that. I didn't necessarily want to follow up on my threat. The point was not to alert the rest of the camp, particularly Bucky.

"This is how you repay me saving your fucking life?" Parker spit in my face.

I tried to make my shrug appear as casual as possible. "Am I grateful that you cut me up without painkillers or any other form of anesthesia?

Yes. And I know you're not responsible for this shit, or else we wouldn't be having a pleasant chat right now. But it would be irresponsible for the powers that be not to have informed you of what exactly is going on with me, which makes you the perfect candidate. Talk."

Parker wasn't done yet, sadly. "If this is because you think I told Hamilton, that's your own fault if he sniffed it out. I said nothing, to nobody. Fucking cun—"

It didn't require more than a subtle shift from Nate to cut Parker off. "If you're done foul-mouthing my wife now…?"

He waited until Parker's face had taken on a slightly red tint before he eased up once more, letting the medic draw a stuttering breath. I wondered if more motivation was required, but, surprise, surprise, Parker seemed to have made the connection that my question meant that I was—literally—off my meds, and that alone gave me more confirmation than I'd wanted to get.

"Most of it is vitamins and other supplements," he explained, still eyeing Nate with unease. "I don't know exactly what. Nothing's strong enough to cause you any harm."

Or not. That was the most anticlimactic non-answer he could have given. He probably thought he was being clever. Well, two could play this game.

Reaching into the baggie, I palmed about half of the contents as I stepped closer. "If that's true, then I'm sure you won't terribly mind demonstrating that, right?"

As soon as my intent registered, Parker started struggling for real, almost managing to tear free. "You fucking insane bitch!" he whisper-shouted, smart enough not to force Nate to silence him again—or pry his jaws wide open to make my job easier. "It's all set for your freak metabolism! That shit would kill me in under ten minutes!"

"And there I thought you couldn't overdose on vitamins," I mused, allowing myself a nasty smile. "Spill it, or I'll see for myself what this shit does to you."

Parker hedged some more, but then seemed to decide that his life—or wellbeing—wasn't worth keeping silent over. "Okay, okay, I'll tell you! But first, you put that away, and you call your attack dog off as well, or no deal."

I thought about pointing out to him that I really had nothing to lose here so why should I negotiate, but Nate already backed up, going for an agreeable compromise. Parker stepped away from the tree immediately, but didn't try to run off. In fact, the way he eyed our surroundings with unease, I wondered if he thought he would get in trouble if anyone figured out he was cooperating with us. Interesting.

"I didn't lie to you," he insisted. "Most of it are vitamins and minerals and shit. Everything that your body needs but won't get from the freeze-dried cardboard that we get to eat. But you're right. There's more." He barked a brief laugh. "Should have guessed that cutting you up would boost your metabolism to where it shot over the threshold."

"Actually, it was the fever that addled my brain so I forgot to take almost two days' worth that made some of that shit you've been feeding me wear off," I remarked, but then thought better of it. "Why, what made you think you kicked my metabolism into overdrive?"

"Because that's what happens to you freaks when you get injured," he said, snorting derisively in Nate's direction. "You better teach her the basics if you want to keep such a charming specimen around." When Nate didn't react, Parker turned back to me. "There's a combination of two pills in there that slows your metabolism to almost human rates, supposedly to give your body time to fully heal before you put it through shit that it won't yet survive. My guess is, they added that so they could control you, to keep you calm and quiet. Judging from what you're doing right now, you definitely should be on a double dose of that. But that's it. Nothing that fucks with your brain." His snark aside, he didn't look all too happy explaining all that, and I didn't get the sense because he was waiting for retaliation from either of us.

"That's all?" Nate asked. When Parker nodded, he jerked his chin to the side. "Get lost. And you better not breathe a word of this to anyone."

"You bet I won't," Parker grumbled as he took another step back. "They'd have my ass before they even considered what to do about you." He turned to go, his shoulders squared, but then paused, the hint of a nasty smile creeping onto his features. "Don't delude yourself into thinking Hamilton's the only one that knows. I know you much prefer Richards to him, but maybe you shouldn't, if you don't like being doped up, none the wiser."

I waited until Parker was out of earshot before I turned to Nate, but he was staring off into the forest behind me, making me guess that the guard on perimeter watch had drawn close. So we waited, and then waited some more, until I started to wonder how else we could have spent that time. I didn't mention that possibility, also because I knew that whoever Gita shared my watch shift with, this wasn't her sector, and the last thing I needed was an asshole like Cole busting us.

"What are you going to do now?" Nate asked, tearing me out of my musing.

I shrugged, not sure how to answer. "I guess doing the same with Richards isn't exactly an option?"

"Remember how many of us it took last night to restrain you? The five of us wouldn't be enough, and I'm not sure Tanner and Gita would be on board. Open confrontation, yes, but Tanner already gave me shit this morning that we're trying to keep things on the down low." At my surprised—and, without a doubt, disapproving—look, Nate chuckled. "Can't hold it against him. From what he told me, they had massive issues with people ganging up on each other before they ended up in California, about to raise New Angeles from the ruins, and some severe trouble since. You know that you don't need to doubt his loyalty, or Gita's. You have it, at least until they're back to report in with Greene. But maybe he has a point."

"So you think it's okay that they tried to keep me sedated?" So much for considering getting up close and personal against that oak tree.

Nate smirked as if he'd read my mind, but then the change in mood was likely easy to read in my body language. "Not without telling you about it. But I understand where they thought they could reason that entire consent issue away."

"It's not just that," I admitted, grunting with frustration. "This shit has been making me paranoid as a nut job." When I caught Nate's doubtful look, it was my turn to laugh. "Yes, I'm inclined to worry about less likely things happening even on a good day, no need to remind me of that. But if the last year has taught me anything, it's to adjust my expectations accordingly. You can't look inside my head. You don't know how it's been." I paused, wondering how much to tell him, but there wasn't any sense in holding shit back. Not after last night. "Ever since we landed on that beach, I've been perfectly miserable. Like, first days after the outbreak kind of miserable. Or, like when I was afraid that Madeline's incessant pushing would make any of you guys expect me to put out as well. That's when I had no confidence whatsoever in my own strength and was too scared and confused to know who to trust." Looking at the pills in the baggie, I let out a miserable sigh. "One thing's for sure. I'm not going back on that shit."

"I don't think they intend you to."

Nate's guess made me frown. "What makes you say that?"

"Just a thought," he offered. "You're no use to them if you can't think straight. You're also no use to them if you're too weak to survive. It's a simple self-solving puzzle. If you pull through and get better, eventually, your metabolism would have started running at a rate fast enough to naturally work through any inhibitors, thus ending the usefulness of this farce."

"But wouldn't that be the point where I needed the other shit more than ever? Those MREs really don't make up for the lack of greens and vegetables in our diet."

Nate gave me a deadpan stare. "You've been subsisting on mostly meat and lots of rice and beans for months. A few more weeks of the same won't make a difference."

I mulled that over some more, but didn't come to a conclusion. "What do I do now? Risk staunching my recovery by missing out on some supplements, or spend the remaining weeks in Europe jumping at shadows?"

"You have no way of telling which pills are what?" Nate guessed.

I shook my head. "Some do look like those bullshit over-the-counter vitamins, but most of them are white with almost identical shapes. Not sure I could keep them separate even if I knew what is what." I looked at the baggie one last time before I let it disappear into my jacket pocket. "I could ask Richards, of course."

"He'd likely deny there was anything in there that would make you go nuts. And there's the chance that once he knew you were off that shit, he'd just tell any of the others to hold you down so they could force them down your throat. Is that really what you want?"

"What makes you think he'd do that?"

Nate hesitated. Never a good thing. "Because that's what I would do in his place, if command had told me to make sure you keep munching your candy," he admitted. "Besides, he doesn't have to. All he needs to do is tell Hamilton, and he'll gleefully set to the task." And there was still the possibility that Parker had been lying.

"So what do I do now?" I asked again, although I already knew the answer.

Before Nate could give one, Bucky's voice sounded from behind the tree where we'd messed around with Parker, his usual sarcastic sneer in full force. "You should really keep your bitch on a leash, now that she's shaken off the shackles we put on her."

I didn't exactly whip around but it was impossible not to tense as I saw that he wasn't alone. Several of his flunkies were along. In fact, it was easier to count who was missing—Aimes, Rodriguez, and McClintock, who were probably on watch detail. I was somewhat relieved when I saw Red among the so far silent onlookers, and relaxed a little when Burns cleared his throat, hoofing it over from the side of the clearing that was closer to our camp. Nate raised his brows at him, Burns quickly signaling that Tanner was with Gita. While my mind wanted to scream in paranoid anticipation of what this might morph into, I forced myself to mentally back down. None of them were wearing extra weapons, and while technically they outnumbered us, none of those who were friendly—like Red, Hill, Murdock, or Davis—had that pinched look on their faces that spoke of some kind of inner conflict. So presumably, we were just about to have a pleasant chat. Yeah, right.

Parker was also missing, but while Bucky was still grinning at unveiling his presence with such a grand statement, I saw him scurrying up behind Red. If that meant he hadn't ratted us out, Bucky had likely been planning this—just as we had been planning to pull Parker aside. Great. I was more than happy to go right off in Hamilton's face, but Nate spoke up before I could, his arms crossed over his chest, his stance at ease.

"It must be close to seventeen years now when I first told you that it says a lot more about you than whoever you're trying to verbally abuse. Just cut the crap. It got old a decade ago."

Bucky grimaced, but it was still a superior grin that shone through, like he was gloating because of something we weren't privy to.

"And, like always, guess who cares?" he shot back, chuckling softly. "It's not like pretending to take the high road ever got you anywhere."

"It usually got me where I wanted to end up," Nate retorted, just a little too confrontational for that relaxed attitude he was trying to portray.

Hamilton chortled, continuing with that same bullshit behavior that was begging for a punch in the face. As much as I wanted to respond, the impassive faces all around held me back. There was more going on than Hamilton just being a fuckwit, and I wasn't sure I still wanted to know what. I was tempted to tell Nate so, but Hamilton spoke up before I could.

"You both owe me, big time. As in, neither of you would still be alive anymore if not for me. So how about you listen up and cut that sneaky bullshit crap. We're all stuck here together and before long, we'll have to rely on each other. Maybe think about that next time you turn your constant whiney moping into action."

That shut me up good. Not the last part about us obviously not being as covert in our undertakings as I'd figured, but then something must have tipped off Hill last night to come over to investigate— likely a muffled scream or two from me. No, it was that first part that burned a red-hot trail of shame through my conscience that made any objection I might have wanted to bring forward die an instant death.

Nate noticed my sudden change in mood, and it was kind of funny to realize what it was that brought his defender urge to the forefront. This once, I could really have done with more stoicism.

"Yeah, right," Nate chuffed, taking a swaggering step forward so he wasn't standing beside me anymore but closer to Hamilton and the others. "Neither of us owes you shit. Do you really need a reminder that since the very first day we met, you've always been playing second fiddle to me? I have always been the better soldier, the better leader. You were always just good enough. If I hadn't thrown in the towel and set things in motion to step out, you'd never have gotten to where you are now. I know that. You know that. Your men know that. More than half of them have the experience and competence to replace you in a heartbeat. You're just here because nobody wanted to make an effort and challenge you. Yet." His tone was hard and held more than just a hint of challenge, making me weirdly proud to stand beside him. The kid gloves had definitely come off. So he had only been holding back until he was sure that I would be okay and able to fend for myself. More than anything else, that was a massive relief to me—and proved that, indeed, I was getting better. Almost dying last night had just been a small bump in the road, nothing more.

Contrary to what I would have expected, Bucky was rather unperturbed by Nate's accusations, his grin never slipping. Oh, there was tension in his jaw as he listened to Nate listing his many shortcomings, but the blow didn't so much glance off as there was no resistance.

"And you're, what? Doing that now?" he asked. "Challenging me?"

"Maybe I should," Nate shot back, his eyes briefly leaving Hamilton to skip along the present soldiers. "It wouldn't be a smooth transition, but I'm sure we'd work out any remaining differences quickly enough. I'm not like you. I don't punish people for questioning my authority. I welcome it, if warranted in particular. Why not air out all our grievances and then see who they'd rather see in charge? Someone who's a competent leader, or someone whose only directive is to follow his orders, with not a care about resulting casualties?"

I knew something was wrong when Hamilton still didn't let himself be baited. And it wasn't that he'd primed his flunkies—enough of them looked genuinely surprised, and while a few didn't seem particularly happy, most seemed intrigued.

"Of course we can do that," Hamilton offered jovially. "But let me remind you of one thing first."

"Which is?"

Hamilton's grin widened but lost a lot of its humor as he started to drone on. "You swore an oath. An oath to never form any emotional connections or attachments. To never fall in love, never marry, never father any children. From this day forward, there is nothing more important in your life than to follow your orders, whatever the consequences, whatever it takes. There's only the program, nothing else."

That sounded like such a load of bullshit that I was hard-pressed not to laugh—until I glanced over at Nate and saw that he'd gone perfectly still, the color draining from his face. Gone was the bordering-on-gleeful lust for confrontation, replaced now by... was that open fear in his eyes? Nate wasn't one to be rattled easily, and except for me dying I'd seldom seen him more than somewhat apprehensive at the most. I knew him well enough to be aware that he was capable of a broader spectrum of emotions, but it likely would have killed him to admit that, or so I'd joked on more than one occasion. There was no hint of that reservation going on now, and that terrified me on a level I hadn't realized I was capable of.

This was not good. So not good. I might not have a clue what was going on, but that much was obvious.

"Decker can't still be alive," Nate rasped out, his voice almost inaudible with strain. "Of all the billions of people that died, he can't have been one of the few that made it. He must be well over seventy now."

Bucky's gleeful sarcasm took on a rather different meaning. This was a bit of information he must have been sitting on for ages, and it obviously made him feel like the proverbial one-eyed man among the blind.

"Seventy-three, far as I know. Rumor has it that, unlike almost everyone else, when the first warnings trickled through the grapevine, he grabbed his favorite granddaughter—supposedly the only member of his family that damn hypocrite found deserving to survive—and disappeared into whatever hidey-hole he'd set up for emergencies. I'm not positive on what happened to the girl but she was still with him when he turned up at one of our bases in early spring." The smile he offered was closer to a grimace. "Who do you think has been running this shtick all year long? Everything we accomplished this year has his stamp blazoned across it." Now that grimace morphed back into a wry grin. "But you do know, don't you? If you didn't outright suspect it, you got mighty cautious after the first few setbacks to keep your name out of the headlines. Too little, too late, I'm afraid. You had your chance and you blew it."

Nate didn't react, still processing whatever that piece of information meant to him.

I could only guess what events Bucky was referring to, but Nate had taken a step away from the stage after the I'd gotten infected at the factory and almost died. For a while, I'd thought he'd lost his drive to help others if it took everything we had just to survive. Then it had been easy to believe that he let me take the lead to exact my bloody revenge on Taggard and whoever else had wronged me. Yet while all that had sounded reasonable at the time, looking back now, Bucky's claim held a lot of weight—and I really didn't like that.

"Who's Decker?" I asked the most obvious question. Silence answered me, Nate and Bucky still locked in their staring match, one gloating, the other still reeling. I cast a questioning look at Burns but got nothing but the same back from him. It was Cole who spoke up to explain, a little bemused after doing his own double-take among his buddies.

"He's a ghost," he offered, snorting when only Hill inclined his head. "Not that I've ever met him. Fabled recruiter of our illustrious ranks. Back when I—and that big oaf here"—he indicated Hill— "were Delta, one of our buddies knew a guy who knew a guy who supposedly was looking for people with a very special skillset. That's closer than most of us ever got to him." His gaze skipped from me to Bucky and Nate. "Except for a few classes of our commanding officers. Good luck with trying to get any intel out of them, though. Never met a single one of them who didn't immediately clam up when he was mentioned."

That explained some things, but at the same time, nothing at all.

Bucky paid us no mind, still fixated on Nate. Somehow I got the feeling that he'd been waiting for this conversation to happen since we'd shown up on their doorstep—or even longer.

"Remember the last words that old bastard said to you, at the hearing for your dishonorable discharge?" he asked.

Nate gave the curtest nod possible, his voice a little stronger than before. "He said that if he ever saw my ugly mug again, he'd kill me. And that I was the biggest disappointment of his life." Unexpectedly from what little information about this Decker guy I'd gotten so far, Nate sounded something between sentimental and laden with guilt.

Bucky picked up on my observation, impossible as it was for me to keep my bewilderment off my face, briefly directing his smirk at me while still mostly talking to Nate.

"You always were his golden boy. His prestige project. He snatched you up right out of the recruitment office, didn't he?" Nate inclined his head but didn't volunteer anything else. "He was your mentor, and you gobbled up every little tidbit he threw your way. You showed interest in something? Why, of course there was a spot opening for you in sniper school or with the Sappers. You wanted to take some months off to take some psych classes in college? Perfect for someone who already had all the ducks in a row to go for PSYOPS next. And like the eager little soldier that you were, you always outperformed his expectations. You always had to raise the bar. Meanwhile, I had to fight for scraps, never being quite good enough simply because I wasn't his psychotic little lapdog. The rest of us had to be bent into shape, broken and reforged. You were perfect just the way you are."

I briefly checked in with Burns. He rolled his eyes at Bucky being so dramatic. Nate still didn't protest, although he looked like he was about to regain his composure. There must have been more to this to explain his outright shock at the news. Then again, I had some experience myself with new information making me rethink my every action for the past, well, years. Might take the best of us a few minutes to come to grips with that.

"Shall I go on or is this enough?" Bucky harped, suddenly no longer that at ease himself.

"No need," Nate was quick to respond. Now there was something I knew I needed to have a chat about with him later.

Hamilton grunted, not done yet—not by a lot. "The only reason you got out was because of me. Did you really think they'd just let you go because you pretended to screw up, and with no casualties to show for it? Come on, you never were that stupid. I didn't get it back then and I still don't to this day, but hey, who was I to stand in my own way? Decker may have believed that he forged you into the perfect weapon, but I've always seen right through you. You wouldn't have made it out on your own without my help. They would have either put you out of your misery, or sent you to be retrained, and we both know how that would have ended." His eyes briefly flitted to me but he didn't elaborate. "So I stuck out my neck for you. Took the guilt and the blame that you couldn't shoulder. Rather than kill you, they decided to shelve you, whatever the old man said. You might still come in handy later, should worse come to worst." He flashed his teeth in a bright smile. "And lo and behold, don't we all know how that went down." That was one way to describe the dead rising once more, after the damn virus killed off most of the world's population.

Bucky allowed himself a moment to gloat—and for Nate to refute any of his claims, which he still didn't—before he went on.

"You made two mistakes," he offered, then included me. "Three." Raising a finger, he counted. "One, you should have come with us back in that godforsaken town right when the shit hit the fan. How you didn't see what was coming before that happened I will never understand, but by then you must have realized that the world was going to hell, and just for sheer survival, your odds would have been a million times better with us than out there alone. Thank fuck not everyone was that stupid." He didn't need to glance at Murdock and Davis to make them hunch their shoulders slightly. Ah, so there was still some residual guilt there that, rather than follow Nate, they'd thrown their lot in with Bucky.

Hamilton wasn't waiting for an answer from Nate, but he nevertheless got one—and one that surprised me in its honesty. "I was heavily relying on intel from one of my associates at the time,"

Nate confessed. "As we all know, she was with those idiots who might have started this shit. She deliberately fed me false information so we'd go through with the mission no matter what. Looking back, it makes sense that she also made sure none of us would snatch up the wrong kind of rumors." Dolores, his tech wizard friend—may she roast in hell.

If Bucky was displeased that Nate didn't argue the point of not joining him having been a mistake, he didn't show it. Instead, he focused on me. "We all know why you joined him." No expected raucous laughter came from the others, and for once I missed it. That damn tension in the air was way worse than getting ribbed. Hamilton cocked his head to the side. "What has always puzzled me is this: did he actually recruit you, or did he just screw your brains out to make you receptive for helping him when he needed you? One of the reasons why I was in that damn town was because you were on a VIP list of people I should fetch. Only found out much later that your status was actually way higher than the random politician's kids that we were also out to collect. Emily Raynor herself set you on that list, and if more assholes'd had the sense to listen to her, you'd have had a special detail pick you up as early as Wednesday afternoon." That would have been two days before Nate and his people locked me up in the Green Fields Biotech atrium with Greene and the other scientists—making it a full three days before it had been too late for all of us.

It was mostly the unease causing my skin to itch all over that got me to answer him. "I had no idea what was going on until I was a hostage in a glass cube. And even then I was only given very limited information." I could have done without Bucky's smirk but didn't concede that point to him. "What did Raynor have to do with that?"

Bucky kept on grinning, letting Red—surprise, surprise—do the explaining. Richards looked vaguely uncomfortable, but so far, he'd watched the exchange with avid attention, making me guess that he was taking notes, just like I was.

"Emily Raynor is probably the only reason why any of us are still alive," Red started. Nobody disagreed, which surprised me. "There was an incident two weeks before that sent her into red alert. She pestered everyone who would listen—which were far too few people—before she grabbed a bunch of scientists, every scrap of lab equipment that she could get her hands on at short notice, and holed up in the Esterhazy base. One of the reasons why she's one of the power players is that her warning hit way closer to the truth than anyone could have expected. She insisted that special troops were sent to key stations to ensure that in the event of a fatal catastrophe, we would be able to prevent worse from happening." He cocked his head to the side when all he got from me was a bland look. "Have you never wondered why the US didn't turn into a nuclear wasteland when the grid went offline and no one was alive to power down the reactors?"

Now that he mentioned that...

I shook my head, unease of a different kind taking over for a second. I sure hoped our European counterparts had used the extra time allotted to them thanks to the slower onset of the apocalypse to take care of that.

"Not getting eaten or infected seemed like the much more pressing issue at the time," I admitted. "And guess I forgot about the rest when no one else brought up any possible dangers." I didn't need to look at Nate to indicate who I was referring to.

"We had teams of two to five people stationed at every single possibly volatile point," Richards disclosed. "That's part of why we lost so many in the first weeks of the outbreak. And why a lot of them chose to set out on their own, ending up on your side of the playing field this year." Bucky's lips curled into a slight sneer. Red ignored him. "I'm not sure how long you'd been on Raynor's radar; probably only for the brief time when you were about to be hired by Raleigh Miller to join his team, but since you never actually got to work on his research, you likely ended up as a note in a file. Yet when she was scrambling to secure all the resources she could, she must have remembered that one of the most brilliant scientists to have ever worked on the serum project thought you a worthy candidate. It took all the favors she could call in to set things in motion. There wasn't enough pull left to escalate your retrieval. If I hadn't accidentally ended up in Lexington as we had to pull back, no one would have spared a second to try to pick you and your girlfriend up."

Gee, wasn't that a nice reminder. That, inevitably, I hadn't needed their help to survive didn't seem to matter to Richards now. That he seemed to be the only reason why Sam was still alive did matter to me.

Tired of someone stealing his show, Hamilton took over once more, raising another finger.

"Your second mistake was showing up on the playing field once more when you thawed out from your bunker in spring." I must have looked surprised that he knew about that, making him laugh— harshly. "Yes, I knew where you were hiding. Never wondered why they had a set of overwhites around that was a few sizes too small for all of them? That was intended for my sister." He grimaced, as if he'd bitten on something unexpectedly bitter. "Back when we built that bunker, we were still tight, but even then we were paranoid enough to keep the undertaking under wraps from everyone who didn't strictly need to know. I didn't have a reason to rat you out. On the contrary. Would have been so much easier for me if you'd just remained dead like everyone thought you were." He barked a short laugh. "But no, you had to be fucking morons who set out to save the world! Some people absolutely deserve the shit that comes raining down on them."

A dramatic pause followed. No one spoke up. This was getting tedious quickly, but considering I kind of knew what was coming next, I could see why he was drawing this out. I had to admit, I was kind of curious about getting his side of things. Not that I expected any huge revelations that could dwarf the bomb he'd already dropped, but so far, none of this had really impacted me. That was about to change.

"Your third and final mistake was to make your return from the dead official," Hamilton recounted. "Maybe they would have ignored you if you'd let her take over the lab in that town in Kansas. What's it called?"

"Aurora," Red and I offered in unison. Hamilton snorted at my glare, easily holding it now.

"That one. Not saying you didn't have a target painted on the back of your head by then, but if you'd stayed behind, Raynor would have put everything in motion to bring you up to her little kingdom, and you would have been out of harm's way at the very least." He chuckled to himself as he focused on Nate again. "Serves you right that of all the billions of cunts in the world, you find the one that matches your crazy—and your utter carelessness, borne from the conviction that you're invincible. Not only did she, quite publicly, throw her lot in with you, no. She had to go the whole nine yards and stress to everyone who wanted to listen, and those who didn't, that you two were a thing. Not going to repeat that quote for sensitive ears here, but that was pretty irrefutable."

"What, you keeping a file on all the shit I say?" I huffed, more intrigued than annoyed.

"Huge file," Bucky succinctly told me. "You signed your death warrant that day."

Now didn't that sound dramatic? I would have loved to call bullshit, but I had the strong—and quite uncomfortable—feeling that, for once, he was telling the truth.

"Then why am I still alive?" I would have loved to proclaim that with a taunting lilt to my voice, but it came out more like a dry rasp.

Bucky's smirk was back in full force. "Why do you ask questions that you already know the answer to?" And fuck, did I hate that he even did a very good imitation of Nate's voice asking me that. He dropped it as he went on explaining. "Guess there are still gaps you're not quite sure how to fill. The moment they knew your dear husband was back on the playing field, they wanted him back in the fold. Not without consequences for his transgressions, but nothing like the end of the world to offer up some second chances, right?" His gaze dropped on Nate. "It was only due to the drag in communication speed that let you get out of both Dispatch and the Silo before they could send me there to fetch you. What comes next, you already know." He allowed himself another chuckle. "Damn, it was great to see the desperation on your face when we cornered you in that factory. Kudos to you. I didn't expect that you'd have it in you to blindly sacrifice several of your men to save her. You still failed. How did that make you feel?" Nate didn't deign to respond.

"The official orders were to bring you both in, and whoever else could be persuaded to come along. Goes without saying that I received my personal orders directly. A kill order for her and anyone you'd ever worked with for more than a single assignment, or who I thought might mean something to you. In the unlikely event of your immediate surrender, I was to take her into custody alive, but we all know that neither of you would have wanted that." He graced me with a sidelong glance. "You think almost dying of getting savaged by zombies was bad? That was child's play compared to what would have happened to you otherwise." He paused, this time to consider, not just for annoying effect. "Guess there was a slim chance that they would have decided to try to use you later on, but nobody thought you'd be useful as a fighter back then. Be glad. You would have hated the husk of your former self that they'd have turned you into. You would have survived that, I guess, considering that you didn't give up just because you started rotting from the inside out. Had they known you were cut from that cloth, they never would have let you go."

"Not much of that 'letting' actually happened," Nate pointed out. "We beat you fair and square, against all odds."

Bucky laughed, for once amused. "Ah, now, did you? Or did I let you go? Let me think." He went as far as to pensively scratch his chin, his eyes never leaving Nate's. "Right. I let you go. Because the last thing I needed was you back in the game, and likely twice as insufferable once you got out of the re-education camp. Or was it sheer sentimentality that made me give the order to fall back and not kill every living soul in that damn building just to hunt you down? Can't be, right? Because we both know they beat that shit right out of us both."

Another nugget, and judging from the harsh set of Nate's jaw, not something he liked to be reminded of.

"You really didn't suspect that they sent us there to get you back?" Bucky asked. "Come on. You turned into a veritable U-boat after that. You must have suspected something."

Nate took his sweet time responding, and I didn't miss that, twice, he cast a cautious look my way. "Suspected? Yes. But the chances that anyone was still alive who had a personal grudge against me were nil. And why would you have let me go in Aurora if you'd still wanted me back in the fold?"

"Why indeed," Bucky drawled. "You know that's not how Decker works."

"I didn't think he could still be alive," Nate echoed his previous sentiment. "Or that anyone would be stupid enough to put him in charge."

Hamilton chortled with mirth. "I don't think it was a conscious decision. You missed out on a lot of infighting behind the scenes. At first, everyone was scurrying to survive. Then there were so many different factions to unite, each one trying to make a grab for control while not giving an inch of what they'd already secured. Trade had to be established, settlements secured, troops redistributed. Who would have paid one single old man much notice? He wasn't stupid. He reached out to us first, secured his base. And by the time anyone else was aware of his return, it was already too late." Another pause. "Not that most minded. The worse the times get, the more people look for a leader, particularly one who pretends to leave them a little more independence than they ask for and is happy to remain in the shadows. Sound familiar?"

It did, and I so didn't like Bucky throwing me that bone to chew on. That sounded a lot like the shit Nate had been pulling for most of the year, if on a smaller scale. I could tell that he knew the damage was done, but Nate didn't give Bucky the satisfaction to look at me, apologetic or not.

"Are you done yet?" he asked instead.

"Not by a mile," Bucky confided. "But I don't want to bore you with the details. Long story short, when I returned empty-handed, they decided to let someone else prove his competence."

"Taggard," I guessed when Bucky didn't volunteer the information right away. I had been wondering where he came onto the stage.

He nodded. "He and Alders—that senile of fuck of a doctor—already had their sick little serum farm set up. No need to ask me about the details, that's one of the factions I never had anything to do with except reading the files after the fact. All it took was to set a trap using that girl from the other scavenger group, and of course you waltzed right in." Another dramatic pause followed, until I was close to going back on my stance not to try to physically harm him. "Far as I know, the kill order on you was still active, but I don't need to repeat that Taggard was barely more than a sock puppet with about as much intellect. Rather than kill you, he took his sweet time locking you up in that tiny cell so he could torment you, and what happened after that he sure had comin'. Still baffles me how he managed to take out most of your merry band of misfits when he was already limping back to the only one who still had his back, for her very own morbid reasons."

Listening to him so casually refer to us losing everyone but the four of us who'd been in the settlement to talk while Andrej had taken up the pursuit—killing one, and severely maiming several others, not the least Andrej and Martinez—made me gnash my teeth hard enough that the enamel should have cracked. I swallowed my ire, instead forcing myself to focus on the new information.

That last bit he'd offered up I could guess at. "So Raynor really knew I was infected back then." Question was, whether or how she'd been connected with Taggard—and Alders—before that.

Bucky graced me with a bright smile. "As soon as one of the lab techs called her from the Silo, after you resurfaced from not biting it. She heard about Taggard's undertaking by accident, and let's just say that she wasn't too heartbroken to get some extra lab results ahead of him delivering you personally. She must have known that was never his intention until she ended up being his only option, but he was an alternative to me. Damned if I know why that woman doesn't like me." Judging from his ongoing smile, he was very aware of said reason.

"So they sent you to the Colorado base to make up for your previous failure, seeing as Taggard hadn't had much more success?" I ventured a guess.

"See, you can be smart if your fucking misguided idealism doesn't get in the way," Hamilton jeered. "Command wasn't happy about the developments that happened over the summer. It was a close to serendipitous moment when we got the news that you were rallying everyone who would follow to come after us. Nobody would have profited from slaughtering the lot of you, and some factions were lobbying that having all the misfits rally under someone they knew had leadership qualities was in our best interest." Nate didn't react to his smirk. "Raynor's insistence got more urgent that you were on borrowed time, so my kill order was rescinded. Why bother when we could just let nature take its course? One invitation, lost in the heat of battle. Stranger things have happened." And he'd likely gotten a commendation for what I'd believed was one of his greater missteps. Ah well. In the light of recent revelations, I didn't give a shit about that anymore.

Nate cleared his throat after a few tense seconds. "What changed?"

Bucky shrugged. "She didn't die quickly enough," he offered. "And the snow storm you encountered on the way to the Silo might have hampered communications."

Wait, what were they talking about now? What change was Nate referring to? Proving once more that he could pretty much read my mind, Nate shrugged. "They could have easily killed you at the Silo. And we never would have made it to the base on our own after the cars broke down. Those ATVs didn't plant themselves out there, fully operational."

"Let's say that I was personally motivated by the idea of gloating into your rotting face one last time after you realized that it was thanks to me that you were dying," Bucky provided conversationally. It was my turn to sneer at him, but I regretted that a second later when his eyes lit up. Uh oh. Dangerous territory. I cast around for what to say to cut this short, but Hamilton was already talking, explaining with glee once more taking over his voice. "And my, did you look pathetic when you couldn't even undress yourself anymore without help. But I have to hand it to you, I hadn't expected you to be such a tenacious bitch. Color me impressed. Impressed enough that I figured you deserved a chance to live."

I bit down hard on my tongue to keep myself from responding. Sadly, Nate had other ideas.

"Like you had anything to do with that," he bit out, heat returning to his tone.

Bucky snorted, unimpressed. I absolutely hated the smile spreading on his face. "You really think that her undying love for you would have been enough to get her through that shit? Guess again. I know, Richards here agrees with you. His idea was to kill you both with kindness. Figuratively speaking, of course." The way he laughed let me guess that he didn't think Red capable of cold-blooded murder. "He wrote your psych profile, just saying," Bucky told me. "Lots and lots of bullshit in there that's absolutely useless. He wanted us to welcome you with open arms. To shame you into cooperating because all of your many misconceptions had led to deaths that weighed so heavily on your soul now, boohoo. That was obvious from all the data they'd managed to gather on you.

But they were lacking one crucial detail that, somehow, everyone overlooked."

I didn't want to, but I just had to bite. "Which is?"

Bucky's smile brightened. "That he"—he indicated Nate—"is the one who indoctrinated you. The one who made you into his perfect little murder doll. Whether consciously or just on instinct, he taught you how to survive, and that at whatever cost. Only makes sense. That's his one defining trait that rules over everything he does. I never found out if he's actually a highly functioning psychopath who's absolutely perfect at pretending to be a semi-moral human being, or the other way round. It doesn't matter. You took your clues from him and made his template yours. Decker never really understood him, not like I did, because some things you only learn about someone if you're really fucking tight. Until that very last resort, you may delude yourself that it's positive thinking that gets you through the day. But once you're at the end of the line, the only thing that will let you survive is cold, hard anger. And my, didn't I give you enough of that to last you for a long, long life?"

I didn't try to refute his claim, not even to myself. Especially not to myself. I couldn't remember when that had occurred to me, but all the denial I had in me hadn't been enough to convince myself otherwise. Yet it was one thing to know, deep down, but quite another to stare the truth in the smirking face.

Uncustomarily for him, Hamilton didn't dwell too long on that, but instead made a grandiose gesture with both arms. "Aren't we all glad I did? I'm not saying I was acting altruistic here. You dying on the operating room table would have turned your husband into a walking bomb. Me killing you outright would have done the same. Decker turning you into a broken and barely put-back-together assassin would have done the same. Anything that would have ended with him losing you would have done the deed. It pains me to admit it, Miller, but yes, you are better than me at one thing: you would have deceived the master deceiver. You would have pretended to roll over and take it, then waited, forever holding your breath, until you were close enough to kill that old bastard and rid the world of him. There wouldn't have been any consequences for me for doing that except having you back around with your superior attitude and your fucking need to excel at everything. Why would I want that? Can't be that, old sentimental fool that I am, I felt like my old friend deserved a shot at a life I'll never have? No, I'd never do that. They made sure that compassion isn't on my list of emotions that I'm still capable of."

He offered the last with a wry grin, but dropped it the next second.

"I consider my debt repaid. I know I said I'd never be able to do that, but that was back when I couldn't fathom you'd ever change. Now you both owe me. And what you will do to work that off is make sure that this mission is a fucking phenomenal success. I don't give a shit if you're moping all over Europe, but you'll do it quietly and efficiently, do you understand? And once we get back to the States, you do what you should have done last year when you had the chance: you will disappear, and you'll make damn sure that no one will ever find you again. I've worked my ass off to secure the position I hold, and I will not lose it to a damn people pleaser and his psychotic bitch. Do we understand each other?"

Nate didn't object nor did he waste a second before he inclined his head. "We do."

"Good," Bucky surmised, looking my way as if he expected me to object. I didn't. Once he made sure of that, he started forward, walking between us back toward the camp. His mostly silent entourage didn't hang back, some of them looking bored, most a little distraught. I didn't miss the fact that Red was foremost pensive.

I'd expected Burns to remain with us, but he mumbled something about filling Gita and Tanner in that nobody had lynched us yet. Well, not physically. One glance at Nate's face, and I wasn't so sure about his mental state—or my own.

"We should have gone to Alaska, huh?" I offered when nothing else came to mind.

"We should have gone to Alaska," Nate agreed with me. It hadn't exactly been a serious plan, but before we'd set out from the bunker, back in spring, I'd jokingly suggested it.

Exhaling slowly—and feeling like this was the first free breath I took in fucking forever—I tried to sort the thoughts racing through my head but it was impossible. So many questions, but none of them vital—except for one.

"What debt was he referring to?" I could tell that I didn't need to explain.

Nate slowly turned to face me, still looking moderately shell-shocked, but didn't hesitate. That didn't bode well. "I lied. I know exactly what soured our friendship. What turned him into the man he is today."

"And that is?" I knew I didn't want to hear this, but that damn tenacious curiosity got the better of me again.

Nate grimaced but complied. "We didn't get stone drunk the night before they shot us up with the serum. Not on our own, that is." He paused, but I could tell it wasn't out of avoidance but because he was trying to think of the best way to explain this to me. "He's right. I had it easy. Easier than him, at least. Not because all doors opened magically for me or some shit. I earned every fucking bit of that, and paid a steeper price for it than he'll ever know. It doesn't matter. He's right when he says I'm good at hiding my emotions. Part of that is due to the fact that I was blessed with a brother who was even better at that. They believed me when I said that I had no emotional ties to anyone whatsoever. My father was dead at the time, my mother had pretty much disowned me for daring to squander my intellectual potential and wanting to join the Army straight out of high school. My brother was wrapping up his studies at the other end of the country and he didn't even call for my graduation. I was the perfect white canvas, and very eager to learn."

"And Bucky?"

Nate sighed. "He pretended to be the same. On the outside, that worked well enough. He came from a family of flaming liberals, if you would believe it." He barked a brief laugh. "Sam and you would have fit perfectly into one of their New York City dinner parties, back before I met you. He was the typical rebel middle child. Bright enough to make it into several Ivy League schools but that wasn't the way he chose. And he did a good job leaving his former life behind— but he couldn't leave behind his little sister, even though he tried."

So many revelations, and none of them pleasant, I figured, considering Nate's somber tone.

"What happened?"

Nate rubbed the back of his neck, a nervous tick if he had one. "For a long time, it wasn't that hard for him to pretend like he didn't care about her. And I guess, right when he signed up, he didn't that much. She was several years younger. To a late teenage boy, that's millennia." He paused, catching my gaze once more. "Is. She's still alive, spoiler alert. The rest of his family cut ties with him easily enough. He wanted to do everything they believed was the downfall of modern civilization, but to her he was her big brother who she adored. Idolized. She tried to write him several times but he managed to always undermine that somehow. I don't even know how she found out about where we were stationed for the inoculation trials, as they called it. They had an official family meeting day before that started. We both knew, of course, that nobody would come to see us. We'd both, each in our own ways, made sure that nobody would come."

I could tell where this was going. "But she showed up."

He nodded, a slow, painful gesture. "That she did. Apparently she'd signed up for some extracurricular program her high school ran just to be in the same state that weekend. It was late evening when she showed up at the base. Why they even let her in, I have no fucking clue. My guess is that they were tracking her for a while already. Else I can't explain how they could organize this on such short notice. We were in the mess hall." He paused, snorting. "Dining facility, of course, at the time."

"So you were getting drunk after all," I intercepted. Damn that uncanny impulse of mine to cut the tension.

"On coffee," he obliged my curiosity. "We both knew that we could die tomorrow. Didn't want to miss a second of what could be our last night easily. Of course we knew we'd make it. You don't live in that world expecting the worst to come true, not after the shit we'd already been through together. I think we both wanted to reminisce about our families but seeing as we didn't dare, we were just shooting shit. Not sure what tipped us off. I think I saw the lights go on over in our barracks. We had our own comfy twenty-bunks building all to our lone selves, seeing as we were the only two officers of the bunch to get shot up the next day. The waiting time would have been so much easier if they'd just stuck us in with the rest."

This time when he fell silent, I didn't prompt him with inane tangents. Nate licked his lips before he resumed.

"They had her bound and gagged, naked on the floor. It didn't take a genius to make the right connections. I'd never seen a picture of her before so at first glance I thought, shit. What are they going to make us do to that poor girl now? Hopefully she's a stripper and they pay her well. But she had his eyes, and his hair. And there was no mistaking his reaction. It was the two of us against seven of the officers who'd gone through the program initiation the week before. We'd had dinner with them once before their great day, with us being envious and jumpy because we still had a week of tests ahead of us, any one of them could have disqualified us for the program. They hadn't really had time yet to completely figure out their enhanced abilities, but it didn't matter. Just meant that half the punches were twice as hard as intended. I managed to take one of them out, Bucky two more. That still left four of them to tie us up and force two bottles of hard liquor down each of our throats. They took turns, and they took their time. Maybe if we hadn't fought so hard they wouldn't have felt like they needed to let off steam on her. You know the irrational anger I warned you about? Two of them weren't even trying to get a handle on themselves. The worst part? Except for the odd kick in the ribs to make sure neither of us managed to roll over and look away, they didn't touch us again. I'm not saying I would have welcomed being sodomized but it would have given me something else to concentrate on. I think you learned that lesson in that white tiled cell."

I nodded, incapable of saying anything else. Hell, not puking up dinner was hard enough.

"It was early morning when whoever was in charge of the program came to fetch us. They dragged us across the base, still trussed-up like Thanksgiving turkeys, and only removed our gags long enough so we could give verbal consent to being admitted to the last stage of the serum program. I almost didn't go through with it, but the general who was presiding over the legal matters was giving us enough warning looks to make it obvious that if either of us refused now, the girl wouldn't make it out alive." He rubbed his neck again. "If it had been my sister, I would have done exactly what Hamilton said I'd do if anything happened to you. I would have waited, and then waited some more, and then I would have killed everyone who was even passingly connected to this, right to the very top. Maybe easy for me to say as I never had a baby sister, and, damage done or not, she was still alive, so they still had leverage on him. I think he eventually accepted his fate. He'd paid the piper. Now all that was left to do was reap the benefits." He gave me a considering look. "I know you don't agree with his side of things. That's one of the reasons why I married you. If you still consider that being a thing."

I knew he was baiting me to tear me out of that nightmare scape of mental images, but that last sentence still perplexed me.

"Why, think that the fact that you had to watch your best friend's sister get raped by the people you most admired would make me want to file for divorce? Try harder next time."

"It's not just that," he hedged, the hint of a sheepish grin crossing his features.

I had to look away for a moment, warring with myself whether to give him a pass or not, but decided that, in the end, it didn't matter.

"That you were, or are, PSYOPS? I'm sure your mother must have been proud." That gave me a pause. "Did you ever tell her?"

He nodded. "After I dropped out. Five months into my freedom, after I'd made sure I was out for good, I tracked her down at a conference she was speaking at. You know, public space, giving her all the chance to just ignore me if she'd wanted. Turns out, she didn't. She had a lot of blame to lay at my feet, some rightfully, some not. Didn't matter. I told her everything. She listened. Then she started asking the questions that no mother should ask but every psychologist will." He grimaced but it turned into a smile. "You know, most people assume that someone with questionable psychopathic tendencies gets that from their father. With my brother and me, it was our mother. And yes, she tested us both, and I hate to break it to you, I can do empathy with the best of them. I just sometimes choose not to. She never told me about herself, but I'm ninety percent sure that she was just acting all our lives, pretending to be the stern if loving parent. That talent I have from her as well. I couldn't connect with her at the funeral. That would have been too dangerous."

That reminded me of something else. "Didn't you tell me that Hamilton had it out for you because you still had a brother and mother who cared for you? How did that work out, when you woke up in the hospital with Raleigh ranting his head off because he found out about the serum."

Nate shrugged. "I woke up. He was there, immediately calling for our mother. Gave me the scare of my life. I needed all of sixty seconds to spill the beans and explain to him why it was impossible for them to be here. He caught on quickly and laid on the outrage very convincingly. I don't think he was acting much, he really was personally offended someone would do something like that to anyone, friend or foe. I never found out how he learned about this to begin with. My guess is someone wanted to recruit him and he took the bait. They must have given him immunity because he joined the research program, and likely made sure to negotiate that our mother was untouchable. You know the rest."

Which answered a question I hadn't expected to ever get an answer to.

"You thought they'd gone back on that promise not to harm him. You thought it was that Decker guy who had simply bided his time to teach you a lesson and had him killed." Nate slowly blinked but otherwise didn't answer my question. Well, that wasn't really needed anymore. "Does that mean that Bucky was right? The only reason we are both still alive is because he was kind of protecting us?"

"He was certainly protecting his own interests. And his own hide," Nate growled. "Don't think I would have passed him over on my way up the chain."

"You really didn't know?" That much was obvious but I still needed him to acknowledge it.

"I didn't," he confessed. "I didn't, and I still can't believe that the old bastard is still alive."

"How can something like this be a thing?" I asked, feeling new anger well up inside of me. "You're all part of the fucking Army! How can there be some systematic, planned, ongoing shit like that inside an organization that's built on the very foundation of protecting the civilians?"

Nate gave another shrug. "It only takes one bad egg to spoil the cake. And that's just it, a few people in the right places, living the power trips of their lives. Not everyone who was working with the program was bad. I'm convinced that the overwhelming majority— staff, soldiers, command, scientists—were decent people trying to do the right thing. That's why I stayed. That's why, once I dropped out, I didn't go on a rampage and went for the soft, easy targets first. I only needed to know where exactly those rotten eggs were hiding."

"Are you sure that it wasn't Decker after all? He could have been pulling Alders's strings for all we know."

"And to what end?" I'd missed that chiding sarcasm from Nate, and almost welcomed it now. "Decker was never officially, directly involved with the program except for recruitment. We were his pride. And no, me disappointing him wasn't enough to change his mind, I'm not delusional enough to even consider that. He's responsible for a lot of shit that went down, but not dooming the world."

"We'll never find out who did that, huh?" I said, half joking— but then stopped. "You caught that part about Raynor trying to alert everyone two weeks in advance of the shit hitting the fan, right?" Nate nodded slowly, trying to guess what I was hinting at. "And now we're here, in France, where she sent us, literally the day she got her hands on me, who she thought was valuable to her efforts." Another nod. "I'm not being paranoid when I'm saying that that's a glaringly obvious connection."

Nate shook his head slowly. "No, you're not."

"So what am I supposed to do now?" I asked again. The first time we'd been at this point in our conversation felt like it had happened to two different people, a lifetime ago. Maybe that wasn't as far off as I liked to think, judging from the latent fear still ghosting through Nate's eyes.

"About your vitamins?" Of course he remembered. It was impossible to sidetrack him, now I knew that for sure. "Keep the pills but don't take them. If in a day or two, you feel any adverse effects, you take them and check if that goes away. Easy as that."

I really didn't like Nate's fatalistic tone. "Trial and error doesn't sound so enticing considering I could have died last night."

"But you didn't," Nate insisted, giving me a hint of a grin. "That was a minor setback. A hiccup, if you will. You've had those before. Your usual MO is to bounce right back from them. You don't need me to tell you that." No, he didn't. I'd come to that very same conclusion. He paused, then shook his head as if coming to a negative conclusion about something he had been wondering about but didn't feel like sharing with me. Ah, so we were back to that. Same business as usual. "Let's get back to the others. If they've actually kept your metabolism firing on only half its cylinders, we need to get more food into you. We still have some extra left that we found at that village."

I thought about holding him back but the moment had passed, and I wasn't sure I wanted confirmation for my guesses. So like the good little soldier that I would never be, I followed him, pretending that I wasn't deeply disturbed.

Chapter 19

Switching to a late watch shift wasn't that bad, at least not tonight. I wasn't sure that I would have been able to sleep after that talk even if I'd tried. Having to take care of food prep and weapon maintenance kept me physically busy and my mind from locking up in memory loops. I was still sore as hell, but as we returned to our packs, I checked on both the wound on my stomach and left hand, finding them healed shut, the scars still angry red and itching but without the threat of tearing the wounds open again. As much as that was a relief, the fact that Parker wasn't a neat sewer didn't exactly make me more fond of him. Well, so much for Bucky trying to shove a wedge between Nate and me by claiming that he's indoctrinated me—which I wasn't a hundred percent sure I could refute, or wanted to—at the very least, that confirmed that my dear husband saw more in me than a pretty face.

Burns had already filled Gita and Tanner in—as much as he'd thought they should know, which likely amounted to barely more than the heavily abbreviated version, so there was no need to rehash anything. I couldn't help but shudder every time my gaze skipped over to where Bucky was sharing his dinner with Hill, Cole, and Russell. I absolutely refused to feel bad for him—nothing had changed about his actions—but he'd given me food for thought. Nate didn't volunteer any further information and he remained quite somber throughout the evening, but I wondered if anyone but me really picked up on that.

We retired late, and I spent almost two hours tossing and turning before I had to get up for my watch shift. Crunching my way through frozen leaves and grass was easier than I remembered from the days before, but that could have been all in my mind. Yeah, right. I did my best not to overthink this shit. That was about as easy as ignoring Cole's muttered taunt when I slipped when we crossed paths in the southern sector, but I forced myself not to give a shit. Nothing I could do about my situation in general, and bristling at every remark only cost me energy that was better spent elsewhere. Right now, someone making fun of the slight mishaps that still happened when I didn't pay attention was really low on my list of priorities. And maybe Burns was right after all. They wouldn't have taunted a nobody they thought far beneath them. I just couldn't sort out my thoughts tonight to make peace with that.

At just after two, I caught a whiff of decay, making me pause and listen. At first, I didn't hear it over the soft sounds of snoring and people turning in their sleep, but there was something out there, slowly drawing closer. I switched on my night-vision goggles, easily making out a few shapes maybe a hundred yards further into the trees. With luck, they might have passed the camp without noticing us, but it was kind of the point to make sure those who weren't on guard didn't have to play guessing games. I hesitated, wondering if I should let Cole know, but we were a good ten minutes from meeting up again, so I decided to set out on my own. Only four zombies, and judging from how dim their signatures were, those weren't fast or strong ones. As a backup plan, I left my M16 leaning against a tree trunk for easy access, then readied my axes. Tactical tomahawks. Whatever. Rolling my eyes at my own silliness, I waded through the snow, aiming for the shamblers, my body singing with the need for some carnage. Anything, literally anything to shut up my mind was welcome.

I didn't try to sneak up on the first but it pretty much happened. I came at it from behind as it bent over to examine something on the ground. The ax embedded itself nicely in its temple, and all it took after that was a shove with my boot against one disintegrating shoulder. It flopped to the ground without even uttering a sound. The other three had seen the motion and started toward me. From up close, I saw that they really were in dismal shape, worse off than most of the shamblers that we'd had to deal with so far. I wondered if maybe they had been locked in somewhere, lack of sustaining food making them rot away faster. I went for the tallest first, to my right, coming for it with a running start. The one next to it followed quickly as it had closed up to its undead companion by the time it fell, lifeless, to the ground. And then it was just the last one. Judging from the height, I figured it had been a woman, but without any hair left and the clothes turned to rags that barely covered the skeletal body, it was hard to tell. It didn't matter. It went down under two hacks with my right arm, and that was it.

Except that, as I stood panting over the corpse, details jumped to the forefront of my mind that I could have done without. Like that left upper arm, the bones visible through the skin where a huge lesion had eaten away what remained of skin, muscles, and tendons, very much resembling my left thigh before Raynor had fixed it up. Or that the hand on that side was missing several fingers, the remnants looking chewed-on and ragged. Or that now that it lay permanently dead before me and what was left of the blouse it had been wearing torn, the torso was half-exposed, showing that the body must have almost completely eaten itself up, reducing everything to whitish, brittle skin, with tendons and what little remained of the muscles standing out starkly. Looking at the face, I found the cheeks sunken in, high cheekbones prominent, not just hinting at the skull underneath. In my memory, the mirror image of how I'd looked just a few weeks ago came up, making me shy away from the corpse fast enough that I tripped, ending up on my ass, still scrambling back—

Until I hit a pair of legs.

Looking up, I found Red standing behind me, an assault rifle in each hand, the one in his left partly covered in powdery snow— presumably mine.

"Having some issues there?"

That was putting it mildly. Swallowing hard, I pushed myself to my feet, absentmindedly brushing snow off my ass and legs after cleaning the ax blades. I tried to school my face into a neutral mask while I was busy. When I turned around, I extended my hand to accept my rifle. "Everything's a-okay," I said a little too cheerily. "Why, any reason it shouldn't be?"

Yeah, that was smooth. The level look I got from Richards told me as much. "You tell me," he prompted. "It's only been twenty-four hours since you had four inches of gaping wound in your stomach."

Ah, that. It wasn't like I had forgotten about it. I was heavily favoring my other side already, and at that realization let my hand drop to the scar, trying a little less hard to ignore the pain. "Hurts, but no surprise there. Would be more disconcerting if it didn't, right?"

Red's lack of a reaction was almost as bad as Nate could get. "Then why were you trying to scramble backwards from a corpse?"

"Tripped," I offered, making a helpless gesture, very aware that I was massively overdoing it, but I just couldn't help myself. With my mind still reeling—and from two separate instances—it was hard to pretend that I was doing fine. "You know, it happens when your balance is off because you have to stuff your boots to make up for missing toes, and half your body is still hurting from past and fresh gaping wounds alike, and such." I should have just shut up. Now it was too late for that.

Red's brows drew together as he frowned. "If you're not feeling well, I'll take you off the rotation, no problem." Like that was an enticing option, after how our evening had started. Thanks, but no thanks. Even giving me the uncomfortable scare of the week, I'd needed that little exertion to burn off some of the latent tension Bucky's revelations had left inside of me.

I gave him wide, hopefully innocent eyes. "No need. I'm good. Actually, I should get back to my watch. Now." It took more effort than it should have to get those words out without starting to hyperventilate. It occurred to me that my mind was trying to compensate, giving me a more concrete target to focus on. Oh great, rather than developing ulcers I was this close to having a panic attack. The way he kept squinting at me made me guess that I really didn't convince anyone. In a visible show of restraint, I exhaled, holding my breath for a few seconds before I tried again. "Thank you for your concern, but it's unfounded."

"You look like you're a second away from running off, screaming at the top of your lungs," Richards observed.

That sounded like a rather apt observation. I wondered if congratulating him on that would help, but doubted it. It was impossibly hard to keep the rising panic at bay—but right along with it came a wave of anger that wasn't any easier to ignore. Hamilton's words echoed through my mind, mixing with months and months of latent misgivings. That feeling of being helpless and vulnerable returned that I'd only just shaken off this morning, having believed it to be gone for good. What a fool I'd been—as if a dash of mental clarity and my body working just a little better could change my general situation. I did want to scream, but with frustration, and it took all my willpower not to let any of that leak out of my mind and turn into physical action. No, trying to sock Red a good one did not sound like the way to go.

"Anything you need?" I asked, my voice pressed, but at least the dismissal I tried to put into it translated well.

Richards blinked, looking genuinely surprised. "I'd say it's more the question whether you need anything," he offered. "Like someone to talk to?"

"And why the hell should that be you?" So much for trying to act civil.

"Who else would you turn to?" There was a note of condescension in Red's voice that was impossible to miss. "To your husband you need to constantly prove that you're at least as tough as he is. You need for Burns not to take you seriously to keep you sane, but that comes with the downside of missing out on some heart-to-heart topics. Gita worships the ground you tread on and you'd rather die than show her that you're only human after all. You don't trust Tanner, likely because you rightfully believe that he proved himself to become Gabriel Greene's second lieutenant. And that's the end of the very short list of people you trust. In many aspects, they all are almost like family to you, and they unwaveringly have your back. But for some things, you need someone who has a little distance. You and me, we have no history, and I think I have proven to you more than once that I have your best interest at heart. It would have been a lot easier for me not to."

The fact that part of me wanted to believe him didn't help. "But I can't trust you, so why would I confide in you?" Red opened his mouth to protest, but I forestalled him. "I didn't say you weren't trustworthy; but you have your orders, and we both know, they supersede your conscience, or else you wouldn't be the lieutenant around here. I get that, and while I personally will never think like that, I can see why the entire lot of you feels comforted rather than alienated by this." And therein lay part of the crux for me, I realized— that the lines were blurring; always had, but it had been so easy to forget with me having been the outsider, and our scavenging team developing its own dynamic right from the start. I'd never questioned how Pia could be in charge as Nate's executing hand without having any military rank. She'd just been. And the others had fallen in line, with minimal squabbling about the hierarchy, or at least none I'd been aware of. Now we had parts of us, and Nate's former teammates, and those that hadn't been with him since he'd dropped out, and it all got very confusing, at least for me, who loved to see the world in black and white, good and evil, us versus them… and now there was only us left, but an "us" I didn't quite feel a part of, which was entirely my own fault—as Red himself had pointed out in the past.

"Penny for your thoughts?" he prompted.

I shook my head, more to clear my thoughts than in denial. "It's not you. Maybe it's not even me. But we both know, if I ask you, again, what this is all about, you won't tell me, and I will be annoyed and suspicious, and that's not a good common ground to have a heart-to-heart. It would go a long way if you gave me just a little."

He seemed tempted, but that smile told me he was seeing right through me. "Guess I should add 'manipulative' to your file," Richards observed. "And there I thought I'd figured you out."

I chuckled, but it wasn't a happy sound. How could he have figured me out when I myself was struggling with the very same thing? That Bucky, of all people, had no problem with that just grated all the more. At least our banter had calmed down my panic, and let most of the anger seep back to the pit of my stomach where it continued to roil.

"Well, if you don't give me anything, why should I behave any differently?" I'd meant that as words of parting, but Red reached for me before I could get away.

"Just tell me what you scrambling away was all about, and I'll drop it."

I considered lying, but antagonizing him if I didn't have to didn't sound all that smart. And what did I have to lose? It was likely not very hard to figure out. After all, he was the one who'd compiled their profile on me. Just perfect. "Guess it took the reminder last night of exactly how close to dying I came to really hammer that message in. Not just dying, but turning into one of them, only with my mind still working well enough to grasp the abject horror of it. Intellectually, of course I knew. I'm not stupid. But I wouldn't have recovered if I hadn't had a healthy dose of denial going on. That's mostly gone now." And damn, didn't that sound like I desperately needed a hug. And let's not forget how Bucky's idea of motivation played into that as well.

Red didn't attempt to give me that hug, but there was conflicted compassion plain on his face that looked too raw not to be real. "I think you're not giving yourself enough credit for what you've managed to do," he offered when he broke the lengthening silence between us. "All of us have had a moment that finally made it real. For most, that didn't come until after the shit hit the fan, but they all volunteered. You only had the choice whether you wanted to give up or have a fighting chance to survive. Even someone who's leading a very balanced life can struggle with that."

"And you're not counting me as 'balanced,' huh?" I teased, surprised that my grin was a real one, if still faint.

Red snorted. "Come on, you get off on that whole 'deranged psycho bitch' pretense that you've had going on for the past few months. Actually, that might be the underlying issue that leads to your deluge of prejudice. You hate that now that you have to work with us, it's very easy to see that you're anything but."

I couldn't help but laugh. "Some of it is true. More so than I like to admit. But please, keep treating me like an intelligent, reasonable person and you might eventually get somewhere."

"Killed, probably," Red mused. "And I wouldn't be surprised if it was your husband who pulled the trigger on me."

"He's not the jealous type," I teased, although there was a hint of truth to Red's suspicion.

"If he really wants back in, I'm in his way," Red clarified. "If asked, I would yield, and gladly, but I get the sense that the people who've dealt with him in the past weren't lying when they said Miller was a crazy, ruthless asshole."

I would have loved to refute that claim—and compared to what I knew of Bucky, Nate really wasn't that driven to reach his goals over the deaths of his men—but didn't.

"Guess you're lucky then that he doesn't," I offered instead. "We both got that memo. Either we disappear, or we might get some unnaturally competent help with that."

A hint of disappointment crossed Red's face. That made me trust him more, actually, although it also begged the question why he seemed to take Bucky's warning a lot less seriously than Nate had. With anyone else, that might have made me question my own stance, but in this, I trusted Nate—and Bucky—a hundred percent. I wondered if I should ask Richards about his opinion. He looked tempted to offer it. Yet what he said was something completely different. "Emily Raynor has more pull than Hamilton will attribute her. If you throw your lot in with her, she will protect you. Some may think her research is a dead end, but a lot of people in the right places believe in her. You could make a difference, you know that."

And again, that siren song, still so tempting even though my survival instinct had already barred that way for good. Still, I had to try one last time. "Well, for starters, if I knew what exactly she is working on, and why we are here right now, that would go a long way toward making me see the faults in my logic."

Red looked away to hide his mirth, but he'd been too slow. "You really don't believe in being subtle, do you?" he remarked, scratching his chin on the shoulder of his jacket. "And you know that I can't, hence you can continue to pretend like I'm the bad guy and you have all the reasons in the world not to trust me. Clever, Lewis, but not really bright."

"Hey, whatever helps me keep going, right?" I jeered, then toned it down a little. "Look, I get it. Orders are orders. But eventually, you will have to tell me, and if it's too late, you're losing a prime opportunity to build some trust between us. You don't need to give me everything. Just give me something. What's the harm? I can't tell anybody, and even if I did, it wouldn't change anything. We can't slink off in the middle of the night as that would get us killed long before we could make it to the coast, and there is the matter of you likely catching up to us by the time the destroyer returns for pickup. Disappearing into the French countryside doesn't really present much of an option. All of us want to survive and get back to our friends and families, which will only happen if we cooperate with you, so what's your problem? I know that your guys all know what's going on. Why keep up this farce of forcing us to tag along, completely in the dark?"

Red considered, but then turned away. "Good night to you, too." And with that, he left me to my thoughts, jumbled as they were.

Well, if he wasn't ready to talk, I would find out another way.

Chapter 20

I was a little bit cranky when I had to get up in the morning, but otherwise did better than I should have had a right to considering my little freakout in the woods. And the rampant paranoia that was simmering in the back of my mind. Funny enough, my previous fear of someone coming after us here was completely gone. My entire right side was sore from smashing those zombies into oblivion, but poking at the scar helped with disbanding the brain fog from too little sleep. Real sleep it had been, no more of that coma shit—a small but considerable consolation prize. It wasn't snowing at the moment but the gray sky overhead didn't bode well, so I put on my overwhites after packing my bag. It had needed some negotiating, but Nate had let me have the ammunition for my sniper rifle back. If I ignored the pain—which wasn't easy—I felt good enough to run all day, but managed to sell him on the idea that in case of us happening upon any issues of the shambling kind, I could just disappear into the snow and pick them off one by one with my M24. But for that to happen, I needed to carry my own ammo, and the rest was history. Part of me felt like hitting myself over the head for volunteering to drag that extra weight with me, but I couldn't have grandiose plans of upstaging—or at least outsmarting—our leadership and then let Nate carry my gear.

That we weren't in a quiet territory became obvious when the early morning light revealed that during the night, we'd had to dispatch more than seventy shamblers. Most of them had been weak ones like those I had encountered, but a few had put up a good fight. Munez had a broken nose and black eye to show for it, and Davis a busted kneecap that forced him to limp rather than run. I was tempted to joke that someone should put him out of his misery, but then realized that I didn't trust Bucky not to and kept my trap shut. Fire team rotations were adjusted to give Davis some respite for today, and before he sent the first teams forward, Red stressed that being careful was more important than making good headway.

We were on the third rotation, mid-afternoon, when we happened upon a few signs as we crossed a road, and I realized a different possible cause for Red's lack of asking for a push: One of the signs indicated Ajou ten kilometers to the south. It didn't take a genius to figure out that rather than look for a campsite for tonight, we'd likely be spending the remainder of the afternoon searching for the source of the radio signal Hill now managed to pick up every time he tried. Even though I had no clue what was waiting for us, the idea that today we might find out a little more helped keep my spirits up. Today might just be a good day.

A sequence of gunshots ringing through the otherwise silent air spoke otherwise. Or maybe not.

I didn't need Nate's cursed direction to turn my radio from receiving only to sending. Technically speaking, that should have been the default setting, but I had no intention of regaling the entire group with our bickering, so I usually switched it off.

"Team Two, was that you?" Red asked over the com.

"Negative," Cole reported in.

"Us neither," I said before Burns could do the deed. "It's coming from somewhere south of us, I think." The low rolling hills were broken up by a thicket in that direction, making it impossible to see farther than half a mile. "We could be there in under ten minutes to check. We're about two miles out from your current position."

"Do it," Red ordered. "But try not to start World War III until we catch up with you."

Nate gave me a hard look, but I ignored his disapproval as I turned from the road toward the open field leading to the trees. "What?" I asked. "We are closest, and we can still run away if this gets too hairy for us."

I took off at an easy lope, but clearly, my action had signaled to Nate that I was on a confrontational trajectory today and he set a much harder pace, forcing me to huff and puff after him. We slowed down as we hit the trees, coming to a complete halt when two more gunshots came from much closer now. Nate listened, then pointed deeper into the thicket. Maybe two hundred yards south, the trees were already thinning again, the murk underneath their canopies minimal. Making sure that nothing else was moving except for us, I pushed forward, flexing the grip on my assault rifle to keep my fingers warm and nimble. It was one thing to go for stealth and use my axes, but I was not bringing them to a gunfight.

The reason the trees were thinning was a steep slope down into a gorge, most of it bare of vegetation. At the top of the slope, it was easy to see over most of the ground below, including the now dry bed of the river that must have taken eons to carve out the valley. I didn't need binoculars to make out where the shots had come from. At the foot of the opposite, much steeper, slope, a huddle of maybe ten people were doing their best to hold their ground—against a sea of shamblers that covered most of the ravine, the free zone around the group disappearing swiftly. That they were human still was obvious, not just because they were carrying guns, but also because of their heavy winter gear.

"I think we just found the resistance," I observed, this time waiting for a nod from Nate to call in. "We have around ten survivors here, about to get overrun by shamblers. They've backed themselves up against a cliff. Opposition is at least several hundred strong."

The frown on Nate's forehead made me guess that he wasn't that enthusiastic about the situation, and I felt my heart sink when I realized what that likely meant—Bucky wouldn't risk our lives on a whim, which would mean we'd come just in time to see the people down there die.

"You know, we could distract them a little while we wait for the others to come to us," I proposed to the guys. "Maybe that will be enough to give the group down there a fighting chance."

Burns's face lit up at the idea, but Nate's mouth twisted into a thin line. "It's still insubordination if you start shooting when you know the 'don't engage' order is coming any moment now."

"Like I give a fuck," I huffed, already working on getting my pack off my back so I could get to the spare ammo and use the pack to prop myself up with my sniper rifle. "And neither do you, if you're honest. Besides, I need a chance to see if I can still hit anything with the old lady." I adjusted the scope, but paused to switch the com back on. "Cole, how far out are you from our relative position? We're on top of the slope, smack in the middle of the ravine."

I half expected the asshole not to respond to me, but his answer came almost immediately, a little winded from running through the snow. "We're maybe half a click west of you. Already seeing the undead fuckers crowding the valley. You got an idea?"

I waited for Bucky to start cursing me out at the top of his lungs, but when still nothing came, I decided to go ahead. "We try to buy them some time to escape by picking out some of the more enterprising shamblers from here. We can still fall back if the tide turns on us. If the shamblers can even make it up the slope to reach us, it will take them several minutes to get here. We have time, and shouldn't let this opportunity slip."

Nate gave a dismal grunt. "Just one problem. I think the group has some injured people down there. They're settling in to make a stand rather than abandoning those that can't climb to safety."

Russell, who was on Cole's team, had his own interjection. "Not sure you see it from your vantage point, but half the cliff's frozen solid, likely from melted snow or a waterfall. Even if they could climb, they won't get out that way. Something must have gone wrong that they got surrounded."

A few seconds later, Bucky's reply finally came. "Everyone, stand down. Do you hear me? Stand down, and do not engage—"

With amusement, I watched as Nate pointedly switched his com off before he got his own sniper rifle out. At a glance from him, I cut the connection as well. Bad for coordinating, but I had a feeling Bucky would soon become a distraction. Burns snickered, readying his assault rifle that he aimed at the shamblers on our side of the ravine. "You try widening that gap over there, I'll give them something to do right here. Any objections?"

Rather than reply verbally, Nate pulled the trigger. A shambler right in front of the cornered group sank to the ground, a substantial part of its head missing. Several of the people shied back, but a rather stocky fellow who was trying to act as a human shield between the undead masses and the others did a great job pinpointing from where the shot had come, raising one hand in a brief wave. That was all the encouragement I needed, although I made sure to choose targets where, should I miss, I wouldn't accidentally kill one of the humans.

It had been a while since I'd been out and about with the sniper rifle, but my aim wasn't bad. With several hundred targets competing for my rounds, it was almost harder to miss than hit, although the first few shots weren't instant kills. Nate didn't pay me any attention, instead doing his very best to build a wall of corpses between the humans and the remaining shamblers. Burns was laughing like a maniac as he picked off zombie after zombie at the bottom of the slope, his job getting easier when they started trying to come for us as well. In short, we made quite the racket, putting the shots we'd heard before to shame.

I was just done reloading for the third time when Cole broke out of the cover of the trees, Russell and Parker in his wake. All three men were panting from running nonstop, and as a single glance revealed, none too happy with us. That was all the attention I was willing to pay them before I picked out my next shambling target.

"Why the fuck are you maniacs shooting?" Cole huffed and puffed beside me. "You had the clear order to stand down!"

"Didn't hear that," I lied as I lined up the next target.

I more felt than heard Cole step up to me, presumably to check the light on my radio unit. "That's not even on!"

"Oops," I deadpanned. "Well, that explains why we didn't hear anything back from you."

Cole wasn't done yet, reaching for the unit to switch it on. "You did that deliberately!"

I didn't respond right away, taking the time to finish off two more shamblers, using up the last of the ammo in the weapon. Only then did I look up, meeting Cole's annoyed look with one of my own. "We can't just let them die."

"Yes, we can. And we will," the asshole insisted—but sounded surprisingly dejected. "Boss's orders."

"It's a total waste of ammo," Russell interjected. "If we shoot them all, we'll easily use up half of our ammo."

I shrugged, nonplussed. "That's why doing it the blunt force trauma way is a lot more effective. We just need to wait for a few more to show up so we don't get eaten the moment we make it down there. The rest should be easy."

Parker gave me a look as if I'd said something crazy, but considering that was the usual way he looked at me, maybe he was just having a bad day.

Cole's snort was shy of derisive. "Oh, and I presume you'll volunteer us for that task?"

I wondered if I should have been talking more slowly. "Anyone who's willing and able to, like a bunch of super strong, super resilient soldiers. But yeah, I'm going, too. Wouldn't want to miss that for the world."

"Status!" came Bucky's bark over the line, cutting our little to-and-fro short.

Cole gave me another hostile stare, but sounded pleasant enough when he responded. "We caught up to the other fire team. They're about two miles from the mouth of the valley, up on the slope." He paused, assessing the view below us. "I think we stand a good chance to bring the assault to a halt with brute force."

"Gee, you're welcome," I muttered, for a moment forgetting that my com was still on—before I realized everyone had already heard my suggestions. "It only makes sense to try to help the people down there. And before any of you great warriors even thinks of calling me a bleeding heart, consider that this might be our best way in. We save them, they're bound to put in a good word with whoever's sitting in Ajou. Considering that they are the first people we've met, and we're only a few miles away from Ajou, they likely belong to that group, anyway. This horde of shamblers must have been plaguing them for weeks, if not months. We clean that up for them, and they might even meet us with favorable feelings rather than suspicion." Nobody had interrupted me yet, so I might as well go for the kill. "Getting that address from the bank and whatever was on that computer in that conservatory only got us so far. If that was enough, Hamilton wouldn't have led us all here. So presumably, we need all the help we can get. That down there is our golden ticket for said help. Think about it. You'll see that I'm right."

I'd expected some serious opposition—and scorn. Bucky delivered on the latter with a derisive grunt, but surprisingly agreed with me. "You really want to do this, Stumpy? Be my guest."

It took me a few moments of gnashing my teeth to realize that he'd just told me to offer up a plan. I hadn't expected that, and I wasn't the only one. Nate beside me paused as he reloaded, if with a hint of a smile on his face. So he hadn't turned off his radio completely.

"Well, not much to plan about this," I said after trying to get a better idea of what was going on down there. No real changes—the humans were still holding out, and more and more shamblers were turning their attention toward our side of the ravine, Nate's sniper rifle causing too much noise for them not to get interested. Burns had mowed down a good hundred by now, creating even more distraction.

"I say, we enter the valley at three points—right here, and about half a click southeast and northwest from here, to pull their attention from a single focus point. Teams of twos and threes, covering each other's backs. Everyone who doesn't go down either gets to lay down cover fire, or works as a lookout to tell those below what parts to avoid or where to head next. Our priority is to break through to that group over there and see if we can extract them. If not, we have a lot of heads to bash in."

Someone grumbled something very far from enthusiastic over the line, but Hamilton's retort cut him off. "We've reached the point Cole marked for us. Sending the others on with Richards except those that will head down with me here. Lewis, you are aware—your plan, your fault if anyone bites it?"

"Well, then you all better not get killed, because I couldn't care less." A lie—and likely one they could all have called me out on, but luckily, nobody did. Oh, indeed, Bucky's speech from yesterday had served more than one purpose, it seemed—or maybe it was just my imagination that now they took me more seriously. Indoctrinated, my ass. I didn't miss the hint of a smirk crossing Cole's face, but when he noticed me glaring at him, he let it slip off his features. He raised his brows at me.

"You coming with us, or what?"

"I already said I would, didn't I?" I pointed out.

"To the third starting point," Cole said. "Makes the most sense that as we're already here and would have to wait another five to ten minutes for Richards, we head over there so that they don't have to go for another half a mile. Or don't you trust us not to smash your head in first?"

I was tempted to hesitate, but got up without any words of protest, quickly brushing snow off my front and legs. I thought about picking up the M16, but I couldn't carry a lot of additional ammunition without a pack; that was staying here. I was doing okay, but not fully-loaded-pack-animal-in-combat good. If we kept making that much of a racket, we'd eventually drown in shamblers. Carrying the assault rifle on the sling across my back would also make for a great way to invite a semi smart zombie to make a grab for it, and I could do without that. My Beretta and Glock would have to do—and my axes, of course.

"I'll keep an eye on you from up here," Nate promised, barely looking up to catch my gaze before he focused on his scope again.

I was taken aback that he wouldn't join us, but quickly shook off my misgivings. He was certainly the best sniper we had along. He was the best man for this job. So he was going to trust Bucky's men to keep me alive. I waited for my usual misgivings to raise their ugly heads, but besides the general unease my idiotic plan conjured inside of me, there was nothing else lurking in the recesses of my mind. Did I personally like Cole, Russell, and Parker? Hell, no. But if I died, they lost a third of the potential shield keeping shamblers off their backs. That wasn't smart. Burns only gave me a wave before he continued shooting—another silent vote of confidence. So this was it—my chance to either prove myself, or remain the incompetent dead weight everyone seemed to see me as.

Really not a hard choice.

"Let's go," I told the other three, hoping that I wasn't making a huge mistake—but I had a certain feeling that I wouldn't get much of a chance to regret it. Parker certainly looked a little green in the face while Cole and Russell seemed mostly giddy. They were probably waiting for me to end up on my ass and in need of rescue so they could spend the next few days making me miserable. Just like Bates would have, I reminded myself. Not for the first time I realized that I'd lucked out with the people with whom I'd run away from that first wave of zombies—but I hadn't yet had the reputation of being an obnoxious bitch then. Or had been gifted potentially near-super strength. I kept reminding myself of the latter as I tried to ignore the former. They wouldn't just let me die, I was sure—no way for anyone to keep gloating at me that way.

As we headed farther along the ravine, the others checked in one team after the other, getting ready. Cole hadn't protested me taking point, so that's what I did. There were no shamblers up here in the trees, but a few tracks showed that they must have joined the large group down the slope not too long ago, the snow, leaves, and earth still freshly churned. The trees started to thin and the ground evened out, and in the distance I saw a road winding toward this end of the ravine—likely the same road we'd crossed before we'd heard the gunshots. It was as good a point to stop as any. When Red reported in ten seconds later that he and the alternate fire team he had in tow had arrived at Nate's position, I knew that the time for hesitating was over.

Looking down into the ravine, I tried to better gauge the situation. The group had hunkered down behind their wall of corpses, doing a good job keeping the odd shambler trying to climb it at bay with long sticks and two hay forks. The only reason they hadn't been overrun yet was that the ravine wasn't that broad, even at the widest part where they had gotten surrounded. Unhindered, I could likely have crossed it within a matter of minutes. The zombies still had the advantage of numbers, but they were a disorganized lot, getting in the way of each other, torn between what target they should go after—including their own dead. Like the four I'd decimated on my unlucky watch shift, they were barely more than skin bags filled with bones. Still a menace, but no match for a healthy, well-nourished human who couldn't get infected. Thinking of that female shambler and the conclusions my mind had jumped to didn't make me feel very comfortable in my own skin, but there was a sure way to make myself stop caring—and that lay maybe fifty feet away from me.

"We're in position," I reported in. "Everyone know what they got to do?"

Bucky's chuff made me wish I hadn't asked. "My, your style of leadership is inspiring."

I looked at Parker rather than deign to answer that. "You can stay up here. Be another spotter," I suggested, trying to keep any disdain out of my voice. Hell, I'd never held back just because of the infection risk. Why did I even think about coddling him now? I was certain that everyone else who could would be heading down there, and Nate would rope Gita into taking my sniper rifle not because she wouldn't be any use otherwise, but because she was the one who would be missing the least as far as brutal strength was concerned. And they sure as hell hadn't hesitated when they'd unleashed all those zombies on us at that factory.

Parker grunted with annoyance, but the tension in his shoulders didn't lessen. "They have wounded people; I'm a medic. I wouldn't be if I always stayed behind."

Cole and Russell grinned at each other, making me guess that I wasn't the first to try to coddle Parker. Like me before, they now shirked their packs and only took their melee weapons of choice with them, plus the odd grenade and handgun.

"Then let's do this," I said with more conviction than I felt—but also gleeful anticipation rising inside of me.

"Ladies first," Cole offered, pointing down the slope with one of his reinforced baseball bats. Over the com, Bucky and Red gave the orders for the teams they were leading. Ah well. Only way was forward.

Chapter 21

We more slid than walked down the steep slope into the ravine, the few trees working perfectly as safety nets so nobody tumbled into the undead horde below. Most of them didn't pay us any mind at first, either standing around, staring at nothing—which now gave me the creeps, considering how much of that I'd done myself of late—or trying to push toward the thickest parts of the horde, around the cornered group and where Burns was still shooting into the thick of the mass.

I was debating with myself how to best start this when I reached the bottom of the slope, only one hop from the thick roots of a tree separating me from the valley floor and its occupants—but Cole letting out an ear-piercing whistle that made heads all around whip toward him took that decision from me. Just as well. Taking a last, deep breath—that stank enough of death and feces to make my eyes water—I did my best to fight down the panic that wanted to claw its way to the forefront of my brain, and launched myself over the roots at the nearest shambler, Cole doing the same to my left.

The first two shamblers were permanently dead within seconds, barely quick enough to turn to face me, too slow to react. From up close, the bad state they were in was even more apparent, some of them barely able to keep upright, let alone defend themselves. There were, of course, the odd stronger ones hiding between the weak, but the first twenty minutes were almost like a walk in the park. A deeply exhausting, strenuous walk that required lots of quick movements that the freshly healed wound in my side wasn't fond of, not at all, but I spent more time trying not to get fountains of congealed blood and gore all over myself than actively having to defend myself. It was a little like chopping wood, although of the truly nightmarish kind. The very small part of my mind that wasn't occupied with hacking at the next limb or skull noted that it only made sense. The shamblers this far back were the runts of the litter, the stragglers who barely ever managed to get more than scraps of what the others left behind. They'd likely spent months subsisting on the remains of their even weaker fellows, who couldn't have been very nutritious. If not for the cornered people clearly being on a very final deadline, it would have been smart to keep decimating the very edges of the undead horde to do away with the easy targets first—but we didn't have that luxury.

"You all need to pick up the pace," Nate's voice alerted us over the com. "The smart ones have figured out that what I'm trying to do is ring the dinner bell for them. The really smart ones are about to ignore all that dead meat in favor of the hot, wriggling snack that's hiding behind it. I don't think they'll have another hour before they get overwhelmed."

Staggering back a few steps to gain some room to breathe, I waited to see if Cole could pick up the slack for me. He gave me a quick signal to go ahead. "How far until we get to the smart ones?" I asked, panting heavily. "We're probably not exactly the closest, but I think we could carve a way through the mass here to meet up with some backup at the wall of bodies."

It took Nate a few seconds to assess, the afternoon eerily quiet as the rapport of his sniper rifle was suddenly missing. Quiet except for the groaning and moaning, interspersed with thuds and other fleshy sounds, of course.

"Depending on how quick you can be, you might just make it. The opposition is heavier in the very middle," Nate offered.

"No shit, Sherlock," came Bucky's grunted response, making me guess he was talking from experience.

"Looks pretty much the same on our side," Hill reported in. "We could try to meet you at the wall. If we miss, what's the worst that could happen?" His laugh was a little winded.

Cole's snort was loud enough that I heard it over his effort to keep the undead at bay. "My thoughts exactly," I agreed on our likely demise. "Can one of you up there tell us if one or the other group is starting to lag?"

"Sure thing," Gita volunteered. "You ready to go? Hill's back to smashing in heads already."

Did she just call me a lazy fuck? Laughing softly to myself, I made sure that nothing was sneaking up on us and Parker and Russell were still doing okay where they were slashing and bashing away a few feet to our left, then joined Cole once more. I'd show her.

It made the most sense to draw closer together as we were trying to push harder, so I ended up next to Russell, with Cole and Parker covering us. For every zombie that we did away with, two more came at us, and now only half of them fell on the corpses to eat, forcing us to confront fighting targets rather than ignorant ones. I really could have done with some extra strength and stamina, but my arms were getting heavier by the minute.

Then the inevitable happened—I slipped on something hidden on the ground just as a somewhat more substantial zombie made a lunge for me. It missed me, but I went down just the same, narrowly avoiding losing one or both of my tomahawks. Deeming me an easy target gave the shambler some extra incentive to come for me, broken, rotting teeth snapping for my face. I managed to get one arm up in time to keep it off me, but it took me two tries to aim a good kick to send it back far enough that I could scramble to my feet. Just as I was doing that, a strong arm came up underneath my left, Cole dragging me the rest of the way to my feet. He didn't waste a second on gloating, just shouted, "You okay?" As soon as I nodded, he was back to bashing the nearest zombie's face in. I finished off the one that had come for me, but my breath was ragged as I straightened again.

"How's your side doing?" Cole hollered after killing his next target. He caught my bland stare with a grin. "Parker's a terrible snitch when you corner him. As you very well know yourself. He told us the details of how that started, too."

Another shambler getting between us gave me some valuable seconds to consider my response. "If you mean, am I too weak to fight? No."

"Not what I was asking," Cole said. "The last thirty minutes proved the contrary, anyway. How much does it distract you? Because you're slowing down, and you really shouldn't be at the end of your strength yet."

"It hurts like hell, but I can manage. Haven't figured out how to mobilize said strength that you think I shouldn't be running out of yet."

That got me a brief bark of laughter, but a couple of shamblers kept Cole from answering for a while. We were a few yards further into the thickening mass of bodies when he drew close enough to respond. "You need to focus. You need to make yourself be able to dip into that well of stamina and strength. Eventually, it'll happen automatically, and very likely instantly when you absolutely need it, but looks like you're not quite scared out of your mind yet."

I didn't try to tone down the laugh that drew from me. "Not quite, yeah." My next slice was powerful enough to sever the trachea of the shambler I was coming after, only a bash with the back of the other tomahawk needed to fully decapitate it. "Make myself stronger, eh? Easy, peasy."

"Brace yourself. I'm coming up behind you. Don't hit me, okay?"

I really didn't like the sound of that, but the onslaught of undead kept me from formulating a reply, and then, it was too late. Cole grabbed my left shoulder with one hand—to steady me, I realized—before he punched my right lower torso hard enough that without his support, I would have likely ended up on my knees. Pain exploded from my side even though he hadn't perfectly hit the scar, just the still healing tissue next to the wound. My senses snapped into clear focus, the stench making me retch instantly, even overpowering the agony radiating through my body for a moment.

"Fight through it," Cole shouted behind me as he let me go. "Push the pain away. Make yourself ignore it. But at the same time, hold on to the sense of hyperawareness. That's what you're going for. Focus on your body. Your muscles. Your arms when you swing that ax, your legs when you kick, pivot. Push everything else away except for the motions. And that's how you do it."

I was so tempted to yell in his face not to be such an asshole, but the lizard part of my brain chose to follow his instructions instead. It wasn't hard, really—I had to try to dull my sense of smell or else I'd start to puke, and that would likely get me killed within moments. Concentrating on the pain and how my body was singing with the need for even more violence was easy. There were more zombies coming at me so I had to first defend myself, then push forward to finish them—and those that came after them—back. The physical motion of my muscles tensing and keeping my body moving forward was easier to concentrate on than the pain still locking up my side, so that's what I did—step by step by step. The next swing didn't go easier or hit harder than the one before, but I felt just a little less winded, and it was just a little easier to react to the next snapping jaws coming for me, just a little faster. Honestly, I'd expected more—particularly after I'd kicked Nate easily across our hangar gym when I had managed to dip deep into my reserves—but this was different. This wasn't about a single punch that could likely send my bare fist through an enemy's skull. This was about keeping going when fatigue was threatening to drop me to the ground—but didn't. It was then that I realized that—at least for me, if not for most others—this was more a matter of tenacity than overwhelming brute force. And if I could claim one thing, it was that being a tenacious bitch who never let go was actually my MO.

"Lewis, you're starting to lag," came Nate's reminder over the com, sounding far away, like a disembodied voice in a dream. I couldn't pay much attention to that, between fighting the pain, fighting the zombies, and doing my very best to keep my position between Russell and Cole as we continued pushing deeper into the crowd. My world narrowed down to just two things—attack and survive. The pain and exhaustion were still there but I could almost ignore it if I tried just hard enough. If I just kept hacking and slashing, I'd get through this in one piece, and everything would be all right.

It didn't really help that it was pretty much my fault that I was in this situation.

Over the com, I heard as one of the other teams got into serious trouble, needing to fall back to where Munez, Davis, and Burns were keeping the tide at bay below our snipers. It didn't matter. We only needed to cut that swath to the group, and then—

Then something happened. We were close enough to the wall of dead bodies—that Nate still kept adding to—that I could catch a glimpse of it whenever a still-moving corpse fell under my axes. It felt like a massive release of adrenaline at first, like startling awake from a dream, only without the feeling of disorientation. There was definitely some dopamine and serotonin in the mix that made me feel light, bordering on high—something I didn't exactly associate with fighting zombies. A more meaty shambler pushed through the others toward me, moving incredibly slow. I raised my left arm—feeling like it was moving through water rather than air—meeting it head-on as soon as it broke free, the blade of my ax cleaving right through the center of its forehead, barely covered with mottled skin as it was. I felt the ax part the air first, then embed itself in the skull, the impact jarring up from my wrist through my elbow to my shoulder. Muscles in my back and arm tensed so I could wrench it free, watching as bone shrapnel and congealed blood sprayed everywhere. It happened so slowly that it was easy to duck. I used the motion to step to the side, bringing my other arm up to go for the shambler's neck even as my torso twisted. The hit struck perfectly, slicing through tendons until the edge of the ax blade grated across and into the spine, severing nerves and blood vessels. The body was folding in on itself as soon as my ax was done slicing through it.

I caught motion from the very corner of my right eye, where my secondary attack had left my back unguarded. My right arm was still moving on the trajectory of the slice, my head turning to follow the arc of gore it left in its wake. Another shambler was about to launch itself at me, using the momentary distraction its peer had provided. Even seeing the danger, I knew I would be too slow to meet it head-on. I had about a second to decide what to do—try to body-slam it with my unprotected shoulder, or let myself drop out of reach. I knew Cole was close enough that if I went down, he'd notice and come after the shambler, but I hated having to rely on that. So I braced myself, tightened my grip on my axes, and hoped for the best.

The zombie smacked right into me, its teeth and claws going for my face. Everything inside of me screamed to turn my head away, but

I needed to see to know where to hit—if I could get enough distance to be effective. The stench coming off that thing was unbelievable, so much worse than what I was already covered in. I tried to get an arm between us but ended up poking my glove into something squishy that I was certain shouldn't have given in so easily—and then my hand was stuck.

"Drop!" a deep male voice shouted, coming from somewhere to my left. Not Cole, but he definitely was shouting at me. Without second thought, I let myself fall to the ground, doing my very best not to end up with the shambler on top of me.

Just in time, I saw the sledgehammer come down. Squeezing my eyes and mouth shut, I turned my head so my face was pointing toward the ground. Something cool and viscous splattered my cheek where it wasn't covered by wool or sturdy fabric. The zombie stopped moving, the hands clawing at my shoulder and torso dropping away for good. With my eyes still closed, I kicked as hard as I could, feeling the corpse lifting off me. Just as I was trying to wipe my face clean—with the back of a gore-splattered glove, which wasn't that effective—someone grabbed my arm and pulled me to my feet. Once I managed to open my eyes, I found Hill grinning down at me, his sledgehammer dripping red.

"My, aren't you a sight for sore eyes," he joked.

Something behind his hip moved. I abandoned my quest for cleanliness and moved as well. My tomahawk buried itself deep in the shambler's chest, enough so that when I pulled, I yanked the thing toward me rather than managed to free my weapon. The angle got awkward, so rather than use the ax, I slammed my closed fist I was holding it with into the zombie's face. Hard. Bone and cartilage gave, and I ended up with yet more gunk covering my hand up to my wrist. Booyah.

Hill grabbed the zombie's head and wrenched it to the side, the spine snapping with an audible crack. I pulled back, finally managing to free my weapon. The thing tumbled to the blood-soaked ground between us. Hill flashed me a quick grin before he went after something to my side. I did the same, coming after an enterprising shambler that tried to jump Cole's back.

We hacked, and slashed, and smashed, and punched some more, until finally, we reached the wall of bodies. It was almost up to my shoulder in some places, and teeming with yet more undead falling on those that weren't moving anymore. Hill came after those with his sledgehammer, leaving it to us to cover him in the meantime. Once Cole and I had secured part of the wall, Parker scrambled over it, presumably to help the wounded. He yelled something at the people in English; they yelled something back in French; it only took them about five seconds to sort out their differences. They all looked scared as hell and very happy to see us, even though they couldn't know who we were. From up closer, I saw that they had three people on the ground, some with open, bleeding wounds. They might have sustained the injuries from falling, but I didn't allow myself to keep my hopes up. The few fit and unblemished guys were eyeing those on the ground with as much caution as us, so I presumed they knew that they wouldn't see two more sunsets. Nobody could be that oblivious and still be alive.

Turning back to the undead horde, I tried to reorient myself and get a better picture of what was going on. There were still plenty of zombies about, but we'd visibly decimated their numbers to something more manageable. Because we were at the wall now, Nate and Gita had stopped shooting, and it didn't take long before Bucky—still somewhere out there—barked for a status report. I missed what Tanner called in as another wave of the undead surged forward, giving us a hard time until we managed to chop them up for good. Hill had come with backup, but even Aimes, Williams, and McClintock in addition to the three of us weren't really enough to hold them at bay for long.

"Can you move the injured?" I called back to Parker, although what I really wanted to ask was whether we could just shoot them and withdraw with those that would still be breathing a week from now. It was then that I realized that this was not how I should have been thinking, but I didn't really care. In fact, I didn't care much about anything except to chase that high—

"Still got some work to do," Parker grumbled back, or at least that was what I thought I heard over the din the not-yet dead made.

Looking around, I tried to gauge how the others were holding up. Not quite a surprise, I seemed to be the most exhausted, but with every second that I got to catch my breath and rest a little, I felt more and more like hurling myself back into the fray. I must have looked the part, too, as when I caught Cole's gaze, he grinned back at me.

"You're one fucking moron, you know that?" I told him succinctly. "Or what else would you call someone who deliberately inflicts pain on the one who should have his back?"

"You should know," he shot back. "You married one." One bashed-in head later, he explained. "They sent me out on my first mission after the inoculation before I'd managed to get a grip on it all. I ended up with several bullets in my leg and arm, in a ditch, unable to attack or retreat. When Miller dropped in next to me, I thought he'd drag me out. Guess what that bastard did? He dug two of the slugs out of my leg so I could keep moving after he patched me up, and with his fingers digging into the bandage, he told me pretty much what I told you. And then he vaulted out of the ditch and went for the bastards that had shot me up, leaving it to me to come after him to help gun the rest of them down. Without my help, they would have killed him; but without moving on, I would have died in that ditch. Never been that glad about anyone putting me through what felt like literal hell that day, but you need to learn that lesson, or you're dead. You can tell that asshole that I consider his favor repaid."

"Go tell him yourself," I shot back.

Cole snorted, but he was still grinning as he glanced back in my direction. "Ready to kick some undead ass? You look like you've got some extra energy to burn off."

Oh, did I ever. Switching the com to send, I asked our lookout, "What direction do you want us to go?"

"Stay," Nate grumbled, but after a few moments offered, "The worst is to your ten. Looks like some of the more crafty ones have been hiding in the thick of the fray and they're making a break for the wall. If you can meet them head-on, you have a better chance of keeping them from breaking through."

"Consider it done." I gave Cole a nod to let him know I was with him, then whistled loudly at where Hill was still doing undead maintenance sweeps. "You game?"

"Always!" he hollered back with way more enthusiasm than any of us should have felt.

"We'll hold the line," Aimes assured me, for once not adding anything with a sneer. And off we went, heading in the vague direction Nate had pointed out. With luck, our advance would leave those at the wall with fewer shamblers pushing on to be easily held at bay.

Everything became a blur. I was out of breath, but I forced myself to keep going. My arms seemed to weigh a ton, but rather than fall back, I pushed ahead. I staggered, stumbled, misstepped, landed on my ass, even lost one of my axes for a short time, but forced myself to go on. There was no turning back now, and no reasoning with the undead. What scared me the most was that not only did I want to go on, but I actually enjoyed it.

We broke through the bulk in the middle eventually, and it seemed like a token of faith that just as I came staggering into the open on one side, Bucky broke free on the other. He noticed me moments after I saw him, both of us staring at the other. I knew this was my chance. Everyone else was too occupied with bashing in heads to notice, let alone aid him. I was shaking with exhaustion, half bent-over in my attempt to catch my breath, but my pulse was going strong, adrenaline making me stupid. I knew I could try to take him down. He'd see it coming, but he must have been just as tired as I was, and while he had height and bulk on me, I was quicker and more agile. I might not win, but with zombies all around us still putting up a fight, I only needed to incapacitate him enough to make him an easy victim—cut the hamstrings, hit him hard enough in the temple that he got too sluggish to defend himself well. What I might have lacked on the physical side, I could easily make up for in craziness. If I let myself—and I was very tempted—I could put all the blame in the world on his shoulders. I could ignore that, while in charge of the soldiers, he wasn't the one who called the shots. He was following orders just like everyone else—and as he'd explained yesterday, there was so much going on that I didn't know. Yet he had been the executing force, and while I might never get a chance at who was controlling him, I could very well try to take out Bucky Hamilton himself.

And he knew it. I saw it in his eyes. The wariness, the worry that peeked out under that mask of machismo swagger. Just like I'd known every single time that I'd crossed our camp, he or his people could have taken me down in an instant, I could turn into an avenging fury now. I could take out all my anger, my grief, my frustration on him, and I had a good chance of taking him down with me. No, I wasn't delusional. I knew that I wouldn't walk away if I did this—but it would be worth it.

"I ain't got time for this shit," I heard him grumble under his breath, then, louder, to me, "Are you going to do this, or not?"

Oh, I wanted to. I absolutely wanted to. Today, right now, the first time in history that I was strong, and capable, and had abso-fucking-lutely nothing to lose. Just me and him, and neither of us would be limping away from this.

Yet instead of coming for him, I let out a primal shout and hurled myself back into the thick of the fray.

I instantly regretted that decision, and I knew that I would keep regretting it for a long, long time—but honestly? My life was far too valuable to waste it like that. The bomb he'd dropped on us could have caused a lot of damage, but this was the lesson I chose to learn from it. I'd beaten the odds one too many times to throw my life away on a whim now, even if it was for a cause I believed in wholeheartedly. That I physically and mentally felt fucking great at the same time that I was choking on my regret helped just a little—and that was enough. Nothing like slaughtering the undead to get your mind off dreams of sweet, sweet revenge. I certainly didn't choose to turn the other cheek, no. I chose myself. And that was worth so much more than all the grievances in the world.

The ravine was cast into the shadows of dusk by the time I dragged my sorry ass back to the wall. It had grown substantially since I'd last seen it. I didn't give a fuck. I could barely hold on to my axes anymore, my fingers alight with agony that surpassed the constant throbbing in my right side by some. A few of the soldiers were still busy hacking away at the remaining zombies, but most of them were dead for good. The few alive were smart enough to play possum, or eat the heaps and heaps of rotting flesh all around them. The stink still made me want to vomit. I'd never get used to that. It was tempting—oh, so very tempting—to just sit down and forget about ever wanting to move again, but I forced myself to get back to the wall. Some of the stagger in my step came from being utterly drained; most from still being high on my own supply. I felt like Hill had worked me over several times with that sledgehammer of his, but I could have run on and on until I reached the very end of the world...

Bucky's roll call over the com dragged me back to the here and now. Right, the wall. We'd sustained no casualties but some good non-debilitating injuries. My own head hurt like hell from where a few shamblers had broken through my cover and punched—and in one case, kicked—me in the face. My nose had stopped bleeding but I would be surprised if it wasn't broken. Cole had a twisted ankle that he tried to ignore. Hill pretended like his left arm didn't hurt like hell. A few more broken fingers, but nothing that wouldn't heal overnight—weren't we the lucky ones? Nate and Gita were the only two who weren't the worse for wear, and decidedly looking it, too. Presumably. Which reminded me…

"Gita? I need you by the wall. Haul your scrawny ass down here," I told her, trusting that the open chatter on the com would make everyone else ignore us. Looking up at the slope, I saw two lone figures scurrying through the snow between the trees. Ten minutes and they would be here—including my pack that Nate was likely lugging with him. Oh joy.

Climbing over the wall was easier said than done. It definitely lacked some good mortar. Zombie guts didn't really work for that. I also had to make sure that none of the building blocks were still able to grab my ankle or try to chew through my boots. A few tried. What we'd accomplished was bordering on a miracle, but technically speaking, we'd maybe killed five to six hundred shamblers, not much more. Incapacitating them had been enough. The problem would take care of itself soon enough, but a part of me resented leaving them like this. It was this very sentiment that made me realize that I was—slowly—coming down from my bender. Compassion for zombies, not exactly a healthy survival trait, but lack of empathy had definitely been part of whatever my body had kicked up into. It wasn't exactly like I felt they didn't deserve to suffer, but it made sense to put them out of their misery.

When I finally managed to get past the bulk of the permanently dead, I found the survivors of the group all staring at me. Parker was off, taking care of what the lot of us was dragging back to him now, and no one else was in earshot. There were twelve remaining of them, and only one of them wounded. The other two hadn't made it, judging from the two heaps of churned earth behind them. Part of me wanted to rail that if they'd had energy enough to bury their dead, they could have fought for themselves as well, but I was wise enough to keep silent. They all looked starved and like they'd been on the go for weeks, sleep deprivation making everything so much worse.

Most of them were young, maybe in their late teens, early twenties, only two men in their late thirties remaining. It was hard to tell with the gear and clothes, but two of the slighter figures looked like they could be women. They all stared at me, and it took me a moment to realize why. I'd started out in my overwhites; some of that outer layer was still intact, but so badly soaked in gore and torn to pieces that I didn't think anything was salvageable. My gear underneath wasn't looking any better, although the integrity of it was still good. Some bleach and water, and lots of elbow grease was all that was needed to make it useable once more. The same couldn't be said for my wool cap, I realized as I pulled it off and let it drop to the ground. Well, at least my hair wasn't completely soaked.

"My name is Bree Lewis," I offered, waiting for a reaction. Not that they'd recognize me, but names sounded like names in all languages. "I don't presume anyone here is speaking English?" I repeated the last in French, hoping I remembered the syllables Gita had drilled into me whenever we'd had time and brain power left in the evening.

Several seconds passed until one of the older men—the stocky one who'd done a lot of defending—shook his head, making a helpless gesture.

I didn't buy it, not for a second. I knew that, historically, the French and the English weren't exactly best friends, but, come on. Most of western Europe had been just as internationally minded as we at home, and unlike us, picking up a second language that was spoken by over a billion people in the world wasn't that much of a stretch. Gita had explained as much. They probably had a good reason for playing dumb now—likely to check if what we talked among ourselves lined up with the bull we tried to sell them. Oh, well. I didn't mind. I also had no intentions of trying to deceive them.

"Can you give me a hand?" I heard Gita behind me as she tried to scramble over the wall.

I quickly turned and hopped back up to help her; I might not mind the odd bite too much. She would, a lot. It was obvious how tired I was when it took her a few seconds to make it through the corpses while I'd needed several minutes. She was shaking all over, her teeth clattering. Lying in the snow for hours will do that to you. Couldn't say I envied her, even if she looked prissy clean while I was… better not looked at too closely.

"Can you translate for me?" I asked quite needlessly. She nodded eagerly. Turning back to the group, I repeated my introduction, only waiting for Gita to offer my name before I went on. "We are from the United States of America. As you can probably see on the neat patches some of us are wearing, and who else would come waltzing through here like Rambo?" I waited for some laughs, but either that didn't translate well, or I was way off my game. I sighed, doing my best not to get annoyed. "I presume you're with the resistance at Ajou? We saw your graffiti when we made land in Cabourg, and have followed the automated radio message." Gita fell silent, and still I didn't get a reaction out of them. Looking back over my shoulder, I saw Bucky striding toward me, glowering. Oops, must have turned off that radio again after hailing Gita. "We're here on a secret mission that's so secret that I don't know anything about it although I really should. We mean you no harm, even if we might have left a different impression. We would like a chance to talk to whoever is still here, sending that message. Please. We just saved your hides, and likely made getting to whatever hideout you have a lot easier. One talk, that's all we ask for. Can be on the radio, too, if you don't trust us with the location of your hideout."

The man listened dispassionately to Gita's stuttered translation, then fired a slew of words back at her. She replied, hesitantly at first, then with more confidence at his response. I didn't bother asking her what he'd said. I knew she would tell me soon enough. It didn't go by unnoticed that several of the soldiers, foremost Hill and Cole, had inched closer, listening in. I gave them a blank stare and got as much in return. Oh, we were back to eyeing each other warily, like wild cats intruding on each other's territory but not yet ready to fight.

I was so fucking tired of this bullshit.

And it was that very sentiment—and where it came from—that made me realize that something had changed. Burns's attempt while working out hadn't done the trick. Nate's admission of guilt over parting ways with them, either. The more or less awkward talks with Red and Hill might have toned down my paranoia, but, if anything, they'd underlined the us-versus-them mentality going on between us. Bucky's big reveal? I still had a hard time wrapping my mind around all of that.

But today? Today there had been no difference. Just as I always trusted Burns—or whoever else Nate had set to babysitting me—would have my back, I'd known that Hill would smash his way through any shambler that tried to eat me, and that any of the others, independent of what they personally thought of me, would do the same. As I would have done for them. I doubted that we'd ever become friends—but we didn't have to. Personal issues only went so far when survival was concerned.

Gita fell silent as she turned to me, getting ready to tell me what they'd discussed, but I forestalled her. "Tell him this. I don't care if they trust us. I don't care what they are up to. There's only one real truth, there are only two real sides in this world left: The dead and the living. We are alive, and so are they, and that's all that matters. On our own, all of us will die. It's only when we work together that we survive. And that's what this is all about, right? Survival."

I caught one of the smaller figures in the back nodding before she caught herself, quick to give me that same impassive stare as before. Gita prattled on, and after a moment's hesitation, the man we'd been talking to inclined his head in agreement. He seemed ready to respond, but then Captain Asshole came trundling in, forcing his way through the barricade of corpses.

"Lewis, you fucking cunt, shut your useless pie hole!" he hissed, his voice partly muffled as he pulled off his gore-soaked balaclava. Like with me, that only added bloodstains and grime to his sweat-soaked face.

I gave Bucky the most neutral look I could muster before I bent over, laughing so hard that I started to wheeze. All that good stuff my brain had produced to keep my body going through pain and exhaustion demanded its tribute now, making it impossible for me to get a grip. Bucky continued to swear, which didn't help, at all. Ah, this was just too precious!

Hamilton finally gave up and turned to Gita. She did her best not to shy away from his scowl, but didn't quite manage. "So you're the one who speaks French, not her," he ground out.

"Never actually said I did," I interjected, chuckling just a little. "You have to pay better attention to what people actually say, not what you want to hear."

He sent me a look that should have made me shut up, but the promise of violence it held only made me want to raise both hands and silently tell him to give it his best shot. I knew that my bright grin only annoyed him further. Ah, this was too easy. A glance at the huddled-together group revealed that they were following the spectacle with rapt attention.

"Way to make a first impression," I jeered at Hamilton, but did my best to do so with a pleasant smile on my face. "All I did was say hello and ask them whether they are part of the resistance at Ajou. You can take it from here." And because he wasn't altogether wrong calling me names, I added, "You're welcome."

Hamilton looked ready to come after me for real now, but visibly pulled himself together and addressed the French instead. Gita's translation sounded more clipped than with me, making me guess that she was doing a more verbatim version now while actually chatting before. The leader of the group responded in equally short, semi hostile sounding sentences, but that could have been my impression altogether. Yes, they were part of those hunkered down in Ajou, and while grateful for the rescue, they couldn't speak for their entire group. They were happy to lead us there and let us talk to whoever was in charge, making me guess that they had a nicely reinforced bunker that was shy of impenetrable. They must have trusted us somewhat not to take them hostage and force our way inside, but then they would all have ended up dead without us, anyway. The woman who I'd seen agree with me earlier did a good job ignoring me as much as Hamilton, but I was certain that they were all watching us.

When it became obvious that Bucky wasn't going to mess this up, I stepped closer to the wall, making me end up next to Cole with just a heap of the dead between us. He listened to the translated answers while standing at idle attention, his eyes never leaving the corpses around us except for when he caught me looking directly at him. That's when he smirked at me, and it was easy to guess just how amused by my antics he was. I gave a silent shrug back.

Any conversation we might have started got cut short when Nate and Burns drew closer; the former lugging my pack along, the latter my weapons. With a theatrical sigh, I heaved myself over the gruesome barrier to relieve them of both. Neither said a word, but it was obvious that Burns was grinning because I'd made another friend. Nate didn't scowl exactly, and with surprise I noted that he and Cole exchanged a small nod before Nate turned to listen in to the three-way conversation as well.

My overwhites were ruined but I was still loath to dump them without trying to salvage at least some parts, so I got a trash bag from my pack and put the torn, soiled clothes in there as I peeled myself out of them. My back was still smeared enough that Burns spent a good minute rubbing me down with snow before I pulled my pack up on my shoulders. It weighed a ton, but just standing there with my empty hands was bad enough—anything would have felt like it was laden down with stones. It was only when we turned to leave, one of our fire teams heading forward where the French guy was pointing, that I realized something: I wasn't cold anymore. Not warm, either, but that deep-seated sensation of freezing to death that had been with me since the beach was gone. My finger and toe stumps were still more sensitive to the cold than the rest of me, but the ache coming from my overused muscles easily pushed that into the very back of my mind. I actually felt better than I had in a long, long time, way before we'd hit the Silo on our journey north for sure.

I could get used to this—and something deep inside of me told me that I would.

The first step on my road to recovery was done. Next up: make Bucky regret he had ever even heard of me.

Chapter 22

We were drawing close to our destination a little after the last rays of the sun disappeared to the west, moderately unscathed from the dropping temperatures. Maybe five miles into our trek, the French had led us into a network of trenches and tunnels, keeping the bite of the wind mostly at bay. Some of those structures could have been remnants from either of the World Wars—or maybe even older; I was a little rusty where French history was concerned—but a lot must have been dug within the last year, judging from the lack of vegetation in parts.

About an hour in, Cole caught up to where I was trundling alongside Nate and Burns. He ignored me as he handed two packs of nuts to Burns. Burns snickered, chucking one to me when he saw me watching. "As usual, half of the spoils of war are yours."

Ah, that explained it, or at least gave me an idea. Smirking at Cole, I observed, "So you were actually stupid enough to bet against me? At the very least you should have the common sense of trusting someone's judgment who's been out and about with me for a year and a half."

"In hindsight, maybe," Cole admitted as he got a third pack out to tear into himself. Some of them seemed to carry an unlimited supply of nuts, probably more than ammo, and we already lugged around enough of that to make random explosions likely.

"Why, what was the bet about?" My question was met with silence, even if it was of the chewing meditatively kind. "Oh, come on! I deserve to know. The least you can do for doing shit like that." It wasn't the first—or even tenth—time this had happened, but usually there was only gloating with the utter lack of holding back involved. And judging from the grin on Burns's face, I wanted to hear this.

Cole continued to debate with himself but eventually relented. "After that misguided attempt of you and Hamilton trying to put each other in your respective places at the destroyer gym, I asked Burns here if it was your usual MO to start something you knew you couldn't finish. He laughed in my face and bet that it would take you less than two weeks to stir up some serious shit."

I shot Burns an amused sidelong glance. "Yeah, anyone could have told you so. Now spill the rest."

Burns chortled at me not being that easily thrown off. Cole grunted. "And he claimed it would be something I felt you were right about. Sounded like an easy bet to win because what shit could you possibly stir up in the middle of nowhere, and even less so something I'd agree with you over a direct order? But turns out, he was right." He paused, markedly to check how far ahead of us Hamilton was.

"You know that, usually, in the field, direct insubordination ends with a bullet between the eyes?"

"Like I care," I chuffed. "If he was allowed to just kill me, Hamilton would have done it a long time ago. Whatever else he ranted about yesterday, he never said he wouldn't kill me if it suited him, only that my death might inconvenience him because of the fallout it would cause. And me accidentally switching off my radio so I couldn't hear any order that might have been given is likely the reason why we'll sleep somewhere warm and cozy tonight, with our bellies full of something other than cardboard."

Cole still wasn't impressed. "If that's how you organized your rebellion, it's a real wonder you didn't all end up getting eaten on day one."

I gave him the most brilliant smile I could manage. "Oh, the others usually do follow orders. Can't take half a lifetime of serving out of a guy just like that. But I'm special."

"Ain't that the truth," came Nate's mutter from up ahead, but I could tell that he was smiling, too.

Cole snorted. "Are you going to keep stirring up shit now that you've proven that you're an eternal troublemaker?"

"Why, would you want me to stop?"

Cole considered his reply, and I didn't like the knowing look he gave me. "It's way more entertaining this way," he admitted. "And kudos to you. You're a way better actress than they told us you'd be."

I didn't quite get that—mostly because, as much as I hated to admit, I did a shit job hiding my emotions most of the time.

Case in point, a frown flitted over Cole's expression. "Shit. You really don't know."

"I usually know more than people think," I offered, trying to bullshit my way through this until he'd drop a hint or two. When he didn't, I shrugged, trying hard to hide my returning annoyance. "Come on. Doesn't all that baiting the bitch get old eventually? Sure, I get it. The guys have told me, time and again, that me having hissy fits like a cat can be amusing, but I think we're past that. I'd be a lot more useful if I knew why the powers that be forced me to tag along. We all know it's not because I'm the most accomplished fighter."

I hadn't expected him to reply—I'd tried the very same spiel more than once and had never gotten an answer, let alone a satisfying one—but after another glance toward the front of our column, Cole opened his mouth.

"You probably remember the part where Miller's brother was looking for a way to stop turning us into zombies once we die?" Both Nate and Burns did a bad job hiding that they were suddenly very interested as well. I nodded. That tidbit was hard to forget, even more so as it impacted my life—and what came after—now as well.

"Yeah, I read his files. Even handed a bunch of them to Raynor," I reminded him.

Cole snorted at my attempt to look like I wasn't ready to jump him and choke the answer right out of him. "Well, rumor has it, he was a lot closer to solving that than anyone else knew. In fact, one of the people he had been cooperating with apparently found the answer." When I just kept staring at him, his face split into a grin. "We're here to get the cure."

"The cure to what?" I asked, disbelief and hope waring for dominance in my mind, almost choking me up with sudden excitement.

Before I got my answer, we had to climb out of the ditch, cross a road, and disappear into the next tunnel, and by that time, Cole had hung back to where Hill and Munez were guarding our rear. I couldn't help but vexedly cluck my tongue, which made Burns chuckle all the more.

"You're too easy sometimes," he professed.

"First time you'd be complaining about that," I offered, deciding to drop the point. I wasn't even sure he could have given me an answer had he wanted to—and it made much more sense to continue to string me along after throwing me that morsel. And what food for thought that was. It was rather unexpected that I could put Cole down on the list of those that might not shoot me in the back of the head out of spite. No idea if that sentiment would survive the next hour or two.

Two more tunnels and through what might have been a forward guard post—now abandoned, the dug-out walls covered in ice—and we ended up at the edge of a small plateau, forest on two sides bordering the overgrown meadow. The French moved forward without hesitation with only the most cursory glance around for danger, making my own paranoia surge. There were no roads leading forward, not even a dirt track, but the snowy grass wasn't undisturbed.

We were way past the halfway point toward the woods when the guy we'd been talking to before stopped, his raised hand a universal gesture that didn't need translation. Bucky still barked at Gita to ask him what was going on, but the man ignored them both. He let out a sequence of whistles that sounded eerily haunting in the cold air of early evening, carrying across the entire open field around us.

A similar sequence answered from somewhere over by the trees, making a few of the soldiers turn that way, hands tightening on weapons. Two short, shrill whistles came from seemingly out of nowhere from the barren meadow to our right. The guy gave a brief nod to his people, then signaled us to follow. He kept heading in the same direction as before rather than ambling for either checkpoint. Ahead, there was a small hill by a ditch—maybe the border between two fields—and it took another minute of us heading in that direction before I realized our path was curving toward the other side of that small elevated point.

It was when we were almost halfway around it that I noticed the group of at least twenty people standing at what looked like an arbitrary point in the next field over, clearly waiting for us. A few of the others drew up short in surprise, but no one was stupid enough to shoot. When the French guy stopped this time, he let a string of words fly at Gita. "He's telling us to wait," she explained. As soon as her words were out, he motioned his people forward, apparently trusting us not to follow. We didn't, although the twist that came to Bucky's mouth was rather amusing. He really didn't like being told what to do. Made it almost tempting to try to weasel a deal out of Raynor on our return that made it mandatory for him to listen to me. Almost.

As soon as our French merged with the other group, the low burr of voices in hushed conversation rose, but I doubted that even Gita managed to catch more than a snippet of that. There didn't seem to be anyone they reported to, several people talking over each other. It took them a good five minutes to sort things out, and a lone figure started off toward us. It was a woman, easily a head taller than me, looking reed-thin even in the layers of winter clothes she was wearing. I didn't see her carrying a weapon but I was sure that she was armed. As she drew closer, I could see her features better; she had a rather symmetric face with high cheekbones that lent her the flawless beauty of a fashion model, except for the jagged scar that ran from her left jaw over her brow to disappear behind the dark, broad scarf that was wound across her forehead, holding back a riot of dark, short coils. Behind her, about a third of the waiting group merged with those we'd followed here, all of them heading toward the mound. There must have been a door leading to a cellar or bunker hidden there because it took them all of a minute to be swallowed up by the ground, leaving us facing the remaining guards. They were armed, if not wearing any kind of discernible uniform. In fact, they reminded me a lot of hundreds of traders I'd met on the road this year.

The woman stopped about ten feet from us, far enough away that should we start any funny business, she might have a head start running, but close enough that we could talk without shouting.

"I am Elle Moreau," she introduced herself. "We have been expecting you." Her voice was deep and full, her French accent obvious while her English was fluent, if with a certain British lilt, and something else that I couldn't place.

Her words made me crack a smile I hadn't known was so ready to appear. Oh, this was going to be good, I just knew it! And judging from the light frown on Bucky's forehead, he knew it as well.

To be continued in

Green Fields #9

Acknowledgements

A huge thank you goes out to my beta reader team. You are amazing, and my books have improved so much since I found you! Also, my sanity.

I'd be lost without my editor and cover designer, because they make this madness look downright professional.

I have the best readers in the world—so thank you as well! I'm reminded of that every time I check my books on Amazon, open my inbox, or log into facebook. If you want to connect with me and other fans of the series, you can now join the facebook fan group. It's an amazing place to hang out and chat!

Oh no, another cliffhanger! And thanks to the feedback I got from my beta readers, it's 2x worse than I intended it to be! Speak about needing book #9 ASAP. Don't worry, I'm on it! One thing I can tell you already: it's going to be one hell of a ride!

If you want to be extra awesome, please take a moment and leave a review on Amazon. Even if it's only one line, it means the world to me and makes a huge difference for us Indie authors! I'm not just saying that because, like all authors, I hunger for feedback and appreciation, but because more reviews mean more new readers getting dragged down into the rabbit hole—and there's nothing wrong with that! I don't have a publisher, PR team, or whatnot—but I have you! And that's the best thing that has ever happened to me. THANK YOU!!

About the Author

Adrienne Lecter has a background in Biochemistry and Molecular Biology, loves ranting at inaccuracies in movies, and spends increasingly more time on the shooting range. She lives with the man and two cats of her life in Vienna, and is working on the next post-apocalyptic books.

You can sign up for Adrienne's newsletter to never miss a release and be the first to know what other shenanigans she gets up to:

http://www.adriennelecter.com

Thank you

Hey, you! Yes, you, who just spent a helluva lot of time reading this book! You just made my day! Thanks!

Want to be notified of new releases, giveaways and updates? Sign up for my newsletter:
www.adriennelecter.com

If you enjoyed reading the book and have a moment to spare, I would really appreciate a short, honest review on the site you purchased it from and on goodreads. Reviews make a huge difference in helping new readers find the series.

Or if you'd like to drop me a note, or chat a but, feel free to email me or hit me up on social media. I'll try to respond as quickly as possible! If you'd like to report an error or wrong detail, I've set up a separate space on my website for that, too.

Email: adrienne@adriennelecter.com
Website: adriennelecter.com
Twitter: @adriennelecter
Facebook: facebook.com/adriennelecter

Books published

Green Fields
#1: Incubation
#2: Outbreak
#3: Escalation
#4: Extinction
#5: Resurgence
#6: Unity
#7: Affliction
#8: Catharsis
#9: Exodus
#10: Uprising
#11: Retribution
#12: Annihilation

Beyond Green Fields
short story collections
Omnibus #1
Ombinus #2

World of Anthrax
new series coming 2022

Printed in Great Britain
by Amazon